ABOUT THE AUTHOR

JUDITH RYAN HENDRICKS is the author of *Bread Alone, Isabel's Daughter*, and *The Baker's Apprentice*. She and her husband live in Santa Fe, New Mexico, where she is at work on her fifth book.

The LAWS *of* HARMONY

Also by JUDITH RYAN HENDRICKS

Bread Alone
Isabel's Daughter
The Baker's Apprentice

The LAWS of HARMONY

A NOVEL

JUDITH RYAN HENDRICKS

HARPER

NEW YORK · LONDON · TORONTO · SYDNEY

This book is for Kate.

HARPER

Excerpt from Jane Hirshfield's poem "For What Binds Us," from *Of Gravity & Angels* (Wesleyan University Press, 1988), copyright © Jane Hirshfield, used by kind permission of the author.

"Handy Man." Words and Music by Otis Blackwell and Jimmy Jones. Copyright © 1959 (renewed) EMI Unart Catalog, Inc. All rights controlled by EMI Unart Catalog, Inc. (publishing) and Alfred Publishing Co., Inc. (print). All rights reserved. Used by permission from Alfred Publishing Co., Inc.

FIRST EDITION

Designed by Joy O'Meara

Library of Congress Cataloging-in-Publication Data is available upon request.

ISBN 978-0-06-168736-5

09 10 11 12 13   OV/RRD   10 9 8 7 6 5 4 3 2 1

. . . see how the flesh grows back
across a wound, with a great vehemence,
more strong
than the simple untested surface before.
There's a name for it on horses: proud flesh,
As all flesh
is proud of its wounds, wears them
as honors given out after battle,
small triumphs pinned to the chest—

JANE HIRSHFIELD, *For What Binds Us*

PROLOGUE

I was born at sunrise on June 3, 1971, on a commune near Taos, New Mexico. Delivery was accomplished with the help of a midwife as my mother squatted, panting, on her mattress, surrounded by her commune sisters, panting in sympathy, cheering her on.

The men had hovered in the kitchen all night, playing cards, drinking, smoking, drifting in and out of the birth room unnoticed, like ghosts. My father happened to be present at the moment that I gushed out from between my mother's legs, and he promptly ran outside to vomit into the rabbit brush. It could have been the sight of blood and birth fluid that got to him, but more likely it was too much Tokay.

In accordance with my birth time, my mother named me Soleil, which is French for *sun*. She neglected to consider that people in New Mexico speak Spanish and English, but very little French. By the time I was twelve, I was sick of correcting the spelling and pronunciation, explaining to people what my name meant and listening to stupid jokes—*So-lay, can you see any bedbugs on me*—so I just told everyone to call me Sunny.

My parents (we were encouraged to call them Gwen and

Rob) had moved to New Mexico from San Francisco, where my mother made paper flowers and my father played bass guitar in a rock band called Driving at Night. They had a rich friend named Danny Oliver who was a music promoter till he got religion and swore off all the materialistic trappings of that life. He changed his name to Moses Strong, bought a 230-acre farm north of Taos, and invited some friends to come live on the land, groove on nature, and start a new civilization. He called it Armonía—Spanish for *harmony*.

People are forever asking me what it was like to grow up in a commune, and it's a question that has no easy answer. Northern New Mexico was Commune Central in those days, and each of the twenty-odd settlements had its own vision, its own quirky dynamics, its own culture. And, of course, no two children ever grow up in the same family, so if you asked both me and my brother, Hart, what it was like, you'd get two completely different perspectives.

I think he was pretty happy.

Part One

It is the image in the mind that binds us to our lost treasures, but it is the loss that shapes the image.

COLETTE

Chapter 1

The heat is a presence. Palpable and relentless, it rolls over Albuquerque like a hot iron.

Right behind it come the spring winds, pushing several thousand tons of dust from Arizona on through to Texas. Whistling around the corners of the buildings. Drying the new grass and flowers to brittle straws. Blowing patio furniture into someone else's yard. Making people yell at the spouse, kick the dog, slap the kid, start smoking again, drink more, drive faster.

Michael's already dressed for work and making coffee when I wander into the kitchen, wrapped in my terry cloth robe, still damp from the shower. I sidle up to kiss his neck, just where his dark hair is starting to creep down over his collar, and wipe away a little smear of shaving cream behind his ear. He reaches around me for his coffee mug and kisses the top of my head absently.

"It's supposed to be hot like this all week," he says. He sits down at the table and submerges himself in the newspaper.

"Want some cereal?" I take clean bowls and spoons out of the dishwasher.

I pull the box of corn flakes out of the pantry and pour

some in my bowl, add milk, and sit down across from him. I've already eaten about half of my cereal when he looks up.

"Hmm?"

"Hmm, what?"

"Did you say something?"

"I asked if you wanted cereal. Since you didn't answer, I took it as a no."

"Sorry. I was thinking."

The coffee maker sighs, announcing the completion of its cycle. I pour some in his cup and set it on the table. "What are you doing today?"

"This morning I'm meeting with Ted Rossmore."

"Who's he?"

"Venture capital guy. Then this afternoon I've got a couple conference calls . . ." The silence is filled with the rustling of the newspaper, the clink of my spoon against the bowl.

After a minute or so, I lay my hand on his arm. "Tell me what's wrong."

He gives me an indulgent smile. "Nothing's wrong."

"Something feels wrong to me."

"Something always feels wrong to you. It's your normal state." He folds up the sports section and smiles at me. The intense blue of his eyes is still startling, even after almost three years of seeing it every day.

"Michael—"

"What? I don't know what you want me to say."

"The truth. Whatever it is."

"The truth is, nothing's wrong." He pats my hand, which I guess is supposed to be reassuring, but it's a gesture so unlike him that it has the reverse effect.

"Okay, everything's great. But I still want us to sit down and have a conversation. Tonight."

He gets up, pours the dregs of his coffee in the sink. "Tonight," he says.

"Come home early, okay? I'll make a big salad and we can have a nice, relaxing—"

"I will." He gives me a quick coffee-flavored kiss.

The door shuts with that hollow sound, and I stir my soggy corn flakes while reviewing the evidence.

Exhibit A. I enter, damp from the shower, smelling of coconut body butter. I brush against him and kiss his neck lightly. His response? Reaching around me for his coffee mug and a mechanical peck on the top of the head. I didn't expect him to rip my robe off and throw me down on the breakfast table, but a real kiss would not have been out of place.

Exhibit B. Monday night. He came home late from his poker game, but I was still awake. I wanted to talk. He said he had e-mails to send. So I left him in his office and went to bed, tending the embers of my hurt feelings and resentment. I heard him come out of his office, walk into the living room. When the TV went on, the embers ignited. I marched into the living room and told him I was sick of his lying. He said, lying about what? I said he didn't really have any e-mails that couldn't wait till tomorrow; he was just avoiding talking to me. I wanted to know why. He said he was tired. I said he was always tired except when there was something he wanted to do. He said this was exactly why he was avoiding talking to me and, for that matter, why he was tired. Why couldn't I just cut him some slack, give him a little room to breathe. I said he could have the whole goddamned apartment to breathe in if he wanted it.

I said I would leave in the morning. I told him I'd go stay with Betsy till he was finished breathing. Then I marched back into the bedroom, got back in bed, and seethed.

He came in about fifteen minutes later, and I pretended to be asleep. He knew I wasn't. He didn't take his clothes off. He just lay down next to me, on top of the covers, and put his hands on me. This was his solution to everything. Touching. Sex. I never knew how to tell him that it was those times when I felt the most distance between us. A yawning canyon full of all the things we never said. But that night I was tired, too. I was sad. I wanted him to hold me. I wanted things to be the way they were before. Before I started getting this panicky feeling that maybe things never really had been the way they were before.

On the other hand it's perfectly true, what he said. A perpetual sense of impending doom is my natural state. I should be used to it by now—this feeling that every next moment is a catastrophe waiting to happen.

So maybe it's just the wind.

I throw the coverlet up over the pillows—about as far as I'm willing to go toward making the bed. I slip on a gauzy Indian cotton dress, slide my feet into old leather sandals, and run a comb through my still-damp hair. Pull a sweater out of the drawer. It'll be freezing in the studio. The last thing I do is grab my medicine bundle necklace and loop it over my head.

It was my tenth birthday present from my father—the last present he gave me. He was always getting stuff in trade for fixing people's cars and tractors. He got this one from an Indian in Taos for putting a new engine in his pickup. It's a tiny deerskin sack that used to be sort of a honey color, but it's darkened with age and the oil from my skin. There's a beaded design on the front in red and white and black. My father said it was a storm design.

When I first got it, it was filled with the corn pollen that Navajos use in their religious ceremonies, but I kept undoing the blue wool tie and spilling the pollen, so now it just holds my Zuni bear fetish, carved from turquoise with an inlaid white shell heart line that represents the path to power in his heart. It's my talisman against drunk drivers, muggers, lightning strikes, inoperable brain tumors, falling down the stairs, or being dumped for a twenty-two-year-old cocktail waitress.

I don't leave home without it.

A crackling dry gust funnels up through the stairwell, lifting my skirt up to my waist, and I'm too hot to care. I juggle the awkward bulk of the Styrofoam cooler, squint against the dust, and try not to breathe till I can get down to the sidewalk. Something white flaps on the windshield of my black Hyundai. Shit. I forgot about street cleaning again. I pull off the ticket and jam it down into the black hole of my purse with all the others.

I drive in the right-hand lane, radio off, running through my warm-up exercises. Breathe deeply. In through the nose, out through the mouth. In through the nose, filling the diaphragm, out through the mouth saying, *AHHHHH.* Touching left ear to left shoulder, right ear to right shoulder. At the first traffic light I turn my head slowly clockwise, then counterclockwise. Then, taking advantage of the long red light, I suck in air and expel it in short, powerful bursts: *Huh! Huh! Huh!*

In the middle of *AAAAA, EEEEE, IIIII, OOOOO, UUUUU,* I remember that my window is partway down. The two men in the blue sedan next to me are exchanging alarmed looks. When I smile sheepishly, their heads snap to the front.

SoundsGood, the studio where I'm recording this morning, is in a bleak-looking strip mall, sandwiched between a daycare center and a Pizza Hut. Half the shops are vacant and boarded up; the other half have burglar bars on the windows and doors. But the heavily curtained glass door to the studio hides a secret world—clean, cozy, and decorated in southwestern pastels, stacked to the gills with cutting-edge technology and staffed by industry veterans.

"A jingle package is going to run you about three grand." Artie Simon sports headphones draped around his neck and a phone lodged between his ear and shoulder. He holds up his coffee cup, raising an eyebrow at me.

I shake my head and sink down on a sand-colored loveseat, extract my copy of the script from my battered leather portfolio. This morning I'm doing a double with Jack Piper, best known for last-minute, flying entrances, so I have plenty of time to look over my dialogue, tuning out the sound engineer's phone conversation. It's the third spot in an ongoing series of commercials for a local furniture chain, and my character is the middle-aged mother of a new college graduate. I look up from the script just as Artie says, "Let me know and we'll get you booked. Yep. My name's Artie." He grins at me and hangs up. "Hi, Beauty. The Beast isn't here yet. Sure you don't want some coffee?"

"No thanks. Too hot. How's everything with you?"

"Good. Just trying to clear the decks here. We're starting postproduction on a film next week."

"Anything I've heard of?"

"Doubt it. It's an indie. Full of people who look about

eighteen. Including the director." Artie drains his cup. "How's Michael?"

"Busy as usual." That much, at least, I'm sure of.

A car door slams outside and seconds later the studio door flies open. Jack, looking impossibly square-jawed and clad in full cowboy regalia, swaggers in ahead of the dry wind.

"Ya wanna buy a car, pilgrim?" He smiles broadly at his own reasonable facsimile of John Wayne.

Artie sighs. "It's furniture, Jack. Bergman's. And you're almost late."

"I know, and I'm sorry." To his credit, Jack never makes up stupid excuses. "But almost late is better than late, is it not?"

"Nice duds, Jack." I smile.

"I'm judging the state chili cook-off at high noon."

Artie heads for Studio A, and we fall in behind him. "Then it's lucky for Sunny we're working this morning."

Artie sits down at the console next to a black metal tower of audio equipment and punches up a display on the computer monitor, while Jack and I take our places in the voice booth, adjust our copy stands and mikes. In a union shop, the engineer would have to come in and adjust the mikes—in fact, touching your own mike normally carries the same stigma as touching your privates on network TV—but then nobody works union in Albuquerque.

Artie dons the headphones. "Let's get a level."

"Okay, Mom, you can open your eyes now. How do you like it?" Once in the booth, Jack Piper is all business.

"This? This is a new apartment?"

"Well, it's new to me—"

"Okay," Artie breaks in. "I'm slating you. Bergman's Home

Furnishings, number three. Cooper and Piper. Take one. We're rolling."

"Okay, Mom, you can open your eyes now. How do you like it?"

"This? This is a new apartment?"

"Well, it's new to me. It's my first apartment."

"There's a toaster oven on top of your television."

"Er . . . yes. That's the kitchen."

"At least you have a walk-in closet."

"That's the bathroom, Mom."

"I see. Well, where's the bedroom?"

"You just sat down on it."

"You're sleeping on the couch?"

"But not just any couch. It's a queen-size sleeper sofa from Bergman's Home Furnishings."

"Ah. Bergman's. Well, maybe there's hope for this place after all."

Artie leans toward his own mike. "Good. But you're at thirty-one-point-five. Can you tuck it in just a bit? And Jack, could you emphasize just the word *Bergman's*. You know . . . punch it, but don't push it. And then you guys can lay down some tags."

At the University of New Mexico, I was obsessed with the idea that I had to be successful at something. Anything. But growing up on a commune presented me with very few role models for success—or even a workable definition of it—in the real world. I was also severely conflicted about the work ethic.

I wasn't excited about promising my time to some company eight hours a day, five days a week, for the rest of my life. Dressing in office-appropriate clothing, taking my one-hour lunch at a prescribed time. Working eleven and a half months to get my two weeks of vacation. Potential employers were not enthusiastic about me, either, judging from the number of job offers I received.

One, actually. With a small office furniture company in downtown Albuquerque. The job was assistant director of marketing. It sounded good in theory.

But the director I was supposed to be assisting made it clear that he wouldn't be in the office much. That I'd be responsible for cranking out press releases and sales brochures, answering the phone, filing, making his travel arrangements, and not revealing his whereabouts to anyone. I'd never had a real job in an office, but the job description still sounded a little strange. The salary he offered me was barely more than I was making on the lunch shift at the Kachina Grill. But he assured me there was potential for "advancement."

I worried, I wavered. Finally I asked my roommate, Betsy, what I should do.

"Wait a second. Let me get this straight. He wants you to do all this work for slave wages and not tell anyone he's not there? Sounds totally bogus to me. He'll probably be screwing his girlfriend in hotels all over the country while his wife's calling you every ten minutes to find out where he is." She shook her head. "Shit, waiting tables is better than that."

I went back to the lunch shift. I graduated to the dinner shift. Tips got better, but I was restless. I was a college graduate working as a server, without even the excuse that I was writing a novel or making sculptures in the basement or going to grad school. Waiting tables was my real, full-time job. I wanted to do something else, but I didn't know what and I didn't know how.

And then one day I went with Betsy to look at a used pickup truck somewhere off of Rio Grande Boulevard, and on the way back we stopped at Garson's—one of the city's biggest florist chains—so she could send flowers to her mom.

While she was looking at plants and floral arrangements, I amused myself by wandering around the shop doing what I thought was a hilarious parody of all the little sayings that were posted everywhere. Like *Say it with flowers, and you'll know she's listening.* Or *Flowers speak louder than words.* Or *A dozen roses are worth a thousand words.*

I noticed a suit hanging around the back of the shop, but I ignored him. I figured he was some guy waiting for his order. When I started in on the book of suggested sentiments for people to write on their gift cards—which I found ludicrous; I mean, you're sending someone flowers and you have to choose what you want to say out of a catalog? Anyway, the guy comes up to me and says, "Pardon me, Miss." He holds out his hand. "I'm George Garson."

Of course, I figure he's going to ask me very politely to get my butt out of his shop, but instead he says, "You have a lovely voice. And very unique. Would you be interested in doing a commercial for me?"

From there, it was only a matter of time before I was voicing Lo-Flo, the ecologically correct, water-efficient, talking toilet for the New Mexico Water Commission.

Much as I like being a voiceover, it's not something you're going to get rich doing—I read somewhere that 10 percent of the VO's get 80 percent of the work—so the rest of us have day jobs. Rather than work for someone else, I started my own little company, Domestic Obligations. I take care of things when people are out of town or otherwise engaged—houses, pets, mail. I stand in line for them at the Motor Vehicle Department and the post office and EventMaster, pick up coconut ice cream for the dinner party, bake and deliver cookies for the knitting group or scones for a writers' workshop. Sometimes I'll even cook lunch or dinner—whatever they can't, don't have time for, or don't want to do, I'll do. The work suits me.

This second job has a lot to do with the voiceover work I've managed to get. Early on I was doing a lot more baking than voicing, and whenever I had food left over from a Domestic Obligations booking, I'd take it with me to the studio. I'm convinced that there have been many times when a choice between me and another VO came down to: *Let's call Sunny Cooper. At least she'll bring food.*

Montoya's Panaderia is visible for blocks—not because of its size, but because its brown adobe walls are splashed with huge, brightly colored flowers. Michael loves their green chile bread.

I leave the car in the gravel lot next to a table with a defunct TV set on top and a couple of old tires underneath, and thread a path through the cluster of kids drinking sodas and eating empanadas on the patio. The scents of cinnamon and chocolate, bread and coffee, envelop me in a friendly embrace.

"Hi, Sunny," Luis greets me from behind the counter, blots his forehead. "Hot enough for you?"

"It's like July, isn't it? You have any green chile bread left?"

"Let's hope that means we'll get April weather in July." He bags the last loaf and throws in a couple of biscochitos for good measure before he rings me up.

I drive home nibbling on a biscochito and park on Mont-claire, under a sprawling cottonwood. Tomorrow the car will be covered with bird shit, but at least it will be cooler. My sandals make a flat, slapping noise on the concrete steps. The slight breeze down on the street hasn't made it to the interior of the complex yet.

Our apartment building, grandly dubbed The Marquesa, was built in the early seventies, which must have been the nadir of American architecture—or at least of New Mexican architecture. When we first moved in, there were more UNM grad students and young faculty, but they've moved on now, presumably to buildings where the plumbing doesn't howl like a coyote after the rain and the windows fit snugly enough in the frames to keep out the fine blown dust. Now most of the tenants belong to the geriatric set, and Michael and I are "that young couple with the loud phonograph."

"Hey, Sunny, where ya been? What's in the bag?"

Sissy Proctor is leaning over the railing across the court-yard. Sissy of the fuzzy orange hair and the fuzzy blue slippers and skin like a lizard. She has to be eighty, but she's got the eyes of a hawk. All the better to spot the yard sale bargains she's al-ways bringing home. That's how I met her. I saw her dragging a gorgeous old pie crust tilt-top table up the stairs one Sunday morning and offered to help. She invited me into her place, which looks a lot like the collection depot for the Salvation Army thrift store. We balanced on the edge of her sofa—a gen-uine Castro convertible nearly obliterated by piles of quilts and afghans—drinking lukewarm tea and talking about collecting. At that first meeting she sang the entire Castro jingle for me in her quavery, off-key voice.

"Hi, Sissy. It's just green chile bread from Montoya's."

She raises her pencil-thin eyebrows knowingly. "Hot date tonight?"

"Any date would be hot tonight."

"You ain't wrong about that. Hey, my cousin just got a new shipment from Miami. You want to check it out Sunday morning?" Sissy's cousin Des has a booth at the swap meet dealing in gently used LPs, forty-fives, and seventy-eights, plus vintage photos and the occasional kitchen gadget.

"Maybe. Let me see if Michael has anything planned."

My key rattles strangely in the lock, and the door swings open with just a push. God, did I forget to lock up this morning? The minute I cross the threshold, I know. Not a sound, not a smell. Nothing I can see immediately. Just a presence. It makes my skin go corduroy.

I stand still, knees fused. I can hear my heart slamming like it's between my ears. Now they come into focus, the things that have been moved. The magazines are on the wrong end of the coffee table. Two CDs are upside down on the floor. I pick them up: Dixie Chicks and Nirvana. They were in the changer last night. I look up quickly at the shelves. The stereo is still there, but my antique wooden tea caddy, where I kept our CDs, is gone.

Down the hall. I nudge open the door to the office, and my breath stops in my throat. The floor is littered with the contents of Michael's desk—pencils and pens, paper clips and rubber bands, rulers, scissors, message pads, stationery, business cards. Both file drawers are open; folders and papers are strewn everywhere.

I know I should call the police, but I'm embarrassed. We

talked about putting a dead bolt lock on, but somehow never got around to it. I've always felt so safe here in the courtyard with half a dozen nosy senior citizens living around me.

I pick up the phone and put it down. Pick it up again. An hour later Patrolman Alan Ramos is at the door.

He's a compact, wiry, no-frills kind of cop. After he introduces himself, he stands with his back to the door looking around at everything with eyes like small, dark marbles. He opens the door, checks the handle, the lock, the jamb.

"Seven-year-old with a library card could pop this," he says matter-of-factly. He sets down the black case he's carrying and pulls out a notebook.

"What was the first thing you saw when you came in?"

"Things were moved. The magazines. All my CDs are gone."

"How many?"

"Probably about thirty."

He walks into the kitchen. "What about in here?"

"Nothing seems to be missing there."

I lead him down the hall to the office doorway.

He says, "Have you touched anything in here?"

"Just the phone."

"Good." He continues on to the bedroom and bathroom while I stand surveying the mess on the office floor. When he comes back he asks, "You notice anything else missing? Jewelry? Money? You have a laptop?"

"Not that I can see. We both had our computers with us."

He scribbles in the notebook. "The men's clothing in the bedroom belongs to who?"

"My—Michael Graham."

"And where's he today?"

"Working. He works here, in the office, but he's out a lot."

"Have you talked to him yet?"

"No. Well, I called his cell phone and left a message on his voice mail."

Alan Ramos rocks back on his heels. "Have you been gone all day?"

"I left about eight forty-five this morning. Michael was already gone. And I got home . . ." I look at my watch. "About four thirty."

"Anybody been in here recently? Like a plumber or something?"

I shake my head.

I follow him back into the living room. More silent looking around. He tugs at the top button on his shirt, like it's too tight.

"Mind if I sit?" Without waiting for my nod, he sits in the leather chair. "Usually burglars take things like stereos, TVs, computers, jewelry." He pauses. "But maybe they liked your taste in music. Or they heard somebody coming. Or thought they did. You and Mr. Graham have the only keys to this apartment?"

"The landlord has one."

"Anybody else?"

"My best friend, Betsy Chambliss. She's in San Antonio this week."

He bends his head to write in the book. His hair is closely cropped and it glistens darkly with some kind of hair goo. He looks up at me.

"That office—seems like somebody was looking for something. Any idea what it might be?"

I shake my head.

"Okay, Ms. Cooper." He stands up. "I'm going to suggest that you get a new lock on this door. A double-keyed deadbolt. You have someplace you can stay tonight?"

"No. But Michael should be home soon."

He picks up the black case. "I'm going to try to lift some fingerprints, then I'm going to talk to some of your neighbors. See if they heard or saw anything unusual today." He heads for the office, but comes back seconds later. "Just so you know . . . chances are we won't recover the CDs."

After he's gone I realize how hot the apartment is. I turn the thermostat down to sixty, take my purse and portfolio back to the bedroom. I know I'm alone, but I keep looking around corners, listening for something. All I see are shadows; all I hear are my own footsteps, muffled by the hall rug.

The mess in the office probably isn't that bad. It just requires wading in and making a start. Normally that's right up my alley. Michael's always letting things fall where they stand, leaving stacks of papers on every available surface, business cards in the bathroom when he empties his pockets, CDs on the coffee table, mail by the kitchen sink. Then I come through, single-mindedly gathering things up, sorting them out, filing papers, shutting drawers. I quit complaining about it long ago, since it never did any good, and now I do it on autopilot. But this is not your ordinary clutter. Someone did this. Someone who shouldn't have been in our home. After studying the scene for another long minute, I shut the door, hurry back out to the living room, put the Dixie Chicks CD in the player, and turn it on. "Wide Open Spaces" blares reassuringly out of the speakers.

In the kitchen I fill a glass with ice, then a picture springs to mind of some stranger handling the glass. I dump the ice in the sink, wash and dry the glass, and get fresh ice. I open the refrigerator. There's a note taped to the pitcher of raspberry tea. It makes me smile in spite of the sick feeling in my stomach. Michael always leaves me messages in the refrigerator because that's usually the first place I go when I come home. It comforts me, reminds me that things will be normal again. I pull the folded paper off the pitcher and open it.

Gone to Taos. Back later.

The note is scrawled in a hurried hand. No signature. No apology. No excuses. No *love you.*

Taos means he's with Kirby Dolen, the guy everyone calls the Software Rock Star. It's about two and a half hours each way, if there's no traffic.

I turn the paper over, hoping for something more. When was Michael here? When did he leave? On the other side is my own handwriting: *garlic, chicken broth, potatoes.*

By 7:30 I've read the newspaper from front to back. The sun is gone, but now the sidewalks and streets and buildings are radiating back the heat of the day. A sudden knocking—it's Mrs. Harriman downstairs, banging on the ceiling with her broom: her way of letting me know the music's too loud. I turn it off and dial Michael's cell phone and get voice mail again.

"Michael, it's me. Where are you? How late is later? I really need to talk to you."

I walk through the apartment, checking all the windows. I flip through the thirty-seven stations we get on cable, catch the tail end of *The Matrix*, and then the happy lady on the Weather Channel says this high pressure area is going to continue to bake Albuquerque at least through the weekend.

By 9:15, I'm pissed off. And hungry. In the fridge I find a Styrofoam box with my leftovers from Tuesday night's dinner. I stand at the sink absently picking pieces of cold pasta out of congealed Alfredo sauce and washing them down with room-temperature white wine. I don't stop till they're both gone, and I feel uncomfortably full, but not satisfied.

Ignoring the tightness in the waistband of my jeans, I cut a slab of frozen Sara Lee cheesecake and eat it out of my hand, watching an old *Star Trek* rerun in which Captain Kirk falls for a gorgeous female alien who turns out to be a robot. I wipe my sticky fingers on a paper towel and try the cell phone again. I hang up before voice mail kicks in.

The eleven o'clock news comes and goes. Why doesn't he call? He knows I worry when he's late. Truthfully, I worry even when he's not late. I'm always convinced he's been run off the road by one of New Mexico's ubiquitous drunk drivers and is lying facedown in an arroyo. Or that he's having an affair, in which case I hope he's lying facedown in an arroyo.

This is the wrong damn night for him to be oblivious. I can't bring myself to go get in bed and turn off the lights. I know I wouldn't fall asleep; I'd just lie there imagining noises. I punch the remote, and the TV screen pops and goes black. I wrap myself up in my mother's old green crocheted afghan— the only thing of hers I brought to Albuquerque with me—and curl up on the couch. Just as my eyes are closing, the telephone jangles, and I race to the kitchen to pick it up.

"It's me," he says.

"Me who? Would this be the stranger who left an unsigned note in the refrigerator?"

"Sunny . . ." His voice is weary and impatient. "Why did you call me?"

"Because somebody broke into the apartment."

There's a long silence.

"Michael? Are you there? I said, somebody—"

"I heard you." Another silence, not quite as long. "Are you okay?"

"As okay as can be expected. They took all my CDs. When are you coming home?" I'm pacing back and forth the length of the cord.

He says, "I'm not."

"What are you talking about?"

"I've got a room at the Sagebrush Inn. I'm too tired to drive all the way back down tonight."

He must be on his cell; the reception's awful. "Michael . . . we got robbed today. All they got were my CDs. For God's sake, what if they come back?"

"I'm sorry, but I just can't drive back tonight. I'm exhausted. I don't think I could make it without falling asleep. Look, why don't you go over and stay with Betsy?"

"Because she's in San Antonio, that's why."

"Did they take anything in my office?" he says.

"It's impossible to tell because they dumped everything on the floor."

No response. If it wasn't for the static I'd think he'd lost reception. "Michael? What's going on?"

"Nothing. I'm just totally . . ." He pauses. "Now this. Christ." But his voice is empty of expression.

"You're acting really weird. Doesn't it matter to you that someone broke into our apartment this afternoon and now I'm—"

"I'm sorry you lost all your CDs, but I can't do much about it tonight."

"It's not the damned CDs." My throat aches from the effort of talking. "I just need you to be here. With me. Why are you acting like this?"

"Well, I can't be there, Sunny. I'm sorry, but I can't."

"Thanks, I've about got that figured out."

"Look, I'll be home . . . before noon. We can talk then. I just don't feel like—"

"Fine." I hang up the phone.

Chapter 2

Michael loves Spanish pie—a thin, double-crusted creation with barely an inch of filling—sort of like pizza with a top crust. I know it's hot to be baking, but I can ramp up the air-conditioning for a while. It'll be worth it. We haven't had that kind of dinner in a while—the kind that ends slowly, the evening shifting seamlessly from the kitchen to the bedroom, the last taste of wine still in my mouth when he kisses me.

I'll apologize for hanging up on him. He'll apologize for not coming home. He'll tell me what's wrong . . . because I know there's something. Whatever it is, we'll talk about it; we'll work it out.

I make pastry the way my mother did—cutting in lard for flakiness and butter for taste—quickly, with two knives, so that it doesn't get gooey in the warm kitchen air. Then an egg and ice water to pull everything together, and into the refrigerator to chill while the oven preheats.

While I stir the almonds in a small skillet, a song pops into my head and I start to hum "Walk on By"—not the one by Dionne Warwick, but the soulful old country-western tune by Leroy Van Dyke.

When the smell of toasted nuts fills the room, I crush them with a rolling pin and mix in sugar and cinnamon. I sweat the onion and garlic in butter for about five minutes before adding the allspice, ginger, turmeric, and cloves. Cumin isn't traditional, but I love its musty, earthy taste, so I throw some in. Then the cut-up leftover chicken, raisins, egg, and wine.

I remember a moonless night almost a year ago. We were on our way home from a dinner with Betsy and her latest admirer. Taking a corner in Michael's truck requires a certain amount of concentration because it's an authentically restored '53 Chevy with no turn signals and no power steering. He was negotiating the turn off Central Avenue onto Montclaire, left arm stuck out the window, when he said conversationally, "You ever think about getting married?"

It caught me off-guard. I kept looking out the window, while the silence lengthened into discomfort.

"Sure, I've thought about it. I think you should have to pass a test first. Like getting your driver's license."

He pulled to the curb and cut the engine, turned off the headlights and just sat there.

I rested my hand on the sleeve of his jacket, feeling his arm muscle tense. "It's been really good. I just don't want to wreck everything."

"I don't see how getting married is going to wreck everything."

"What if it doesn't work?"

"If it doesn't work, we get divorced, like normal people. Can't we burn that bridge when we come to it?" When I didn't laugh, he said, "That was a joke, Sunny."

"I know." But my stomach was churning.

"I want you with me—"

"I *am* with you."

"I want you to be my wife."

"Couldn't we just be . . . like domestic partners?"

"Fuck." He said it under his breath. "It sounds like we have a housecleaning business." He finally turned to face me, leaning against his door. "Look, if it's the money, things are getting better. Pretty soon we'll be able to move out of this dump. In fact next weekend we should go look at some townhouses or—"

"It's not the money. You know that."

"What the hell is it, then? Do you love me?"

I said, "You know I do."

That was as close as I ever got to saying it out loud . . . I love you, Michael. The thing I'd never said to him. It was too much like pushing your luck. He always seemed to understand.

I remember that night because that's when it started to change. As slowly and imperceptibly as continental drift. Nothing appeared to be moving at all, but one day everything was different. Michael and I were suddenly as distant as Africa and South America, but you could still see the outline of the way we had fit together.

The dough is just cool enough. It rolls out smoothly. I spread the sugared nuts over it, then the filling, then I roll out the top crust and settle it gently over everything. Slash three steam vents, crimp the edges, brush the whole thing with egg wash, and stick the baking sheet into the oven.

We'll have it room temperature with a glass of cold white wine.

I'm scraping the last vestiges of dough off my hands when the doorbell rings.

The New Mexico state trooper is young. He has a blond crew cut. His features look newly minted and sharp without a softening frame of hair. My first stupid thought is that they found my CDs.

"Mrs. Graham?"

I stare at him. "Um . . . no. Sunny Cooper. Is this . . . about the break-in?"

"No ma'am." He checks a card in his hand. "Does a Mr. Michael Graham live here?"

"He's not here right now. Can I help you?"

"My name's Sergeant Tim Bagley. May I come in, ma'am?" He holds out his ID badge.

I step back without a word.

After we sit down—me on the couch, him on the edge of the leather chair—he sets his hat on the coffee table. My hand goes automatically to the medicine bundle, pressing it to feel the small hard kernel of the bear inside; underneath it, my heart works slow and hard.

"Ms. Cooper, can you tell me if Mr. Graham owns a blue 1953 Chevrolet pickup truck with"—he pushes a piece of paper across the coffee table toward me—"this license plate?"

My fingers leave traces of flour on the table when I reach for the paper. It's Michael's vanity plate: BLUEDOG.

"Do you know where Mr. Graham is, ma'am? Is there any way you could contact him?" He takes a small notebook and pen out of his shirt pocket and writes something down.

It's the truck. Somebody stole the truck. It happened once before. It's a classic '53 five-window with three-on-the-tree and a completely rebuilt engine. Michael never locks it. He says he'd rather have somebody steal it than screw it up trying to break in.

I reach for my cell phone.

This is Michael Graham. I'm sorry I can't take your call right now . . .

His recorded voice is reassuring. Everything's okay. It's just the truck.

"He's not answering," I say.

The sergeant picks an invisible speck of something off his trousers. "When did you last speak to Mr. Graham?"

"Last night. About eleven thirty, I guess." I sit forward. "Please. Is something wrong?"

"When you spoke to him, where was he?"

"Taos. The Sagebrush Inn. What's wrong?"

He looks directly into my eyes. His are gray with little sun-yellow flecks. "This truck was involved in a very serious accident sometime early this morning, just outside Trinidad, Colorado. On Interstate Twenty-five. The vehicle flipped and rolled and then a fire began from the leaking gasoline. The driver was killed."

"Well, then, it couldn't be Michael." I hear my own voice, obscenely cheerful. "Because he wasn't in Trinidad, Colorado. He was in Taos at the Sagebrush Inn."

"Any idea what he was doing up there?"

"Meeting with some software guru."

"Do you happen to know the guru's name?"

For a minute I blank. Then I say, "Kirby Dolen." And the trooper writes it in his little book.

"Is there anyone else who might have had reason to be driving his vehicle?"

"I don't know. It could have been stolen. It was a classic thirty-one hundred. It had the original sun visor—"

"Yes, ma'am. Can you tell me when Mr. Graham was expected home?"

"Today." I bite down hard to keep my teeth from chattering. "This morning."

"And you have not seen or heard from him since the phone conversation last night?"

"No."

He writes down something else. "We'll check with the Sagebrush Inn." His voice is measured, kind, but impersonal. "But at this time, ma'am, we believe that Mr. Graham was the driver of the vehicle. I'm very sorry."

I can't help noticing his uniform. It's dark and looks heavy. Nice material, but it has to be terribly hot. In this weather . . . why don't they have something lighter? Seersucker.

"Ms. Cooper . . ." He's looking at me steadily, and I can't breathe.

No, I'm breathing. I'm just not getting any oxygen. I feel lightheaded. I press both hands to my mouth, hard, to stop the shaking.

"Are you going to be sick?" he asks.

My head moves from side to side.

"Can I get you a glass of water?"

"No. Thank you." Then the tears pool in my eyes and spill over. He offers me a handkerchief, but I reach blindly for the green afghan and hold it to my face.

After a few minutes I manage to stop crying by biting on my lower lip till it hurts. He asks if there's someone I want to call. Gwen? She still doesn't have a phone. Betsy's out of town.

He asks if he can take me somewhere.

"No. I'm fine. I'll be fine." But my breath continues to jerk weirdly. I just want him gone.

He lays a business card on the table. Central New Mexico Crisis Center. "In case you want to talk to someone," he says. "I'm very sorry for your loss, Ms. Cooper."

Cold air is pouring out of the air vent above the couch and I'm shivering. I wrap the afghan around myself and sit, mindlessly rubbing the scalloped edge along the jagged scar that runs down my left forearm. Someone's crying. Me. Louder and harder till I think I'm going to gag.

A pounding noise. When I realize it's Mrs. Harriman banging on the ceiling with her broom, something inside me goes off like a bomb. Suddenly I'm in the middle of the floor screaming—*SHUT UP, you stupid old cow!*—jumping up and down as hard as I can, till my feet tingle and my knees hurt. After a minute or two I see myself acting like a total lunatic, and it scares me so badly that I stop. I sit back down on the couch, crying and hiccupping. Mrs. Harriman's broom is silent.

I don't know how long I sit there, but finally the pungent smell of burning pastry reaches my nose and a few seconds later the smoke alarm begins to shriek.

When I met Michael, I was a junior at UNM. Working mornings at a coffee place—Java Junction—and sharing an apartment with Betsy. I was also at the end of a long string of bad choices in men—the latest one a married anthropology instructor, Roy Addison. The affair had progressed to Stage Five— near death—where every meeting consisted of sex followed by an argument, but I was still convinced that he would divorce his wife and marry me. And in fact, he had moved out of his house and into an apartment.

He and Michael had known each other since their undergrad days, and they were regulars at Java Junction. They were an interesting duo. Based on appearances, you would have thought Roy was the MBA candidate—all tweedy and preppy—and Michael the anthropologist. Michael's good looks had a more exotic cast—thick dark hair and olive skin, but startlingly blue eyes and a smile that flashed like lightning. I was too absorbed in my soap opera romance with Roy to pay much attention to him, but Betsy got all sparkly and animated whenever the two came around.

When Roy informed me that he was going back to his wife, things got ugly. We had the nasty breakup scene, complete with door slamming, broken pots, and neighbors calling the police. Betsy nursed me with wine, chocolate, and a sympathetic ear, and I finally started sleeping through the night. Three weeks later I was leaving Java Junction at one thirty on a Saturday afternoon, just starting out the door, when Michael started in and we nearly collided.

"Sunny, hi." He stepped back out and held the door for me, aiming his wonderful smile at me. "Where are you headed?"

"Home. I just finished my shift."

In our brief mutual hesitation, I wondered how much he knew about Roy. Two women approached the door, waiting for us to move out of the way. "Well . . . Nice to see you." I moved past him, but he touched my elbow.

"Can I buy you a coffee?"

I floundered for a minute. I was hot and sweaty and I knew my hair smelled liked burnt toast.

"Oh, for God's sake, have coffee with him," one of the women said. "Just get out of the doorway."

Instead of coffee, we ended up drinking margaritas on the shady patio of a small café off Romero Street.

"So you and Addison broke up."

I studied the menu. "You knew that."

"Yeah. I helped him move back in with Claire."

I slid the knife and fork off the napkin and placed it on my lap. "That's what married men do, isn't it? Just pick right up where they left off—" I stopped.

He ordered guacamole and chips and more margaritas. The waiter brought a pitcher and two icy glasses with salt on the rims.

"I shouldn't be doing this," I said.

"Why not?"

"It's the middle of the afternoon."

"The only difference between a margarita at night and one in the afternoon is the ambient lighting." He smiled. "Besides, I've always thought that if everybody did something they shouldn't at least once a month, the world would be a better place." He filled our glasses. "Don't worry, they're ninety percent ice."

I took a sip, sloshing some on my nose, and we both laughed. He reached over to dab the tip of my nose with a napkin, and I set down my drink. "Why are you doing this?"

"Doing what?"

"Look, I'm sure Addison told you all about how I broke the pottery and the neighbor called the police—"

"He didn't tell me anything."

"But it's okay. I'm fine. In fact, the whole thing was getting pretty boring—"

"Is that what you think this is about? Believe me, I'm not that nice."

I drank a big gulp of the margarita. It was icy cold, but it made my stomach feel warm. "I'm not sure what this is about. I just don't want to be your good deed for the week."

"Sunny, cut it out. Or I'll get pissed off. And you know what happens when a Cheyenne gets pissed off . . ."

I shook my head.

"The Little Bighorn."

It was the tequila that was making me laugh. "You can't be a Cheyenne. You have blue eyes."

"Actually I'm a 'breed. My mother was an Indian maiden and my father was a fast-talking son of a bitch from Chicago."

"Where are they now?"

"My mother? Inside a whiskey bottle. If she's alive. My father—I don't know. He left before I was born. I grew up on my grandparents' farm in Illinois."

"What was that like?"

"It was okay." He shrugged. "They did their best to make a good little white boy out of me."

"And did they succeed?"

"More than I would've liked. Less than they would've liked."

I used a tortilla chip to shovel up a chunk of guacamole, chased it with another gulp of margarita, and then frowned as the cold twinged between my eyes.

"Where are you from?" he asked.

"Arroyo Embuste. It's sort of near Taos."

"I know exactly where it is. My undergrad roommate was from Taos. I used to go home with him for the holidays. You go back much?"

I shook my head.

"Where exactly did you live? I know that area pretty well."

"At Armonía."

"The commune?" Now I had his undivided attention.

"Yes. I was born there."

The waiter brought my chicken with dark mole bubbling at

the edges of the plate. I cut a big piece and put it on Michael's plate.

"I'm not hungry," he said, but I knew he'd eat it.

We floated down the afternoon on a slow river of margaritas and conversation. He told me matter-of-factly about helping his mother up the stairs to their front door when she was too drunk to walk. About coming home from school when he was in first grade to find her giving some guy a blow job on the living room couch. He told me how, when he was eight, she drove him in a borrowed car to a farmhouse in a small town far from their home and told him to stay with the two white people who lived there while she went to the grocery store.

He sat on a swing that hung from a big tree, watching the cars go by in the warm afternoon. The white people came and told him to come inside for dinner, but he stayed on the swing while the shadows grew longer and darker and the sun disappeared and the first stars came out. By then he knew. So instead of waiting for the white people to come outside and tell him, he got off the swing and went into the house.

I told him about growing up on the mesa, always knowing I didn't belong there, always feeling alone in the middle of a constantly changing crowd. I told him about my father leaving when I was ten, how my mother taught me to cook, how Hart and I picked apples in the early fall. I actually started to tell him about Mari—which should have been my first clue that I was drinking too much—but at the last minute I changed the subject. I think he knew there was more to the story, but he didn't push.

I didn't realize just how drunk I was till he asked for the check and I got up to go to the bathroom and knocked my chair over. The noise startled me, and I laughed. The two other couples on the patio politely ignored me.

Stepping into the street from the shade of the patio, we slammed into a wall of late afternoon heat. I stopped. "Ohmigod. It's so hot out here."

"Yeah, it is. Are you okay?"

"No, I feel like . . . I'm in a tunnel. You know?"

He guided me past a fountain where a little cement boy peed water into a turquoise pool.

"I'm so sorry. This is terrible."

"It's not like you were dancing naked on the table." He paused to light a cigarette and for the first time in my life, I liked the smell of tobacco. "Can you make it to the car?"

"I think so."

The last thing I remembered was him fastening my seat belt.

A wedge of light split my head open. I moaned, covering my eyes with my forearm.

"Are you okay?"

I tried to push myself into a sitting position, but the room rushed away from me and I lay down again. The floor moved. Not a floor, a bed. Not my bed.

"Where am I? And why is the bed moving?"

He laughed. "At my place. And it's a water bed."

"What am I doing at your place?"

"Well, I don't know where you live, and you were in no condition to give directions."

"Michael, I'm so embarrassed. What time is it?"

"About ten."

Panic seized me. "In the morning? Oh God. I have to go to work."

"Saturday night."

I removed my arm from my face and peered out from the slits of my eyes. He was sitting next to me, propped up against a pillow, a book in his lap. My hand went automatically to my shirt, which was untucked and twisted around. I sat up slowly. "I should go home."

"Why? It's late, we're comfortable. You can just spend the night, and I'll take you home in the morning."

"I can't. Betsy—she'll be worried."

"So call her."

I got up unsteadily, the water bed heaving under me, and walked into the bathroom. I took a healthy swig from a bottle of Scope sitting on the counter, splashed some water on my face, tried to rub out the creases made by the pillowcase.

When I came out, he was gone. I sat down on the bed. I had absolutely no recollection of how I got here. Did he have to carry me or did I walk? How long was I passed out? I remembered it was four o'clock right before we left the café, but surely I wasn't unconscious for five hours. I was hoping we hadn't had sex, because I liked him, and I didn't want to end up breaking his dishes some night.

I looked around. The room was a typical apartment bedroom. Beige carpet, white walls. The only art was a framed map of New Mexico when it was still a territory. The closet door was open, and I could see boots: cowboy boots, hiking boots. A dusty backpack leaned against the wall.

A movement in the doorway, and he was back, a plate in one hand and two glasses in the other. "I didn't think you'd want wine, so I opened a bottle of my finest Albuquerque tap water."

I took a glass and drank half of it at once, then looked over

at the plate bearing cheddar cheese, bologna, and white sandwich bread. My stomach rumbled ominously.

"I don't keep a lot of gourmet stuff around." His tone was
apologetic.

"That's okay, I'm really not hungry."

"You should eat something. Even if it's only bread."

I dutifully took a white spongy square, ripped it in half,
pinched off one small bite.

"I like that," I said, nodding at the map.

He laughed. "I bought it in La Mesilla right after I graduated. The guy in the shop told me it was very old—1879, he
said. I can't remember how much I paid for it, but it seemed like
a lot at the time. I was so proud of that thing." He took a drink
of water and set the glass on his night table. "When I took it to
be framed, I told the woman that I'd gotten it from a collector,
and that it was very old and valuable, and she laughed. She said
it was a reproduction. She told me how these guys use tea to
simulate aging, how they make the wrinkles with a steam iron
and sell them to suckers like me."

"Did you ever go back and confront the guy?"

"No. I was too embarrassed. And I just figured it was a lesson. The lesson was that I didn't buy a map; I bought a feeling.
That's why I keep it around."

"I have to ask you something." I was still rolling the bread
between my thumb and index finger. "I don't remember if . . .
did anything . . ."

He took the tiny cylinder of mashed bread out of my hand
and put it on the plate. "No. You're still a virgin."

I set the glass down on the bedside table and slipped my feet
into my shoes. "I've got to go."

"Sunny, it was a joke. I didn't—"

"No, really." I spotted my purse on a chair draped with T-shirts and jeans. "You're a nice guy and I like you. I don't want to get involved with you."

"That's a very interesting philosophy. You prefer to get involved with guys you don't like?"

"Apparently."

He stepped in front of me just as I reached the door. "I'll drive you."

"I can get a bus."

"Not many buses running on Saturday night." He took my arm gently. "Come on. I'll drive you home, and that'll be it. I promise."

He called me about a week later and left a message on the machine—did I want to go for a hike up at the Pecos National Monument. I debated whether to call him back. I didn't know how to tell him the truth. That it had become too easy for me lately to invest everything in somebody else's world. That Roy was the fourth one in just over two years, and I was tired of ending up in Betsy's intensive care unit for the lovelorn. Guys didn't want to hear stuff like that. They thought you were being coy. So I didn't return his call, and he didn't call again.

Chapter 3

I spend the next three days sitting on the couch with the television on. I watch Katie Couric and Matt Lauer. I watch Martha Stewart and Oprah. I watch *All My Children* and *Geraldo*. At night I watch the cop dramas—*Law and Order* and *CSI*. I like their compactness, their symmetry. I like the fact that even when the good guys don't win, at least they know what happened, who's to blame. Evil may not always be punished, but at least it's identified.

The phone rings and I listen to the messages, but I don't pick up. Betsy returns my call, her voice unsteady. She'll be home the day after tomorrow. Artie wants to know if I'm all right. Can we reschedule the session I no-showed yesterday? A woman from the Weavers Guild wants to know if I can do "light refreshments" for a gallery opening. Bobbi Hazeltine says Smedley the poodle misses me. I delete them all.

Except Sergeant Bagley. I call him back right away. Because some part of me still believes he's going to say, we've made a mistake. It wasn't Michael in the truck. It was just some nameless car thief. Instead, Sergeant Bagley asks if he can stop by again.

He fills the doorway—not as tall as Michael, but square and muscular—saying, "Hello, Ms. Cooper," in his polite southern voice. "How are you getting along?"

I mumble something unintelligible.

"I wonder if I could ask you a few questions."

This time we sit in the kitchen at the table and drink lime iced tea from my blue Fiestaware pitcher.

"I just want you to know this is all strictly routine," he says. He's not wearing a wedding ring. He looks younger than me, but acts older. I wonder if there's anyone who loves him, who would stomp on the floor and scream at an elderly neighbor if he happened to get killed.

"Can you tell me about Mr. Graham's medical history? Was he generally in good health?"

"I guess so. I don't remember him ever going to a doctor."

"Did he ever have any kind of seizures?"

"No."

He scribbles in his notebook. "Did he ever have any psychotic episodes?"

I frown. "Like what?"

"Acting irrational. Seeing or hearing things that weren't real."

Only money, I think, but I say, "No, nothing like that."

"Any history of depression?"

"No." I wonder abstractly how many times he's had to do this. Dissect some dead person's life.

"What did he do for a living?"

"He started companies."

"Beg your pardon?"

"I know." I rest my chin in my hands. "It sounded strange

to me, too. When he first told me. He liked to call himself a serial entrepreneur. Basically he would start companies and then
when they were going well, he'd sell them."

"That's a new one on me." The sergeant shakes his head.
"Everything going okay with his . . . companies?"

"Fine. I guess. It was kind of hard to keep up with."

"Did he have any hobbies?"

"We used to go hiking. Baseball. He loved the Cubs. And
poker."

He writes this down and underlines it, and suddenly I feel
disloyal, talking about Michael to this stranger.

"You mean like Texas Hold'em? Did he play at the casi-
nos?"

"No, no. I mean, I don't know what they actually played,
but it was just a bunch of guys getting together on Monday
nights."

"You know any of these guys?"

"Roy Addison. He's a professor at UNM. He's about the
only one I know."

"They never played over here?"

"Well . . . no. Michael said they played at somebody's house
who wasn't married."

"Makes sense." He flips a few pages in the notebook. "Did
he use any type of drugs or alcohol?"

"Beer. Wine."

"Did Mr. Graham have life insurance?"

"I don't know."

"How long were you and Mr. Graham married?"

"We aren't—weren't married. We lived together almost
three years."

Sergeant Bagley drains his glass. "Is there any other family?"

"I don't think so. He wasn't in touch with anybody." I reach for the pitcher behind me on the counter and realize that he's staring at my arm.

"That's a pretty mean-looking scar."

Patches of heat erupt on my face. "I had an accident. A long time ago."

He looks at me steadily. "And your relationship with Mr. Graham, how was that?"

I'm too exhausted to lie. "Not as good as it used to be."

"In what way?"

I stir the ice around in my glass with my index finger. "I don't know. First he wanted to get married and I didn't. Then I sort of wanted to and . . . We stopped talking. I don't know— the usual stuff, I guess."

"Did he ever cheat on you?"

"No." I hesitate. "I mean . . ."

"You mean, if he did, you didn't know about it?" The sergeant is very good at interpretation. "He ever hit you?"

"Never. Why do you need to know all this?"

He taps the top of his pen on the table. "We talked to the folks at the Sagebrush Inn. Mr. Graham checked in late. Just after eleven. He paid in advance, so they don't know what time he left. The maid did say that the bed was wrinkled, like he'd laid down on top of it. But it wasn't really slept in."

I stir my ice some more while I digest this.

"How did Mr. Graham sound when you talked to him Wednesday night?"

"Tired."

"Anything else?"

"Reception was terrible. I couldn't hear him very well. He seemed stressed, but there was a lot of that lately." My chin trembles. "Somebody broke into the apartment that afternoon and stole some CDs. I was afraid they might come back. I was pissed off that Michael wasn't coming home. That he didn't seem very . . . concerned. I hung up on him."

He waits a moment. Then, "Can you think of any reason why Mr. Graham would want to take his own life?"

I look at him, startled. "Is that what you think?"

"Not necessarily. He probably just fell asleep."

"I don't have to . . . see him. Do I?"

"Make an identification? No ma'am." He finishes his second glass and stands up. "If you can give me the name of his dentist . . ."

The memory of Michael's smile brings me up short, embarrassed. "I don't think he ever saw a dentist. Since we were together."

"Then maybe I could take something of his . . . a hairbrush or a hat, maybe. For a DNA analysis. It's just routine. I think we can be reasonably certain the driver was Mr. Graham, so we're going to release the remains to you for burial."

In our bedroom I pull out the top drawer on Michael's side of the dresser. I haven't looked at his things in ages. He always put his own clothes away. Socks in a jumble—he never tried to match them up till he needed to wear them—his nail clippers, an old wallet full of sample business cards from all his companies, a small pueblo pottery dish of pennies. God, there's the birthday card I gave him last year. I never imagined he kept things like that. A travel dispenser of dental floss, the faded blue bandana he used to tie around his neck when we went hiking.

What am I supposed to do with all this? The clothes, shoes. The Chicago Cubs hat, his hiking boots. The silver ring with the nugget of green turquoise that he bought in Cerrillos but rarely wore.

My head feels like an echo chamber. I keep hearing Sergeant Bagley say, *Can you think of any reason why Mr. Graham would want to take his own life?*

No. Michael wouldn't.

But then, I can't think of any reason why he would have been driving north on I-25 at three in the morning, either. Why don't I know what was wrong? Because something was definitely wrong.

I lie back across the bed, propping a pillow under my head and letting my eyelids fall shut of their own weight.

I dream that we're at a motel, a roadside tourist cabin. Michael loved those relics of pre–interstate highway days, and whenever we discovered a new one, he had to spend the night there. He never minded the smell of ancient cigarettes and moldy mattresses, the banging of the metal wall heaters and the squealing pipes. Mornings would find him in the office, drinking horrible coffee and pumping the desk clerk for local history. In the dream I'm sitting on the bed watching TV, and he goes outside to get something from the car. Then he's knocking on the door. The knocking gets mixed up with something on the television, and I can't tell where the sound is coming from. I hear him calling me. He keeps saying, *Sunny, are you there?*

And then I realize that I'm not asleep anymore and someone really is calling me.

"Sunny! Are you there? It's Betsy." Her voice sounds far away, muffled by the door.

I roll off the bed, fuzzy-mouthed, in a haze of sleep, and stumble out to let her in. Her face registers alarm. "Oh God, Sunny. You look like hell's blue plate special. Did I wake you up?" She hugs me hard, and I feel her tremble a little.

Her leather shoulder bag slips off her arm and onto the back of a chair. "This weather sucks." She brushes at the damp wisps of hair plastered to her forehead. "All my good blouses are getting rotten under the arms."

She follows me into the kitchen. "Have you got any tea? No, forget that, I need a beer." She opens the fridge and pulls out a Dos Equis. "Want one?"

"Not now."

We retreat to the couch, and I sink back down into the spot that still holds the imprint of my butt. Betsy sits sideways at the opposite end, regarding me anxiously. "Are you eating?"

"Corn flakes."

"Sleeping?"

"Not much."

"I've got some pills the doctor gave me last year when my dad died and I couldn't sleep. They put me out like a light. I know you don't like drugs, but why don't I bring you a few tomorrow?"

"I figure when I get tired enough, I'll sleep."

"What have you been doing?"

"Watching TV mostly."

"Speaking of drugs." She shakes her head.

I run a hand through the greasy strings of my hair, realizing only now that it hasn't been washed in five days. My head feels like it's on somebody else's body. "God, if I could just make myself believe it . . . maybe I could function. I keep expecting him to walk in the door." I look at her, my eyes filling up. "I was making dinner when the cop came."

She scoots down next to me and puts her arm around me, resting her head on my shoulder. "I know, honey. I'm so sorry. This is such a terrible shock. I'm so, so sorry." Suddenly she's crying, and I'm comforting her.

She pulls a tissue from her pocket and blows her nose. "What can I do?"

"I'm having a hard time . . . with this funeral thing."

She jams the crumpled tissue back in her pocket. "What do we have to do?" This is so Betsy. Give her a task to accomplish, a problem to solve, and then get out of her way.

"Choose a funeral home. Give them Michael's name and tell them to contact the Medical Investigator's office."

"Where's your laptop?"

We sit, side by side on the couch while Betsy scrolls through pages of funeral consumer websites, FAQs about funerals, and an incredible number of options for disposing of the Loved One. I had no idea. Besides the traditional burial and cremation choices, you can have your loved one launched into space, have his ashes sent off in a helium balloon, or have them mixed with cement to create a "living reef" in the ocean. There's a process called plastination, which sounds almost like taxidermy. I guess that's if you want to keep him around, maybe seated in his favorite chair.

"My God." Betsy shakes her head in disbelief. "You can have his carbon remains compressed into a diamond, so you can wear him on your finger!"

When I start laughing, she puts her arms around me and lets me sob.

The second time I met Michael was almost four years ago, when Betsy had her catering company, Savoir Fare. She was doing the grand opening for some new luxury condos in the Sawmill District and she asked me to work for her as a bartender that Sunday afternoon.

"I don't know anything about mixing drinks," I said.

She said, "You don't have to mix. All they're having is wine, beer, and soft drinks. I just need you to pour and look cute."

So there I was in the penthouse, wearing a white pin-tucked shirt with the sleeves rolled up, black pants, and black bow tie, my hair pulled back severely, asking, *merlot or chardonnay?* And reciting the three different beers and two mineral waters they had on ice.

During a brief lull, I looked over at the French doors that opened out onto the terrace, and this great-looking guy stepped inside. He was wearing faded jeans, a white shirt, and a navy blue blazer and looking completely out of place. Most of the men were dressed in suits, as if they'd come directly from church and brunch; a few others sported Italian designer slacks with sweaters tied around their shoulders, and two, who were obviously there just for free refreshments, wore grubby jeans with the knees ripped out.

The guy stood there studying the brochure with the floor plans, and I kept thinking, *I know him.* And then he looked up, right at me, and I saw recognition flicker in his indelibly blue eyes, and I remembered. I'd seen Michael Graham only once since the long night of margaritas—it was right after I graduated from UNM. He was in the Satellite on Central Avenue having coffee with a very pretty blond woman, and he didn't see me. I was too shy to walk up and say hi. And probably afraid he wouldn't know who I was.

At that point, a very wide guy in a Western suit stepped up to the bar and ordered a bunch of drinks, which he kept turning around and passing back to his friends, effectively blocking my line of sight to the door. When he and his posse finally wandered off, Michael was gone.

Later, when we were cleaning up and loading boxes of supplies into Betsy's van, I said, "Did you see Michael Graham?"

She heaved a carton of plastic wineglasses into the back and turned her head to me. "No. Was he here?"

"I'm pretty sure it was him. Those killer blue eyes."

She sighed. "I didn't see him. Actually all I saw was myself, coming and going. This is the second time that little twit Caroline has no-showed me. It'll be a cold day in hell before I ever—"

"There you are."

We both looked in the direction of the voice.

Michael Graham said, "Betsy and Sunny. The dynamic duo. You two have more staying power than most marriages I know."

We both laughed.

"So you're caterers?" he asked.

"Yes," Betsy said.

I said, "It's her company. I'm just the hired help."

"You did a great job. Great food."

She said, "Thanks. Too bad we didn't get to eat any of it."

"That doesn't seem fair. Why don't you stash all this stuff

and come to Hank's for a burger with me?" His cobalt eyes rested on each of us in turn.

I was starving, but Betsy shook her head. "I'd love to, but I've got to get all this stuff back to the kitchen and cleaned up, and then I have to do the final accounting and put the bill together."

"I'll help you, and then we can go," I said quickly.

"No, you don't know the system. It's easier to do it myself than try to explain it. You guys go ahead. If I get through in time, I'll come over and meet you."

"Okay," I said, and I felt the tiniest jab of guilt for being glad she wasn't coming.

"You up for walking?" Michael asked when we came around the corner of the high-rise and onto Grand Avenue. It was a mild spring evening, with only a slight breeze to stir the blossoms on the redbud and crabapple trees.

"Sure." We stood at the corner, not talking, and when the light changed and we stepped off the curb, the touch of his hand at my elbow gave my heart a little jump-start.

We found a corner booth at Hank's, ordered burgers and their special batter-dipped fries.

"And to drink?" the waiter said.

Michael shot me a wicked grin. "Margarita?"

I felt the heat rise in my face. "I think I'll have a Tecate with lime."

"Make it two," he said and the waiter left.

"So will I ever live that down?"

"Probably not." He slouched down in the booth. "It's really funny running into you like this. I was just at Miguel's the other day—I hadn't been there in probably a year—and I wondered what you were up to."

"I've got this little business going: home security, personal assistant stuff. A few commercial voiceovers."

"Did you by any chance do the Garson's Flowers spots?"

"How did you know?"

"I never forgot your voice."

I looked down at the silverware, rearranging it. "What are you doing now?"

"I'm a serial entrepreneur."

"You mean like corn flakes?"

He laughed. "No, not that kind of cereal. Like one after the other."

A different waiter came and set down two cold glasses and two bottles with lime wedges sticking out of the tops. "So what does that mean exactly?"

"I start a business, then sell it, then start another one."

"Really?" I looked at him curiously. "What kind of companies?"

"Oh, let's see. First I had an art importing business, then a sportswear imprinting company. I sold both of them and started a long-distance reseller company—that's the most recent one. I haven't sold it yet, but I'm working on a software company—"

"I didn't know you were a computer geek."

"I'm not. Kirby Dolen is."

"Kirby Dolen . . . Isn't he the guy who got kicked out of school for hacking into the admin computers?"

"That's him. He's brilliant."

I sat back and looked at him. "That's pretty interesting. But why don't you just start a business and run it?"

"Because I'm not good at management. I like the ideas. I

like getting something off the ground. I'm good at beginnings and endings and not so good at middles."

The food arrived then, and for a minute we busied ourselves with ketchup and mustard, salt and pepper. He asked where I was living.

"I have an apartment on Tillman. Where are you?"

He looked sheepish, almost uncomfortable. "Actually I'm still in that same crummy place."

"Why haven't you moved?"

"Too busy."

"Think you might buy one of those condos?"

"Nah. They're overpriced. Maybe in a year or so, when half of them are still vacant, you'll be able to get a deal."

"They don't give you a feeling?"

He looked puzzled, and I felt foolish. Why did I imagine he'd remember what we talked about one night five years ago? For that matter, why did *I* remember it?

"I just . . . I remembered your map of the territory of New Mexico. How you said you didn't buy a map, you bought a feeling."

"What I remember about that night is that you left too soon."

In the moment before I looked away, we had a whole silent conversation.

When we came out of the restaurant, it was dark and cool. I rolled my shirt-sleeves down.

He said, "Can I give you a ride home?"

"Thanks, but my car's in the parking garage."

We walked slowly down the Sunday night vacant street watching the traffic signals change from red to green and back again. A blue band of twilight lingered on the horizon and stars were beginning to pop out. The sky was perfectly clear, but I could feel the electric charge building, like a coming storm. The garage elevator wasn't responding, so we walked up three flights of stairs to find my car the only one on the floor.

By the time we got to it I was breathless, but not from stair climbing. I was already pawing nervously through my bag in search of the silver concha that anchored my key chain when he took my arm, turned me around, and kissed me. It surprised me—the way I wanted to slide my hands inside the back pockets of his jeans and hold him against me—but then I hadn't been with anyone in a while. I probably would have gone home with him that night if he'd asked me. Instead, he let me go. He took the keys out of my hand and opened the car door.

"I'll call you," he said.

In the end, it's a very small funeral—a graveside service.

Me and Betsy. A tall no-neck guy wearing a pinstripe suit who introduces himself as Matthew Herzog, Michael's attorney. My old flame Roy Addison. He's got the beginnings of a paunch, a seriously receding hairline, and a new, young wife.

He hugs me for a second too long and says, "I'm so sorry, Sunny." New Young Wife gives him a warning look.

There's a spray of flowers from Brookfield/Remington, one of his companies, and one from somebody named Milton Kaplan. The name is vaguely familiar.

After the generic minister gives his final New Age, nondenominational blessing, Betsy and I each throw a handful of dirt on the plain wooden box and watch as the cemetery workers lower it the rest of the way into the ground. We hug and cry.

When I look up, the others are already milling around. They walk past us, directing their murmured condolences somewhere between me and Betsy.

Addison says, "Is there anything I can do?"

"Could you just let everybody know? The poker group."

He frowns. "I will if I can find them. It's been a while since we've gotten together."

I look at him. "You guys haven't been playing on Monday nights?"

"Not lately. It's probably six months or so since . . ." His voice trails off.

"It's okay," I say quickly. "Just if you happen to talk to anybody."

We're still looking at each other when New Young Wife tugs at his hand and they turn and walk toward their car.

Betsy takes me to Graze, and we sit by the windows, nibbling on artisan cheeses and chickpea fries, watching the parade of people on Central Avenue.

"Are you surprised no one else came?" she asks me.

"Actually I'm surprised it wasn't just you and me. Did you call Addison?"

She flushes slightly. "I thought he'd want to know. They were pretty tight in school."

I twirl my wineglass on the cocktail napkin. "I thought about calling some of the people we used to hang out with, but we haven't seen any of them in over a year. I never met any of his business partners. And Michael just didn't have any real friends. That I know of." A little nubbin of a thought sticks in my mind. About the poker group. I start to say something about it, but Betsy gives my hand a quick squeeze.

"He was lucky to have you."

I look at her. "What did I do for him that was so wonderful?"

"You loved him," she says.

Water brims in my eyes. "Did I?"

She looks disconcerted. "Didn't you?"

I spread some goat cheese on a piece of bread. "Something was wrong. I know it. But he kept saying things were great. I don't know . . . You couldn't tell?"

She chews a garbanzo carefully. "It's hard to tell what goes on inside somebody else's relationship. Shit, sometimes it hard enough to tell what's going on in your own. Whenever I was around you guys, he seemed happy."

"How did I seem?"

"Well, girlfriend, you've never exactly been Little Mary Sunshine."

"What?"

"Here, drink some more of this." She edges my glass toward me and rests her elbows on the table. "You've got this melancholy streak as wide as the Rio Grande. I always figured it had something to do with growing up on the mesa."

"But you never asked me."

"I don't poke around in my friends' past lives. If you wanted me to know, you would've told me."

I stare at her, astounded at how nonchalantly she's zeroed in on the central fact of my life and never questioned me about it."

"Anyway, I still think he was lucky to have you. You guys had a couple of great years together. Which is more than a lot of people ever get." She picks up her glass and her eyes fill again. "To Michael. God bless him."

Chapter 4

I probably should have let Betsy give me some sleeping pills, but I hate them. The state they induce seems more like a coma than sleep, and I always feel hung over the next day.

So now I'm lying here, wondering why the room is so light, picking out the familiar shapes of furniture: The hulking dresser we stripped and refinished. The chair in the corner, draped with my clothes. The red lacquered night table I found in a junk shop . . . Oh, right. It's the ghostly green of the illuminated clock radio. Michael slept on his side, his shoulder blocking the light from me. Solving this puzzle satisfies me on some basic level. It means I haven't totally lost my ability to observe, to reason.

But I have lost my ability to sleep through the night. I stay up late, watching old movies till I can hardly hold my head up, then I go to bed, sleep for about an hour, and wake up on my back, eyes wide open, ears attuned to the dripping faucet in the bathroom, the occasional car whizzing past, dogs knocking off a garbage can in the alley.

It's only 5:30 a.m., but I know I'm not going back to sleep, so I pull on a sweatshirt, pad out to the kitchen, and start the coffee. I open my Day-timer. Today: blank. Except for my usual afternoon date with Smedley the poodle.

I flip through the week, all the little blocks of time, subdivided into a.m. and p.m., then further, into a grid of hours. That keeps it manageable. Dealing with a whole Tuesday is too much, but I can do Southwest Women's Empowerment group coffee 10:00 a.m. In the afternoon, record public service announcements for the Mother's March Against Birth Defects.

Wednesday I've got a training tape booked for a small software company in Rio Rancho. I haven't given much time to the script; I was planning to delve into it over the weekend, but somehow I didn't get to it. The Warrens are still out of town, but Joan Ruiz is back, and the Cosgroves are gone for two weeks. I close the Day-timer and set it back on the counter with my sunglasses and keys.

It's 6:30 now and the paper will be here. I open the front door, intending to swoop down and grab it, but the sight of a man leaning against the railing directly across from my door stops me in mid-swoop. His dark hair is receding a little on top, short over the ears and disheveled, as if he's been driving with the car window open. Fatigue scrims his blue eyes. He's wearing faded jeans, a Colorado State T-shirt, a blue windbreaker, and jogging shoes.

His smile is tentative. "You must be Sunny."

It takes me a minute to recall that I'm wearing only a long sweatshirt over my nightshirt, and I edge slightly behind the door.

"Sorry," he says. "I guess I'm catching you at a bad time. I drove all night, and I've been sitting out here waiting till I thought you'd be awake."

"I'm sorry, too, because I don't have the faintest idea who you are."

He pushes himself off the railing and holds out his hand. "I'm Frank Graham," he says. "Mike's brother."

I straighten up slowly and lay my hand in his, but I can't feel it. I'm at a total loss for words.

"I was up in Montana fishing when he called. I didn't get his message till day before yesterday, when I got back into cell phone range. I came as quick as I could. Is he awake yet?"

I detach my hand, reach down to pick up the newspaper in its thin plastic bag. I hug it to my chest and push the door open with one foot.

"You'd better come in."

I leave him in the kitchen with a cup of coffee and the news that his brother was killed in a car accident ten days ago and I go off to the bedroom to find my jeans.

When I come back, the coffee is sitting on the table exactly where I left it and he's standing at the sink, apparently fascinated by my windowsill herb pots with their pale, spindly arms reaching for the light that never quite makes it around to this side of the building.

"Those need more sun," he says.

It pisses me off. "There's no balcony. I wish I had another place to put them, but I don't."

"Sorry," he says, hearing my tone. "I think I'm in shock."

"Sit down and drink the coffee." I refill my own cup and boost myself up to sit on the counter by the sink. "So, where do you live?"

He rubs his eyes. "Manitou Springs."

I wonder, but not out loud, if that's where Michael was headed that night. "You said he called you. When?"

"I'm not sure what day. I've been gone three weeks. There were a ton of messages."

"What did he say?"

"Just that there was some kind of problem. He needed my help. I figured it must be pretty bad for him to call. We haven't talked in a long time."

"He didn't say what kind of problem?"

He raises his eyes to mine. "So you didn't know?"

"No. He wasn't talking much lately. When was the last time you spoke to him?"

Frank Graham shrugs. "About a year ago, I guess."

"I don't understand. Why did you know about me, but I never knew about you? Is there any other family?"

"Not anymore. Our father died about fifteen years ago. Mom passed away last year."

"Was she . . . um . . . Native American?"

He looks at me blankly. "You mean like Indian?"

"Yes. Cheyenne."

He shakes his head. "What did he tell you?"

"That his mother was a Cheyenne, and he never knew his father. That his mother was an alcoholic and he was raised by his father's parents. On their farm in Oak Park, Illinois."

"Well, he got the town right."

We both fall silent.

"I'm sorry I didn't . . . I'm sorry you weren't at the funeral."

"Oh, hey. There's no way you could have known." He slaps the tabletop lightly with his open hand. "Well. I've taken up enough of your time. I should hit the road."

"Don't you want something to eat first? I could fix you some eggs."

"I guess I am pretty hungry. But I don't want you to

cook. Why don't I buy you breakfast? Is there someplace we can go?"

At Flying Star he plows through a full stack of blueberry pancakes and a side order of bacon and talks about his brother, while I listen, nibbling halfheartedly on a bran muffin and sipping lemon rose tea.

"Dad was a contractor. My mom stayed home. They weren't a good match. It wasn't that they argued or anything. They just didn't seem to like each other much. Michael and I both spent a lot of time at our grandparents'."

"On the farm?"

He grins ruefully. "It wasn't exactly a farm. Oak Park is officially a village, but it's really just a suburb of Chicago. Anyway, from the time Michael was about ten, they practically raised him. I guess he was closer to our grandmother than to anyone else. She died when he was in high school, and after that, he just couldn't wait to get out of there. He left right after graduation."

"And you never saw him after that?"

"Oh, he'd turn up every once in awhile. Sometimes he needed money. Or he wanted me to invest in some business deal. Sometimes he just wanted to talk." He loads the last forkful of pancakes into his mouth. When a server comes to clear his plate and refill his coffee, Frank looks at his watch.

"I should hit the road. I've got a lot to do." He hesitates. "I was wondering if you might give me directions to Mike's . . . to the cemetery."

"I could take you by there."

He mulls it over. "I think I'd rather go alone."

"Of course," I say quickly. "It's Fairview Memorial Park. Not far from here."

I drive us back to my apartment building and let him out at his car, a dirty blue Jeep Cherokee with Colorado plates.

"What happened to your Jeep? God, it looks like you had a run-in with an immovable object."

His eyes darken. "I hit a deer. Driving back last night. That's never happened to me before. I felt awful."

"Oh, I'm sorry."

"I was thinking about Mike. Wondering why he called. I probably wasn't paying attention." He shakes his head. "Well, thanks, Sunny. I'm glad I got to meet you. I feel so bad about all this . . ." The card he hands me says only FRANK GRAHAM and a phone number. "It's my direct line. If you need anything or . . . if you just feel like talking. Anytime. I hope you'll call me."

The phone's ringing when I step out of the shower. I'm tempted to let the machine pick up, but then I think it might be Jill Bloomberg, my agent, calling with some work, which I could certainly use, especially after I blew off my last session. Artie said the client was very understanding once they found out why, but it's not something you can get away with too many times if you want to keep working.

"Mrs. Graham?" The guy sounds like he has sandpaper in his throat. "Milton Kaplan." An awkward pause, then, "Do you know who I am? Milton Kaplan. From Denver?"

"Oh, right. You're—were Michael's partner. Thank you for the flowers."

"I'm just sorry I couldn't be here for the service. But I'm in town today, and I was hoping I might stop by for a few moments and pay my respects . . ."

I bend to dry my legs. "That's very kind, but this is sort of a bad time for me."

"I do apologize, but I need to talk to you about something."

"Can't you tell me now? Or I could come to the office. Maybe tomorrow . . ."

"The . . . no, things are fairly disorganized around here at the moment. And I have to fly out to New York tonight. Tell you what. I have an appointment over on your side of town this afternoon. Is there someplace we could meet for coffee?"

"I have to go to work, Mr. Kaplan. If you could just tell me whatever it is you want to tell me . . ."

He clears his throat. "Of course. The reason I came down— it's a bit complicated, but as you may know, in the last several months we've been working with a software designer from Taos on some new accounting security software. I don't know about you, but I don't really understand all that stuff. And I don't want to. I mean, as long as it works, right?" His laugh sounds like it hasn't been used in a while.

"The . . . the situation is that I believe Michael had the program loaded on his laptop, along with a lot of other proprietary information. Apparently the computer wasn't in the truck, so I was just wondering . . . do you know where it is?"

"No idea."

"It's not at your home?"

"I haven't seen it." I glance down the hall at the closed door to Michael's office. After Sergeant Bagley left that first time I just closed the door on the chaos and I haven't set foot in there since. Theoretically, anything could be in there under all the mess.

Big pause. "Well. I'm certain he would have made backup

CDs. Michael was very careful about things like that. Do you think the software might be in his office there at home? It would be on a CD. The label would say 'Dolen Consulting' or 'DolenWare.' It might have Michael's name on it, too."

"I haven't seen any CDs." I shift my weight and adjust my grip on the towel. "But when I get it all sorted out, I'll drop off everything that's work-related at the office. It shouldn't take me more than a day or two."

"You know, I'm in a bit of a time crunch here. Is there any way I could come over and maybe look through Michael's office myself? I could tell very quickly if what I'm looking for is there."

This strikes me as a very odd request.

When I don't respond, he presses on. "It would only take a few minutes; in fact"—he stops, as if the thought has just occurred to him—"I'm not that far away. I could be there in, say fifteen minutes?"

It's obvious that unless I suddenly become less polite, he'll be knocking at my door momentarily.

"I don't mean to be difficult, but I have to go to work and I'm not really comfortable with this."

"I understand completely." Now the voice is subdued. "Perhaps I could call you next week, when I get back from New York?"

"I'm happy to take everything over to the Brookfield office—"

"I'd rather you didn't," he says quickly. "Things are a bit— everyone's upset about Michael's death, and I'd prefer that nobody here know the CDs are missing. No point in worrying them. I'll call you when I'm back."

By the time I hang up I feel heavy in every limb, and the

shower's dampness has evaporated, replaced by a film of new perspiration. Back in the bathroom, I blot myself with my towel and finish dressing. I'm pulling a T-shirt over my wet hair when I get a singing telegram from the left side of my brain.

How did Milton Kaplan know the laptop wasn't in the truck?

I finish dressing, then pull one of the Brookfield Investment Technologies business cards out of Michael's top drawer. I sit on the edge of the bed, pick up the phone, and dial. Two rings, then a click and a mechanically cheerful voice announces, "The number you have reached is not in service. If you feel you have reached this recording in error, please check the number and try again."

Since I have no one to see today except Smedley the poodle, I make a pot of coffee and spend what's left of the morning cleaning the apartment. It's dirty and cluttered, but it's so small, that it doesn't take long to put things in order. I collect all the dishes, cups, and glasses, load them into the ancient dishwasher, and crank it up. I push the vacuum around, give the furniture a half-assed swipe with my microfiber Miracle Dust cloth, and gather all the dirty clothes in the plastic laundry basket. The two washers in the little laundry room downstairs have been out of order for almost a week, so I'll stop by the coin laundry while I'm out.

When I first see my car, I stop in the middle of the street. It looks like it hosted a crow convention during the night. Closer inspection reveals that it's not bird shit; it's eggs. Somebody has egged my car with many eggs and great enthusiasm. I spend twenty minutes scraping off the windshield with my Visa card so I can see to drive.

"Honey, somebody don't like you," the guy at the car wash says. The monogram above his shirt pocket reads VICK.

"Woo-hoo," his buddy joins in. He has no front teeth and no shirt, thus no name. "Who'd you pith off?"

They run my abused vehicle through the wash three times, and when they're finished, there's still an interesting lacy pattern on the hood and the roof.

"I've got to get rid of that stuff before it eats through the paint." I give them my best damsel-in-distress look. "What should I do?"

"Bug Off," says Vick, and his buddy nods.

I'm just about to say something uncomplimentary about their manners, but then he adds, "They carry it at the auto parts store. For getting bugs off the windshield and the grill. It'll help, but you're probably still gonna have some clearcoat damage."

"Don't wait too long," says the nameless one.

The address listed on the Brookfield card is 4171 West Clayton Avenue, #531. I locate the street in my Thomas Guide and, following my afternoon rendezvous with Smedley and a stop at Manny's Auto Parts for a can of Bug Off, I drive on over. West Clayton is a sleepy suburban village street shaded by big cottonwoods and a few Russian olive trees. Small, sixties-vintage professional buildings line the sidewalks, with a café, a shoe repair shop, and a bakery tucked among them.

Traffic is light, so I cross in the middle of the block and walk toward the ascending numbers. I don't see anything that looks like an office building—certainly nothing five stories tall. I pass a convenience store and a one-chair barbershop with a faded sign on the front door that says, BACK IN 5 MIN. A small hardware store is next, and then a display of birthday cards in a window knocks loose a memory. Sunday is my mother's birthday.

I don't see anyone when I step inside, setting off the door chime. The place feels lost in a time warp—a fine dust sits on the glass cases showcasing fountain pens in fancy boxes, bottles of ink, and a few expensive-looking ballpoint/pencil sets. The birthday cards in the display rack have yellow edges from the sun, but I flip through them determinedly till I find one with a picture of a garden and some not-too-sappy verse. The envelope has been sitting there so long that the back is a different shade of blue from the front. I dig four dollar bills out of my wallet and lay them on the counter. Just as I'm starting for the door, a woman's voice says, "Never fails, there's nobody on the street till I have to go to the bathroom. Find what you were looking for?" A Raggedy Ann doll with frizzy red hair and green eyes comes shooting out of a curtained doorway in a motorized wheelchair.

"I did, thanks. The money's on the counter."

"Here, let me ring you up officially and give you a receipt and some change." She zips around the tables, racks, and counters to a cash register on a computer desk.

"Do you by any chance know where Four-one-seven-one West Clayton is?"

She laughs. "You're standing in it."

I look around, thoroughly disoriented.

"Who are you looking for?" she asks.

I take out the business card. "This company, Brookfield Investment Technologies. I was looking for an office building that might be tall enough to have a fifth floor."

"They're a box holder here." She takes the birthday card from me and drops it into a small brown bag along with a receipt. "Five-three-one is their box number."

She nods toward the back of the shop, and it suddenly materializes out of the gloom—a whole wall of mailboxes.

She smiles. "I do it all. U.S. mail, FedEx, UPS, DHL. Packing, shipping, receiving. Mail-forwarding. Good thing, too, 'cause I'm not selling a lot of birthday cards."

"So, in other words, people don't even have to come pick up their mail?"

"Not if they pay for the forwarding service."

"Can you tell me if this company has their mail forwarded?"

"No." She shakes her head emphatically. "No, meaning I can't give out information about my clients. It's all strictly confidential."

"Of course. I wasn't even thinking. Well . . ." I turn toward the door. "Thanks for your help. I guess that's what I need to know."

"Hey!" She scoots around the counter, waving the brown bag. "Don't forget your birthday card."

Michael Graham. What made him so different from all the other men I knew . . . besides being more beautiful? He seemed somehow more worldly or sophisticated than the others—if you could use those words about someone who'd spent most of his childhood in Illinois and his entire adult life in New Mexico. He liked German cars, but drove a classic pickup truck; he loved Italian clothes, but most often wore jeans and a blazer; he appreciated French wine, but usually drank Mexican beer.

He liked jazz and baseball. He actually read the Sunday *New York Times.*

There was an aura about him—daring, adventurous, carefree, almost joyful—but with a darkness just under the surface. Like you could scratch him with your fingernail and find something you might not really want to see.

It was mid-September, an absolutely perfect Rocky Mountain fall weekend, and we were headed for the Blues and Brews Festival. The road to Telluride snaked through the San Juan Mountains, past miles of pristine ponderosa pine, Douglas fir, and aspen forests. He was driving my little Hyundai and we had Eric Clapton blasting out "Layla." The aspens had begun to turn and they winked in the bright sun like new copper pennies. We were very goofy in love.

About fifteen minutes out from town the CD ended and I was reaching for the Eject button when I noticed that I couldn't reach the button because I was flattened against the passenger door. I remember looking at Michael, the concentration on his face, the way his knuckles were white on the steering wheel.

Each moment was a frozen image, like a series of photographs. The other car racing toward us from what seemed at first like a long way off—an old Chevy convertible, blue and white, the top down. The two couples in it—both women were blond, both men were wearing baseball caps. I remember noticing slowly, the way an image through a camera lens comes into focus, almost with a sense of wonder, that we were on the wrong side of the road. Michael already had his foot on the brake, and both cars were spinning toward each other, then away—them toward the rock wall, us toward the edge of the road.

I felt the crunch as the front tires gripped gravel and slid, the back end swung around and stopped. Across the road, the Chevy was stopped, facing the wrong way, on the shoulder next to the rocks. Michael got out, but I sat, afraid to move or even to draw breath. The other driver was running across the road, looking like he wanted to kill us.

"Is everyone okay?" Michael hollered.

I don't think the guy even heard him. "You stupid jackass! You son of a bitch! You just about killed us all! You fucking idiot!"

Michael held up both hands. "Hey, I'm sorry." He actually chuckled. "I swerved to miss a big rock and sort of lost it. I'm sorry."

Now I could see the guy was older. His hair was gray and his face was white under his tan. He started to calm down, but he stood there and lectured Michael for five minutes. He said this was a dangerous pass, that every year there was at least one fatality, some yahoo driving too fast, losing control on the curve, and going over. When he nodded toward the flimsy guardrail, I followed his gaze and my stomach came up to keep my heart company in my throat. We were so close to the edge that I couldn't see any ground between my side of the car and the drop-off. I leaned my head back and closed my eyes.

Finally he left, and we drove very slowly down into Telluride. I don't know what actually happened. I didn't see a rock in the road, but I wasn't watching the road. What stays with me more than the near miss is the contrast of our reactions.

Michael was absolutely wired. We must've been up till one in the morning, him drinking micro brews, sharing a joint with some cowboy, dancing with anyone who'd dance with him, while I sat paralyzed, clutching a plastic cup of warm beer in one hand and my medicine bundle in the other.

When we finally stumbled back to our bed-and-breakfast, I was too exhausted for sleep. I wanted him to hold me. I wanted comfort, not sex.

But Michael had other ideas. He was gently insistent, and finally I relinquished myself to his hands and his mouth, to pure sensation, to forgetfulness, spiraling down into that other kind of death—the kind from which you usually come back.

Afterward, he brushed the hair off my face and kissed me and fell asleep without a word. I lay there in the dark watching the lighted sign outside our window flicker and listening to him snore. Every time I closed my eyes, I saw us going over that cliff, bouncing on rocks, end over end, exploding into flames.

At eight in the morning, he was wide awake and ready for round two. I shrugged him off, rolling myself into an upright position, feet on the floor. Undeterred, he got up and began looking for his clothes and a cigarette. "Let's go eat, then. I'm starving."

When I didn't immediately jump up and start dressing, he came and sat down next to me, pulled me into his arms. "It's okay," he said. "It was scary, but it's over."

I looked at him. "We could have been killed."

"But we weren't. Remember what Churchill said: There's nothing as exhilarating as being shot at and missed." He kissed my hair. He got up. He picked my clothes up off the chair and handed them to me. "So let's go have breakfast."

From the very beginning, his business dealings were incomprehensible to me. Some people would find it strange that I'd never seen the Brookfield offices. But he did most of his work out of the apartment, going to Brookfield only for meetings. It was just the newest of several companies in various stages of evolution.

I never met his partners or co-workers—except for Kirby Dolen. Michael would talk about Steve in marketing or Harry, the operations VP, or Maxine, the financial whiz. A few lived in Albuquerque or Santa Fe, but others were in Phoenix or Denver or Dallas. They all seemed to be independent entrepreneurial types, like Michael, and they did their business via phone and computer, coming together virtually for an intense period of start-up, the search for financial backing, initial operations, and then fading into the background. I quit trying to understand who they were and what they did. By the time I figured it out they would be gone.

Most of the businesses were virtual; transactions were conducted by phone or over the Internet. Michael said the lesson he'd learned with his imprinted sportswear company was that businesses requiring a physical plant, with workers producing a product, incurred too much overhead. Dealing with real estate, facilities and maintenance, payroll and benefits, workers' comp, warehousing, and shipping was doing things the hard way. It was much better, he said, either to sell services through telemarketing or the Internet, or in the case of the chef's equipment website that he and Betsy had been talking about, simply to act as a marketing company and have the actual merchandise drop-shipped from the manufacturer directly to the consumer. Theoretically all his company had to do was promote the business, place the orders, and collect the payments. These businesses were also easier to sell, because without a lot of costs, they looked good on paper.

There was never any logic to his earnings.

When he was flush, we'd eat out four or five nights a week, he'd buy a membership in a wine club, get himself a leather flight jacket, bring me antique turquoise jewelry or a deerskin shoulder bag so soft I wanted to curl up and sleep in it. Other times we'd be shopping for groceries at Costco and buying boxes of wine instead of bottles.

A few months after we reconnected, he moved from his old grad student flat to a beautiful three-bedroom condo on the top floor of a brand-new building with underground parking, a swimming pool and health club, and a coffee bar. And he moved me in with him.

That first year with Michael was a revelation for me—the only time in my life I'd ever been able to forget that chaos is only a ripple of butterfly wings away—well, maybe not to forget completely. But somehow to coexist with the knowledge.

Then something happened. I never found out precisely what, but suddenly we were getting increasingly nasty reminders about late credit card payments, our phone got shut off, his BMW was repossessed, and we ended up selling the condo and hosting the mother of all garage sales. By the time we moved into The Marquesa, I was so stunned and disoriented that I didn't press him for explanations beyond his terse "Financing dried up and we got overextended."

The "setback," as he called it, affected me more than it did him. He was already off and running on the next venture with great optimism, enthusiasm, new partners, fresh infusions of cash from somewhere. He was high as Charlie Parker. Whereas I was having trouble sleeping; I started forgetting things—such as going to the grocery store or picking up the laundry. I never quite got around to unpacking the moving boxes that held all the kitchen stuff, so we ate a lot of cheap Chinese takeout and pizza off of paper plates. He never complained.

Then one evening I dragged myself home from a long session in the studio. When I opened the door to the apartment I stood absolutely still for a minute, halfway convinced that I'd somehow opened the wrong door.

The aroma of a long-simmering marinara sauce greeted me warmly. The living room was spotless. All the pictures that had been stacked against the baseboards were hung on the walls. Michael appeared from the kitchen wearing a dishtowel tucked into his jeans and his thousand-kilowatt smile.

"What's going on?" I asked.

He didn't say anything. He just pulled me into his arms and held me for a minute. Then he put my coat and purse on the couch and led me into the kitchen, where the little table was set for dinner with candles and a small bouquet of flowers in a jelly jar. All the kitchen boxes had been unpacked and the dishes put away.

He gave me a glass of red wine and made me sit down while he broke the dried spaghetti in half and pushed it into a pot of boiling water. Then he pulled out the other chair and moved it over next to mine. He sat down and held both my hands. He said, "I know this has been hard on you, but it's temporary. You need to understand that when you do what I do, shit happens. You deal with it and move on. I know I get moody or preoccupied, but it has nothing to do with us. You just have to accept that's how it's going to be sometimes."

Maybe another woman would've heard a warning in there. What I heard was the reassurance that I was going to be part of his life, so I would have to learn how to keep my balance. Suddenly I was ravenous.

We ate huge plates of spaghetti with freshly grated Parmigiana-Reggiano, twirling the golden strands around our forks, and drank Barolo till I was lightheaded. I wobbled a little when I got up to clear the plates, and when I was standing at the sink, he came to stand behind me. To kiss my neck and untuck my blouse and slip his hands inside, one rising to find my breast, the other descending under the waistband of my slacks. We left the dishes in the sink.

Chapter 5

Betsy Chambliss and I are so alike physically that we've been mistaken for sisters—both of us dark-haired and dark-eyed, but with the kind of skin that turns terra cotta after ten minutes in the sun. We share a lot of interests, like food and garage sales and movies and music and falling in love with the wrong men.

We could wear each other's clothes, but we don't. Her wardrobe consists of a lot of silky, drapey things, while I'm your basic jeans person—I guess that comes of growing up in Armonía, where most of my clothes came from the Free Box. It could also be because she attracts money, while I seem to repel it like a duck sheds water. She's the eternal optimist; I'm the incurable pessimist. She's active and energetic; I'm what she generously calls laid back.

We both majored in communications. We both worked in coffee bars and waited tables to get through school. Now she ends up owning a hip café in Nob Hill while I end up schlepping cookies to sound engineers and picking up dog poop in other people's yards to subsidize my fifteen seconds of fame.

Betsy's new condo is north of town, in Rio Rancho. The complex, called Vista Laguna, is huge, a sprawling maze of tastefully landscaped fake adobe stucco. She greets me at the door with a big hug and a white wine spritzer and the pronouncement that I look much better.

"Let me show you what I've done," she says, taking my tote bag and hooking her arm through mine.

What the place lacks in charm it makes up for in sheer square footage. Her unit is more than twice the size of the one Michael and I shared for the past year. And she's already begun to make it her own, with paint and upgraded flooring, her funky collection of folk art, and furniture gleaned from garage sales and thrift stores. That was the first thing that brought us together: our shared love of trolling for junk.

Tour completed, I perch on a bar stool at the kitchen counter while she washes greens for our salad. "I can't believe the weather," she says. "I'm so glad this heat wave's finally broken. I hope it's not a taste of what's coming this summer."

I squeeze more lime into my drink and stir it with my finger. "At least you've got a pool."

"You know you can come over here anytime. In fact"—she rummages in a drawer—"take this key. Since our schedules are so different, you can come whenever you want, and I don't even have to be here."

"That's really sweet of you, but it's kind of a long drive for me. I'd probably never come if you weren't here."

She layers the dripping romaine leaves in her salad spinner and pulls the cord. "In fact, you ought to think about getting a place here. Payments probably wouldn't be much more than your rent."

"It's too far from all my jobs—"

"Not really." She snaps the spinner's cord energetically. "And you don't even have to get on the I-Twenty-five. I can show you all the shortcuts I've found."

"It's all academic anyway, since I could never get a mortgage."

"I know a mortgage broker who could probably help you out. Or you could rent. A lot of people have bought here just as an investment; they don't live in their units. You wouldn't believe how much the prices have gone up already. Besides," she rattles on, ignoring my protests, "you need to get out of that firetrap you're in. Not only is it a total tear-down, but it's just a garbage pit of memories."

"I just don't seem to be able to muster the energy to make any drastic changes right now."

"Inertia," she says, stuffing the spinner into the already full refrigerator. "A symptom of depression. Okay, that's done. The chicken's cooked; we can just nuke it when we're ready to eat. Let's go get wet."

For every three buildings at Vista Laguna, there's a swimming pool with a couple of Mexican tiles imbedded in the coping. We put on our bathing suits, collect beach towels, bottled water, SPF 30 that smells like piña coladas, and go down to her designated pool.

It's surprisingly crowded for a weekday afternoon, all the chaises longues occupied by brown bodies glistening with sweat and Tropi-Tan. We spread our towels on an unoccupied patch of grass. The sky is studded with puffy clouds, so in spite of the fact that the deck is wall-to-wall bodies, the pool is nearly empty. The cold water is a delicious shock. We swim a few laps and then climb out, goose bumps springing up as dry air meets wet skin.

Betsy shakes her head to one side to dislodge water from her ear. "Tell me honestly, how are you doing? Are you okay? Because you know you're more than welcome to come stay here with me. As long as you need to."

We drop down on our towels and immediately begin slathering on sunblock. Her offer is both touching and embarrassing. "Oh, thanks, Bets. I appreciate it, but I'm fine. Really."

She shakes her head. "Don't lie to me, Sunny. How could you possibly be fine? Maybe you should take a little vacation? Go to Hawaii or Mexico. Lay on the beach and drink margs."

"Right. And come back looking like shoe leather. And I don't have any money. Besides, I need to be here right now."

"What on earth for?" She turns on her side, facing me, propping herself up on one elbow. The tan swell of her hip in the lime green thong bikini reminds me of some Mesoamerican fertility goddess sculpture.

"For one thing, I need to work. And for two things, there's just a lot of stuff going on that I don't understand."

"Like what?"

I roll over on my side to face her. "Like what was Michael doing in Trinidad?"

"I can't imagine." She sets down her sunblock and looks at me.

"And that's not the only thing." I tell her about Milton Kaplan and the disconnected number. The mail-drop address.

"And yesterday this guy shows up on the porch at six in the morning telling me he's Michael's brother."

Her eyes get very round. "I thought he didn't have any family."

I squirt some water into my mouth and some of it dribbles

down my chin. "So did I. The way he talked about his mother
. . . it was heartbreaking. And all those stories he told me about
his grandparents. About the farm. I feel like an idiot. I hardly
knew anything about his companies. The only person I ever
met was that computer guy, Kirby Dolen. What if nothing was
ever what I thought it was?"

She looks away from me. "Does it really matter now?"

I follow her gaze toward the pool, where a guy stands at the
end of the diving board staring into the water. He stands motionless for nearly a minute, oblivious to the urgings of his two
friends behind him to just go on and do it. Then abruptly, and
seemingly without any effort, he rises from the board, bends
into a perfect jackknife, and disappears into the water with
hardly a splash.

When I push open the door at SoundsGood, Artie is talking to
Ron Wyler, another engineer I've worked with.

"Hi there, Sunny." Ron's voice is a little too hearty, and as
soon as I say hi, he scoots down the hall.

Artie's greeting is more subdued. "You doing okay?"

"Pretty good."

"Maybe you haven't seen this?" He holds up today's *Albuquerque Journal*, folded open to a story with the headline "FCC
and SEC Move Against Remington Telecom."

I take the paper from him and scan the first paragraph.
Something about responding to allegations of stock manipu-
lation. But what catches my eye is a URL for a website that
promises more information for those who believe they were
victimized by the company.

"You can take the paper with you," Artie says gently. "But

I checked out the website this morning. It names Michael as CEO but neglects to mention he's dead. And they've got your home address and phone number posted."

"Shit." It's more whimper than expletive.

"Shit indeed." he says. He tugs on his earlobe. "Maybe you should think about moving. Even if it's only temporary. If nothing else, you need to get your number changed to an unlisted one." He looks at me closely. "Are you okay? We don't have to do this today. I can call Ray and—"

"No, really." I fold up the newspaper and set it on the couch, thumb through my papers, and pull out the script for the New Era Computer Academy spot. "It'll be good for me to think about something else."

"I want you to take this." He reaches in his pocket and hands me his business card.

"I already have one of your cards."

"This one's got my home and cell numbers on the back," he says. "I want you to keep it with you. Call me anytime." His eyes shift away and then back to me. "I mean if you need help or anything. You know?"

I smile at him. "Yes, I know. Thanks, Artie."

There are twenty-seven messages on the machine when I arrive home tired and grouchy from too many ins and outs of the car, inspecting the yards of my house clients, and taking Smedley for a long walk. Probably more than twenty-seven, but the thing is at capacity. I delete them all and unplug it. Then I have a better idea and pop the phone cord out of the jack.

I pour myself a very large glass of white wine and sit down to read the story in the *Journal*.

It takes me a while to read the story. One, because it's really long and boring. And two, because I don't make a lot of long-distance calls, so I don't pay much attention to all the deals floating around. The reporter drones on about "slamming" and "cramming" and a bunch of other practices ranging from questionable to downright fraudulent.

In a related story on the facing page, a different reporter writes about the promotion and sale of Remington stock. This piece is even harder to decipher, since it assumes the reader knows all about OTC stocks and something called the Pink Sheet and expressions like "thinly traded," none of which means anything to me. This reporter also mentions that Michael was "unavailable for comment."

What I'd love to know is, where's all this money that Michael and company were supposedly fleecing the good citizens out of? I certainly haven't seen any of it. I had a hard time scraping enough together for his funeral. After a handful of roasted peanuts and a piece of cheddar cheese, I sit down on the couch again, fire up my laptop, and pull up the Remington Revenge Blog.

There it is. Michael's name, address, phone number, and e-mail address. There's even a picture of him, an old driver's license photo, it looks like. How do these people get all this stuff? The only good news is, they have our old address, because Michael never changed his driver's license when we moved. Scrolling down through the posts, it quickly becomes obvious that there are some pissed-off people out there—not that I blame them. Some of the messages are full of garbled rage and misspelled words, but one in particular is reasoned, articulate, and haunting. The writer calls himself MetalMan.

Graham and his partners are real pros. Their ingenuity almost inspires a grudging admiration. The slamming and cramming of long-distance customers was just their opening act. The pièce de résistance was the engineered "sale" of Remington to Brookfield Investment Technologies—a company in which Graham is also a partner. Rumors and news of the sale were fanned to drive up the price of Remington stock so that the partners and their buds could unload their shares at a healthy profit before the whole house of cards collapsed. A classic pump-and-dump with a twist. Long may they burn.

The last line makes the hair rise on the back of my neck.

I believe in baking the way some people believe in God. It's usually what I turn to on those days when the very thought of reality is enough to send me diving back under the covers.

Fortunately, I have to bake today anyway. I'm making raspberry brownies for the Friends of the Rio Rancho Library annual tea; I adapted the recipe from one of Betsy's café desserts. I pulled the ganache and the berry purée out of the freezer last night, so all I have to do this morning is bake the brownies, glaze them, and deliver them to the library by 3:00 p.m. I measure out the flour, brown sugar, white sugar, and salt. Cut up the stick of butter, beat the eggs with an old fork, and unearth my ancient Sunbeam mixer. It has that postwar streamlined look that was big in the fifties, and one of the beaters is just slightly bent. I found it at a yard sale—Betsy wanted it too; it's the closest we've ever come to fighting over a find. Anyway, that was six years ago and it still runs like a champ.

I smash the chocolate with my old wooden meat mallet, put it in a small metal bowl, and set it on top of a pan of water on the burner. I throw in the pieces of butter and stir, zoned out by the swirling patterns of buttery gold against deep, glossy brown.

I keep thinking about the newspaper articles, all the blog entries, and it just doesn't compute. The Michael Graham I knew once turned around and drove five miles back to a restaurant where he thought he'd undertipped a waiter. He appreciated nice things, but he was no high-roller. He liked walking down by the river on Saturday mornings. He could spend hours polishing the truck or patiently trying to teach me to ski up on Sandia Peak, and his idea of vacation was exploring the silence at Chaco Canyon.

How could this be the same person who supposedly masterminded a stock scam?

When the ganache has set, I mark and cut the brownies into squares, and cover them loosely with waxed paper. It's only about a thirty-minute drive to the library, but if I go early I can stop by Betsy's on the way home. Bathing suit and purse go into my big tote bag, and I sling it over my shoulder and head downstairs, balancing the pan of brownies.

I'm being so careful with the brownies, opening the passenger door, arranging them on the seat, securing them with the pieces of Styrofoam block I keep in the car, then putting my tote on the floor, that I don't notice till I shut the door that the right front tire is flat. Then I notice the right rear tire is flat, too.

I walk around to the driver's side. Both tires are flat. I squat down on the blacktop for a closer look. Slashed. All four tires.

I get in the car and call Triple A on my cell phone. Then I call Betsy. Then I put my head down on the steering wheel and wait for the tow truck.

By the end of the afternoon, I have four new retreads, which I put on my MasterCard, trying not to think about what I'll do when the bill arrives. Betsy took me to Rio Rancho to deliver the brownies and has now dropped me off at the tire place before going to work. She leaves me with a hug.

"I think you need to get out of town for a while." She looks at my four shiny black tires and the white blotches on the hood where the egg dried.

As she drives away, I see her looking at me in her rearview mirror, and I know she's thinking I won't really do it. She's probably right. Where would I go?

I climb in the car and toss my tote bag on the floor, and that's when I see it, sticking up between the console and the seat, a sun-faded blue envelope. My mother's birthday card.

Her birthday is Sunday.

Chapter 6

I leave early after a cup of coffee and a leftover brownie. Fortunately I still have the travel carrier in my car with my dozen favorite CDs . . . now my only CDs. Heading north on I-25, I keep the needle on eighty, turning up Trisha Yearwood till the bass line vibrates in my chest, barely noticing as Albuquerque shrinks in the rearview mirror.

I fly past Rio Rancho and think of Betsy, probably sound asleep after a busy Friday night at the café, past the pueblos—San Felipe's Hollywood Casino boasting *Saturday! Paul Revere and the Raiders!*; Cochiti and Santo Domingo, their stations advertising cheap gas and cigarettes; past Traditions, the strange tourist marketplace where tourists never stop and most of the stores sit all lit up, but empty.

A billboard for laser tattoo removal shows a girl's body clad in low-rise jeans. On her hip is etched a prominent red heart and a guy's name. Across the top in big letters, ERASE YOUR PAST!

Santa Fe beckons seductively. I could have breakfast at Tecolote. The thought of their atole piñon pancakes with four berry sauce tempts me to continue on to the St. Francis exit, but I veer off onto the 599 bypass for Española and Taos. I could take the high road through the mountains. Stop at Chimayo, visit the weavers, but my goal is Arroyo Embuste, and I'm afraid that if I stop somewhere, my resolve will crumble, and I'll never get back in the car. I'll find some dark little adobe bar, cool and damp with the smell of spilled beer, and sit there drinking tequila till I fall off my stool.

So I keep driving, and the closer I get to Taos, the thicker the air becomes with the past, until it practically coalesces in the passenger seat—a reckless rider, smoking a joint, refusing to fasten his seat belt. Or *her* seat belt. Because, for me, the past begins and ends with my mother.

By Embudo Station my bladder is making strong suggestions that I stop. The café patio is empty, and I stand in the shade drinking a glass of lemonade and watching the Rio Grande trundle south out of the gorge. I try to make my mind a blank, but it doesn't work. A crowd of memories is already lined up, ready to take turns banging on the door.

The last time I stood in this place, Gwen was standing next to me. It was June of 1989. I had just turned eighteen and I was on my way to Albuquerque. Fall term at UNM didn't start till August, but there didn't seem to be any reason to hang around Armonía when I could take a couple of freshman courses in summer school and look for a job. Gwen drove me down in Boone's red-and-black '71 Barracuda with the windows open and the tape deck blaring the Allman Brothers.

"Berry Oakley was Rob's hero," she said, dangling her arm in the warm air like it was bathwater.

"Who?"

"The original bass player for the Allmans. He was killed in a motorcycle accident the year after Duane."

It irritated me the way she talked about these people like they were close personal friends. "I thought Duane was married to Cher."

"That was Gregg."

"Oh."

I think that was about the extent of the conversation for the whole drive, except when we stopped for lunch and she asked me what I wanted on my cheeseburger. She probably thought I was pissed off at her, but I was actually terrified.

I was getting exactly what I wanted, what I'd been planning for the last ten years. Out of Armonía. I wasn't happy there, but it was all I knew. UNM was a big school—huge, by my standards—in a big city, and there were hundreds of things I was going to have to do that I didn't know spit about.

I wanted to feel like I could tell her all this. I wanted to think that she'd say something like, *don't worry, you'll be fine.* Or *you can always call me, you can always come home,* but I knew she wouldn't say those things, and I knew I'd never go back to the place I called home, no matter how bad it got. So I just sat sweating, watching the mileage signs slip past and wishing the car's air conditioning worked.

Once we'd moved my three boxes of clothes and books into the ugly cement-block dorm room, Gwen took me to Del Norte Savings and helped me open a checking account with the five hundred dollars I'd saved over the last two years working at a souvenir shop in Taos.

I was ready for her to leave so I could go look for a job, but she didn't seem in any hurry. My skin prickled with heat and impatience. Finally she took me back to the dorm, but instead of leaving, she opened her backpack and drew out a wrinkled envelope. From the pay phone on our hall, she called a phone number that was written in pencil on the flap. It was a short conversation and then she said, "Come on, let's go."

"Where?"

"We're going to get some money."

The lawyer's office was hushed as a church. The receptionist's wrinkled nose reminded me that we probably didn't smell too fresh. She stared openly at my mother's embroidered cotton dress and gypsy shawl, her gladiator sandals and unshaven legs.

Finally she showed us into an office full of blond-wood furniture and a wall of windows that looked out toward the dust cloud at the base of Sandia Mountain. My mother chatted easily with the lawyer about the weather and the traffic. Was she actually flirting with him?

I concentrated on watching the tropical fish in the aquarium on top of one of the bookcases. I'd seen pictures of fish like these—red and orange and electric blue, black-and-white zebra stripes, long fins trailing like silk scarves between tiny green plants, and bubbles rising from a little hose to the surface.

"If I could just have your signature on a couple of forms," the lawyer said. He opened a file folder and pushed it across the desk. I looked at Gwen, waiting for her to take the pen from his outstretched hand.

"Go on," she said to me. "You have to sign the papers."

"What?" It had never crossed my mind that this was about me. I looked down and through the jungle of single-spaced words a number came into focus: twenty-five thousand dollars. It came to me suddenly that my mother had somehow finagled me a loan, and my first thought was that she'd slept with this guy. "It's too much," I said. "I'll never be able to pay it back."

The attorney laughed, and I really looked at him for the first time. His ruddy face and perfectly groomed hair. His manicured nails. "You don't have to pay it back, Miss Cooper," he said. "It's yours."

"It's from Nana," Gwen said. "In her will she created a college fund for you."

I gripped the arms of the chair and stared at her. The lawyer got tired of holding the pen out and set it down next to the folder. "Just go through the pages and sign your name and date everywhere you see a blue marker. Oh, and I'll need a certified copy of your birth certificate."

Gwen was already drawing a folded piece of paper from the envelope, pushing it toward him. I flipped through the pages in a haze, signing and dating. Then he flipped through them to make sure I'd found all the blue markers.

"Now, if you'll give me a voided check, I'll have just one more form for you, and we can wire the funds to your account."

I sat there feeling my damp blouse cold against my back. *Twenty-five thousand dollars.* When would I ever see that kind of money again? I didn't want it wired to my account. I wanted to carry it into the bank myself and hand it to the teller.

"Could I have it in cash, please?"

"I'm afraid not." He smiled patiently. "The money's coming from a bank in California. It's much easier and safer to have it transferred directly to your account."

"When will it be there?"

"It should be there by Monday morning."

"What if it's not?"

He picked a card out of a leather tray on the desk and handed it to me. "If it's not, please call me."

Gwen stood up. "Don't think she won't."

• • •

In ten minutes I'm back on the highway. Past Dixon and Ranchos de Taos, with its squatty little bulldog of a church that you see in art galleries and on postcards all over New Mexico. Starting there, in Ranchos de Taos, billboards line both sides of the road and traffic slows to a crawl. I eject Trisha from the CD changer and insert an old folk rock compilation, cruising into Taos while Joan Baez sings "The Night They Drove Old Dixie Down."

As I cross Kit Carson, a poster leaps at me from a gallery window: IMAGES IN SHADOW, NEW PHOTOGRAPHS BY PILAR MONAHAN.

I slow down to stare at it until the guy in the SUV riding my bumper starts honking. I pull over and wait for him to pass, still staring at the poster. It has to be her. How many Pilar Monahans can there be?

The gallery has just opened for the day. The woman behind the desk, dressed in the requisite long black dress, is talking on her cell phone. She slips it quickly into her bag.

"Hi, how are you? Excuse the disarray; we're still setting up for the reception." She smiles and flips her blond hair over her shoulder.

I look around. "That's okay. I'm just browsing."

"Are you familiar with Pilar Monahan?"

"I've seen her work before."

"Oh, good. That piece about her in *New Mexico* magazine last fall?"

I nod.

"We have a few prints from that series, and this new collection was all done in Africa. Also we have a very few excellent examples from her book on Taos commune life. She grew up north of here, on the mesa."

"Is that right?"

"Yes. Those ones are right on the other side of that partition."

"Thanks." I step around to the other side of the wall and come face-to-face with myself. It's an odd and not entirely pleasant sensation. There I sit on my bed at Armonía, long hair obscuring my face, reading Hart's textbook on making adobe bricks. The photograph is a black-and-white, and the background is slightly grainy. I stare at it a minute, willing familiar objects out of the fog. The chair with the broken leg that I kept next to my bed. You couldn't sit on it, but I used it like a night table and to drape my clothes over when they were wet. The ugly still life of flowers in a vase that I did in art class is tacked to the wall.

The woman joins me. "That's a great one. She took it at Armonía, which was up near Arroyo Embuste. This one came from there, too."

It's the carcass of Bubba, our yearling steer, being hauled up on a singletree to bleed out after being butchered.

"It's a little grisly, I know." The woman makes a delicate face. "But I guess that's what life was like in those communes. The amazing thing is, Pilar was only about thirteen when she shot this series."

"She's very talented," I say.

"Yes she is. She really captures the essence of her subjects."

"Just out of curiosity, what are the prices running?"

"They range from two seventy-five for one of her small bird shots to seventeen fifty for some of those large scenes of the South African veld. If you're interested in any of these commune photos, we're probably talking about five hundred dollars or so. Of course, we're flexible."

"That's good to know," I say. She walks tactfully away to let me ponder a decision. I look at a few of the others, just to be polite, and then I head for the door.

"Pilar should be here in about an hour, if you'd like to meet her or talk to her about any of her work."

"I'll try to stop back by. Thanks."

I retrace my steps to find a machine-generated ticket on the windshield of my car. I get in and sit for a minute reading it through the glass. Thirty-five dollars for parking in a loading zone.

In the seventh grade, I wanted to be Pilar Monahan.

Everyone did. She was beautiful: small and slender, with the smooth olive skin of a Spanish aristocrat, long, straight, black hair, and eyes like brown velvet. If she had a flaw, it was her thick, dark eyebrows—Brooke Shields was still a few years away from making that look hip. Her father was an architect and her mother's family had been in northern New Mexico forever.

I met her in the school library, a tiny room with a motley collection of books housed in six bookcases and presided over by a fat, sleepy librarian who kept herself semi-awake with endless cups of coffee.

We were looking for the same book, *Tides and the Pull of the Moon*. I was taller, so it was easier for me to see the books on the shelf labeled *PHYs. SCIence*. Pilar was balanced on tiptoe, and as I reached for the battered paperback and pulled it off the shelf, she uttered a soft little sigh of disappointment.

"I wanted that one." She looked at the book in my hand.

"Are you writing a report on astrology, too?"

When she shook her head, her hair rippled like a dark liquid. "I just wanted to read it."

"You can have it as soon as I'm through." I stepped up to the check-out desk and slapped the book down, startling the librarian out of her doze.

"Or we could share it." Pilar had followed me to the desk and stood next to me, looking up at me through her thick lashes.

"Share it?"

"Yeah. You know, we could go to my house after school and take turns using it." She smiled.

I stared. Was she making fun of me? It was my first and only invitation to somebody's house.

"You want to?" she persisted.

My pride would not allow me to act as thrilled as I felt, so I just shrugged and said, "I guess."

From the road, the house looked like a fort. Adobe, of course, with massive walls the color of wet sand. The windows were set deeply into them and covered with Taos blue shutters carved in a lightning bolt design. When Pilar pushed open the heavy door, it was quiet. No music, no voices, no children screaming, no animals squawking, braying, mooing, barking— just a deep and welcoming silence. I thought I'd stumbled into heaven.

She hung our jackets on a wrought-iron wall rack that was hammered into petroglyph designs. "You want a Coke or something?"

"Yes, please." I followed her down a long hallway, lit by skylights, whose walls were covered with black-and-white photographs in frames. Not pictures of family or friends, but pictures that were art. Stark landscapes of the mesa, close-ups of rocks, clouds, dead trees. Some of them were beautiful. There were one or two small color shots of birds and lizards that stood out like jewels against the white walls.

Pilar noticed me looking. "My mother took most of those." A pause for effect. "And I took some." She pointed out hers. "I have my own camera now. It's a Canon SLR. That stands for single-lens reflex."

We spent an hour or so seated on opposite sides of her desk. I copied out quotes from the book while she worked on her spelling list. At some point I looked up to see Pilar pointing a big black camera at me, twirling its snout back and forth.

"Look at the book," she ordered. "And sit very still. I have to use a really slow shutter speed for indoors."

I sat motionless while she clicked off a few shots, and then I pushed the book across the desk.

"Are you through already?" she asked.

"Yeah. There's not that much I can use."

"Bummer. Hey, do you need to call your parents or anything?"

"No." I didn't want to tell her there was only one phone, out in the workshop, and at this time of day, there wouldn't be anyone out there. I put my notebook and pen away.

She leaned forward across the desk. "So what's it like, living there?"

"It's okay, I guess. It's just so noisy all the time."

"How many people live there?"

"About twenty-five."

"Are there lots of kids?"

"Five or six. And a couple of babies."

"What does everybody do?"

I looked at her sharply, trying to decide if she was asking about sex and drugs. My mother had drummed it into me that I was not to discuss those things with outsiders. "What do you mean?"

She set the camera down carefully and curled the woven shoulder strap into a tight coil. "I mean like what kind of jobs do people do? How do they make money?"

"The same things people do anywhere. Grow food, build houses, fix cars. Some people make things to sell, like jewelry or quilts or candles. There's one guy who paints pictures."

"Is he good?"

"Actually, his stuff is gross. It looks like he let his dog drink paint and then pee on the paper."

She laughed, showing her tiny, perfect doll's teeth, and began to pepper me with questions, like she was writing a report. She wanted to know what we ate and who cooked and who did dishes. She wanted to know what my father and mother did. I told her Rob used to farm and work in the shop—he could fix anything that had a motor—but that he was gone now. I told her Gwen was in charge of cooking; I was too embarrassed to say she took care of getting us food stamps.

"Hi, there." The woman standing in the doorway could have been Pilar's older sister, but I knew this was her mother. She was wearing a long dress and a shawl woven of iridescent yarns that changed colors as she moved. "Are you guys doing homework or just chatting?"

Now, there was a word you didn't hear much at Armonía— *chatting*. There it was called "rapping" or "shooting the shit."

"Both," Pilar said. "Sunny's sharing her book with me. She lives at Armonía."

Mrs. Monahan raised one dark eyebrow and said, "That's very nice of you, Sunny."

I pushed the hair out of my eyes, suddenly acutely aware of the ugly flowered shirt that I'd gotten from the Free Box, the obviously hand-crocheted vest that Wendy had made me.

Then Mrs. Monahan politely pointed out that it was almost suppertime and she asked if I needed a ride home.

"Oh, no thanks. I like to walk."

"I've been to Armonía, and it's too far for you to walk," she said.

"You've been there?"

She smiled. "Yes, we went to a party there a couple of years ago. A friend of my husband's was in some band that was staying there." She stood up and straightened her skirt. "Come on, I'll drive you."

"No, really, I can walk." I didn't like the picture forming in my mind: Gwen meeting Mrs. Monahan.

"Absolutely not. It'll be tomorrow morning before you get home."

As it turned out, on the way through Arroyo Embuste, I spotted the white bakery truck with flowers painted all over it, known as the Dream Machine, sitting in front of the saloon, and I knew somebody from Armonía was there buying cheap wine for the weekend—"Tokay is Okay" was the saying around the circle. Mrs. Monahan seemed dubious, but I finally convinced her that I could get a ride home with whoever was driving the truck that night.

So she dropped me off, and I stood in the street waving at Pilar, who was hanging out the window of her mother's Volvo waving back at me.

• • •

In the weeks that followed, Pilar began fishing for an invitation to Armonía. And Gwen was bugging me from the other side to invite her. Caught in the middle, I held out as long as I could, and then I ran out of excuses.

It was October—one of those fall days like they have no place else but in New Mexico. Sky blue and sun gold, the air so clear that every rock and tree was razor edged, and the Taos Mountains seemed to spring from the ground directly behind our barn. The sun was warm, but a chill hovered in the shade, warning of nights below freezing soon to come.

I waited at the top of the road for Pilar's mother to drop her off, and we walked down to the pueblo, her camera bouncing against her hip. In the commune kitchen, my mother was putting the final layer of cheese on three huge pans of enchiladas.

"You cook on a wood-burning stove?"

My mother smiled. "Hi, I'm Gwen."

Ten seconds later Pilar had the lens cover off and was shooting pictures of my mother, the stove, the Circle Room with its massive dining table and benches, the drumming room, where Wendy was doing yoga.

"This is so groovy," she bubbled. "Show me your room."

I cringed.

Hart wasn't there, but evidence of him was. His gunboat sneakers, Blue Streaks Boogie poster, dirty underwear on the floor, which I attempted to kick under the bed before Pilar noticed it.

"You share a room with your brother?" She was too polite to say, *How weird* . . . "I want to get a shot of you sitting on your bed reading." She looked around. "But I don't know if I'm going to be able to get back far enough."

I picked up Hart's book *Building the Adobe House*, and pretended to read it while Pilar snapped away, plastered into the corner by the door. It was hard to believe that seven years ago there'd been another bed in here. The little cot where Mari used to sleep.

I heard footsteps, and before I could warn her, Hart stepped through the doorway just as she pressed the button. The click startled him and he whirled around.

"Hi. I'm sorry. I was just taking a picture of Sunny."

For a second, he seemed unable to talk, and the look on his face was one I'd later learn to associate with a surplus of adolescent male hormones.

I introduced them. Pilar was charming; Hart was inarticulate. He did manage to ask if "we" could show her around. She said she wanted to see everything, so we started with the animals. There were a couple of goats in the garden. Hart shooed them out to join their friends who were grazing in the pasture, and we followed the irrigation ditch past Jimbo and Kath harvesting corn and beans, Boone driving the tractor in the upper field, getting ready to plant winter rye. Pilar recorded it all on film. Down by the river we came to Hondo's tipi.

Sort of a nice guy, but with weird moments, Hondo was our Vietnam vet who came back without all his parts. He lived alone in his tipi and wore mostly fatigues. And he had guns—a rifle that he carried around like a baby sometimes, and a handgun that I'd never seen, but Hart had told me about it. It was some kind of fancy German gun that Hondo supposedly took off a dead guy in Nam. A couple of times the men had talked to him about his penchant for getting loaded and shooting into the air. Right at the moment, he was standing on the riverbank watching us.

Pilar made a move for her camera and Hart smoothly turned it toward himself, mugging into the lens.

"I want to take a picture of him." Pilar was looking at Hondo, who was still watching us.

"He was in Vietnam," Hart said. "It's not a good idea to point things at him."

"Oh," she said. Then she smiled at Hondo and waved.

We took her to the shop, the only place in the compound that had electricity. That was where Rob had worked fixing cars and other mechanical stuff. That was also the location of two washing machines, which sometimes worked, but not at the moment, and a big upright freezer, a studio where Harpo made jewelry, Chuck made leather belts and shoes, and Trish and Wink made candles, hanging them over the spokes of a salvaged wagon wheel.

I could tell Pilar was enthralled with the Happy Hippies in Commune Heaven.

She couldn't know about the scene last Saturday night when Kath went off with the drummer in the band, and Frog got pissed off and drunk and threw up on the dinner table. She wasn't here when the kitchen sink backed up because Dave put the pipe in wrong, and the skylight over the stove started to leak and we didn't have any money to buy Plexi to fix it. Or the night when the two crazy, filthy monks stopped in for dinner and spent the night talking weird Bible stuff on the floor of Wendy's room. She wasn't here when my mother had it out with Aura Lee, who never helped in the kitchen or garden, and had no money to contribute, but sat on her butt crocheting ponchos to give to her friends.

When we rounded the corner of the barn and heard the sharp crack of a rifle I remembered: the men were butchering today. Bubba, our yearling steer, was about to be turned into packages of beef for the freezer. I grabbed Pilar's hand, but she pulled away.

Over by the big cedar tree, Tucson was just lowering his rifle. Bubba had fallen to his knees, probably already dead. At least I hoped so, because Harpo charged in with a knife and slit Bubba's throat under the jaw. When the blood spurted like a fountain, the men all cheered because he'd done it right. Two of them rushed in with buckets to catch the blood.

I heard the camera clicking and I looked over at Pilar. She was a little pale, but she kept shooting.

"Do they drink the blood?" she asked breathlessly. "Like the Masai warriors?"

Hart and I shared an alarmed look. When he explained that it would be mixed with sawdust and linseed oil and used to seal the floors, she seemed disappointed.

Hart proudly showed her the garden, the greenhouse that was under construction, and the root cellar, where carrots and potatoes were buried in sand for the winter. She helped my mother and me peel and slice apples for drying. She fed the chickens with Wendy's kids, Corona and Kachina. She was squeamish about using the five-seater outhouse, waiting until she was in pain before whispering to me that she had to pee really bad. So Hart and I stood guard, keeping anyone else from going in while she was using it.

That night, after enchiladas and coleslaw and chocolate

cake with walnuts and raisins, Topper and Jimbo got out their guitars, Tucson retrieved his bongo drums, and Boone had his harmonica. They played a little Dylan, a little Grateful Dead. Hart threw a big log on the fire, and people drank wine. Carl fixed his pipe with some homegrown and passed it around—a pretty mellow scene.

I was just beginning to get warm when the door swung open with a rush of cold air that made the fire sputter and surge. Hondo walked in and stood there with that fixed stare that meant he was totally flying. The room got quiet except for Topper, still playing the bass line to "Sugar Magnolia."

"Hey, Hondo. Come on in, man," somebody said. "Shut the door; it's cold."

"Want some chocolate cake?" Kath asked him.

He was wearing his fatigues with an old poncho wrapped around his shoulders. And then he took out his fancy German gun, put it in his mouth, and pulled the trigger.

The silence was cold and solid like a block of ice, except for the click of the pistol. Hondo started to laugh. It was this wild noise like the coyotes make, and he laughed till the tears ran down his face. He doubled over and kept slapping his thigh while everybody stared. Finally he choked out, "Somewhere in here, there's a bullet. Who wants to play roulette?"

Boone and Harpo were on him amazingly fast for two guys who'd been smoking dope; then Topper and Dave. They hustled him outside.

Wendy got up and ran out of the room, crying, and Kath went after her. I laid my hand on Pilar's arm, but she sat frozen, gripping her camera to her chest like a shield. She didn't even know I was there. Then, abruptly, she looked at her watch and said she had to go; her mother would be waiting at the top of the road.

Hart and I pulled on our jackets and walked with her. We didn't talk. She hugged her camera to her chest, and I could hear her teeth chattering. When we saw the lights of her mother's car sitting just outside our gate, she ran to it, opened the door, and got in, slamming the door behind her. She never said goodbye or waved or even looked back at us.

I stood there with Hart in the light from the full hunter's moon, watching the car turn around and head back down the road till the taillights disappeared.

And I knew instinctively that on Monday, when I saw her in the hall, she would look at me and smile, her gaze slightly unfocused, just above my head, and she would keep walking.

Chapter 7

I drive past Cid's, the yuppie grocery store, north toward Arroyo Embuste and the mesa. It occurred to me somewhere between Velarde and Dixon that I don't know where my mother lives. When they turned Armonía into a bed-and-breakfast last year, she sent me a letter telling me she'd moved, but the return address was a P.O. box, and I'm quite sure she didn't give directions, never dreaming that I'd actually come to visit. The last time I was up here was three years ago, when I brought Michael to meet her.

He was quaintly insistent that if we were going to live together, he should meet my mother. She disliked him on sight—good looking, well dressed, clean-shaven, ambitious: Satan personified.

Arroyo Embuste has one four-way stop at the south end of town, and you rarely see two vehicles at the intersection at the same time. The biggest building is Valdez Feed and Hardware. Just down the street is the Arroyo Café and General Store, which also houses the post office. Next door to that is the saloon, which used to be called Dirty Ed's. Ed and his wife, Trish, lived upstairs and the volunteer fire department stashed their equipment in the back room. Now the place is called El

Bosque, but it looks pretty much the same. The macrobiotic grocery where we used to swap handmade jewelry for cheap vitamins still survives, with its tiny clinic in back.

I park in front of the general store, careful to leave the hitching post clear for anyone who might ride up on a horse. I don't need another ticket. The door squeaks raggedly when I push it open. A young girl sits at the counter drinking coffee and reading, oblivious to the flies swarming over her partially eaten breakfast. A woman in a long dress and a Sherpa hat pulled down over her gray braids stands behind the counter. Watches me. Says nothing.

I smile. "Hi. I'm looking for Gwen Cooper."

"Don't know her." This is the high mesa version of screening visitors.

"She lives here. She has a post office box here. She used to live at Armonía."

The woman picks up the girl's plate and sets it gently in the bus tray. "More coffee, Benny?"

"Sure, thanks."

This ritual is designed to let me know, just in case I missed it, that I'm the outsider. I sit down at the counter, smile at the girl. She smiles shyly and goes back to her book.

"Can I have a Coke, please?"

The woman sets a warm can in front of me and doesn't bother to open it. Her name comes to me: Terry. She owns the café now. I vaguely recall her, long-haired and naked except for a squash blossom necklace, dancing at one of the parties they used to call "boogies." She obviously doesn't remember me.

"I'd like a glass of ice, please."

She gives me a hard stare and eventually a glass with two ice cubes.

"Are you rationing ice?"

"It's high desert here. Water's scarce." She turns away and begins wiping dust and crumbs off the counter.

The can opens with a sharp hiss and a fine spray of Coke. I pour it over the two lonely ice cubes and take a swallow. "I know it's a desert," I say. "I grew up here."

This causes them both to turn my way.

"Gwen's my mother."

The girl is twirling a piece of honey-colored hair, gazing at me with open curiosity. The woman's mouth twists into something like a smile.

"Soleil?"

"Sunny," I correct her.

"Does Gwen know you're coming?"

I shake my head.

She sighs and gives an answering head shake. "You kids."

I take another drink. "Do you think I could get some more ice?"

She digs the metal scoop into a bucket of ice and fills my glass with it.

I follow the map that Terry drew on the back of a paper bag. When I see the sign that says, COUNTERCULTURE BED & BREAKFAST, I turn the opposite direction. I wonder if they serve beans and tortillas for breakfast. I wonder if their guests have to use the five-seater outhouse, if they lie awake, freezing, listening to ten guys drumming and chanting till 2:00 a.m. At least I didn't have to pay for the privilege.

At the end of a rutted dirt road, I find my mother's house. Like most of the buildings out here, it looks like it's in the process of melting back into the earth. A Dodge minivan with a flat tire and a WHO WOULD JESUS BOMB? bumper sticker sits in the yard. I park next to it and get out, wiping sweaty palms on my jeans. I catch myself tiptoeing toward the door, which is propped open with a black work boot.

It's ridiculous. I'm not trying to sneak up on her. And anyway, she will have known someone was coming even before she heard my car. It's a sixth sense you develop when you live in the middle of nowhere. I used to have it, too.

A gray cat, snoozing on the threshold, jumps up at my approach and disappears under the portal. My mother sits at a small table by a window, head bent over something; long brown hair streaked with gray curtains her face.

"Hi, Gwen."

She looks up and smiles. "Why, hello, Sunny." Like I'm a friend who's just stopped by for a cup of tea instead of the daughter she hasn't seen in three years. When I step inside, I see that she's beading, something she took up after my father left.

She gets up and comes around the table to hug me. She's put on weight. I feel a small frisson of satisfaction.

"You doing all right?" she asks.

"Okay. How are you?"

She pushes her hair back. "Staying busy." Then she looks past me. "You're by yourself? Where's what's-his-face?"

"Dead."

I know it's a cheap shot, but when I deal with my mother, I feel justified in using whatever means are necessary to produce a reaction. And this works very well.

She breathes in sharply, then waits. Studies my face to make sure it's not some sick joke. "What happened?"

"Truck accident."

"I'm sorry. Really. I didn't like him, but I certainly didn't wish . . ." Her voice trails off. She takes off the skinny glasses perched on the end of her nose and lets them nestle against her denim shirt, suspended on a beaded chain. "When did it happen?"

"About three weeks ago."

She hugs me again. "Who's been taking care of you?"

"I have. I'm pretty good at it. And my friend Betsy Chambliss."

"Wasn't she your roommate for a while?"

"Right. She owns a café now. In Nob Hill. She's been great."

"I really am sorry, Soleil."

All this sympathy is making me itch. "What are you working on?" I nod at the table.

"Oh, just a belt."

I walk over to look at it. "Just a belt" is an intricate, graceful floral pattern in tiny beads of turquoise, brown, gold, and green. "It's pretty."

"Yeah." She stretches her arms to the ceiling, which is so low she can almost touch the darkened log vigas. "My technique's gotten better. But my back's killing me. This one's for a rich old hippie from L.A. Some of those beads cost a fortune."

I look around at her. "I hope you got some money in advance."

"Always so trusting." She laughs. "He'll pay me. He's a good guy."

"I remember a few good guys who stole food and money from us after we fed them and gave them a place to stay."

Her serene smile always made her look like a Madonna in

an Italian painting. In spite of the added years and pounds, it still does. "Nobody took much. I figured they needed whatever they took. Most of them paid us back. One way or another."

This is the point where we could slip effortlessly into one of our old arguments, based on diametrically opposing views of life, so I swallow my response and let her offer me tea. While she bustles around the tiny kitchen, I check out her new house. It has the packed-dirt floor common to old adobes, but it has electricity and running water. A small, black wood-burning stove occupies one corner, obviously for heating, not cooking.

"I'm getting too old to be chopping wood and hauling water," she says, reading my mind.

The couch cushion, covered in a wild yellow-and-green paisley and draped with handmade afghans, sinks like quicksand when I sit down. "You should get a phone."

"Too expensive. Anyone who wants to talk to me can find me easy enough." She raises her head to look at me. "Obviously."

"What if something happened? What if you got sick or hurt yourself?"

The teakettle screeches, and she pours boiling water into an earthenware pot.

"I have friends," she says. "We check on each other."

She brings the pot and two rustic mugs over to the couch, but when I reach for the pot, she puts her hand on mine.

"Five minutes," she says. "It has to steep."

"You don't seem very surprised to see me."

"I dreamed about you two nights ago. You were walking down a long, dark flight of stairs by yourself. I should have known what that meant." She looks at me sideways. "But you didn't come all the way up here to put your head in my lap and cry. What's going on?"

I sigh. "Michael. He was apparently involved in some . . . business stuff. It wasn't all exactly kosher. There are a lot of pissed-off people coming out of the woodwork." I steal a look at her face; her expression is neutral. "They put our address and phone number on the Web."

"You mean like on the computer?"

"Right. So anyone who wants to find him . . . or me—"

Her gray eyes flash. "That's outrageous. Fucking computers. It's like Big Brother. You know that's all controlled in Washington." She scoots forward on the couch and pours the tea.

"Is there any sugar?"

"Of course not. I have some honey, but this stuff is better plain. Here, just try it." She hands me one of the cups, and I burn my mouth on the rim.

"Careful," she warns belatedly. "That micaceous clay holds the heat."

I touch the burned place with the tip of my tongue. "I just wanted to get away for a couple of days. So I could think about what to do. And . . ." I fish in my purse for the blue envelope and hold it out to her. "It's your birthday."

"So it is. I'm not counting, though." She takes the card out and reads it, smiling slightly, stands it up on the coffee table. "Thanks for remembering."

I try the tea again. Two tiny sips. It's good. "What is this?"

"Jiaogulan. It's the immortality herb of Chinese medicine. It has more than three times the saponins of ginseng."

She stops, the cup nearly at her mouth, and looks out the

window. I follow her gaze. There's nothing outside, and all I hear is the high desert wind rounding the softened corners of the adobe.

"What are you looking at?"

"This guy."

"Who?" I twist around to look.

Finally I see him. Walking slowly toward the house. From this distance, only his walk is male, that peculiar rolling onto the balls of his feet that some guys do.

We watch him until he reaches my car. He doesn't touch it but circles it, looking in the windows. He's wearing gray slacks and a white short-sleeved shirt, which immediately brands him as not local. I get up and walk outside. He's busy inspecting my vehicle, so he doesn't see me till I'm practically on top of him.

"Who are you?"

He pivots his bulky frame so fast he nearly loses his balance and faces me, breathing raggedly. Under the flush of exertion, his face is gray and doughy, and sweat trickles into the rolls of flesh on his neck.

"Lessing. Tom Lessing." He holds out a business card, which I refuse to take, so he stuffs it back in his pocket. "And you . . ." Significant pause. "Are Mrs. Michael Graham."

"I'm afraid not."

"Well, you might not be married to him, but you definitely live with him."

"What are you doing here?"

"Trying to locate Michael Graham."

"Try Fairview Cemetery."

He studies me with colorless eyes. "You're saying he's dead?"

"That's usually why people are in the cemetery."

"How convenient." He takes a step closer, and suddenly I can smell him. Holy Mary, his body odor could drop a buffalo.

"Feel free to check with the New Mexico State Police. He was killed in a truck accident three weeks ago."

"I'd like to ask you a few questions. About his business activities."

"I don't know anything about his business activities."

He looks over my shoulder. "So . . . who's in the house?"

This guy is getting on my last nerve. "None of your damn business."

"Actually, it is." His smile is more like a smirk, and I can't help thinking that he looks exactly like a mole, with his pointy nose and jutting little teeth. Or he would if moles wore glasses and sweated. "I belong to a group called the Remington Restitution Committee. Our members are people who were swindled by your boyfriend and his partners. We intend to get our money back and see that the perpetrators are punished."

"I just told you Michael's dead. I don't think there's much more you can do to him."

"Maybe not, but I can still collect information about his activities, so we can try and recover some of our money."

"Well, you're going to have to collect it from somewhere else."

"You expect me to believe that you lived with him and you don't know what he was up to?"

"It doesn't matter whether you believe it or not. It's the truth."

"You could be an accessory to a federal crime, lady. If you're smart, you'll cooperate with us." He's jabbing the air in my general direction with his index finger and it scares me that I'm imagining the rubbery crunch of it between my teeth.

"What seems to be the problem?" I turn to find my mother standing beside me.

"Gwen, please go back in the house."

She ignores me. "You're trespassing here, so why don't you tell me what this is all about."

"Sure, I'll tell you what it's all about," he says. He proceeds with a litany of grievances against Remington and Michael while Gwen listens patiently. He implies that I was at worst complicit and at best willfully ignorant. He says Michael's probably not really dead, just hiding out till things cool down. Then he tells her about his group of vigilantes, who are determined to see justice done. In case the government fumbles the proceedings.

I glare at him. "Stalking's against the law, too, you know."

"We're not stalking you," he says indignantly. "We are the victims of a confidence—"

"Not to mention egging my car and slashing my tires. That's called vandalism. Also illegal."

"I don't know anything about that," he says primly.

My mother lays a restraining hand on my arm—as if she thinks I'm about to attack him. "What proof do you have that she's involved in any way?"

"She lived with the man."

"Okay, she lived with him. They slept in the same bed. They had sex. So while they're in the middle of getting it on, he's gasping and panting and saying, oh god, Sunny, let me tell you the great scam I thought up today—oh god, yes, do it again, baby . . ." She smiles disarmingly. "You think that's how it went?"

The Mole's face is flushed with the effort of imagining. "I think she—"

She cuts him off. "You know, people who get scammed are usually people who are looking to make a fast buck and aren't particular about how it's done. Then they're the first ones to scream when something goes wrong."

He pulls a dirty white handkerchief out of his back pocket and mops his forehead. "We thought it was a legitimate invest—"

"Investments!" She gives him a withering look. "That's what's wrong with the whole damn country. Everybody always worrying about their damn investments. If you're so hot to invest, why not pick some green companies, ones that are doing some good, helping to heal the earth instead of polluting it? It's all one, you know. Humans may be at the top of the food chain, but they're still part of it. Have you ever given any thought to the interconnectedness of all the species on the planet?"

I'm starting to worry that she's going to invite him in to drop some acid, but Mole is inching backward. I think he finds my mother scarier than me.

"I'll be in touch," he says, not looking at her. He jams the handkerchief back in his pocket and lumbers away, the heels of his Hush Puppies slinging up dirt. When he disappears around the bend in the road, we go inside.

"Now the tea's cold," Gwen grumbles. "I hate to throw it out, too. It's expensive."

"If you had a microwave—" I begin.

"Those things cause sterility."

"You're not planning to have any more kids, are you?"

"And cancer," she says. "I'll drink it iced. You want some?"

"No thanks. For someone who used to ingest peyote, you're pretty picky about a few microwaves." I go back to the couch.

"Typical materialistic, greedy bastard. Fucking capitalists are taking over the whole—"

"You should've just let me handle it."

"I was afraid you were getting ready to tear his throat out. Then you'd get arrested, too. I just can't believe—"

I look up. "*Too?*"

She joins me on the couch with her iced tea. "Your brother's in jail in Kentucky."

"What for?"

"Passing bad checks. He wrote me for bail, but I don't have that kind of bread."

"It's money, Mother, not bread. Bread is something you eat. Why didn't he get in touch with me?"

She says, "He probably didn't know how."

"If that fat jerk-off could find me, I'm sure Hart could. I'm listed in information."

"I'll give you his address. You can write and ask yourself."

I lean back into a squishy pillow and prop one foot up on my knee. "You can't be too surprised that at least one of us ended up on the wrong side of a jail cell door. You're the one who taught us that the law was irrelevant. It was okay to bust the system because the system was corrupt and meaningless."

She gives a short, wry laugh. "I never knew you were actually listening to me."

I rest my head on a saggy cushion. "Aren't you going to ask

me whether I really knew anything about what Michael was doing?"

"Of course not. You were never a good liar."

"I just can't believe he was involved in anything illegal. I mean, yes, he wanted to make money, but he would never knowingly have—"

"He wasn't what you thought he was."

I look at her. "You have no idea what he was. The only time you ever met him you were incredibly rude and you acted like you couldn't wait for us to leave."

She rattles the ice cubes in her glass testily. "I have good intuition about people, Soleil."

"We were going to get married."

"It would have been a huge mistake."

"He loved me."

"He would've sucked the life out of you," she says. "He was plastic—"

"He was not—"

"When you brought him up here, I saw immediately that you'd lost your center. Men can do that to you, believe me—"

I can't suppress a laugh. "What makes you think I ever had a center?"

She sighs noisily and drains her glass. Then, "Are you planning to spend the night?"

I hesitate. As usual, I can't tell if she wants me to stay or not.

She says, "I don't have an extra bed, but you can sleep on the couch."

I guess that's an invitation.

Dinner is the green chile stew that I smelled simmering on

the stove when I walked in the door. Gwen gathers up her beading tools—needles and push pins, thimble and threader, containers of beads—some in shot glasses, some in an old vitamin
dispenser. I make cornbread while she tosses a salad with her
favorite sesame dressing. We move around the tiny space easily,
in the way of women who are used to cooking together, and for
a brief space of time I'm back there—six years old—helping my
mother, the queen of the kitchen. Hart is sitting in a ladder-back
chair, feet hooked behind the rungs, reading R. Crumb comics.
My sister, Mari, two years old, sprawls on the floor playing with
the wooden animals my father has carved, corralling them in a
big saucepan. A scene from *Little House on the Mesa.* I push the
memory away.

Even though it's late April, the nights are cold up here, and
before we sit down, my mother makes a fire in the woodstove—
one piece of wadded-up paper, a handful of kindling, and a dry
piñon log. I wonder if I could still do it that fast. There are only
two electric lamps in the whole place, so she lights a kerosene
lamp and places it on the table between us while I fill the re-
cycled glass tumblers with cheap red wine. The food relaxes us,
blunts our sharp edges, and the wine lowers my defenses.

Conversation becomes easier; I find myself confiding more
about Michael than I intended to, but it's a safe topic. Safer than
acknowledging the ghosts who come out of the dim corners to
sit with us in the warm yellow light, safer than talking about
the one whose undeniable presence we both ignore. My sister.

Her name was Mari. Rhymes with sari, not Gary. It was
short for *mariposa,* the Spanish word for butterfly. Another one
of Gwen's flights of fantasy. At least it was Spanish, not French.
Actually Gwen named her for the mariposa lily, a wildflower

that grows on the mesa . . . sometimes. They don't always bloom. Conditions have to be just right. After an especially snowy winter, you can find them in the early spring, three pure white petals on a slender stem, blooming in some rough patch of rock and sand. She was a beautiful child, growing in a rough patch of life, and like her namesake, she didn't last very long.

After dinner, Gwen makes decaf and then produces a cookie tin containing ZigZag papers, a Bic lighter, and a small pouch of marijuana. She rolls a joint, efficiently, matter-of-factly. She's had lots of practice.

She flicks the Bic and inhales deeply, holding the smoke in her lungs.

I ask, "Have you heard from Rob lately?"

She shakes her head, finally exhaling. "Not in a year or so. Last time he wrote me, he was in Fayetteville. Hart was there. Rob's married again. I guess she's younger. Had a couple of kids by her first husband; now they've got one together. He's got himself a little appliance repair shop."

"Perfect. 'The Handy Man.'" I've had just enough to drink that I start humming the old Jimmy Jones song. We sit for a while without talking, both of us drifting on the past.

A sudden smile lights her face. "Remember that time you got sick and he made a vaporizer out of a peanut butter jar and the spout from the oilcan?"

For an instant I'm there. The damp cold of a late-winter storm, white frost on the windows. The comfort of Vicks and steam. I take a sip of wine. "He was so good at that; I don't know why he ever wanted to do anything else. Why did he want to be a musician?"

"That's what everybody wanted to be then. A guitar man."

She offers me the joint, even though she knows I won't take it. "He seems happy now."

I wave the smoke away from my face.

"I've got his phone number around here somewhere, if you want it."

"No thanks."

I haven't talked to my father in twenty-two years. I don't know what we'd say to each other. I wonder if he can picture me as an adult, or if he still sees the skinny, clumsy ten-year-old who clung to his hand the day he left, dark hair matted with tears.

I stir milk into my coffee and watch her body visibly relax, wondering if the dope makes her forget. Years ago she told me she wished she would get Alzheimer's, that her memories were unbearable. But how would it be if she had none? What if she just stared at me out of empty eyes?

Deep wrinkles fan out around her mouth like spokes of a wheel when she takes a last toke. She says, "He asked about you. No, really. He did."

Chapter 8

Thunder wakes me in the night. I don't open my eyes, but the lightning is so bright I can see it through my eyelids. The rain starts as a gentle patter, then gathers force, rattling against the adobe's metal roof like machine-gun fire. I try to remember if I rolled up all the windows in my car. My eyes flutter, and I'm about to sit up, when a flash of lightning reveals my mother, standing at the window. She seems unaware of me, twisted up in a blanket on her couch. She's just standing, staring out into the storm.

In the intermittent bursts of light, all the signs of aging—her softening chin, the lines around her mouth, her drooping eyelids—are muted. I see her the way she used to be. Heart-shaped face, delicate nose, full mouth, long dark hair. I can picture her at the Berkeley antiwar protest where she met my father. She would have been barefoot, holding an armful of the brightly colored paper flowers she always sold at peace marches. No wonder Rob loved her.

I shut my eyes tight and concentrate on the purple star-bursts against my eyelids.

• • •

The next time I wake up, light is filtering through the gauzy curtains and the door is open. The breeze is cold and clean, and carries the sharp, fresh scent of big sagebrush. I shiver and wrap myself tighter in the faded blanket. I slept with my socks on, but my feet are still freezing. I reach for my jacket, slip my arms into it.

"Gwen?" I pull on my stiff jeans, tucking in my T-shirt and stuff my feet into jogging shoes.

Her bed is neatly made, spread with an ancient quilt I recognize as one she got in trade for some goat cheese. The door to the bathroom is open, the room empty. I return to the front window. The rain has sluiced the dust from the air and scoured everything, if only temporarily. My car glistens, black and pristine in the sun; from here you can't see the white splotches left by dried egg. Then I see her coming up the path that curls around the back of the house. Her long skirt ripples in the wind and she walks slowly, deliberately. She walks as if something hurts and she doesn't want it to show.

She steps inside. "I was down by the river. Doing my Tai Chi."

She'd never say it, but I'd be willing to bet she was down where we scattered Mari's ashes on that wild, windy day, November 2, 1979: El Dia de los Muertos, The Day of the Dead.

That's the day when the Mexican people bring food and liquor and cigarettes to deceased loved ones. They hang around the graves and talk to them, play their favorite music. Rob used to say it was just an excuse for a party, but I'm not so sure. Maybe it's an old knowledge that we no longer admit to—that the dead never really abandon the people and places they loved and that loved them.

I say, "That was some storm last night. I guess you needed the rain."

She shrugs and heads for the kitchen. "I didn't hear a thing. I sleep like a rock."

I stare at her back. Did I dream her standing by the window? Another memory: how her absolute certainty always made me doubt myself.

"Wheat grass or carrot juice?" she asks.

My stomach turns over. "Why don't I take us out to breakfast? For your birthday."

At the café, Gwen has carrot juice and herbal tea, sprouted wheat toast (dry), and organic oatmeal with honey and soy milk. Meanwhile, Terry whips up French toast and bacon for me and keeps my coffee cup filled while she leans her elbows on the counter and trades gossipy tidbits with my mother about who's playing musical beds, who's pregnant, and who's leaving to go out to California or just got back from Florida.

When they've run through everyone they know, Terry shifts her weight and turns to me. "Sunny, it sure is good to see your face around here. You gonna hang for a while?"

Amazing how fast I went from being *turista non grata* to the prodigal daughter. I smile and chew.

"Well, actually—"

"She's at a turning point," Gwen interrupts. "Her guy just got himself killed."

"It's not like he did it on purpose. He was in an accident."

"Just a figure of speech," she says mildly, then turns to Terry. "Anyway, a lot of strange people are turning up on her doorstep claiming Michael screwed them out of money or some such thing."

"Really?" Terry's attention is now fully engaged. "Man, it sounds like a movie. Have they threatened you?"

"Of course not. It's just—"

"One of them actually followed her up here yesterday. I had to run him off."

"I just needed a break," I say. "To think about what to do."

Terry and Gwen lock gazes. "I Ching."

Before I can swallow the food in my mouth, Terry whips the dog-eared, food-splattered book and her worn velvet coin purse out from under the counter.

"Come on, you guys, I want to finish my breakfast."

My mother pulls a sheet of paper off the little notepad she always has in her backpack. "Think of your question and write it down."

I take a purposeful sip of coffee. "I don't believe in this crap."

"It doesn't matter whether you believe in it or not," Terry says. "It works anyway."

She dumps the three dirty coins out of the velvet bag into her hand and fondles them like jewels.

"I really don't want to do this. It's a waste of time—"

"Sunny," my mother interrupts. "It's my birthday. Humor me, okay?"

Terry looks at her accusingly. "You didn't tell me it was your birthday."

"I'm not celebrating them anymore, but Sunny decided to come up—"

"Then it's the least you can do," Terry says. She pulls the pencil out from behind her ear and thrusts it at me like a sword. "Here. Write down your question."

"God." I snatch the pencil and scribble *How can I put my life back together?* on the paper. Gwen folds it in half without looking and tucks it under the edge of her toast plate. Terry presses the coins into my hand.

"Hold the question in your mind while you're throwing," she says.

I throw the coins six times and my mother records the totals and builds the hexagram. This was the way decisions were made at Armonía, except they always used the yarrow stalks, which took about four times longer. I remember nights spent with two dozen people gathered around the huge table, the common area thick with smoke, all of them hanging raptly on the adventures of the corrupt King Shang and the virtuous King Wen.

"Okay, your present hexagram is Number Twenty-six, Da Chu."

"Gesundheit." I laugh but they ignore me.

"You have one changing line, but we'll read the present first."

Terry reads from the book. "Present Hexagram Number Twenty-six, Da Chu, Great Gains—"

"Isn't that a breakfast cereal?"

"Sunny, shut up and listen," Gwen says. "You might actually learn something."

Terry coughs and starts again. "*It is advantageous to be firm. It is disadvantageous to enjoy luxury and leisure at home. It is advantageous to cross the great stream. Do not think about it; do it. Have courage and step into the great stream.*" She and my mother exchange a Significant Look.

"And the changing line is number one . . . let's see . . . Oh, my . . . *The situation is perilous. Peace can be deceptive. The dan-*

ger has not been completely eliminated. Remain cautious. Do not be taken by surprise."

Gwen says, "The Future Hexagram is Number Eighteen. Gu. Decaying."

The slap of the screen door makes us all turn around.

"Hey, Terry. Hiya, Gwen." The guy approaching the counter is tall and barrel-chested with a ratty gray ponytail coiled over his shoulder like a pet snake.

"Can I get a cup of coffee and one of your cinnamon rolls?"

"Hi, Chip. It'll be a few minutes. We're throwing the I Ching."

He looks like he just farted in church. "Oh, sorry." His voice drops to a near-whisper. "I'll run over to the feed store, and come back."

Terry flips backward through the pages. "Eighteen, you said? *Gu indicates a corrupt enterprise. When food is rotten, it must be replaced. The analogy denotes a turning point, the moment of change when King Wen replaced the rotten Shang.*

"It is advantageous to cross the great stream. If your situation has soured, it's time to move on."

Terry and Gwen shake their heads in tandem. "Wow," Terry says. "Pretty amazing."

"You couldn't ask for a plainer reading," my mother says.

I stare at them. "You're joking, right?"

They stare back at me.

"No, we're not joking." Terry sounds offended.

"I don't see that it told me anything specific." I look at Gwen. "Tell me what you think it says."

"Well . . ." Gwen arranges her skirt and hands me the paper

with my question on it. "I assume you asked something on the order of *What should I do now?* Right?" I nod. "It's telling you to step into the great stream—"

"I thought it said to cross the great stream."

"There's different ways to interpret it," Terry says. "When it says to enter the stream and it will carry you along, it's like life. Get back into life."

"But if I cross the stream, then I get out again."

"Quit being so literal." Gwen glares at me. "Try to see the metaphor."

"Wait a minute!" Terry looks like she might start jumping up and down. "What if it means the Rio Grande? It could be telling you to go west."

"So maybe it means get back into life, and maybe it means head west. How am I supposed to decide?"

"Intuition," Gwen says. "You must have some kind of gut feeling about it."

Terry slaps the counter. "Turn off your radar," she intones. "Use the Force!"

My mother and I don't talk on the ride back to her house. She turns the radio to some oldies station that's playing Joe Cocker, and her fingers tap the armrest with the driving beat. His voice always reminds me of a large waterfowl being poked with an electric cattle prod.

When the song ends, she says, "You could come back here." Her voice rises on the end, like a question.

"Why on earth would I do that?"

She looks straight ahead, and I can tell by the set of her jaw that I've finally managed to hurt her.

"I don't know why you feel so shortchanged," she says.

I grip the steering wheel tightly and then loosen my hold. "How about because I had to learn how to tie my shoes and tell time from teachers at school. Because I had to have people tell me I stank before I knew you were supposed to take a bath on a regular basis. Because—"

"I taught you what I thought was important."

"Like how to roll a joint."

"You know what, Soleil?" She presses her lips together and I pray she doesn't start crying. "The world is going to cut you only so much slack because you think you had a lousy childhood." She turns her face to the window.

There's not much I can say to that. Or rather there's too much I can say, and if I say one thing, I'll have to say them all. And she'll have to defend herself. Then we'll fast-forward to the same old accusations and denials, recriminations (hers) and guilt (mine.) So I don't say anything.

When we get back to the house, I gather my spare T-shirt and my toothbrush and my jacket and toss them in the backseat of my car. She follows me outside and settles a brown shopping bag on the front passenger seat. It holds something heavy and bulky, wrapped in newspaper.

"What's that?"

"The bean pot," she says.

It's the micaceous clay pot that we cooked beans in for years. Made by a Taos potter who fired his vessels at such a high temperature that they can go in the oven or over direct flame. It cooks dried beans in three hours flat, no pre-soaking, and gives them a slightly smoky taste.

"I can't take it," I say. "You need it."

She laughs. "I don't make beans anymore. They give me gas."

There's a split second where I hate her for knowing exactly what I want and deciding to graciously bestow it on me. Because that's just what she does. Has always done. She gives things away. It's never mattered what or to whom. It's not like I'm special. I'm no different from any of the stragglers who wandered down the road to Armonía looking for something.

I hug her quickly, awkwardly, and pull away just as quickly.

I say, "When are you going to get the tire fixed on your van?"

"When I need to drive somewhere." She smiles like we've just had a really fun visit. Maybe we have. Maybe this is about as fun as it's going to get for us. "Safe home," she says.

Chapter 9

I find the check register under some file folders while I'm trying to put the office back together. I start to toss it into one of the drawers, but something stops me. Michael and I each had our own checking account, and there was a joint household account for major expenses like rent, utilities, and food. All three accounts were at Bank of the West. All three check registers were white with the bear logo on the front. This one is different. Pale gray, not white. CAP ACCOUNT REGISTER is printed on the cover, and in the lower right corner in tiny letters: *Reorder online at www.firstdallas.com.*

The starting date is January 20 of last year. I open it and scroll down the neat columns of check numbers, payees, and amounts. There are lots of J. Smith and T. Jones entries. J. Henry, T.D. & H., Garson F., Campos Syndicate. When my eye lands on the ending balance, dated March 13, of this year, I hear my own startled intake of breath.

$367,416.32.

It must be some kind of business account. But why was he banking in Dallas? And where are the checks? I survey the floor. Somewhere in this mess.

I stand up the two photos he kept on his desk. The frames and glass are pristine, since I cleaned the black fingerprint powder off them with 409. The pictures themselves look dingy by contrast. One of Michael and me at the New Mexico State Fair, stumbling off a stomach-churning ride, holding hands, laughing. It's hard to remember him ever wearing a cowboy hat. I can't even recall who took the picture. The other is a shot of his Monday night poker group that one of the guys took with a digital camera. It's printed on thin paper, with muddy and faded colors, but I wouldn't let him throw it away. It was my favorite photo of him—his hair was longer then, down to his collar. He's frowning at his cards; a cigarette dangles from his mouth. If he just had a black hat, he could be the proverbial Mississippi Riverboat Gambler. Two of the others hold longnecks aloft— one is Addison. The other guy, standing behind Michael, looks familiar. Sort of. He's got long hair, too, a narrow jaw, and high cheekbones. But I can't place him. The host—I think his name's Brian—pretends to take a bite out of a cheese ball.

I set the register on the desktop, gather up all the empty folders, and put them back in the file drawers, sort through the papers, making two heaps, one for all Michael's work stuff and one for everything else. And finally, reluctantly, I sit cross-legged on the floor and begin sifting through the chaos—income tax documents for both of us, piles of paid bills that used to be organized by category, my medical records and health insurance (Michael had neither, preferring to think he lived a charmed life), information on his truck and my car, and warranty cards for every appliance either one of us ever bought, from the battery charger to the stereo.

But it's becoming obvious that there's not much left of Mi-

chael's paperwork. Just a few bills, mockups of promotional brochures, Xerox copies of articles from *StartUP* magazine and the
Wall Street Journal. I've now lifted up every piece of paper on the
floor and there are no checks to match the alien check register.

I stand, stretching my cramped legs, then sit down in the
desk chair and study the register more closely. Could Garson
F. be Garson's Flowers? I turn the pages backward. One, two,
three, four checks to payee Garson. Not one under a hundred
dollars.

And what's the Campos Syndicate? In January, February,
and March, the payee is listed as Campos Syndicate. The checks
are spread out, one, maybe two a month, for several hundred
dollars. By October they've become more frequent; the payee
is listed as Campos. The amounts have increased to a thousand
dollars, then three thousand, then ten. They seem always to
come close on the heels of a deposit in the same amount. The
last check recorded follows three deposits of one hundred thousand each, spread over the course of a week. The check is for
$325,000, and the payee is listed as C.S. The amount of the
check was never subtracted from the balance, so the actual account balance is $42,416.32.

So who does the money belong to now? Would Michael
have made a will? Very nice, Sunny. He's barely in the ground
and you're thinking about money. I feel truly sordid. Anyway
I doubt he would have had the foresight to "put his affairs in
order." Michael didn't think in those terms. And I'm also fairly
certain that he planned never to die.

I stick the register in the middle drawer and go back to
the pile of papers on the floor. I just don't have the energy to
organize all this stuff, to redo two years' worth of filing in one

sitting. Instead I stack it all neatly in the top file drawer and put the few remaining papers of his in the bottom.

Noon. I slap some peanut butter on a piece of whole wheat toast, wash it down with the half glass of milk that's left in the refrigerator, and call it lunch.

It's time for my poodle rendezvous.

All the time I'm driving to the Hazeltines' house, while I'm feeding the goldfish, walking Smedley, refilling his water dish, cleaning up his deposits on the minuscule patch of grass, watching his forlorn face in the window as I leave, it's nagging at me. Those checks to Garson's. Four of them since August. None before that. It's like that one little piece of grit that lodges in an oyster, and now layer after layer of my imagination is coating it, embellishing it with ever stranger explanations.

He could have sent flowers to clients, I guess. And Gwen could be secretly taking correspondence courses to become a commodities trader. I keep thinking about the messages on the answering machine. Maybe I should have listened to them before deleting them wholesale. On the other hand, what difference does it make? He's dead. If he was seeing someone else— do I really want to know? Why can't I just think of the good times and forget the rest?

But I remember the argument we had when I brought home a twenty-dollar bunch of tulips from the grocery store; meanwhile he was dropping a cool hundred on flowers at Garson's— not once, but four times. And who were they for, dammit? I bite down hard, crushing the peppermint I stole from the dish on the Hazeltines' coffee table.

If Michael Graham wasn't already dead, I might have to kill him.

By the time I park under the big cottonwood tree on Mont-
claire, I have a plan. It's not so much that I want to know; it's
more that I need to know. I sit down at the kitchen table and
call George Garson's office.

Leila, his assistant, answers the phone. "Sunny! Oh, sweetie,
how are you? Artie told me about Michael. I'm so sorry. I feel
just terrible."

"Thanks. It was a pretty big shock . . ."

"So are you okay—God, what a stupid question. Of course
you're not okay. I'm an idiot. Is there anything I can do? I know
there's not, but I wish I could."

"Thanks for your good thoughts, but I guess it just takes
time." Then I ask casually, "Is George around?"

"Nope. He and Evie went to Chicago for a christening.
Their newest grandkid. They won't be back till next Wednesday. What do you need? I can help you."

"Well . . . I hate to bother you with this . . ."

"Oh, come on. What can I do?"

"To be honest, Michael's financial stuff is a bit of a mess,
and I'm trying to sort things out. I mean, I hate to even be
thinking about this stuff, but—"

"Hey," she says, "it's gotta be done, right? Just tell me what
you need and I'm on it."

"I'm trying to finish pulling together some expense docu-
mentation to give the attorneys; I really don't understand why
they need it—"

"Yeah, well, who knows why lawyers do anything."

"True. So I was just wondering . . . there seem to be a lot
of receipts missing from his tax files, and I think he sent a few
arrangements to clients last year. I was wondering if it might be
possible—"

"Is that all you need? No problem. I'll run off copies of his charges and pop them in the mail to you."

"Would you? That would help me out so much." I pause. "Oh—actually, I'm coming out your way this afternoon. Could I just stop by and pick them up?"

"Sure. I'm leaving early, but I'll put them in an envelope for you and leave it with the receptionist. What else can I do?"

"I really appreciate your help, Leila. That's all I need."

By the time I let myself into Betsy's condo, I'm limp with exhaustion. As if somebody had removed my skeleton, leaving a wobbly mass of skin and flesh. I could have a glass of wine, I suppose, but that would make me a total rag doll. I sit on the couch and somehow, exactly the way it always happens when I'm sad or angry or afraid . . . or just tired, my right fingertips find the scar on my left arm, jagged and puckery, like embroidery done by a beginner.

I lean back against the bright patchwork of pillows and wait, watching the room darken until the lamp that's on a timer suddenly gushes light into every corner. A minute later she's there. Keys jangling, arms full of mail and her purse and a bag from the café, she bumps the door open with her hip. She doesn't see me at first and then she gasps.

"Sunny! Shit, you scared me. I didn't think you'd be here till later." She dumps all her stuff on the counter between the dining area and the kitchen. "I brought us some shrimp and couscous." She goes to the fridge and takes out an open bottle of white wine. She pulls two glasses off the shelf over the sink and sets them on the counter. "What's going on?"

I want to say, "Nothing much. You want to have dinner or go to a movie? You want to go down to Navarro's and listen to reggae? Want to make popcorn and watch *Law and Order*?" I want it to be last night.

About this time, she's tuning in to the fact that I haven't spoken. Can't speak. That I look weird. That something's wrong.

"Sunny?" She pours the wine and brings it to the couch. "Are you okay? You don't look like you feel good." She sits down next to me and puts her hand on my forehead to see if I have a fever.

When I manage to make my voice work, I say, "I have something to show you."

"What is it?" Her eyebrows draw together.

I pick up the envelope, open it, withdraw the copies, and hand them to her. She lifts each piece of paper, carefully, almost delicately, while I watch her face. I know her so well I can read each thought as it appears. *Deny everything* is the immediate reaction, just as quickly rejected. *It's not what you think, I can explain* comes next. To her credit, she moves on to the only remaining choice.

She lifts her eyes to mine and they're brimming with tears, which spill down her pale face. "I'm sorry, Sunny. I'm really, really sorry." And she starts to sob.

I sit, dry-eyed. She gets up and goes into the kitchen, comes back with some tissues.

She drinks half her wine in two gulps. The tears return. "I didn't mean it to happen. You know I never meant to hurt you."

"Then why did you?"

She lays her face in her hands, muffling her answer, but I hear it loud and clear—maybe even before she says it. "Because I loved him."

She cries harder now until she's practically choking, and part of me wants to put my hand on the back of her neck and stroke the fine, dark hair. But I don't.

When there's a lull between sobs, I say, "Why couldn't you just tell me how you felt?"

She looks startled. "How could I tell you? I didn't want to hurt you."

"So instead you went behind my back and slept with the man I was living with. Like that wouldn't hurt me."

"I know it sounds crazy. It *was* crazy. I didn't want it to happen, but I couldn't stop it. I loved him for . . . ever. Ever since we were at school and he used to come into Java Junction."

"How long was it going on?"

"August," she says. "But it was over. Long before he—before I went to San Antonio."

"You pretended to be my friend."

"I didn't pretend. I was your— *am* your friend. But I—"

"Whatever you are, Betsy, you are not my friend."

More sobbing. I wait for her to stop. "I have to know how this happened. How did it start?"

The look she gives me is agonized. "I can't tell you all this shit."

"You owe me an explanation. At least."

She draws a deep, miserable breath. "Last summer when— I guess you guys started having problems—or that's what he said—he came into the café one night. I think you were working an event. He had dinner. After the rush, I went over and had a glass of wine with him." She twists the tissue in her hands, shredding it.

"He just started talking to me. About you. He said that

you weren't ready to get married and he didn't know if you ever would be. He thought you were unhappy. He didn't know what to do. Stuff like that. He asked me if I knew how you felt."

"I don't suppose he said why he was asking you and not me."

She shakes her head. "I thought . . . I thought I was helping. There was no harm in that, and I didn't want you to . . . worry."

I catch her with a stare. "Why would I worry? He loved me. You were my best friend. What could I possibly—"

"Stop it, Sunny. For God's sake. I feel horrible enough."

I want to slap her. "How the hell do you think I feel?"

A few more tears slide down her cheeks. "It's a terrible situation."

Love that word. *Situation*. It sounds so neutral. So no-fault. It's just a situation; no one's to blame.

"So then what happened?"

She drinks more wine. "He started coming by the café every once in a while. Usually in the afternoon. We were talking about that chef's equipment website. Mostly. Then he came in one night almost at closing. He said you guys had had a fight. You got mad and walked out. We were short-staffed, and I couldn't talk to him. I felt bad, so I asked him"—she pauses for a quick inhale—"to come over for a cup of tea. That's when it happened the first time."

She finally looks at me again. Her expression reminds me of nothing so much as Smedley the poodle and I almost laugh. She says, "I was so ashamed. I felt so awful."

"Not awful enough to quit doing it."

"Don't you get it? I was the consolation prize. I always knew he didn't love me. It was always you."

"Oh, bullshit! If he loved me, why was he sleeping with you?"

She winces. "I don't know how to explain it. He was frustrated. He was lonely."

"How could he be lonely?" I have to make a fist so my hand won't shake. "I'm there every day, begging him to tell me what's wrong, and he keeps telling me everything's fine. It's all my imagination."

"That was later," she says quietly.

"Later than what?"

"I hadn't seen him in over a month when I left for San Antonio."

"How did—when did you . . . meet?"

"In the mornings usually. Before he went to work."

"What about Monday nights?"

"Never at night. Never." She gives me a puzzled frown. "Sunny, please, don't hate me. It was a horrible mistake, and I've been miserable about it ever since the first time."

She looks so thoroughly wretched that my interest in torturing her is beginning to wane. I stand up, my purse still hanging from my shoulder, and nod at the coffee table. "I left your key."

She reaches for my hand. "Sunny, please believe me. I wish with all my heart that it never happened."

When I look at her, I don't see Betsy, my best friend. I see a stranger with red rimmed eyes, her cheeks tracked with mascara.

I say, "I wish that, too, Betsy. I'll probably miss you more than him."

. . .

Fly or drive. That's the only decision left to make.

I'm terrified of flying. I've been on a plane exactly once, from Albuquerque to Denver, for a business communications seminar. It was a short flight, but so rough that I spent the entire hour and fifteen minutes with my face in the barf bag and I refused to fly home. Not only did the airline decline to refund my return ticket, but I ended up renting a car and incurring an immorally astronomical drop charge to turn it in at the ABQ Sunport. That was eight years ago, and I haven't set foot on a Jetway since.

On the other hand, I'm not really excited about driving alone from Albuquerque to the West Coast. I imagine myself falling asleep and driving across the center line into an oncoming eighteen-wheeler. Or the Hyundai breaks down in the middle of a Kansas cornfield and the nice man who stops to help me turns out to be a slobbering psychopath who has a thing for blondes.

Yes. I bleached my hair.

I was seized by a sudden desire to not look like Betsy Chambliss, so I went to the drugstore and bought a kit called Ultra Sun Blonde. I spent the evening stinking up the apartment and then discovered I'd fried the ends, so I gave myself an impromptu trim. My hair has looked better, but I remind myself that it will grow out. Meanwhile, I avoid mirrors and large windows and anything shiny enough to show me a reflection.

I go to the clinic and tell them about being afraid to fly. The doctor on duty gives me a prescription for the most popular tranquilizer in all the land. She says that if I take one right after I go through security, I should sleep through the entire flight. By the time I finish reading the list of possible common and uncommon side effects—including: drowsiness (which I thought was the whole point), vomiting, nervousness, aggression, behavior problems, burning tongue, changes in sexual drive, chest pain, confusion, constipation, delusions, depression, diarrhea, disorientation, dreaming abnormalities, exaggerated sense of well-being, hallucinations, impaired urination, inappropriate behavior, incontinence, itching, loss of appetite, loss of sense of reality, memory impairment, nightmares, rapid heart rate, ringing in the ears, skin inflammation, and jaundice—I decide to flip a coin: heads I fly, tails I drive.

The black Hyundai gets sold to a guy from Belen—a high-school graduation present for his daughter. I donate most of the furniture to La Luz, a halfway house for women in drug rehab; and all Michael's clothes and a lot of my own to the Hospice Thrift Shop. I sell the Melmac Azalea dessert plates and matching coffee mugs, the mercury glass Christmas ornaments, and the lusterware sugar and creamer to Sissy Proctor. And for everything else, I have a yard sale on a cloudy Saturday in May.

I sit in a lawn chair drinking coffee from my commuter mug and watching the early birds—those pushy (mostly) women who always show up before the scheduled start time. Some of them are antique dealers wanting to skim any real finds to mark up and sell in their shops. Some are yard sale entrepreneurs who load up on the most popular stuff—tools, sports equipment, books, LPs, and CDs—and then have their own garage sale with the loot. Some are just survivors, made aggressive by hard times.

Betsy and I were usually among them—with us it was the thrill of the chase. It seems wrong that she's not with me today. Helping me make change, pulling unsuspected treasures out of my junk, squealing, *I didn't know you had one of these!*

It's hard to sit here and watch strangers pawing through my stuff—metal measuring cups with small dents, wooden spoons with handles worn smooth, recipe books spattered with grease, a beautiful teacup with a tiny chip in the bottom, a beaded evening bag with braided fringe on the bottom and an oxidized mirror inside, a scrapbook with a carved wooden cover and black pages full of sepia-tone portraits of unsmiling people I never knew—somebody's family and friends.

All these things have a patina of age and use. They don't look as if they just came off a conveyor belt in some factory, assembled by a bunch of robotic equipment, dropped into a carton and shipped out to Wal-Mart. These objects have been handled by real people in families with traditions and history, and now the history includes me. I'm sad to watch it go.

By three o'clock everything that's going to sell has sold, and I'm bagging up the remainders for Goodwill and the Dumpster. I've already taken the signs down, sealed the money into a manila envelope, and put it in a shopping bag with my leftover price tags, scissors, and tape.

"How much for this, please?"

I look around, then down. A young Hispanic girl. About eight years old, wearing faded pink shorts and a white sleeveless blouse. She's holding something I had forgotten I owned until this moment. Two crossed Popsicle sticks with three different colors of yarn woven laboriously in and out in a circle. Dark blue in the center, then alternating bands of yellow and green. I stare at it without answering her, so she asks again.

"How much?"

I set down the shopping bag and take the Ojo de Dios from her.

"You know what this is?" I ask.

"Sí. It is the Eye of God."

"My brother made it," I say. And the memory washes over me in a cold wave. Hart had made it for Mari. To hang over her bed. It was supposed to signify that God was watching over her, keeping her safe. At some point during the blurred and senseless weeks that followed her death, I ended up with it.

"It's not for sale," I say.

She doesn't budge. "It was in the box."

"I know, but I forgot it was there. Pick out something else. Whatever you want. You can have it for free."

"I want the Ojo de Dios." Her eyes are dry and dark and bottomless.

"Felicia!" A woman calls from a white Chevy Nova at the curb. "Let's go!" A few more beats. "Now! Or there's big trouble!"

Reluctantly, the girl turns away, headed for the car. She climbs in the back while the woman holds the front seat forward, and then I yell, "Hey, wait!"

I jog over to the car. Felicia's face peers out from the backseat. I reach in and hand her the Ojo de Dios.

I won't be the one to tell her it doesn't work.

Sissy is adamant that I have dinner with her and spend the last night on her Castro convertible rather than go to a motel on Central Avenue.

"Lotsa weird stuff goin' on in those places," she says. "Drugs and such."

I resist the temptation to tell her I grew up knowing how to roll a joint, make hash brownies, and talk someone down from a bad acid trip. In honor of my going-away dinner, she's cleared off the dining room table and we sit on the delicate Queen Anne chairs eating pizza and drinking a truly awful red wine that becomes less offensive the more we drink.

She keeps pouring and sighing and telling me how sorry she is about Michael and how she still can't believe it. After three glasses she begins questioning the existence of a Supreme Being. That's my cue to yawn elaborately and mention that Super-Shuttle is picking me up at 8:30 in the morning.

I wake up at 3:15 a.m., partly because I'm nervous about oversleeping and terrified of flying and partly because my throat is so dry it hurts. I drink chlorinated water from Sissy's tap, lie back down, and try to stop the panic that's ringing in my head. What am I doing? This is insane.

I can't just leave like this. It's ridiculous. I'll get up at seven and call Mr. Martinez and tell him I've changed my mind. He'll bring me the key. I'll move back in to my apartment. Fine. Settled. I turn on my side and pull up the cover. A wave of heat rushes over me. My body seems to sink into the Castro convertible and I imagine it folding back up into a sofa, swallowing me whole.

My apartment is empty. I'll have to start over. Buy furniture and sheets and towels and dishes and cups. Set up phone service, utilities, a bank account. I'll have to look for a job, since I've

turned all my accounts over to a home security company. Artie's
going to think I'm a total squirrel.

God. Where should I go? What should I do? I'm thirty-
one years old. What is it that I want from my life? Why can't I
make some kind of decision?

And then, somewhat belatedly, it comes to me. I *have* made
a decision. I've bought my ticket, burned my bridges. I've sold
or given away everything because I wanted to make it impossible to stay here. And I have.

The fingers of my right hand find the scar on my left forearm, cool and rounded like silken cord. I drift back into an
uneasy sleep.

Sissy's up at six fixing oatmeal, toast, orange juice, coffee. I
have to force it down because my stomach is still cowering from
the wine. When the shuttle arrives, she walks me out to the
sidewalk and watches the guy toss my backpack into the luggage compartment of the van.

"Sissy, thanks for everything." When I hug her, she starts to
cry and presses a damp piece of paper into my hand. Her name,
address, and phone number.

"Call me, okay?" she sniffles. "Let me know how you're
doing. Tell me about all those adventures you're gonna be having. Damn, I wish I was going somewhere."

"Me too," I say.

The guy behind the glass window looks bored.

"Help you?" he says without looking at me.

When I hesitate, he pushes his glasses back up the bridge of
his nose and focuses on my face. "Where you getting off?"

"I'm not sure." I slept in the Seattle airport last night and spent most of the two-hour shuttle ride to Anacortes semiconscious. My teeth feel like they're all wearing little fuzzy sweaters; the ferry terminal is cold, and I have that disoriented feeling you get when you wake up somewhere other than where you went to sleep.

He pushes a hank of reddish hair up off his forehead, and his mouth tightens into an impatient line. "I can't help you if you don't know where you're going."

I pull out my wallet. "What's the farthest west I can go?"

"On this ferry?" He turns to the map tacked to the wall behind him and sticks his finger on a large brown amoeba that seems to float among friends in the green ocean. "San Miguel. Harmony."

I think I've misunderstood him. "I'm sorry, did you say, 'Harmony'?"

"San Miguel Island. The town of Harmony." He enunciates each syllable with exaggerated care, like I'm a slow learner.

"Harmony." I can't believe it. Maybe I *am* a slow learner. I stare at the map.

"Miss, you want to go there or not? We're gonna be boarding pretty quick here."

I swallow and open my wallet. "Yes. Harmony. Please."

He punches a few keys on the computer and a tiny metal mouth spits out a ticket. "Ten dollars and twenty-five cents. Board through that door in a few minutes."

I sit down on a wooden bench next to a woman with long, straight blond hair. I lean my backpack against my legs. When I yawn, she looks over.

"Me, too. Can't believe I missed the express. This damn milk boat stops at every island."

I try to look sympathetic, but I'm kind of glad. I crossed through a lot of territory yesterday, most of it with my eyes shut. Now I'm ready to start looking.

The woman seems about to say something else, but the guy behind the window picks up a microphone and calls for all walk-on passengers to proceed to the embarkation ramp. I stand up and shoulder my pack and become part of a wave of bodies heading for the double doors.

Everybody else rushes ahead, apparently knowing exactly where they want to sit. I follow the smell to the café, get myself a greasy bacon-and-egg sandwich and take it to an empty seat up front. The boat shudders with the exertions of the big engines as the pilings on either side of us begin to slide away and the window in front of me becomes a giant movie screen of water and sky.

All around me people eat and talk, read newspapers and kiss, play cards and pound on their laptops, oblivious to the gentle pitch of the boat and to the fantasy world just outside the windows—rippling blue-green water, rocky islands upholstered in conifers, shreds of mist. Each time I start to eat, there's something that distracts me, makes me pause with the sandwich halfway to my mouth—a perfect, toylike red lighthouse or a log cabin tucked into a secluded cove, or the white ellipse of a boat lying at anchor on a glassy bay. I stare transfixed, finally forgetting about the sandwich.

Then a hearty baritone over the P.A. system announces a pod of orcas to starboard, and I try frantically to recall which side that is. As it turns out, all I have to do is follow the crowd, which surges to the right side of the ferry in such a rush that I'm sure the whole boat will tip over.

It's like something on The Nature Channel—giant black-and-white bodies, gleaming wet in the sun, huge tails slapping the water and sending up fountains of spray. Each time the whales breach, there's a collective gasp of wonder, like you hear at a fireworks display.

I've entered a different world, and my heart suddenly lifts. It seems I've finally slipped the gravitational pull of New Mexico, and the past is dropping away behind me like a spent booster rocket.

Part Two

It is a curious circumstance, that when we wish to obtain a sight of very faint star, we can see it most distinctly by looking away from it, and when the eye is turned full upon it, it immediately disappears . . .

DAVID BREWSTER

Chapter 10

"What's happening with the Players this year?"

Chuck Bettis is the mail carrier for Harmony and its near environs—meaning the south end of the island of San Miguel. His summer uniform consists of baggy surfer trunks, a white T-shirt, and TEVA sandals, although he's been warned repeatedly by Amanda Howell, the postmistress, that he is not in compliance with official USPS uniform standards. He knows she could write him up for it, and after enough write-ups he could be put on probation and then fired. He also knows that she won't do any such thing. Chuck Bettis has not missed a day of work in twenty years, and he's been known to double-back on his route to deliver a postcard that escaped his attention, and to kick in additional postage out of his own pocket when Mrs. Kozlowski's letter to her son in Schenectady turned up in the drop box with a twenty-eight-cent stamp from 1972.

"We're a little late getting started because Tracey was off island all last month, but Laura and I are trying to round everyone up for a production meeting in the next few weeks," Hallie says. She takes the mail from him and hands him two outgoing bills.

"Any ideas?" He helps himself to a chocolate chip cookie from the paper plate by the register.

"I'm thinking *Our Town*." She holds up a book for his inspection.

"That old chestnut?"

"Hey, it's a classic. And we've never done it. I think it would attract a lot of people."

"Whatever. Let me know when auditions start?"

"Sure thing."

The bell jangles after him and Hallie looks at the stack of mail in her hands. A catalog of women's athletic wear, a statement from Baker and Taylor, a catalog from Poisoned Pen Press, a solicitation from the UCSB Alumni Directory.

A postcard. An eerily beautiful photo of the little town of Mendocino, perched at the top of its bluff, overlooking the gray Pacific Ocean and a lavender twilight sky. The windows of the old hotel are tiny points of light. Even before she turns it over, her heart thuds painfully in her chest.

Thought of you here, the message says. The signature is just an *E* with a long tail. Eric.

The bell over the door signals another customer, and Hallie smiles automatically at the woman in a broomstick skirt and sleeveless shirt who immediately heads for the bestseller rack.

"If you don't see what you want, holler at me." She feels like one of those old dolls, the ones they called Chatty Cathy. You pulled a cord in the stomach and one of a dozen taped sentences would play.

If you don't see what you want, holler at me.

No, we don't carry Cliffs Notes.

Maps and navigation charts are in the rack next to the window.

Postcards are a dollar twenty-five.

. . . And so forth, as the King of Siam said.

She rips open the statement from Baker and Taylor and stares at the page without seeing it. All she can see is Eric. The gold glinting in his red hair, the cool green eyes, the dimple that embarrassed him whenever he smiled.

She bites the inside of her cheek. Ridiculous. It's been almost two years, and a postcard can bring her to the edge of tears. She opens the athletic wear catalog and slaps it on the counter, startling a teenaged boy browsing in Science Fiction.

The sudden deep blast of a whistle makes everyone in the shop turn to the window that faces the waterfront. A customer looks at her watch and smiles. "Here it comes!" she says to no one in particular as she darts toward the door.

At 10:40 a.m. the *M.V. Tacoma* bounces gently against the pilings, fifteen minutes late, and the steel car ramp clangs against the wooden pier. Over at the Ale House, Piggy Murphy stops loading CDs into the changer and watches the cars and trucks and motorcycles clatter off the ramp and onto the pier. The parade turns right on Front Street and proceeds left up Sumner, tourists looking for parking places, locals anxious to get around them and out of town.

It's a typical spring morning: cold and damp. Billows of fog roll in and drift away. Foot passengers are still straggling off, groups of hikers and cyclists, a couple of kayakers wearing their craft like weird, oversize hats. Clusters of kids fan out and then clump together, laughing, snapping pictures of each other on their cell phones. Piggy can see Laura, huddled in her down jacket, waiting for them all to descend on her booth.

The cars in line for the 11:05 to Lopez and Anacortes are already rolling up the ramp into the vessel's belly when a woman steps out of the drifting mist, adjusts the straps on her backpack, and follows the crowd headed for Laura. Something about her draws Piggy's attention, produces an eerie sensation of familiarity.

Maybe it's the way she walks: carefully upright, like she's turned her back on something that she hopes is not following her. Standing in line, she surveys her surroundings by making two complete rotations. When her gaze falls blindly on the front windows of the Ale House, Piggy knows instinctively that it's himself he recognizes in her. Himself three years ago, running both from and toward things he couldn't name.

The woman talks to Laura for a few minutes, leaning her elbows on the booth's tiny counter. Then she shoulders her pack again and walks across the street, up the rise to the Ale House. The door's unlocked even though they don't start serving till eleven thirty. She hesitates in the vestibule till Piggy says, "'Morning. What can I do for you?"

She steps up to the bar and smiles at him, a thin glaze of earnest politeness laid carefully over a cold river of nerves. He can smell it.

"Are you Brendan Murphy?"

"That's me."

"My name's Sunny Cooper. I'm looking for a job. Laura— at the booth—said you might be able to help me."

"She did, huh?" He looks her over: thirtyish, medium height, interesting face but not what you'd call pretty; kind of funky hair, obviously a bottle job. The most striking thing about her would have to be her voice, clear and low and musical. "What kind of work you looking for?"

"I've done some catering. I've worked as a prep cook and a server."

"How much experience have you had?" He leans forward, resting his arms on the bar so she can see the death's head tattoo.

She slips her pack off and climbs up onto a barstool. A necklace hangs on a leather thong around her neck. Some kind of Indian thing. Red, white, and black beaded design on the front.

"I worked my way through school in restaurants. The last few years my main job was voiceovers, but it wasn't always enough, so I—"

"Voiceovers?" He takes the towel off his shoulder, polishes an invisible water spot on a pilsner glass.

"You know, commercials, elevator voices . . ."

He nods. "Well, Sunny, we're still trying to figure out how much summer staff we're going to need. Probably be another few weeks till we see how the season's shaping up."

She tries to hide her disappointment, but she's got one of those faces that shows everything. "Maybe I should check back with you then."

From a cubbyhole beside the antique brass cash register, he pulls an employment application and lays it on the bar with a pen. "That'd be good. In the meantime, why don't you go on and fill this out. That way it's done."

She takes the cap off the pen and begins filling in the blanks with square block printing.

"Where are you from?" he says.

She looks up briefly. "New Mexico."

His thick eyebrows lift. "You're a long way from home."

"That was sort of the point. Could I possibly have a glass of water?"

He fills a glass, places it on a napkin in front of her. Her glance gathers up the whole room—beamed ceiling to wide-planked floor, freshly scrubbed tables with chairs tucked neatly underneath, the oak bar with its brass fittings, the posters promoting ales, lagers, stout, porter. She gulps half the water, looking out the wide windows at the harbor, and turns back to the form. He watches her hesitate over the references section, twirl the pen between her thumb and forefinger, and then print in careful capitals, BETSY CHAMBLISS.

"Whereabouts in New Mexico?" he asks.

"Albuquerque."

"You got a place to stay here?"

"I have a couple of possibilities." She pulls a folded page of *Island Times* classifieds out of her windbreaker and lays it on the bar. Two ads are circled in red.

He bends over the page. "This one here is up in Rocky Harbor. You got a car?"

"Not anymore."

"Then I'd go for this other one. It's in town here. Just a couple blocks away. If you want, you can use the phone to call."

Thanks, Brendan." She signs the application and pushes it toward him.

"Everyone but Laura calls me Piggy," he says.

I follow Piggy's directions to Booker Avenue, one of those tree-lined, green-lawned, and flower-bedded streets that I always thought existed only in old TV sitcoms. The house is an aggressively pretty white bungalow, the white picket fence bordered with purple and yellow pansies. Not a blade of grass out of place.

It's disorienting. In New Mexico the houses that confer the

most status are old adobes with porches hanging at odd angles and rusted hinges on weathered gates. At home people don't try to get rid of weeds, they let them be and call them landscaping.

I pass under the arched trellis, where a climbing rose snatches at my jacket, and up to the front door. A woman is waiting.

"Hi. I'm Sunny Cooper. I called about the room for rent."

"I'm Sarah Lakes." A faded denim jumper hangs on her lanky frame, and a red shirt buckles under the armholes. No smile, no extended hand. "How long will you be staying in Harmony?"

"I'm not sure yet. At least a month."

"Are you vacationing?"

"Looking for a job."

"I'll show you the room."

The white garage is connected to the back porch of the house by a covered walkway. Inside, the temperature drops at least ten degrees and I can feel the cold, unyielding concrete slab under the beige industrial carpeting. Sarah bustles around pointing out the kitchen, which consists of a tiny refrigerator and a two-burner stove shoehorned into a corner by a small sink. The room contains a bed, a three-drawer chest, a small wooden table, and two uncomfortable-looking chairs. When she starts going on about the casement windows and the gas log fireplace, I interrupt her sales pitch.

"I'd like to rent it."

She pushes her thick iron-colored hair back with one hand. "I don't allow smoking."

"I don't smoke."

"This is a very quiet neighborhood."

"I'm a very quiet person."

"There's to be no drugs or alcohol."

I sigh. "Anything else?"

Sarah Lakes regards me suspiciously for a minute, focusing on the medicine bundle necklace. "I don't like hippies." She manages to make the last word sound like something you don't want your dog to leave on the sidewalk.

"Coincidentally, I'm not fond of hippies myself. How much of a deposit do you need?"

"First month in advance." She eyes the pack. "Is that all your luggage?"

"I travel light." I smile at her.

She doesn't smile back. "I guess you can go ahead and unpack, then come over to the house and fill out the tenant information sheet."

When she's disappeared out the door, clutching her deposit, I bounce down on the bed. At least the mattress is firm. Lying back, I pull a pillow onto my stomach and hug it to me.

Once I tried to talk Michael into going to a resort in Jamaica for a week. He said that water made him nervous, and being on an island would feel like being in prison. He loved New Mexico—the buff-colored desert studded with somber green juniper and piñon, silvery chamisa; the red mesas and purple mountains; that trick of the thin, bright air that makes everything appear closer and smaller than it really is. He liked his blue in the sky.

The bathroom reeks of disinfectant so strong it scratches the back of my throat. Sarah strikes me as the type of woman who'd use a nuclear device to eliminate roaches. Looking for a place to hang my cosmetics bag, I discover a piece of cheap yellow newsprint thumb-tacked to the back of the door.

HOUSE RULES

1. *no liqor or drugs of any kind*
2. *no smoking only*
3. *as a curtsy to the neighbors, no loud music*
4. *no more than 3 occupants at a time, two of which must be of the same sex*
5. *septic system no flushing any personal items down the toilet*
6. *do not use fireplace more than two hours*
7. *no dirty dishes or otherwise in the sink*
8. *garage must go out daily to prevent bugs.*

I stare at the last one for a minute before realizing it's supposed to be *garbage.*

I take the plastic baggie from my kit, pull out a sage bundle, and light it with Michael's old lighter. As it begins to smoke, I walk through the two rooms, waving it to what I think are north, south, east, west. The smell of burning juniper and sage is cleansing and comforting—something familiar, even if it won't last.

Carpet freshener is the dominant fragrance in Sarah's house. She leads me through a kitchen full of ruffled curtains and plastic flowers and into the living room, where a gas log flames behind glass doors. A low, growling noise directs my attention to an elderly Jack Russell, curled up under the chair by the fireplace that she's pointing me toward. I hesitate.

"That's Paco," she says. "He's very friendly."

Friendly little Paco is baring his canines at me, so I stand still. Sarah gives me an impatient look. "Are you afraid of dogs or something?"

"I was attacked by a Chihuahua when I was a baby."

She brushes past me, making annoyed little clicking sounds with her tongue, scoops up Paco in one arm, and hands me a clipboard with a form attached to it. I sit down. The pen is out of ink and she gives me a look that says it's somehow my fault before striding off down the dark hallway in search of another. I look around.

The room is crammed with dark-wood furniture and every surface is covered. Doilies on all the tables, antimacassars on the couch and chairs, carpeting on the floors, braided rugs over the carpeting, sheers on the windows, and drapes over the sheers. Every naked patch of wall space is hung with pictures and fussy little shelves full of porcelain animals and birds.

Sissy would love the hulking old television, its big wooden cabinet and tiny screen. The top is crowded with photographs, all of them featuring a beautiful blond girl. There are pictures of her on a bicycle, astride a horse, on the deck of a sailboat, her dark glasses bigger than the top of her bikini. There's one of her in a cheerleader's outfit with a red *H* on the sweater. In another, she's wearing a cap and gown. There's one of her in full bridal regalia, but it looks more like an ad from *Brides* magazine than an actual wedding photo. She's shining a brilliant smile into the camera lens while the groom stands slightly behind and to the side, looking dazed.

Sarah bustles back in with a new pen and catches me looking.

"My daughter," she says with obvious pride. "Mary Beth. She's in Seattle now. She's a personnel manager with a computer company, and her husband's an attorney with a big law firm."

"She's lovely." I reach for the pen, but she's using it to point out another photo. Mary Beth with a small Mary Beth clone.

"My granddaughter Bree."

I can't imagine naming a kid after a cheese, but I haven't got a lot of room to talk in the name department.

"Adorable," I murmur, trying again for the pen.

"And smart as a whip, I can tell you," Sarah says, pointing the pen at the mantel. "My late husband, Henry." A humorless-looking man in some kind of uniform. "He was an engineer on the ferries," she says. "He passed five years ago next month. Heart attack." Next to Henry, a small unframed snapshot leans against the chimney. It's a young boy, squinting into the sun, sitting on a dock with his legs hanging over the edge into a rowboat. His hair is fair and curly as a cherub's.

"My son, Johnny," she says. She hands me the pen and retreats to the kitchen with Paco tucked under her arm.

The village of Harmony seems to doze in the afternoon sun, a photo from a travel brochure with its picturesque harbor and cozy shops. I go inside a few places. The bakery, a video rental store, a couple of inns and cafés, and a coffee bar down on the waterfront. I ask about a job. Everyone is polite, but noncommittal. Things are pretty slow right now, they say, but hopefully they'll pick up in a few weeks, when the summer tourist season begins. They invite me to check back.

I wander past a little museum, housed in an old cottage. The grange and the courthouse, city hall, library, a high-school football field, green and lush. I stare into the window of a knitting shop, at the baskets overflowing with rivers of colored yarns: turquoise and mauve and salmon and heathery purple.

I buy a turkey sandwich from Jake's Deli, take it down to the park at the foot of Front Street, and sit on a low stone wall, watching tourists photograph one another in front of a totem pole that, according to the plaque below it, symbolizes the interrelation of humans and animals. The pole sits on a lawn that's a minefield of Canada goose shit, which strikes me as funny. Since not much has been striking me as funny lately, I hoard the image like treasure.

After lunch I stroll past the ferry landing and out onto the marina pier. Harbor seals sun themselves on the breakwater while gulls screech, whirling and diving for food among the forest of bobbing masts. About halfway down the pier, people are lined up for fish at a tiny stand where an orange cat dozes on top of a cooler.

The fishmonger, a guy in a wife-beater undershirt and cutoffs, rests one bare foot on a metal box and jokes with his customers. He seems comfortable in this getup, despite the fact that it's probably only sixty-five degrees and a brisk wind is whipping in off the water. I watch, fascinated as he casually wields a thin bladed knife, carving a chunk of fish into filets, pausing every few minutes to take a drag from a cigarette that he keeps wedged between a wooden block and a glass tank full of shellfish.

After the last customer has taken her package of fish and headed for the street, he looks up and sees me perched on one of the pilings.

"Hi. Need something for dinner?"

I walk over just as he's wiping the remains of his last fish into a bucket. He throws the head to the orange cat, who attacks it with gusto.

"What kinds of fish do you have?"

"If it swims in this water, I got it." He nods out toward the ocean. " 'Course, earlier is better. I haven't got a lot of stuff left today: some blackmouth, some lingcod, maybe three or four halibut steaks. Some clams . . ." He nods at the glass tank. "No oysters."

"What's blackmouth?"

"Juvenile king salmon. From San Juan Island. I'll be getting some more of that here shortly." He appraises me coolly. "You're new on the island, am I right?"

"Yes."

"Thought so. Where're you from?"

"Albuquerque, New Mexico."

Eyebrows lift. "You're a long ways from home, aren't you?"

"Yes."

"Just visiting?"

I hesitate. "Yes."

"I always like a gal knows how to say yes." He grins.

"Then I hope you find one." I turn back toward the street.

"Aw, don't get your knickers in a twist," he says. "I was kidding. Hey, really, don't you want something for dinner?"

"Not tonight, thanks."

He hollers after me, "Come on back when you do. Mine's the best. You ask anybody in town, they'll tell you Mick Holzer's got the best fish."

Chapter 11

Whenever I go to sleep in a new place, I dream about my sister. This time we're waiting for a bus up to the mesa. Hart's with us, too, and it's snowing, fast and thick. The bus is crowded, and there's not room for all of us. Hart and Mari get on ahead of me, and while I'm trying to explain to the driver that we three have to stay together, he closes the door in my face. Mari is waving frantically from the window as the bus drives away, and when I try to run after it, I nearly fall out of bed. It's 6:40 a.m. I lie back and pull up the covers.

Sometimes I pretend that she didn't die.

That we're sharing an apartment in Albuquerque, shopping for clothes, eating ice cream, and watching movies, taking walks at the Rio Grande Nature Center, hitting garage sales on Saturday mornings. There might be occasional road trips up north to visit Gwen and Rob. Hart would drive up from Ocala to join us in our filial duty, but mostly it's an excuse for the three of us to be together, to ride horses on the mesa and play in the river, to sit up after Rob and Gwen and have gone to bed and drink beer and talk about what it was like for each of us, growing up at Armonía, and where we're all headed.

It's fantasy, pure and simple. Rob and Gwen would have split anyway. Mari's death probably accelerated the process, but even before the accident, their marriage was unraveling faster than an old sweater. On the infamous road trip to California, the vague awareness that something was wrong became a certainty that even a six-year-old could hardly have overlooked.

That June my mother's favorite cousin, Allison, was getting married in Long Beach, and she asked Gwen to be her maid of honor. Rob didn't want to go. He said there was too much to do at Armonía, but Gwen insisted, and as usual, he went along.

We drove one of the commune vehicles, a VW Westfalia camper bus with psychedelic animals painted all over the original faded beige. Hart and I called it the Zoo-Mobile, and it was probably the only one of the dilapidated cars, trucks, and buses at Armonía that had any chance of making the trip to California and back. Rob packed his toolkit and whatever spare parts he thought might be useful, and we took off one morning in early June.

The trip was brutally hot, and our progress was slow, because the camper didn't go over about fifty without rattling like a percussion ensemble. Drugged by the heat, I slept, waking up periodically in a pool of sweat to drink the warm water Gwen poured out of a plastic bottle.

We rolled into Long Beach at sunset on the fifth day and wheezed to a stop in front of a house. It was huge. Bigger, it seemed to me, than any building in Taos. The neighborhood was full of big houses. All different kinds and colors. Shiny new cars sat in driveways. Lawns were green and the streets were lined with palm trees. There were flowers everywhere, masses of them in sizes and shapes and colors I had never imagined.

"Who lives here?" Hart demanded.

Gwen sat still for a minute. "My mother and father," she said.

"And who else?" he asked.

"Nobody else," she said. "Just them."

It was inconceivable to us.

"Where are their animals?" I said.

"Hush," Gwen said. The front door had opened and a man and woman were coming down the walk.

My grandmother was wearing black shorts and a striped T-shirt. She was beautiful, with dark wavy hair and dark eyes. My grandfather had gray hair and looked like a giant. When we got out of the van he towered over Rob.

"This is our family," Gwen said. "Hart. Soleil. And Mari."

I can only imagine the sight we must have presented: Gwen in her gypsy skirt and embroidered blouse, no bra, barefoot; Rob with his beard and shaggy hair down to his shoulders; Mari in her undershirt and dirty diaper; and Hart and me, looking like we'd been raised by feral dogs.

But my grandmother smiled. "It's so good to see you. Please come in." She put both her hands on Gwen's shoulders and kissed her cheek. Gwen kissed her back.

"We've been camping," she said. "We're probably a little dirty." Which had to be the understatement of the year. She handed Mari to her mother, and we started to walk toward the house. I was trailing Hart, but then my grandmother shifted Mari to her left hip and reached her right hand down to me.

"Soleil is a lovely name," she said.

"What's your name?" I said.

"It's Willa. But I hope you'll call me Nana."

After dinner, Nana took me upstairs, through her yellow bedroom with the gigantic bed and into her bathroom. It was bigger than the kitchen at Armonía.

She peeled off my clothes, which were caked with sweat and dust, and bathed me twice. Once just to get the surface dirt off. The second time, after she'd washed the mud down the drain, she made a bubble bath and popped me into it. She shampooed my hair and piled suds on top of it and let me look in the mirror. She sang a song about a little white duck. She toweled me off and let me use what she called her dusting powder. It didn't smell anything like dust; it smelled like powdered flowers, and it shimmered on my skin like glitter.

"Can I sleep with you?" I asked while she was combing my hair.

She plugged in a fat plastic gun that blew hot air on my head. "You'll have your own room," she said over the noise. "I hope you like it."

When my hair was dry, she took me across the hall to a pink bedroom where a white canopied bed seemed to float like a cloud. It had pink sheets and lots of pillows and three teddy bears.

"This was your mother's room," she said.

She tucked me in and kissed my forehead with her cool, thin lips. I was planning to get up as soon as she left. I wanted to know what was behind the closet door, what you could see out the window if you opened the white shutters, what was under this bed that made it so high—all of those things. But then she turned out the light and said, "Sweet dreams, Soleil," and I was asleep before she closed the door.

I learned a lot of things in the next few days. I learned that I had a second cousin named Kendra, two years older than me. I learned that lots of people—not all of them related—called my grandmother Nana. I learned that my grandfather smoked a pipe, but he didn't get stoned. I learned that Rob didn't get along with anyone in Long Beach. When I got up the next morning he was already on the phone with some musician buddies, making plans to meet them in a place called San Pedro. Hart went with him.

I learned that things could get tense between my mother and her mother. I kept walking in on conversations that stopped as soon as they noticed me. Conversations about sleeping arrangements (Hart and I were too old to be sharing a room, according to Nana) and clothes (she couldn't believe I was running around in those rags) and school. Drugs. Religion. Politics. (My grandmother loathed Jimmy Carter. She referred to him as "that peanut farmer who pardoned all the draft dodgers.") There wasn't much they agreed on except food, and cooking seemed to be the one thing they could do together without arguing.

On Thursday morning, when Gwen went to get fitted for her bridesmaid dress and have lunch with all the ladies in the wedding, Nana left Grandfather and Rob in an uneasy truce to look after Mari and Hart. She bundled me into her big green car. She pulled out into traffic, drove a few blocks, then hit a button and the windows went down by themselves. A startlingly cold breeze rushed through the front seat.

"There it is, Soleil. The Pacific Ocean. The most beautiful ocean on the planet."

I loved watching her drive, the way she rested her elbow on

the open window, a cluster of silver bracelets against her tan wrist, her diamond ring throwing off sparks of light, the wind ruffling her hair. Her nails were painted a pale orange that matched her lipstick.

At Fashion Island there were shops and restaurants and a movie theater. An ice cream store. A bakery. Escalators to ride. There were fountains and flowers and tables and benches, and the air was thick with a delicious combination of flower scents and food and the sea.

We sat at an umbrella table on the patio eating grilled cheese sandwiches, and she asked me about school.

"I hate it," I said.

"And why is that?"

"Nobody likes us."

I had a hot fudge sundae for dessert and told her about helping Gwen cook. About spraying the floors with water in the morning. I told her that Hart worked in the garden and sometimes he helped Rob in the shop. I told her about the outhouse, how we kept the seats by the fire in the winter so they'd be warm in case you had to go. I told her about Hunter, who didn't talk, so he drew pictures for everything he wanted to say. I told her about Fred, who was bad and stole things and so they'd made him leave, and about Olivia who knitted scarves and mittens for everyone.

"Nana," I said, when I had told her all about Armonía, "can I stay here with you?"

That was the only time she looked away from me. She bit her lip. She took a drink from her water glass. Then she leaned over and pushed my bangs off my forehead.

"That would be lovely," she said. "I would like it so much.

But your mother and father and brother and little sister couldn't get along without you."

After lunch we went to a special store full of gauzy, frilly dresses and I tried on a dozen or so. I loved every one, but Nana would look at me thoughtfully and purse her lips.

"I don't see her in that color." Or "That one's a bit too fussy." Or "No. Too old-looking."

The sales clerk went away and came back with another armful, and she didn't even get to put them down before Nana spotted one in the pile and pulled it out. "This color would be wonderful on you, Soleil."

The dress was brown (Nana called it chocolate) and was in two pieces: a plain, dark underdress with skinny straps, and a long-sleeved, high-necked overdress (the clerk called it a cage) that was completely see-through. The dress had pink roses embroidered on the top and around the hem. It floated when I moved and twirled after me like a shadow when I turned around.

"What a good eye you have," the saleswoman said. "It's perfect for her."

I wanted to wear it home, but Nana persuaded me to let the clerk wrap it up in pink tissue paper and lay it carefully in a flowered bag with ribbon handles. In a shoe store we found pink satin slippers to match the roses. I was so happy I felt like I hovered just above the car seat all the way home.

My mother was in the kitchen drinking iced tea when we came in the back door. When she saw us and our many-colored shopping bags, her face got dark as a thunderstorm on the mesa.

"What's all this?" I knew that tone of voice.

"Nana took me shopping," I chirped. "We had lunch at a restaurant and I got a dress for the wedding."

"You already have a dress for the wedding." Gwen wasn't looking at me, but at her mother.

Nana didn't blink. "I saw that dress. It's not appropriate for an afternoon wedding."

Gwen looked down at me. "Soleil, go upstairs and see if Mari's awake and if she needs to be changed."

"But I want to show you my new dress—"

"We'll look at it later. Get upstairs."

"Gwen, I saw the ocean!"

She stopped then, and smiled just slightly. "You can tell me all about it later. Go on upstairs."

I climbed the stairs slowly, listening to the rise and fall of the voices in the kitchen. The sound made a hole in my stomach that swallowed up all the brightness of the day.

Saturday dawned cloudless and still. By four o'clock it was hot, and the Bayshore Congregational Church was packed. We left Mari screeching in the nursery with the other little kids and I wished I could stay with her. The nursery was nestled in the shade of five or six huge old trees and it was much cooler than the sanctuary.

Before my mother left the house to go dress with the bridal party, she'd laid out my old yellow dress with the daisies on it and told me that I was to wear it to the wedding. Somehow, between then and my bath time, the dress disappeared from my bed and in its place was the new dress, all pressed and ready to wear, along with my new underthings and the pink satin shoes. Nana helped me dress and pulled my unruly hair into a French braid. Rob whistled at me when we came down the stairs, and

Hart's eyes bugged out. Mari cried because she didn't recognize me.

Now, as we sat in the stuffy church, on the hard wooden benches that Nana called pews, I felt the first tremor of doubt. My mother was going to be angry when she saw me.

Up front, three women were playing violins while people came in and found their seats. The church was full of flowers, and their perfume in the enclosed space was overpowering. Nana waved her handkerchief in front of her face.

"Tuberose," she whispered to Grandfather. "She should have stayed with something unscented."

Suddenly the three women put down their violins and a great, rumbling chord vibrated in my chest.

"Look," Nana said in my ear. "The bridesmaids are coming."

There were four of them, all wearing yellow dresses and carrying bouquets of white and blue and pink flowers. Nana named them for me as they went by—my cousin Kendra, looking self-important, was a junior bridesmaid.

"That's Heather Davis, Allison's roommate. Cindy Franks, I believe she's another college friend. There's your mother. Isn't she beautiful?"

Gwen was gliding down the aisle, serene, nodding at her friends. Then her gaze landed on me and her mouth tightened. I waved shyly. She seemed to remember that everyone was looking at her, and she smiled benevolently.

The ceremony was brief, with the bride and groom mumbling things I couldn't hear, a song I couldn't understand, then a kiss, and it was over.

Nana guided me through the receiving line at the yacht club. Everyone shook my hand and said how pretty I was, just like my mother. When we got to Gwen, she bent down and kissed my cheek and then smiled at Nana and said through gritted teeth, "I just don't believe you, Mother."

Nana smiled back. "That cute little daisy dress had a stain on it, dear. I had to throw it in the wash and it didn't get dry in time." She stepped gracefully down the line and embraced the bride.

We sat at big round tables and ate chicken with brown sauce while two men played guitars. Then the guitar players left and a band came in and started tuning up onstage. Rob got up and went to shake hands with them.

The bride and groom danced by themselves to the slow first song, but when the band suddenly started playing rock 'n' roll, the tables emptied out onto the dance floor. I danced with Hart, then I danced with Grandfather till Rob tapped him on the shoulder and took his place. I could smell that he'd been drinking beer, but he wasn't drunk yet.

"What song would you like to hear?" he asked me.

"You know."

"I do?" He pretended to think. "It wouldn't be that old song about the handy man, would it? Oh, yeah, *now* I remember. Before this party's over, I'm going to sing it just for you."

My mother came and got me and took me around to meet everybody at the bride's table. Everybody touched my hair and said I looked just like Gwen. While I was being patted, I happened to look up at the band and there was Rob, playing the guitar and singing. In his one good shirt—white with ruffles on the front—and his best jeans, cowboy boots polished, and his hand-tooled leather belt with the silver buckle, he looked like the rock star he'd always wanted to be.

All Gwen's friends started clapping and yelling for Rob.

Cindy said, "Oh my God, he looks just like James Taylor, only cuter."

Gwen smiled and waved at him, and he blew her a kiss. He played with them for the whole first set, dedicating songs to me—although not the one I asked for—and Gwen, and drinking steadily. I knew he was getting drunk when he dedicated a song to Nana. Finally the band took a break and he disappeared with them.

The sun was setting out the big window, turning all the boats golden and pink, and somebody announced that the bride and groom were going to cut the cake. When everyone was gathered around watching them, I pushed the handle on one of the big doors and stepped outside. I had to find Rob before he got totally messed up. The wind blew my overdress up from underneath like a big bubble. I ran down the side of the building, turned the corner, and came to a little patio where the band members plus Rob were sitting passing around a joint.

"Hey, princess," Rob said. "What are you doing out here? Come to find your old man?"

"The doors won't open," I said. "Can you come help me?"

"We're just going back in for the second set. You can come with us."

"Uh, Rob . . ." One of the guys stood up. "The first set was cool, man, but . . ."

He trailed off and another one stood up. "We're just gonna do our thing now, you know?"

Rob's smile was lopsided. "Guys, guys. No problem. You just gotta let me do one more song." He grabbed my arm. "One for my girl. I promised her."

I pulled at his hand. "Let's go find Gwen."

"No, a promise is a promise. And I always keep my promise. Just one last song, come on, guys? How 'bout it? For my little girl." He got unsteadily to his feet and tried to keep from swaying. "You guys know 'Handy Man,' right? I gotta do it for my girl."

The others looked at one another and shrugged.

The band got up on the stage and started tuning up. Rob picked up the wrong guitar and laughed loudly. "Just testing you." He traded with one of the other guys. The people on the dance floor rocked back and forth in anticipation. Rob slung the strap over his shoulder and stepped up front to the mike.

"This is my little girl's favorite song," he said, slurring a little. "So I'm dedicated to Soleil."

He took one more halting step and pitched forward off the stage.

We had planned to leave Monday, so Nana said we'd go to the beach on Sunday. Saturday night I dreamed of walking barefoot on the white, sugary sand, splashing in the cold water, of Grandfather teaching me to swim. It helped me forget about Rob lying on the yacht club floor with a bloody nose and a broken guitar, sparks popping as cords got yanked from amplifiers, and the earsplitting buzz that came from the amplifiers, the silence in the van on the way home.

But I woke up to find Gwen in my room stuffing my clothes into the duffel bag and Mari tugging on the covers, trying to climb up in bed with me.

"You need to get up and get dressed. We're going home today."

"Tomorrow," I corrected her sleepily.

"Your father and I decided we need to get back."

"But Nana's taking me to the beach."

She tossed a pair of shorts and a T-shirt on the bed. "I'm sorry, Soleil, but we have to go home."

"Why?"

She resorted to the age-old fallback of mothers everywhere. "Because I said so, that's why. Now get up and get dressed."

I peered over the edge of the bed at Mari, her sweet little upturned face. She had this way of looking at you—solemn and watchful. It was as if she had seen and understood everything, felt the full weight of life, but she just hadn't decided what to do about it yet. I started to cry.

Gwen turned to look at me. I think she must have been surprised. I was not the sort of child who cried a lot. "What on earth is wrong with you?"

I wasn't old enough to know what was wrong with me.

Ostensibly I was disappointed because I'd been promised today at the beach and now it would be spent in a suffocating van, lurching across the desert toward New Mexico. The truth I didn't know how to articulate was that I didn't want to go back at all. I wanted to stay in California with Nana beside the most beautiful ocean on the planet. I wanted to wear clothes that hadn't come out of the Free Box. I wanted to live in a house where you didn't have to water the floors in the morning or eat dinner with people you didn't know. I wanted to go to the toilet in the house.

"Soleil . . ." Gwen sighed deeply, as if she had so many things to tell me she didn't know where to start. Then she said, "Just get dressed."

It didn't take us long to pack up because we didn't have

much stuff. Nana and Grandfather were in the kitchen making eggs and toast that nobody wanted to eat. Nana handed Gwen a bag. "Sandwiches for lunch," she said.

"Thank you, Mother."

Rob filled up the water bottles. His face was bruised and swollen and he hadn't said a word to anyone. Now he went out and cranked up the van. We all walked down the front walk. The grass was still wet with dew, and the palm trees cast tall, skinny shadows on the street. Gwen hugged her mother and father and shoved open the back door of the van. Hart said his thanks and goodbyes and clambered in. Gwen was waiting for me so she could close the door.

"Goodbye, Soleil," Nana said. "I hope you'll come see me . . . again."

The little hiccup in her voice held everything that I felt but couldn't say, and instead of hopping into the van, I started crying again—sobbing, actually. I threw myself at her, clinging to her knees and I kept saying, "Let me stay, let me stay with you."

Nana was stroking my hair; she was crying too. She was talking to me, but I couldn't hear what she said with all the noise I was making. When Gwen had recovered from the shock, she grabbed my wrists and pulled me off her mother and set my butt firmly on the backseat next to Hart, who looked at me with eyes full of pity.

The back door closed.

"Thanks for everything," Gwen said. Then she got in and the Zoo Mobile pulled away from the curb with a long, shuddering slide into first gear.

We drove in absolute silence until Rob gunned it up the ramp onto the freeway, and then I remembered.

"Where's my dress?"

Gwen didn't turn around. "You can't wear that kind of dress in New Mexico. I left it with Nana."

I don't think we ever forgave each other.

Six years later Nana died from complications following heart surgery. It was a cold, wet winter on the mesa and Gwen was in the hospital with pneumonia. Rob was gone by then, so none of us made it to the funeral. Less than a year after that, my grandfather died in his sleep. My grandparents slipped out of my life as easily as they'd slipped in, leaving only the memory of a summer wedding in California.

Chapter 12

While I wait for the coffee to brew, I pour cream into the stained white mug and study the tiny kitchen. The contents are all in plain sight on open shelving. Four place settings of chipped and faded plates, bowls, and cups. Water-spotted glasses, mismatched flatware standing upright in a crock with a can opener and a plastic spatula. One frying pan and one sauce-pan, a colander, and two flimsy steak knives.

I have a brief but intense pang of longing for my own familiar kitchen stuff. The dishes I painstakingly collected at flea markets and antique malls and church rummage sales over the years. All my baking gear and cast-iron pans. The warped wooden spoons. My heroic little Sunbeam mixer. All gone now.

I wanted to believe that it would be liberating, this lack of possessions. I told myself I wouldn't have to worry about taking care of things, packing them, unpacking. But the truth is, it feels very much like loneliness.

I pour coffee into the mug, slip into my rain parka, and step outside, locking the door behind me. The fog is dense and gray and I nearly trip over Sarah in her baggy gray sweats, down on her knees snipping individual leaves off a perfectly oval shrub.

"Where are you going?" The question sounds interrogatory rather than friendly.

"I just thought I'd take a walk before breakfast." I smile.

She doesn't. "Well, don't lose that mug. Or break it."

I resist the urge to lob it into the street. "Don't worry, I've handled lots of coffee cups. I'm actually pretty good at it." I make it to the end of the front walk before she calls out, "And shut the gate. Otherwise I'll have every stray dog in town in here ruining my lawn."

I walk up Booker Street and turn north on Second, away from town, taking small sips of coffee, wrapping my hands around Sarah's priceless coffee mug. In the next block I notice a small knot of people standing at the end of a driveway, and I wonder briefly if someone's been hurt. Then I see the signs and balloons and I remember that it's Saturday—yard sale day. It would probably be smart to avoid any nostalgia trips just now, but I seem unable to resist the siren song of chipped teacups and water-stained books. I drift over to join them.

A woman about my age, dressed in a red-and-gold Harmony High School tracksuit, is showing a little girl which price stickers go on which books and dishes. An older boy, probably twelve or thirteen, is selling coffee and donuts at a separate card table, while a gray-haired man wearing bedroom slippers mutters that at the last sale he went to the coffee was free.

I stand for a minute in front of a table loaded with housewares: a rusty box grater, an old-fashioned egg timer, the kind with sand inside; a blue-and-white teapot with no lid; some chipped jelly jar glasses that are almost retro enough to be worth something. A yardstick that's not really a yard, but a meter.

My favorite item is a white toilet plunger that has a clear

plastic handle filled with rice. On top are a plastic bride and groom, arms linked, with a tag that says "We took the plunge."

Then I spot the cookie jar. Betty Boop sitting on the Empire State Building. Betsy would kill for that. She has a whole collection of Betty Boop stuff—clocks, dishes, a teapot, dolls—some of it valuable. When she first starting collecting them I used to call her Betsy Boop. I pick up the lid and check inside for the price. Ten dollars. It's probably worth at least twice that; Betsy would know for sure. Sissy always said Betsy had a good eye.

An image forms in my mind. A warm summer morning—could be any one of a hundred. Betsy's driving; on my lap is a street map of Albuquerque dotted with red *X*s. The car radio is pumping out Willie Nelson, the cup holders sag with Venti Frappuccinos.

Was that the day we fought over the Sunbeam mixer? The time she found the kitten in the alley? Or one of the many days we quit early to take refuge from the heat at an afternoon movie. The day we got caught with tuna sandwiches in the multiplex and she stuffed the entire quarter sandwich in her mouth so she wouldn't have to give it up? I laughed so hard I nearly wet my shorts, and they asked us to leave anyway.

The memory makes me smile for a second, but it's like a picture in an old high school yearbook, viewed with amused disbelief. Who are those funny girls, anyway? I feel like I should know them.

"That's really cute." The woman standing beside me is talking while stuffing a donut in her mouth; the clear red jelly oozes onto her fingers. I smile and head for the street, leaving the cookie jar to her.

In minutes the village is behind me and I'm entering a tunnel of tall evergreens, silent except for my footsteps, a few musical birds, and the steady dripping of water. At the corner of an unnamed, unpaved road a rickety wooden structure sits like an altar with an offering of a half-dozen egg cartons stacked precariously. The hand-lettered sign reads EGGS $2/DOZ. I open one of the cartons. No all-white, grade-AA, extra-large uniformity here. It's a United Nations of eggs. White, ivory, brown, and a delicate shade of blue-green. Large pear shapes, perfect medium ovals, and fat round spheres.

The metal box behind the sign is full of small bills and change. I gaze down the road till it disappears into green darkness. No sign of anyone. Do they actually leave all this out here? I suppose they can't afford to hang around here all day waiting for somebody to come buy eggs, but it seems incredibly trusting. Gwen would love it.

Pavement gives way to gravel, and the woods to meadow. The roadsides are thick with spring growth of yarrow and Queen Anne's lace about to bloom, tufts of purple clover and rambling wild sweet pea vines. Bursts of fragrance drift up to me as I step on wild mint or brush the delicate fronds of fennel.

It's May, and days are already long here, and amazingly cool. I've learned not to go anywhere without a jacket or sweatshirt, because a brisk wind can rip through or the fog roll in at any time. Even after a week, I still feel vaguely jet-lagged, but I sense it has less to do with the time difference and more with the strangeness of this place.

You can't even see the ground, which—in stark contrast to New Mexico—is completely covered with growing things. Hills draped with the forest primeval, moss growing on bark, giant prehistoric-looking ferns, berries and herbs growing wild in the ditches. And some strange life forms, like banana slugs—huge snail-things without shells—that leave slime tracks all over the porch during the night like weird nocturnal elves.

It doesn't bear much resemblance to my fantasy of strolling on a white-sand beach while gentle waves wash over my bare feet. Most of the San Miguel coastline consists of what the locals call "high-bank waterfront," meaning steep bluffs that drop down to the ocean. Beaches are few, small, and covered with gravel and shells, boulders and piles of driftwood. Not conducive to walking barefoot. And the water is cold.

I was in such a hurry to put New Mexico behind me that I didn't take any time to investigate what was in front of me. I might as well have thrown a dart at a map, blindfolded. But now I'm here, too mentally exhausted to pack up and leave. And I can't escape the irony of having run so far, crossed "the great stream," as the *I Ching* advised, and ending up in a place called Harmony.

Different Drummer Books occupies a small storefront on First Street between Crystal Cavern Aromatherapy and Jake's Deli. The woman behind the counter looks up and smiles when she hears the door.

"Hi. If you don't see what you want, yell at me."

The place smells of paper and freshly brewed coffee and some kind of potpourri suggestive of rain in the woods. Undoubtedly from the Cavern, next door. I head for a sign that reads LOCAL INTEREST. There are maps and sailing charts, Audubon books on birds and plants, the usual tourist guides, and skinny paperbacks of island lore written by local history buffs.

I'm tempted by one called *The Island Gardener*, but I have no place to garden except for one window box. Thinking of the wild mint and fennel I saw on my walk, I pick up a weighty volume called *Wild Edible Plants of the Pacific Northwest*. The problem is it's roughly the size of *War and Peace*, not something you'd want to carry around in the woods.

"Looking for anything special?" The woman from the counter is standing behind me now, tall and athletic, with a pretty smile gleaming against her tan skin. I can't help wondering how she gets a tan in this climate.

"Do you have anything on edible wild plants—preferably something that doesn't weigh eight pounds?"

She laughs. "We usually have one called *Native Harvest*. Let me just trade places with you for a sec. Hmm . . ." She flips through the books on the top shelf. "Looks like we're out. We should be getting some more in a few days. If you want to give me your name and phone number, I can let you know when they come in."

"I'll just check back with you. I don't have a phone."

"Should I hold a copy for you?"

"Um . . . sure. Sunny Cooper."

She holds out her hand. "Hallie Winkler. I'm Laura's sister."

"Laura?"

"In the Chamber booth by the ferry." She smiles and tucks her thick, dark hair behind one ear. "Sorry. I always assume everyone knows Laura."

"Oh, right. So how long will it take? To get the book?"

"The distributor usually has this one, so probably about a week. Our deliveries come on Wednesdays." She rests her arm on the ladder that leans against the bookcase. "So how's it working out over at Sarah's? You getting settled in?"

I stare at her. "How did you know where I'm staying?"

She looks thoughtful. "I think maybe Laura told me."

"How did she know? The only person I talked to was . . . the bartender at the Ale House."

"Piggy." She smiles broadly. "He and my sister live together." She laughs at the expression on my face. "It's the Harmony telegraph. Don't tell anyone anything you wouldn't like to see on the market bulletin board."

The hardest part of unemployment so far isn't the shortage of funds—I figure if I'm careful, I can survive about a month without work—it's the surplus of hours and nothing to occupy my brain. With the future unknowable, and even the present somewhat out of focus, the past leaps onto the screen to fill the void, like a movie that's too disturbing to ever completely forget.

A few years ago I read a story in the paper about this guy in New York who murdered his pregnant wife and blamed it on burglars. The woman who lived next door got suspicious when she came over to bring him condolences and a casserole. She told the cops his wife's two German shepherds were acting strange. They came right up to her as soon as she walked in, but they wouldn't have anything to do with the husband, even when he tried to feed them.

The story just reinforced my belief that you can tell a lot about a person by how they are with animals. My brother, Hart, is almost part animal himself. His name is actually another name for deer. With his warm brown eyes and that soulful smile just on the edge of sadness, he was the kind of guy women always wanted to hug. He never developed a protective shell and he couldn't handle conflict. In the heat of sibling battles, if I yelled that I hated him, he'd be crushed. If something was wrong with one of the animals, he blamed himself. When Rob and Gwen got into one of their scenes, Hart always thought it was his fault.

He was willing to work hard, but he never seemed to figure out what to work hard at. He left the mesa when he was seventeen, just days before his high-school graduation. He got a job working for a veterinarian in San Antonio, and for a while he sent postcards with funny little messages or poems. Eventually they stopped.

He called me one night at the end of November during my freshman year at UNM, and I went to meet him at Danelli's, a local pizza hangout. He was standing out front in the gray drizzle, hands tucked into his armpits for warmth. I didn't recognize him at first. In fact I walked right past him, but he touched my arm and said, "Hey, Sunny Bunny . . ."

It took a few seconds for me to connect my brother with the gaunt, bearded guy in the dirty parka. His embrace smelled of cigarettes and stale sweat, and I forced myself not to cry.

Danelli's was dim inside. Only a few tables were occupied. Some guys were playing foosball in the corner and Clint Black's nasal "Killin' Time" twanged out of the jukebox. I ordered a large pizza at the register and went to join Hart at a booth in the back.

He looked disappointed when I set down two Cokes. "I could use a beer."

"You'll have to get it yourself. I'm not legal." I took off my jacket and tossed it into the booth ahead of me. "Give me your jacket." I stretched out a hand.

He hunched his shoulders. "I think I'll keep it on. Kind of cold in here."

I settled myself across from him, and he smiled. One of his front teeth was chipped.

"Bar fight," he said, and I remembered the time when we could finish each other's sentences. "You look great."

"Thanks," I said. "You don't."

He smiled again, this time with his mouth closed. "Yeah, I know. Things have been . . ." He pushed his hair out of his eyes with dirty fingers. "But they're getting better."

"Where've you been living?" I said.

"Florida. A horse ranch near Ocala."

"What are you doing there?"

"Taking care of the barn and the horses. You know—mucking stalls, grooming, feeding, giving them their meds."

"You like it there?"

"It's great." He said it a little wistfully. "They breed and train quarter horses. They're the best little guys. You should see how they teach them to work cattle. They're so damn smart—and fast, too. God, I love 'em." His face glowed. "There was this guy there, Ned Crow; he's a Seminole. He was going to teach me how to shoe. He said a good farrier could always find work."

"So what are you doing up here?"

He looks away from me. "I'm sort of in transition." Then quickly: "I'm just on my way to take a new job."

I pulled the paper off a straw and stuck it in my glass. "Where?"

"At the greyhound track in Colorado Springs. Taking care of the dogs."

"Hart, how could you work at a—"

"Because I need money." He cut me off. "Besides, the dogs are there. Nothing I can do about that. I figure at least there'll be one person there who loves them. How's school? What are you studying?"

I gave him a long look before I answered. "It's okay. I'm mostly taking boring freshman requirements."

"Mostly?"

"I only get one elective. I'm taking drama."

"Drama? Really?" He leaned back against the hard wooden booth. "You want to be a movie star?"

"God, no. I just sort of like acting."

"I never would've thought that. You. Getting up on a stage in front of a bunch of people . . ."

"When you get up onstage in front of a bunch of people you're not you anymore. How come you left Florida?"

His eyes went to the bar, where our pizza had just appeared. "I'll go get that."

He set the metal pan on the scarred plastic table between us and before I could pull two napkins out of the dispenser, he'd grabbed a piece and taken a huge bite, stringing cheese between his mouth and hand like little suspension bridges.

"Why did you leave Florida?"

He made a big show of chewing and swallowing the pizza. "Whew, that's hot. Why did I leave Florida? Well, because. There was this guy there that didn't like me. He got me fired."

I separated a wedge of pizza from the pie, pulled a round of pepperoni off the top, and laid it on my tongue. "How did he do that?"

Hart looked at me, annoyed. "He told lies about me, that's how."

"Like what?"

He took a long drink of Coke and another bite of pizza. The way he was inhaling food made me wonder when he'd had his last meal. "He said I was doing drugs."

"Were you?"

"Oh, give me a fucking break, Sunny." He crumpled his napkin and threw it on the floor.

"Is that a yes or a no?"

"No!" Under the layer of grime, his skin was flushed and damp. "I mean, I'd already quit by that time."

·I took a small bite of pizza and chewed it slowly.

"Don't look at me like that," he said.

"Like what?"

"Like you're so goddamned disappointed." He dropped his pizza and just looked back at me. "I'm about fucking sick and tired of everybody being disappointed in me."

I folded my arms on the table. "Hart . . . have you really quit?"

He nodded, keeping his eyes on mine, but I didn't believe him.

"Can you loan me some money?" He picks up the slice again. "Just until I get settled? I'm going to get my GED and then I'm going back to Florida and learn how to be a farrier."

"You probably don't even need the GED," I said. "You fin-ished all the classwork. I bet if you just called the Taos school district they'd let you take a proficiency exam or something and give you your diploma."

Something came alive in his face. "You think?"

"Yeah, I do. When does your new job start?"

"I need some new clothes and stuff. In three weeks. About."

I studied him. "At Christmas? How can they race during the winter?"

His hesitation was brief but definite, and it told me what I didn't really want to know. It was all a lie. There was no job.

He drank some Coke and his hand trembled when he set down the glass. "No, I mean three weeks after Christmas. I mean, they still have to take care of the dogs, even when they're not racing."

"So what are you going to do in the meantime?"

"I don't know. Maybe go see Gwen. Or maybe just hang out here with you." He tried on a grin, but it didn't go with the rest of his face. "So, how about it? Can you loan me some money?" He started to sing. *"I need money, Sunny. That's what I want . . ."*

"How much do you need?"

He licked his lips. "Couple thousand."

I almost laughed, but then I saw he was serious. "I've got an idea. Why don't I go shopping with you? I'm good at picking out clothes—and we can have lunch. It'll be—"

His face got dark and still, like a mask, and the words seemed to eject from between his clenched teeth. "Don't you talk to me like I'm some kind of fucking idiot. You don't believe anything I've said, do you?" I was certain that everyone was listening to us. "You think I'm going to buy drugs."

"Come on, Hart. I don't think that." I almost whispered it, hoping he'd get the message and lower his voice. "I just want to spend some time with you. You act like all you want from me is money."

"Well, you're the only one in the whole fucking family who's got any. You're the girl with the *college fund*." The last two words came out hissing with venom, and my heart clenched like a fist.

I got to my feet, but he grabbed my arm. "Sunny, wait a second. Don't—"

I pulled away. "I'm just going to the bathroom."

I stayed a while in the bathroom, washing and rewashing my hands till they were red and chafed, trying to think about what to do with my brother. No obvious solution came to me. When I got back to the table, he'd eaten all the pizza except for the piece I'd been nibbling on. It seemed to have mollified him. He'd ordered two more Cokes.

"Sorry. I was really hungry."

I slid into the booth. "That's okay. I wasn't." I ate the rest of my slice and sipped at the new Coke while he pillowed his head on his arms and closed his eyes. I thought about how he'd looked the last time I saw him—when we were still sharing our little bedroom off the kitchen at Armonía. When he was just seventeen, handsome and sweet, with little downy whiskers on his cheeks and long, dark eyelashes. I thought about how he'd complain when I wanted to read after lights out, the way he'd snore like a toy motorboat.

He sat up abruptly and looked straight into my face. His eyes were bleary and his voice shook. "You ever think about her, Sunny?"

There was no need to ask who he meant. "Not very much."

"I do," he said. "I think about her a lot. Sometimes I can't sleep."

I put my hand on his sleeve. "Listen, why don't you come back with me. I'll sneak you into the dorm and you can take a shower. I have a big sweatshirt you can—"

"No, that's okay. I sort of met this girl . . ."

"Well, tomorrow, then. Meet me at the Del Norte Savings on Central and we'll go shopping. Get you some decent clothes. And we'll go to lunch. There's a great burger place . . ."

"You don't have to do that."

"I want to. Hart . . . about the money. I didn't know till Gwen brought me down here for summer school."

"Hey—it's okay. Nana probably knew you were the one who'd use it."

"You could've used it too. You could've gone to veterinary school."

He shook his head. "I don't have what it takes. Animals love me and I love them, but it takes more than that to get through vet school. Besides, I can always find work. There's so many animals and not enough people who know how to take care of them. I can always get a job."

I pulled on my jacket, paid for the extra Cokes, and we walked outside. The rain had stopped and the sky was a black dome, studded with ice. I turned to him.

"So we'll go tomorrow? Take a shower so you can try on some clothes, and I'll give you some money to take with you. Just please, please, don't spend it on drugs. Okay?"

He laughed. "What a trip. Here we grew up on the mesa where we could've had any drugs, anything—pot, hash, peyote, acid—whatever we wanted, for nothing. Now you gotta pay twenty bucks for a nickel bag of shit that's half oregano."

"Hart . . ."

He kissed my forehead with his chapped lips. "Okay, okay. Don't worry, Sunny Bunny. I'll meet you tomorrow. What time?"

"Ten thirty. In front of the Del Norte Bank on Central. Can you find it?"

"Yep. G'night, little sister."

He walked away like he knew where he was heading, and I hoped he did. I hoped there really was a girl and that he had a warm place to sleep and that he'd take a shower.

The next morning, after a cup of coffee, I got dressed and dropped my checkbook into my backpack and walked down to Del Norte. It was still cold, but the sun was shining and it warmed me. I stood there by the bank door for two hours, waiting for my brother, till the guard came over and told me to move along.

I still have the piece of paper Gwen gave me with his address, some post office box in the Kentucky penal system. Several times since I landed here, I've sat down, intending to write him a letter.

Hey, Hart—Guess what! I'm living on an island . . . in a town called Harmony—how's that for ironic?

That's always my first line. Then I falter.

Sorry to hear you're in jail. Made any good license plates? Ha, ha.

No, it's not funny, I know that. But how can I be serious?

Did you ever really stop doing drugs? Why were you passing bad checks? Why didn't you call me instead of Gwen? Are you mad at me? Do you ever want to see me?

Has it been too long or not long enough?

I tell myself he could already be gone from there, anyway. He could have gotten probation. Or community service. If they knew how good he was with animals, maybe they'd let him work off his sentence at Animal Control or something.

A few more days, a few more letters not written. I quit trying.

Instead of spending my mornings in an uncomfortable wooden chair in my room, I spend them on an uncomfortable wooden bench by the totem pole, watching ferry passengers disembark.

When the sun arrives in the afternoons, I explore. Without a car, I'm limited to places within walking distance, although I did hitchhike to Whale Watch Point one afternoon. Through sheer dumb luck I got there at low tide, and joined the half dozen other beach walkers scrambling around on the exposed ocean bed. We watched long-legged shorebirds foraging in the tidal flats, cormorants spreading their wings to dry in the sun.

A woman with a huge straw hat and baggy jeans rolled up above her ankles pointed out hermit crabs to me, tiny jellyfish the size of marbles, flowerlike anemones and spiny urchins and huge purple sea stars. I examined every creature carefully, while the baggy jeans lady examined me, as if I were some interesting new specimen washed up by the tide.

Two hours later I was exhausted and sunburned and stag-

gering drunk on salt air. And it was time to find my way back
to the village. That's the problem with hitching. That afternoon
I ended up walking close to six miles before some guy in a cement truck finally came along.

I've visited the organic lavender farm, toured the sculpture
garden and the two-room Island History Museum, hiked out
to the old island cemetery, on a bluff overlooking the harbor,
checked news and e-mail at the library—three messages from
Artie, all ending the same way: *Miss you . . . and the brownies!*—
and spent lots of time reading the menus posted in restaurant
windows and wishing I could afford to try some of them.

The highlight of my day—or at least the benchmark
by which I know I've made it through another twenty-four
hours—is my trip to the marina to buy fish for my dinner. I've
been gorging on salmon and halibut, lingcod, clams, because
it's so different buying it here from buying it frozen or shrink-
wrapped on a slab of Styrofoam. Mick Holzer told the truth.
His fish is the best—cut to your specifications, right before your
eyes. Mick's obnoxious, but he knows fish, and he's given me
some good suggestions for cooking, even showed me how to
shuck the clams I bought day before yesterday.

By the time I get to the marina today it's after four o'clock
and the fog is beginning to roll in, along with some heavy,
gray-bellied clouds. When Mick sees me, he hollers, "Hey Albuquerque . . . got some bitchin' lingcod here. Just came in a little
while ago. How 'bout a piece for dinner?"

"Sure."

He cuts it, wraps it, takes my money, all the while running
his mouth, never noticing that I haven't said a word to him. I
take my package with a brief "thanks" and turn to leave.

"Hey, Albuquerque, wait a second. What's your real name?"

He pulls a half-smoked cigarette from his shirt pocket and re-lights it.

"Sunny."

"Sunny What?"

"Cooper."

"That's cute. Listen, Sunny Cooper, I'm closing in a few minutes. Why don't you stick around. Have a beer with me."

"No thanks."

"Why not?"

"I don't drink beer," I lie. This is what's known as a no-win conversation; God only knows why I participate.

"I've got wine. Vodka. Bourbon." He lowers his voice and wiggles his eyebrows at me. "I've even got some pretty good Maui Wowie if you're—"

"Thanks, but I need to get home."

He hooks his thumbs in the side pockets of his dirty jeans. "I been seeing you almost every day and I don't know one damn thing about you."

"You sell fish, I pay in cash. What else do you need to know?"

"That's not a very friendly attitude." He blows a plume of smoke into the air and the wind whisks it away.

I fold my arms. "I'm not a very friendly person. Now you know something about me."

"And after I showed you how to shuck clams and every-thing." He shakes his head. "You got a boyfriend?"

"It's really none of your business."

"True. But, hey, where are you staying?"

"Neither is that. Good night, Mick. I need to get home before it rains."

"Rain? Shit, it's not gonna rain tonight. It's just messing with you. Don't worry about that."

" 'Bye, Mick."

"Okay, no problem. I can take a hint. Good night, Sunny Cooper." He's still chuckling to himself as I head up toward the street, regretting that I even told him my name.

I manage to get inside my room without running into Sarah, although I'm pretty sure I see the kitchen curtains flutter as I come up the driveway. I can't imagine what it is she thinks I'm going to do that would be so interesting. I strip off my clothes, pin up my hair, and head for the shower. The bathroom is freezing cold, and I stand motionless under the hot spray waiting to warm up. This has always been my favorite indulgence—probably a consequence of not ever having enough privacy or hot water at Armonía. Sarah will no doubt be complaining about my water usage as soon as she gets her next water bill.

While I'm drying myself with the skimpy towel, I realize that it *is* beginning to rain. I pull on a turtleneck and jeans and stand by the front window for a minute watching the sidewalk darken and the shrubs quiver and the flowers nod their heads.

I lie across the bed and try to think about cooking dinner. I'm hungry, but it seems like too much effort to get up and deal with the lingcod. I close my eyes and listen to the gentle, intermittent rain, inhale the damp breeze coming through the partially open window. It smells of seawater and evergreens. In New Mexico the rain smelled of sage and rabbit brush. And it was rarely gentle.

Out on the mesa, rain was an unpredictable lover. He stayed away too long and came back whenever he felt like it. Sometimes in July and August the clouds would hover far to the west, the sharp line between black sky and red earth would blend and soften, and you knew he was giving himself to someone else. It was provocative, infuriating, frustrating, but what could you do? No prayers, tears, or curses ever moved him.

Then one day he'd just show up. Sweet and quiet at first, soon he'd overwhelm you, exhaust you, never giving you a moment to catch your breath. Raindrops would become buckets, sheets, torrents, and the river would race by, swollen and angry, looking for a place to climb out over its banks. Great slabs of the mountains would drop away, sliding down into the valleys, obliterating roads, uprooting trees, swallowing buildings and pickup trucks. Just when you decided you hated him and never wanted to see his face again, the rain was gone. Leaving you with the nagging feeling that you'd be missing him a long time before he reappeared.

I turn on my side, hugging the pillow against me. It smells of fish. That's the only downside to having fresh fish for dinner every night. There's no vent fan over my tiny stove, and the smell tends to linger. It's a nice smell when it's cooking, but it's not so attractive the morning after. Even opening the windows doesn't completely take care of it, so after dinner every night, I smudge the place with my juniper/sage bundle just before I crawl under the covers to read until sleep comes.

My eyes open wide and for a few seconds I don't know why. I also don't know where I am or what time it is. I squint against the glare of the bedside light. The banging on my door takes care of the why.

"I'm coming. Just a minute." I look at the clock. 11:20 p.m.?

I just closed my eyes for a minute and then slept for almost three and a half hours. More banging on the door. I'm so out of it that it never occurs to me to wonder who might be coming to call at this hour until I open the door and am nearly knocked over by the smell of beer.

Mick sags against the door frame. "*Geeezus,*" he slurs. "Thought you were dead in there."

"I was asleep. What do you want?"

"Your light was on."

"Sometimes I fall asleep with the light on. Now go away before my landlady comes down here and kills us both."

"Thought ya might like a drink." He shows me both hands—one holding a half-empty bottle of Michelob and the other some kind of whiskey. "Ever have a boilermaker?"

I'm now fully awake. "I do *not* want a drink," I hiss. "Now get your ass out of here before you wake up Sarah."

"Don' chew worry about Sharah. She's my bud—"

"And how the *hell* did you find me?"

He smiles sloppily, eyes at half mast. "Issa small island, Sunny Cooper."

"Mick, I'm not kidding. *Go away!*"

He gives me a hurt look. "I brought this stuff *all* the way over here just for you and now you won't even drink it. Not even a teeny weeny?"

"I swear to God I'm calling the cops if you don't leave *right now.*" Never mind that I don't have a phone.

Big sigh. "Okay." He pivots smartly then lunges against the porch post, leans over and vomits into Sarah's flowerbed. *Shit.* He turns back to me, wiping his mouth on his sleeve. "Sorry about that, chief."

"Never mind. Just get out of here."

His attempted salute causes the whiskey bottle to slip from between his fingers and shatter on the porch, splashing booze and shards of glass all over. The lights go on in the kitchen.

By the time Sarah comes lumbering out, clutching her bathrobe up to her throat, Mick is weaving his way down the sidewalk.

"What in the name of heaven is going on?" When she gets closer to the flowerbed, she recoils. "Oh dear Lord Jesus, what is that horrible—"

"Sarah, don't come any closer, there's broken glass all over the place."

"What are you doing out here?" Her voice is rising, so I lower mine.

"I'm not doing anything. Some drunk wandered in here and started banging on my door. When I tried to make him leave, he . . . threw up in—"

"Oh, God," she wails, "my peonies."

"And then he dropped the bottle and broke it. The flowers will be fine. I'll hose them off tomorrow and clean up the glass and stuff, but it's too dark now."

She gives me a hard look. "Who was it?"

I hesitate.

"I told you no alcohol, no men visitors."

"He wasn't a visitor. I didn't invite him over. He just showed up drunk. I was already asleep."

"Do you always sleep with your clothes on?" she huffs.

"Look, there's nothing we can do tonight. I'll explain the whole thing tomorrow."

"It had better be a good explanation." She turns and lumbers back inside.

• • •

At 10:30 a.m. Thursday I'm sitting in front of the bakery, treating myself to breakfast since I've just spent two hours cleaning up broken glass, scrubbing the porch, and hosing off Sarah's peonies while she took turns micromanaging the operation and grilling me about my male visitor.

My sidewalk table is just big enough for a book—a silly mystery about drug smuggling written by some local guy—a cup of coffee, and a giant, still-warm chocolate chip cookie, its caramelized edges and gooey chunks of chocolate making me want to cram the whole thing in my mouth at once. I force myself to break off little pieces and chew them slowly until they disappear. This is not the way I learned to eat.

Gwen, in spite of her back-to-the-earth lifestyle, had been raised with table manners, which she tried halfheartedly to pass on to Hart and me. But the reality of life at Armonía was, the last one in the dinner line got more rice and less chicken, more lettuce and fewer tomatoes, cukes, mushrooms, and green peppers. I learned to get it while the getting was good, and shovel it in quickly to make room for seconds.

I remember the first time I had lunch with Betsy, looking up, suddenly embarrassed by my clean plate, while she was still languidly spearing bites of asparagus, cutting an olive in half and smushing it against a crumb of Roquefort cheese. She's really the one who taught me to savor food, all the contrasting aromas, tastes, textures.

I pull my eyes back to the book and banish Betsy from my mind.

Suddenly a fat, blatting roar rips into the peaceful morning, and a motorcycle careens around the corner, stopping neatly in front of the Ale House. It's Brendan the bartender, clad in jeans and a leather jacket, a red bandana tied around his head. He knocks the kickstand down with his left foot and rises from the bike all in one fluid motion. While I'm still marveling at his unexpected grace, he starts across the street toward the bakery.

Inside the shade of the awning his eyes focus on me. "Hey. Just the person I was looking for."

"Hi, Brendan."

"Piggy," he corrects me. "I just came from your place."

"Great. My reputation as a slut is now secure."

"What?"

I tell him about Mick's midnight visit.

He laughs. "Yeah, Sarah's a bit of a tight-ass."

"You could have warned me."

"True. But then you might've left and you wouldn't be here now and we've got an opening at the Ale House. A server quit Tuesday night. You still interested?"

"Yes," I say, without thinking.

He drums his fingers on the back of the chair across from me. "Let me go grab a coffee and we'll talk about it."

Michael had a theory that anything you say yes to without thinking falls into the category of Fate, and you might as well accept it as such. So here I sit, having just verbally accepted a drive-by job offer.

I swivel in my chair to watch Piggy through the bakery's front window. Almost everyone on both sides of the counter speaks to him. He smiles easily, seems comfortable with people; he's apparently the man in charge at the Ale House. But there's something about him . . . something that has to do with the skull tattoo on his right forearm and the big-ass motorcycle parked at the curb and the way he walks, leaning forward, as if he's heading for trouble and feeling good about it.

In a few minutes he's back, pulling out the extra chair, setting down a roll that oozes cinnamon and sugar, and a giant industrial-size coffee, black and steaming. He sits down and opens a napkin, settling it on his lap. It seems an odd gesture for someone who looks like an extra from a biker movie.

"What kind of motorcycle is that?" I ask.

His proud grin is instantaneous. "Forty-seven Indian Chief."

"Forty-seven as in 1947?"

"Yep."

"I've never seen one with fenders like that. It's kind of pretty."

"*Pretty?*" He snorts. "Nah. She's beautiful. Those fenders are an Indian trademark." He empties a tiny plastic container of cream into his cup; it sinks to the bottom without effecting any noticeable change in the coffee.

"Why do men always call their machines 'she'?"

He gives me a look tinged with impatience. "I don't know about 'men.' I only know about myself. Sometime, when I get to know you better, I might tell you." Then he smiles. "So, how do you like the island?"

"I'm not quite sure what to make of it," I say, and he nods.

"Different from New Mexico, I guess."

"Very."

He blows on his coffee, takes a big bite of cinnamon roll, and chews contentedly. "Think you might be bored working as a server?"

"I wasn't thinking of it as entertainment," I say. "I need the money."

"It's the dinner shift," he says. "Three thirty to midnight. You mind working nights?"

"No."

"Think you'll stay through the summer?"

"Probably."

"Probably?"

"Right now that's my intention." I look at him sideways. "In the food business that's about all the guarantee you can expect."

He gives me a rueful grin. "True. Can you start tomorrow?"

"Yes."

"Come in about three and we'll get you set up. Meanwhile, I'll call your reference," he adds offhandedly. I look over the rim of my cup and into his cool green eyes.

"Okay."

Business concluded, he gathers up his coffee and cinnamon roll and heads back across the street. End of job interview.

Chapter 13

Promptly at three on Friday afternoon, I push open the back door of the Ale House and step inside, my stomach tense and growly. It's been a while since I waited tables, but it's sort of like riding a bicycle. You don't forget how. And the Ale House is pretty casual. It just seems important now. I need the money, true, but it's more than that. I need a focus, something to anchor me in the present.

Piggy is lounging against a worktable talking to a couple of guys. When he sees me, he comes right over. "Hey, Sunny."

"Hi." I roll up the sleeves of my white shirt and unbutton my vest. "I forgot to ask what I should wear."

"What you've got on is fine," he says. "When we get our new batch of T-shirts, you can pick out a couple of those. Come on, let's get you an apron."

I love restaurant kitchens. Something about a gleaming stainless-steel backsplash, fire-blackened pans, the mellow golden grain of well-scrubbed butcher block, the smoky scent of the grill, always makes my heart beat a little faster. This one is small but efficiently plotted. You can just about stand at one station and with one or two steps in any direction, reach everything you need.

"This is Justin," Piggy is saying. "He's the main man back here. Justin, Sunny, our new server."

A short guy with curly black hair and eyes like pools of melted chocolate grins at me. "'Scuse me for not shaking your hand." His plastic gloved hands are sunk in a stainless-steel tub of some kind of batter, arm muscles rippling as he mixes it.

Piggy hands me a long white apron, folded stiff and flat. I slip my head through the loop, pull the strings around to tie it in front. Two women are having an animated conversation in front of a small stainless-steel sink, while the taller of the two puts on lipstick in a wall mirror. They both look up when Piggy says, "Where's Heather?"

They shrug simultaneously.

"This is Sunny Cooper. She's starting tonight, replacing Kathy. This is Barbara Fedora." The short one is dark-haired, chubby, and sullen looking, but she has luminous skin; her cheeks are the pinky rose color of a baby's feet. She allows me a careful smile. "And Freddie Russell."

"Hi there." The tall blonde has nice blue eyes and a soft voice with a nasal twang that I recognize as originating in west Texas. If she wore white shorts and a whistle on a long black cord, she'd look like your favorite P.E. teacher.

"Freddie, Sunny's tailing you tonight. Barbara, you're gonna have to handle upstairs by yourself till Heather shows."

"Oh . . ." Her head falls back with a groan.

Piggy turns back to me. "Look over the menu, get the specials from Justin. You shouldn't have any problems, but if you do, ask Freddie or me. After your shift I'll need you to fill out a couple of forms."

He goes back to the bar, and I ask, "What's upstairs?"

Freddie finishes smoothing her fine blond hair back into a ponytail and fastens it with a red Scrunchie. "A teensy dining room. Four four-tops and a couple of deuces. For folks who don't want to mix with the trashy element in the bar."

Barbara sniffs. "I'd rather wait on the trash than run up and down those stairs all night. Clean spilled Cokes off of rug rats. And the tips are never as good up there."

The screen door bangs and a young woman wearing jeans and a barely there halter top presents herself.

"Heather." Barbara gives her an evil smile. "So glad you could join us. Too bad you didn't have time to get dressed."

The girl ignores her and smiles at me. "Hi. I'm Heather Forsthoff. Trent's my dad." She grabs an apron and pulls it on, frees her long dark hair from the neck strap.

"Who's Trent?"

She gives me a look. "The owner of this place. I love your vest. You must be from Arizona."

"Thanks. New Mexico, actually."

A frown wrinkles her smooth forehead. "So are you legal?"

"Legal?" At first I flatter myself with the thought that she thinks I'm underage.

"You know, do you have like a green card or whatever?"

Freddie turns to hide a smile, but Barbara snickers. "We own New Mexico, Heather. Did you cut history class that day?"

Heather flushes deeply and glares at her. "I know that. It was supposed to be a joke." She disappears through the swinging doors.

"Daddy's little girl." Barbara looks at the ceiling, poking her index finger into the side of her cheek. Then to me. "We call him The Trent."

Freddie hands me a scratch pad and a plastic card with a magnetic stripe. "You ever used the DinnerWare system?"

"No. We used HotPlate."

"You won't have any problems with this one. It's pretty basic. I'll show you when we take our first order. You get two fifteen-minute breaks and a thirty-minute dinner. Tonight you can take your dinner with me if you want. Be sure to let Justin know what you want about fifteen minutes ahead of time." She looks over at the prep area. "Justin, honey, whatcha cookin' tonight?"

"Soup is corn chowder. Pasta is linguine with clam sauce. Fish is grilled swordfish or pan-seared salmon with my super secret Cajun spice rub. And"—a pause—"no lemon tart tonight."

I meet Manolo and Gus, the line cooks, and Jack, the dishwasher. Freddie gives me a time card and shows me where to clock in and then promptly at 3:30 she tucks her pad in the back waistband of her jeans. "Okay, y'all let's go. And be careful. It's a jungle out there."

She holds open the swinging door. "Ah. First victims." She nods at a table where three men are laughing and punching each other in the arm like a junior high football team on their first road trip. One of them is Mick Holzer.

"Howdy, gentlemen," Freddie drawls. "You too, Mick."

He grins when he sees me. "Hey, Albuquerque. Good to see you're keeping off the streets and out of trouble."

Freddie pulls me closer to the table. "This is Sunny. As some of you already know. It's her first night, so she's following me around. By tomorrow night I'll probably be following her around." She reaches for her pad and flips the page. "Mick, you know what you want?"

He winks at her. "Your face in my lap."

Freddie smiles sweetly. "Not on the menu. What's your second choice?"

"Guess I'll have a porter, then. Hey, Freddie, you know what the medical name for Viagra is?" He looks at me. "Mycoxafloppin."

"Sounds like a personal problem, darlin'." She's trying hard not to laugh. "Bobby?"

"Why does a squirrel swim on its back?"

"To keep his nuts dry," she says. "What are you drinking?"

"Hey, you ruined my punch line," he grouses. "I guess I'll have a Coors. And bring us some chicken wings to start."

"I got a new one," the third guy says. "How did the Dairy Queen get pregnant?" He pauses. "The Burger King forgot to wrap his Whopper."

This sets off a whole new round of shoulder punching.

When we're in the kitchen fixing setups, Freddie turns to me. "I see you've already met the local bubba contingent."

"Just Mick. I was buying fish from him till he suddenly decided we should be drinking buddies."

She laughs, brushing her bangs back from her eyes. "He's mostly harmless. But he'd just about hump a pile of rocks if he thought there was a snake under it."

At nine fifteen, Freddie and I take our dinners to the tiny room off the kitchen where two small tables with folding chairs serve as the staff dining facilities. I set down my Caesar salad with grilled shrimp, unscrew the top on a Perrier, and lower myself into a chair with a sigh.

Freddie blows on a spoonful of corn chowder. "You have

to try this sometime. It's *so* good. How's it going? You doing okay?"

"Fine." I deposit a shrimp tail on my bread plate. "I'm just not used to being on my feet this long at a stretch. My legs are killing me."

"You might want to get some support hose. They're gross, but I wear 'em every night." She tears off a piece of sourdough bread and slathers butter on it. "So how long did you live in Alberquacky?"

I tip back the bottle of water. "Since I was eighteen."

"What brings you to this little corner of creation?"

"I don't know. I was just ready for something different, I guess." I push the salad around on my plate.

"Well, being from Texas, which is sorta like New Mexico only more so, I can tell you, it doesn't come any more different than this."

"How long have you been here?" I ask.

"Be two years next month."

"So, you must like it."

She wipes up the last dregs of her soup with a piece of bread. "Yeah, I do. I mean, I miss Texas—sometimes I miss it a lot. Miss my family, my friends, my horse—not necessarily in that order. But for now, I'm staying right here." She pushes the soup bowl aside and pulls her dessert plate closer. The plate is nearly hidden by a huge slab of chocolate cake.

I must be staring at it because she pushes it back toward me. "Go on, take a bite. It's worth every calorie."

"No, if I start, I won't be able to stop. I want to know how come you don't weigh two hundred pounds."

"I take after my momma. She's a little bitty thing, eats like a truck driver." She puts a forkful in her mouth and closes her eyes. "Damn that Justin. Sexy, funny, and he cooks like a maniac."

I study her for a minute, her tall, blond, cowgirl good looks—like an ad for Tony Lama Boots—and I try to picture her with Justin.

"I think he looks like a little elf."

"I dated one of those little Cajun elves one time, and let me tell you, honey, it's true. They can do magic." She gives me a knowing smile and licks the fudgy icing off her fork. "What do you think of this place?"

"The Ale House?"

"No, silly. Harmony. San Miguel Island."

"It's . . . beautiful."

She nods. "Yeah. Takes some getting used to. Believe me, I know. You divorced?"

I chew a bite of bread very slowly. "No."

"Okay, no more interrogation tonight." She laughs good-naturedly and sets down her fork. "I'm saving the rest of this for my last break. Come on, we better get back to the chain gang."

Like most small town markets, Forsthoff's—another piece of The Trent's empire—carries a little bit of everything. Everything except the *masa harina* and chiles, the *queso fresco* and tortillas that I'm craving. All they have is a few cans of Old El Paso enchilada sauce and some Zapata mild green chiles.

I stand in the long line for one of the registers. It's Saturday morning and the aisles are clogged with locals and tourists playing bumper carts. There are only three clerks, and they stop to chat at the slightest provocation. I'm the only one who seems to notice or mind. Everyone else is drinking coffee and gossiping like it's the county fair.

As I stare into space, my eyes focus on a patch of green by the front door. Herb seedlings. I abandon my cart to check out the display. Basil and thyme, parsley, oregano, sage. They actually have cilantro. Six is probably all I can fit in my window box. Even at that, they'll be cozy.

"So you're planning to grow your own." Startled, I wheel around, and a pot flies out of my hand.

Hallie from the bookstore smiles at me with her white, even teeth. She retrieves the seedling from the floor and glances at the white plastic label. "Cilantro, huh? Do you cook a lot of Mexican stuff?"

"Southwestern," I correct her. "And it looks like I won't be doing much of it here. They're kind of shy on ingredients."

She laughs. "I would imagine so. I went to school in Santa Barbara, and I really miss that kind of food, too. Of course, I'm not up to cooking it, but it would be great if somebody opened a café here. In the summer we get a lot of tourons up from California, I bet it would go really well."

The checker calls out, "Whose basket?"

"Sorry." I head back to the counter. "I need a small bag of potting soil." I reach for my wallet.

"I'll ring it in and you can just grab one on your way out."

I count out the change, and a teenage boy with an eyebrow ring bags my groceries. Hallie's disappeared, but when I step out to the sidewalk, she's opening the hatch of a green Subaru Outback.

"Need a ride?" she says.

"No, thanks." When I reach for the potting soil, a box of

spaghetti falls out of my plastic grocery sack. I bend for it, but she's quicker. "Thanks."

"Sure you don't want a ride?"

"No, that's okay."

"What a beautiful necklace." She's staring at the deerskin pouch.

"Thanks. It's a—"

"Medicine bundle?" she says, and I nod. "See, we're not all total ignoramuses." Her smile takes the edge off the words. She tucks the bag under my arm.

"Thanks. See you."

"Probably will. It's a small island."

The Ale House door opens, admitting a cool gust of air and an attractive middle-aged couple. On their way to a table near the bar, they stop to speak to almost everyone they pass. They sit in my station, but I hang back, watching Freddie talk to them before I pick up two waters and move to the table.

"This is my pal Sunny." Five nights at work and we're pals. "This is Trish Carver, the best haircutter in town."

The woman is pretty, but she'd look even better without the overdone makeup.

"And Scott Carver." The guy nods. His sandy hair is shot through with gray and his smile is friendly. He looks older than his wife, but maybe it's just wear and tear. When he gives back the menu, I notice his hands: worn and scarred like my father's, only more so. And he's missing the tip of his left index finger.

"You already know what you want?" I ask.

He laughs. "I don't need a menu. I always get the same thing."

Freddie turns to me. "Fried shrimp platter and an IPA. Strawberry shortcake for dessert, if we have it, and if we don't, chocolate brownie sundae. Decaf with cream, no sugar." She looks over at the bar. "Oops. The boss man's calling. *Hasta*, y'all."

"Didn't realize I was so boring." Scott laughs again. "Where are you from, Sunny?" His wife is still studying the menu.

"New Mexico."

"Oh, such a great place." Trish's mascara-laden eyelashes droop expressively. "We drove through Santa Fe and Taos on our honeymoon."

"Thirty-five years ago," Scott says. The two of them share a look that surprises me.

"Thirty-six," she says. "And you're almost off probation." She grins at me. "How do you like our island?"

"So far it's great."

"You just here for the season?" Scott asks.

"Probably."

Trish smiles. Actually she hasn't stopped· smiling since they walked in. Antidepressants, maybe. "Everybody stays here longer than they plan to," she says. "That's the first law of Harmony. Hard to get to, harder to leave. I think I'll have a glass of sauvignon blanc."

"What part of New Mexico are you from?" Scott asks when I set his beer down.

"Albuquerque." I put Trish's glass in front of her. "Do you know what you'd like to eat?"

Scott says, "My aunt and uncle used to live there. Nice town, isn't it? Where did you live?"

"Near the university."

"They lived over by Sandia. 'Course that was years ago. Wasn't much out there then. You ever ski there?"

"Once or twice." I tap the pad with my pencil. "Actually I'm not much of a skier."

Before he can say anything else, Trish laughs. "The girl is trying to work for a living here, honey. She can't stand around jawboning with you about Albuquerque." She hands me her menu. "I'll have the Chinese chicken salad."

Scott looks charmingly sheepish, and I escape to the kitchen.

At four o'clock every afternoon, conveniently scheduled in the lull between the three-fifteen and the five-thirty ferries, a large black dog comes trotting up the dock from the marina and sits down at the curb. Sometimes cars stop for him, but he refuses to cross until they move on.

Once I start looking, I see the dog everywhere. He gets French bread at the bakery, big, craggy soup bones at the market. At the herb shop, I spot him scarfing down herbal dog cookies. I see him at the bookstore sharing Hallie's lunch. He gets his picture taken with tourist kids, and they let him lick their ice-cream cones when their parents aren't looking.

Then one afternoon, at about 4:15, I'm fixing setups in the kitchen when I notice Justin heading for the back door with a nicely grilled hamburger patty. He pushes the screen open and there sits the black dog, waiting patiently to be served. When Justin turns around and sees me, he shrugs.

"That's Bailey. He likes my cooking."

I smile. "Perfectly understandable. I just didn't realize we had curb service. Who's his owner?"

He looks down at the spot where the burger has already

vanished and shrugs. "Bailey don't have an owner. He's a citizen."

Sunday.

Just before noon I finally roll over and open my eyes from a black and dreamless sleep. My toes are cold and there's a dull ache down low in my spine. Eleven hours of sleep and I feel like I spent the night doing calisthenics in a meat locker. I hate to waste the whole morning sleeping, but I can't seem to muster the energy even to sit up, much less get out of bed.

Freddie invited me over for a drink after work, but making conversation with Freddie can be exhausting, and I just didn't feel up to it. Her questions are innocent and natural enough, but I feel myself pulling away like one of those sea anemones that retract at the slightest touch.

I've just filled the coffee pot and set it on the burner when a scraping noise outside the door startles me and sends me to the window to peer out through the crack between the shade and the wall.

It's Sarah. Dragging my newly planted window box around the side of the porch. Paco is parked on the top step keeping watch for evildoers.

I open the door. "Is there a problem with my using the window box?" I try to keep it pleasant.

She looks up. "Of course not. We just need to keep it on the other window where I had it."

"Why is that?"

She stands up slowly, wiping her palms on her beige knit slacks. "Because that's where it belongs."

"That's the north side of the building," I say calmly. "There's no sun."

"That's where it belongs," she repeats, more firmly this time.

I bite the inside of my cheek. "It doesn't make much sense to have a window box on the north side, since nothing will grow there."

"Ferns. Pansies. Impatiens."

Can I explain this without letting on that I find her excruciatingly stupid? "These are herbs for cooking. They need full sun."

"As you can see from my yard, I'm an experienced gardener," she says stiffly. "I'm well aware of light requirements for herbs. However, I do not want that window box over here."

I let my eyes close for a second. I take a deep breath. "Fine. I'll buy myself a planter and put the herbs in it. Is there a problem with putting my planter over here by the door?"

Her eyes narrow while she considers the request. "I suppose not. As long as you put a saucer underneath." She bends down to the window box.

"I'll do it today. As soon as the market opens. In the meantime, would you please leave that over here so I don't have to haul things back and forth?"

"The market's not open today." There's no missing the satisfaction in her voice.

"It's not?"

She smiles, lips pressed together. "Not open on Sundays till June fifteenth."

She disappears around the corner, dragging the window box, and I close the door. I stand there gripping the doorknob till I realize that my heart is racing and I feel sort of spacey. I need some protein. I take the butter and eggs out of the fridge and set them on the table, but instead of doing anything with them, I sit down in the chair.

Tears that I didn't even know were waiting inside seep from my eyes and begin to run down my face, splashing on my bare thighs, soaking my shirt. In the bathroom I stare at myself in the mirror. With everything else that's going on in my life, I'm crying over a window box. What the hell is wrong with me?

Chapter 14

Hallie's got her nose in a book, but she looks up when I come in.

"I don't know how you can listen to that bell all day without going off the dock," I say.

She smiles and reaches beneath the counter for the copy of *Native Harvest.* "It's the sound of money," she says. "Sorry it took so long to get this. It was back-ordered at the distributor."

"That's okay." I take the book she's holding out, trying not to look disappointed.

She picks up on my expression immediately. "I know it's small, but there's a surprising amount of information in it. Even a few recipes. And remember, you didn't want big."

"I was hoping there might be some middle ground."

She says, "The thing I really like about this book is the way the plants are illustrated with photographs as well as botanical drawings. I hate it when you're out there with a field guide and none of the plants looks like any of the drawings. But if you decide it's not what you wanted, bring it back."

"I'm sure it'll be fine." I hand a twenty-dollar bill over the counter.

She counts out my change and drops the book and register

receipt into a paper bag bearing a woodblock stamp of a drum. She pauses. "By the way, a friend of mine leads nature hikes about once a month or so. Always a different place, usually really interesting. It's more or less the same half dozen of us every time, but anyone's welcome. Since you had an interest in that book, I thought you might like to come next time."

"Thanks, but I'd like to read a little first. Since I'm new here."

"There's no prerequisite level of knowledge," she persists.

I sigh. "You know, I just can't get enthusiastic about the idea of tramping through the underbrush with a bunch of other people."

"Six," she says. "Not a bunch."

"I'd be seven. It's too many. That's not a nature walk, it's a parade."

She laughs at me. "Why are you so antisocial?"

It startles me for a second, hearing this classification of myself.

"Hey, forget I said that." She shakes her head. "Sometimes I just . . . it's like there's a direct pipeline from brain to mouth, no filters. I apologize."

I look into her wide-open gaze. "At least you're honest. So here's an honest answer: I grew up on a commune in New Mexico. I spent my first eighteen years surrounded by an ever-changing cast of characters. Group work, group play, group meals . . . group sex, on occasion. Even our outhouse was a five-seater. It made my brother the kind of person who'd strike up a conversation with a guy who's mugging him at gunpoint. It made me into somebody who thinks three people is a mob. That's pretty much all there is to it."

Her eyes are full of questions, but she just nods. "Makes sense, I guess. I hope you're not—"

"No. I'm not."

We trade smiles as I back out the door.

It's only one o'clock, but I can't face going back to my little room, so I wander down the sidewalk, aimless, eventually falling in behind a woman and two young girls, obviously tourists.

When she stops to unlock an SUV parked at the curb, the woman gives me a friendly smile. It's an inclusive gesture—as if she knows me. I wonder what makes her think my life bears any resemblance to hers. I feel reasonably certain that she didn't grow up in a house with dirt floors. That her first driving experience wasn't in a psychedelically decorated former bread truck. That her mother was nothing like Gwen.

I don't know why, but I miss my mother sometimes. In spite of the fact that I don't like her, I'm drawn to her, pulled by the attraction of shared blood, I suppose. Up close, only our conflict is obvious. But at a distance, all the other tiny bits— like pointillist dots in primary colors—describe a whole picture with all its shadings.

I remember a day when I stood next to the chair where she nursed Mari, wishing the baby would hurry up and go to sleep so Gwen would pay attention to me, look at the potholder I made in art class, the picture of Rob and Boone that I drew in my notebook.

It's one of those memories that trips a switch, illuminating another darkened image. The picture I had drawn was of Rob and Boone fighting. Not having an argument, but actually throwing punches out by the barn. When I showed the picture to Gwen, she studied it for what seemed like a very long time. She still had Mari at her breast, but she pulled me to her side, put her arm around me, and stroked my hair gently while I tried to stand absolutely still, afraid that if I moved she would stop.

It's two o'clock. In the Ale House kitchen Manolo and Gus are cleaning up from lunch and starting prep for dinner. Justin's back in the storeroom unpacking a delivery and singing along with a scratchy sounding Zydeco cassette on an ancient tape player.

He smiles at me. "Hey. What're you doing here so early?"

"Nothing special. You need some help?"

"Don't have to ask me twice."

I cut open a carton with the utility knife he hands me and start stacking cans of tomatoes on a metal shelf. "You miss Louisiana?"

He laughs. "I never lived there in my whole life. I grew up in San Francisco, but *ma mère* was a pureblood, top-of-the-line Coon-ass. She had this stuff going day and night. Still does. When I call her on the phone, I can hear it blastin' in the background."

"She's still in San Francisco?"

"No, not for a long time. Too cold for her bones. She lives in San Diego now. Not in the city, but a little beach town. Leucadia. Ever hear of it? She's always trying to get me to move down there."

"So why don't you?"

"Too many people for me—Southern California. And half of 'em are up here in the summer. You wait till July. You won't believe how it gets around here. I do miss her cookin', though." He shakes his dark mop of hair. "Hoo boy, the woman, she can cook."

I throw the carton on the pile of empties, slit open another one.

He's still talking. "Gumbo. Jambalaya. Étouffé. Big ol' steaks cooked in olive oil on the griddle. Calas—that's sweet rice cakes . . . Oyster po' boys. Makes me hungry just thinkin' about it."

"Do you ever cook like that?"

"Not here. But at home I do. Me and Vicki—that's my wife—we'll make up a shrimp gumbo of a Wednesday night. Always have jambalaya on Christmas Eve. Hey, you'll have to come over sometime. Vicki's from Detroit, but she cooks like a Looziana girl."

I stack bags of bow tie pasta on a shelf and try to gracefully ignore the invitation. "So why don't you cook that way here?"

"Ahhh . . ." The way he rolls his eyes lets me know that this discussion is a tired old horse—you can flog him all you like, but he never goes anywhere. "Trent hired some menu consultant when this place was in the works. To come up with a menu that was gonna go good with beer. This is what we got. Some daily specials and, you know, the fresh seafood, but mostly . . ." He gives an exaggerated yawn.

Two more boxes and we're done. He says, "Thanks for the hand, Sunny."

I follow him out to the kitchen. "Sure. Anything else I can do?"

He looks at me. "You on the clock?"

"No. I just—I was bored. Didn't feel like hanging around my place."

Didn't feel like thinking about my dead fiancé and my dead little sister and my cheating best friend and my jailbird brother and my missing father and my crazy mother. Didn't feel like sniffing sage smoke and crying till my eyes swelled shut. Didn't feel like sleeping anymore or arguing with my landlady about window boxes.

"Well . . . if you're just itchin' for something to do, you can peel some shrimp. Drag that stool over here and I'm gonna get you going."

It takes about fifteen seconds for him to figure out that I don't know shit about peeling shrimp. "Lemme show you somethin'." He grabs a shrimp and decapitates it with a flick of his thumb. "Then you pull off his feet, and then if you squeeze right down here, just above the tail, that little fishy just pops right outta his shell."

On my first try, I succeed only in smashing the shrimp.

"Don't push your fingers together so hard, just kinda press and slide 'em forward. That's it. You got it." He peers into a big stockpot on the back of the stove. When you get a full bowl of shells and heads, dump 'em in this pot and we'll make us some big-time shrimp stock."

After two or three more, I get the feel of it, and it makes me irrationally happy to be able to shoot the shrimp into the huge aluminum bowl.

I notice him as soon as I come through the swinging door from the kitchen. Sitting alone at a window table. I can't see his face, but the line of his shoulders, the way he leans over the table, focused on something in front of him, rivets my attention. He hasn't been here before—at least not on my shift. I would have remembered.

When I set down a menu and a glass of water, he looks up from a pile of papers. It's even more remarkable close up: my father. Not as he'd be now, but the way I remember him. No, maybe he doesn't really look like Rob, but there's something . . . The directness of his gaze or the tilt of his head. Maybe it's just the wire-rimmed specs. Or maybe I'm thinking too much.

I smile at him. "Can I get you something to drink?"

He looks at me—studies me, actually. Appraises me. His look is cool, analytical. And very off-putting.

He says, "How would you describe the '02 Woodward Canyon merlot?"

Since I've been working here, I've been asked a lot of questions about wine . . . which red wine is my favorite or if the white zinfandel goes with steak or if the house chardonnay was California-style. One guy wanted to know why the pinot noir wasn't cold. Those I can handle, but this is an essay question. The guy is either a wine aficionado or a self-impressed jerk. Or possibly both.

"I guess I'd call it intense and tannic but amusingly pretentious."

"I'll try it." His gaze doesn't flicker.

"We don't sell that one by the glass."

"I don't want a glass. I want a bottle."

"Shall I bring two glasses?"

"Not unless you're planning to join me."

"Um . . . no. Thanks." I leave him perusing the menu.

I bring the wine and his glass, which I've polished to a gleam with a clean bar towel. I open it slowly, being careful to center the corkscrew and not crumble the cork. I wipe the mouth of the bottle and pour a little for him to swirl and taste, which he does, almost mechanically. Then he nods, and I pour him a glass. He orders Manhattan clam chowder and sourdough bread, and goes back to reading his stack of papers.

"How's the wine?" I ask.

He doesn't look up. "Edgy and unsophisticated and annoyingly underdeveloped."

This seems a good opportunity to keep my mouth shut.

When I pick up the menu, I get a look at his reading material. It looks like a photocopy of a magazine article, the headline of which is "FCC Punitive Actions in 2003." Okay, I forgive him. Anybody who's forced to read something like that is entitled to be a little crabby.

He goes through the soup and bread hurriedly, as if he's fueling a machine. He doesn't seem actually to taste anything. Then he sits for another hour and a half, staring out the window, nursing the wine, his papers forgotten. I check back with him from time to time, refill his glass, ask if he wants more bread. When I pour out the last of the bottle, he looks at me as if he's trying to remember something.

"Am I being hustled for a tip?" There's no smile to make it a joke, and I'm quite sure he's not flirting.

"I can't imagine hustling you for anything else."

He doesn't seem to register that he's just been insulted, but I resign myself to this being a no-tip situation. He goes back to his reading material and again I think of Rob. Drinking alone so many nights. Even when there were other people in the room. His capacity was astonishing, and most of the time he didn't seem drunk—just unreachable, adrift in the middle of some vast ocean of sadness. Eventually he'd get up and stagger off to bed without a word. It makes me wonder if this guy's going to get in a car and take out a utility pole. I figure on my next pass I'll ask where he's staying. If he needs a ride. He'll probably be offended, but at least I'll have a clear conscience.

But when I come back, he's gone. Under the empty bottle are five ten-dollar bills.

The village is dark and still except for the clink of rigging on the boats and a distant barking dog. In spite of my tired feet and aching back, I always enjoy the walk up Front Street to Booker, watching the fog curl in off the ocean, letting the cold, silky wetness slick my face. My arms and legs don't get dry and itchy here like they did at home. There's no wind-driven dust to cake my skin, stick in my eyes, line my nose, and crunch between my teeth. I hug the rain parka around me and breathe in the night air.

Then I turn the corner onto Booker and I freeze in midstep. There's a light on in my room.

Before I can begin thinking rational thoughts like, *Did I forget to turn it off?* there's a moment of unreasoning panic. I picture my new address posted on the Remington Revenge Blog.

Then common sense kicks in. I probably left the light on myself. If I didn't, I should have. I will from now on, although Sarah will probably get her nose out of joint about my wasting electricity. And then I see the unmistakable lanky form of my landlady silhouetted against my window shade. *Damn* that woman. I run toward the garage, arriving at the same instant that a car pulls to the edge of the pavement and kills its headlights. I ignore it, flinging the door to my room open. Sarah wheels around with an alarmed squeak.

"What are you doing in here?"

"I was just walking by and I smelled smoke." She rubs her hands together.

"You were just walking by? At quarter to one in the morning? That's a load of horseshit."

"Don't you talk to me like that."

"I'll talk to you any damn way I please when you're breaking into my—"

"I did not break in. I own this place and I have the right to protect—"

"Okay, ladies, let's just quiet down now." A man's voice, deep and slow.

My head follows the sound to the doorway. A shock of silver hair under a cowboy hat, flinty eyes in a weathered face.

"Oh, Zack, thank God you're here." Sarah bursts into tears and runs to him.

I toss my purse on the bed. "Who are you and what the hell is going on around here?"

He looks at me. "Young lady, I understand you being upset, but I really don't like cussin'. I'm Zack Eden, island sheriff, and I was responding to a call. And I'd like a bit of information from you."

"My name is Sunny Cooper and I live here. And she's just entered my room illegally." God, I sound like a bad courtroom drama.

Eden looks at Sarah, whose tears dried up the minute she ceased to be the focus of attention.

"I thought I smelled smoke. I told her no smoking, no dope, but you know how they are these days. A decent woman can't—"

"I don't do dope."

Eden hooks his thumbs behind his belt buckle. He gives the overall impression of being slim and muscular, but you can see a hint of stomach pushing out just slightly over his belt. "Hush, now, both of you." He walks from one side of the room to the other, then diagonally from corner to corner, nose in the air. "Well, I do smell something . . ." Sarah gets her little moment of triumph before he says, "But it ain't marijuana."

"It's sage. Dried sage."

"I told you when you rented the place, no smoking here." She folds her arms across her breasts. "No tobacco, no marijuana, no sage or parsley. No nothing. It's a fire hazard."

"It's so damp in here, the place couldn't possibly burn down. And I wasn't smoking it anyway." I feel suddenly exhausted.

"What were you doing with it?" Eden's voice is more curious than accusing.

I look at him, somewhat calmer, now that I know he's not going to haul me in for drug trafficking. "You light dried sage and you take it to the four directions of a room—north, south, east, west. It's for purification."

"This place doesn't need purifying," Sarah says. "It's absolutely spotless. Or it was till you—"

"It's spiritual purification," I interrupt her. "Something you obviously know nothing about."

"Don't you talk to me like that, you little hippie."

"I am *not* a hippie!"

"Hush!" Eden's voice thunders out. "Both of you. I'll fine you both for disturbing the peace, and don't think I won't." He appraises me. "Where are you from, young lady?"

"New Mexico."

"Is there a town?"

"Albuquerque. Look, I haven't done anything except come home from work and find her—"

"Nobody's saying you done anything. That sage business, that's Indian custom, isn't it?"

"My . . . fiancé was part Cheyenne."

"And where is he now?"

"Dead."

He looks around the room for a few minutes while the silence settles. Sarah fidgets with her rings, and I shift my weight impatiently.

"How long you gonna be around here?"

"I don't know for sure. I work at the Ale House."

"You workin' for Piggy?"

"Yes."

"Well . . ." He yawns. "It's getting kinda late, so let's cut this party short. Miss Sunny Cooper, Sarah here's the landlady, and so long as you're renting from her, you have to play by her rules. And Sarah, just because you own the property doesn't give you the right to come bargin' into somebody's room in the middle of the night without any warning." He looks from me to her. "We all clear on this?" We both nod, refusing to look at each other. "Good. Now let's go get some sleep and forget all about this misunderstanding."

He takes Sarah firmly by the elbow and steers her out, shutting the door behind them. All the way down the drive, I can hear her running her mouth about troublemakers and hippies.

Time to rethink my housing options.

Freddie has invited me out to lunch, to Whaler's for a drink. She's asked me over to her apartment for dinner and she wanted to meet for coffee one morning. I can't think of any more good reasons to say no, so when we both score the same Friday night off, I finally have to say yes.

I've been dreading the evening all week, quite sure that it's supposed to be one of those cozy, get-to-know-you, girlfriend kind of evenings filled with wine and chocolate and confidences. At least I'm sure about the wine and chocolate part, since I'm bringing both. It's not that I don't like her; it's just that I'm not ready to be exchanging life stories with anyone. Not even with Freddie, who's been my mentor at work and the closest thing I've got to a friend here.

Being with her is getting easier. Fortunately she likes to talk, so now I ask the questions and she takes the ball and runs. I already know that she lives in a studio apartment over Hallie's bookstore. That she moved here from Big South River, Texas—just across the county line from Little South River—leaving behind her beloved gelding, Two Gun, a dashing cowboy husband named Junior who couldn't keep his jeans zipped, and a bewildered family who belonged to the Church of God and didn't believe a little ol' thing like adultery was grounds for divorce.

"My momma was so pissed off when I left him, she didn't speak to me for a year," she told me. "Lord knows my daddy was no saint, either. Sometimes I think that's what made my momma mad. Like if she had to put up with it, I should, too."

At 8:15 Friday night I'm negotiating a narrow flight of stairs so steep it's almost like climbing a ladder. She opens the door before I knock.

"Welcome to my abode. For a quick tour, turn around once. The only thing you won't see is the bathroom, and that's just because the door's shut."

Happy yellow walls set off by crisp white trim. A blue denim loveseat with bright throw pillows. A stack of old suitcases for a coffee table, and the bookcases every college student has—cinder blocks and wooden planks. The dining table had a former life as an industrial spool for some kind of wire or cable, and it's flanked by two white director's chairs.

"So where's the bed? Is it the couch?"

She points to what looks like a cabinet built into the wall. "That thing flips down. Called a Murphy bed. It's old, but it's actually a lot more comfy than one of those damn hide-a-bed couches. You want wine or beer?"

"I'll have a beer."

She opens two longnecks and hands me one. "Have a seat while I finish up with dinner."

Instead of sitting, I check out her books—mostly bestsellers and romance novels. But one whole shelf is given over to bird books and wildflower guides, a few volumes on the natural history of the San Juan Islands, some scruffy-looking biology textbooks, and a copy of *Walden*.

Wall space is limited, but every square inch is covered with framed photographs of people in cowboy hats, mostly with dogs and horses and pickup trucks.

"Are all these your family?"

"And friends." She sighs. "At least they used to be. I been gone so long, they probably forgot who I am."

She comes over to stand next to me. "That's my momma. She pretty much runs the ranch since Daddy checked out. That's my older sister, Ginger, and her husband, Johnny, also known as Fat Jack. Would you believe he tried comin' on to me right before I left Junior?" Without waiting for a reply, she moves to the next photo. "There's me with my horse, Two Gun. My dogs, Jeepers and Creepers. This is me when I was a barrel racer. And here's me in my majorette getup."

"Freddie, you've got all these hidden talents. And what's with all the nature books?"

She looks over at the shelf and smiles. "That was my other life. Before I dropped out of UT to marry Junior." She points to a wedding photo in an ornately carved frame.

Freddie, wearing thick, black eyeliner, blond hair spilling over her shoulders, and holding a bouquet of white lilies stands next to a handsome cowboy, somewhat older and slightly weather-beaten. At least *I* think he's handsome. As an embellishment, Freddie has blacked out his front teeth with Magic Marker and added horns sticking up out of his hair.

"I should've never carried lilies. My momma warned me about it. Said they were bad luck."

"You think that's what it is? Luck?"

"What else?"

I follow her through the kitchen and out onto the tiny balcony that overlooks the harbor. We stand side by side, resting our elbows on the rail. She pulls a single cigarette out of her shirt pocket and cups her hand around a small plastic lighter.

"I didn't know you smoked."

She laughs a deep, throaty laugh. "Honey, all cowgirls smoke. It's a job requirement. My only vice lately." She exhales up into the wind.

The blue of the sky is beginning to wash into pearly lavender and a few wispy clouds are frosted pink. The boats in the harbor seem to be sitting on a mirror.

"Great view."

"This is why I rent the place, small as it is. Long as I can come out here and have my coffee in the morning and my wine at night, I feel like a zillionaire. When I sell my book, I'm not moving into a bigger place unless it has a view like this."

I turn to look at her. "You're writing a book? Is it a nature book?"

She laughs again. "Nature books don't sell too well. Mine's a romance novel. Every now and again I feel like throwin' it against the wall to see if it sticks. Sometimes Laura and Trish Carver and Barbara and I get together and drink wine and I read 'em the latest installment. You'll have to join us next time."

"I've heard it's hard to get published."

"I know, but somebody's got to make it. Might as well be me. Besides, if I don't believe in my stuff, who's going to?" A timer buzzes in the kitchen and she says, "Let's eat. If you want some wine, glasses are in the cupboard by the fridge. I think I'll stick with beer." She drops her cigarette and grinds it out with her shoe.

From the oven she extracts a pan with two little packets of brown paper and she puts one on each of our plates.

"Okay, stand back. I learned this from Justin, but this is the first test run." She picks up a knife and pokes the packet, releasing a cloud of fragrant steam. "Now peel back the top . . ."

Inside is a plump salmon filet covered with finely chopped carrots, onion, and a paper-thin slice of lemon. She dishes up Cajun dirty rice, fresh asparagus, and a basket of buttery brown rolls, and then clinks her longneck against my wineglass for a toast.

"I know it was yesterday, but happy birthday," she says.

"How did you know it was my birthday?"

"Your employment app, of course. Piggy asked me to enter it into the computer, and I just happened to notice . . . Don't look at me like that. He was all set to have Justin bake you a cake—we do that for staff birthdays—but I told him I thought we should just let it ride this time."

"Well, thanks for that." I take a sip of wine. "And for the wish."

The next few moments pass in silence—one of those food silences where everything is too good to comment on, the only appropriate response is to eat. Then a door slams downstairs. Freddie goes to the front window and waves.

"Is that Hallie?"

"Yeah. I asked her to come eat with us, but she volunteered to help sort shelves at the library tonight."

"You see her much?"

"We're practically on intimate terms. She can hear everything I do up here. She even knows when I flush the john. Every once in a while she'll stop by for a glass of wine. I think she's really lonesome. She misses that boy she used to be with. Eric."

I don't ask, but she tells the story anyway.

"He's an artist. Painter."

"I'd think this would be a great place for that."

"He never took to it. Some people just can't live on an island, I guess. If it's in your blood, like Hallie, you can't live anywhere else. He wanted to go back to California, and Hallie didn't. The day he left made me sadder than when I left Junior. They were together a long time. I don't think Hallie's ever got over it."

"Maybe you don't. If you really love somebody."

"Well, that's a cheerful thought."

"You ever dated anyone here?"

"One or two. Nothing serious. There's not a lot of variety in the gene pool." She brightens. "But that's okay. There's always Bob."

"Who?"

"B-O-B. My Battery Operated Boyfriend. Best friend a girl ever had."

When she takes a bite of her brownie, she doesn't say anything, she just moans, which I take to be a good sign. She takes another bite and says with her mouth full, "How do you do this?"

"They're not hard to make. It's a little bit time consuming because you have to make the berry purée and the ganache, but you can do that in advance. You want the recipe?"

"No way. And don't be giving it out to anyone else, either. You need to enter these puppies in the Island Fair. These are blue-ribbon material for sure. Then you can give out the recipe if you want."

When I laugh, she says, "I'm serious. That's exactly what you need to do. Want some more coffee?"

"No, thanks. Let me help you with the dishes before I leave."

She looks up abruptly. "Well, eat and run, why don't you."

"I'm sorry, Freddie. I've just been so sleepy lately. I can't seem to get my internal clock synchronized to working at night."

"That's okay. Next time I'll invite you to lunch." But I can tell she was anticipating a late-night wine and gabfest. "You should get yourself some vitamins with iron. Hey, don't worry about the dishes." She smushes the last crumbs of her brownie with her index finger and deposits them gently on her tongue. "I'll forgive you if you let me keep half the leftovers."

Chapter 15

Curl Up and Dye has only two styling chairs. Trish is sitting in one of them, reading *Elle*, a half-empty Coke bottle dangling from her fingers. When she raises it to her mouth, she sees me and laughs.

"Busted!" She gets out of the chair.

"I just came by to see if I could make an appointment for a haircut."

"I can do it now if you want. Kind of a slow day."

Before I can protest that I haven't really decided what I want to do with it, she's got me in the shampoo chair, a towel draped around my neck, head leaning backward into a small sink. I slip into a half-doze under the perfectly warm water and the rhythm of her strong, deft fingers.

She presses my hair in a soft towel. "Did your own color?"

"Is it that bad?"

"Basically, yes."

"I guess I was bored."

"Next time try a good book. Why don't you let me put a toner on it? Just a little damage control."

"I'm short on funds at the moment."

"Okay, but I'm going to give you a deep conditioner. At

least give it some shine and body." Then she adds over my objection, "It's on the house."

"What's going on?" she asks when the conditioner is rinsed
out and I'm sitting captive in the chair at the mirror.

"I've got a new place to live. I move in this weekend. It just
wasn't working out over at Sarah's."

"Yeah, she's a regular bitch."

I laugh. "I wasn't going to say it."

"Might as well call it as we see it." She runs a wide-toothed
comb through my wet hair. "So what are we doing here?"

"Well, all my life I've been thinking I had straight hair." I
pick up a wet strand and let it flop back down. "Now all of a
sudden, it's curling, and I don't know what to do with it. I was
just hoping we could make it a little easier to deal with."

"It's the humidity here," Trish says. "A little different from
New Mexico. What you do with it is, you let it curl." She
scrunches a handful between her fingers. "Ideally, I think I'd
layer it a bit more. If you had a cut that followed your natural
line, you'd hardly have to do anything to it."

"Except keep getting it cut."

"Right. There is the maintenance factor."

"I can't afford a haircut every month."

"We can do long layers. You won't need a trim but every
two or three months, except the bangs, and I'll show you how
to do those yourself."

"Remember, not too short." I look nervously in the mirror.

"One blow and go, coming up. I won't take too much off.
Just shape it a little—hmm . . . nice trim job. You do that, too?"

"Yeah. It was a bad day."

"Seems like." She pushes my head down and forward

slightly and begins trimming along the nape of my neck. The scissors are cold.

"So what does Scott do?" I ask.

"He's a cabinet maker. He makes furniture and does finish work carpentry. Whenever he can drag himself away from the boat, that is. He's got a twenty-four-foot Islander, and he crews for a lot of the people who bring their big boats up here in the summer. You like to sail?"

"Before I came here, I only saw the ocean once. When I was six years old. I can't even swim."

She looks at me speculatively. "What on earth made you come up here?"

"Just wanted to try something different."

"Where's your new place?"

"I'm renting a little cabin from Trent Forsthoff. Off Lavender Road."

"Really?"

"What's the matter?"

"The only rental cabin I know up there is pretty . . . rustic."

"I'm sure it's fine."

"Haven't you seen it?"

"No. Trent said he was fixing it up."

Trish looks at the ceiling. "His idea of fixing up and my idea of fixing up are two different things. Is it furnished?"

"He said it was partly furnished."

"What's partly furnished: comes with walls and ceiling?"

"I don't have much choice at this point. Everything's rented out for the summer. And even if I have to sleep on pine straw on the floor, it would be better than living under Sarah's nose."

"True." Trish sections off some more hair in the back and

clips the rest up on top of my head. "But I think we should go
over and take a look at it when we get through here. You working today?"

"Not till three thirty. But I don't need—"

"That's plenty of time. We can—"

"No, Trish, really, I can't ask you to—"

She stops what she's doing and rests her hands on her hips.
"Damnation, Sunny. You didn't ask me. I offered. And don't
argue with a woman who has scissors in her hand. We'll just
hop in the Vee-Dub and go see what Mr. Trent's idea of fixing
the place up entails."

The driveway to the cottage is a long, narrow allée cut into the
woods. Filtered sunlight dapples the gravel road. "How are you
going to get back and forth to work?" Trish says, turning the
car's engine off.

"It's only a couple miles from town. I can walk."

The small shingled house nestles in an embrace of evergreens and another kind of tree—tall and slender, twisted into
strange angles, their pale, smooth trunks mottled with green
and red bark that peels like peanut skins.

"Walking to work at three in the afternoon is one thing,
but walking home at midnight is something else." She looks at
me with something like pity. "There's no streetlights, except in
the village."

"What are those trees?"

"What trees? Oh, they're just a bunch of madrones."

"Madrones?" I repeat the pleasantly magical word. "They're
beautiful."

Trish shrugs. "Yeah, and they're messy as hell. They drop
leaves and bark all year long and the stuff takes forever to

decompose. You need to get yourself an island beater. There's always a few for sale in the *Island Times* want ads. Check the bulletin board at Forsthoff's market, too."

"I will," I say absently. My attention strays momentarily from the madrone trees to the sunny meadow where a small pond glistens, jewel-like in a setting of spring green grasses. "I could put a garden right there."

"You're gonna have to hurry and get it in the ground. Our days are long, but the summers are short. Well, let's have a look."

Before I can say that I don't have a key yet, she grabs the handle and pulls the door open. A long strand of spider's silk hangs across the opening like a ceremonial ribbon, and I walk through it.

The cool, dark main room smells of ashes from a long-cold fire. To the left is the kitchen, furnished only with a red-handled pitcher pump, a woodstove, and some shelves.

"How's your wood fire cooking skills?" she asks.

An involuntary smile lifts the corners of my mouth. "It's how I learned."

She turns to me. "Really?"

"I grew up in a commune."

"Really?" This *really* is about an octave higher than the last one.

"No refrigerator."

"You talk to Trent," she says. "Just be really up front about what you need."

"I don't think I have a lot of leverage."

"Sure you do. No summer people are going to rent a place like this. Partially furnished, my great aunt's fanny."

I'm busy admiring the handsome rock fireplace in the corner. "Mm-hmm."

We walk through into the bedroom. It's completely bare. No closet, not even pegs to hang things on.

"Well, never mind. We've got some furniture in the garage you can use. From Scott's folks' house, when they moved into a retirement place a couple years ago. I don't even know what's out there, but you're welcome to it."

I look at her, momentarily astonished at my good fortune. I open my mouth, but before anything comes out she snaps, "And if you say you can't one more time, I'm going to take you back to the shop and shave your head. Just repeat after me: Thanks, Trish."

I smile, feeling slightly foolish. "Thanks, Trish. Really, that's so nice of you."

She waves her hand. "The number two law of Harmony. When you need something, you just have to ask."

Saturday morning at seven o'clock Trish hands me a pair of work gloves and pushes open the door to her garage.

"I'm going to leave you to it," she says. "I've got to get my breakfast and get to work. Got a full day today. If you need help with anything, Scott'll probably be out back in his workshop. Pull out whatever you need, and one of us will drive it over there tonight in the truck. Did you do anything about getting yourself some wheels?"

"I'm supposed to go over to Piggy and Laura's tomorrow. He said he had a bike I could use till I can find a car."

"Piggy has a bike?" Trish laughs. "That I would love to see. Be like King Kong with training wheels. Okay, have fun. See you later."

"Trish, I can't tell you how much I—"

"Then, don't. You're embarrassing me."

The furniture is stacked neatly, but it probably hasn't been touched since it was put here. The thick layer of dust over everything makes me sneeze repeatedly and brings water to my eyes. Most of it is just secondhand furniture, but there are a few pieces that have real value—like the twin maple spool beds. Betsy and I admired a similar pair in an antique store in Nob Hill. Priced way out of our range.

The thought of Betsy opens the door to more memories. Summer in Albuquerque can be brutally hot, but it's also the season when she's got plenty of help at the café. This will be the first summer in five years that there won't be a girls' road trip to Ruidoso or Creede. No hanging out at the pool; no weekend garage sales, afternoon movies.

At least a couple of times a month Michael and I would go to the Twin Oaks for dinner. We always sat outside, where it was quiet enough that you could actually hear Betsy's thoughtfully chosen jazz tapes. The huge cottonwood trees that shaded the patio during the hot afternoons at night glittered with hundreds of twinkle lights, and Betsy'd always send us a surprise for dessert—molten chocolate cake or banana crème brûlée. The depth and breadth of my contentment on those nights was something I'd never anticipated. How lucky could you get? The two people in the world who loved me actually liked each other.

After our meal, she'd come sit down with us for iced coffee, the three of us laughing and talking in the balmy night while the staff cleaned up around us. Now I feel like an idiot. Were they playing footsie under the table while I swooned over the hazelnut gelato?

I untie the bandana around my neck and blot my eyes with it.

"Hey, come on. The furniture's not that bad."

Scott stands smiling just outside the door.

"It's the dust."

"Trish said you might need some help pulling things out. There's a lot of stuff in here you probably can't even see. You taking the beds?"

"Just one."

He picks up a headboard in his right hand and the footboard in his left. "Maybe you can grab the rails and slats. You need the mattress?"

"Is there one?" I look around.

"Yeah. It's in the house. So it wouldn't get mildewed. What else?"

The wooden chairs are easy, but the table takes both of us, and it's still a push. When it's finally in the truck we stop for a minute, panting.

"This thing must be steel painted to look like wood."

He laughs. "Solid maple. My dad made it."

"I guess he never intended to move it."

"What else?"

"That's it."

His eyes survey the shelves. "I know there's more stuff you probably need. You're not thinking hard enough." He pulls down some old file boxes from a high shelf. "Let's see what's in some of these. Shit, this one weighs a ton." He lowers it carefully to the ground.

The label reads KITCHEN. Scott lifts the lid and shakes his head. "Dishes. Really, really ugly dishes."

I laugh. "I don't know; they're looking pretty good to me. Better than Spode."

"Better than what?"

"Spode. It's fine china."

"Not my department."

By seven thirty the sun has moved across the meadow and is beginning to settle slowly into the long twilight. I sit on the steps, hugging my knees, every muscle knotted with fatigue, wishing for a cold beer and a phone to call for pizza delivery.

Now I have to think about making a fire and cooking my dinner.

I inspected the stove early in the week, figuring if there was bad news I needed to let Trent know right away. The seams all looked tight. One small crack in the top appeared to have been expertly welded. The grates looked almost new—obviously replacements. The firebox was in good shape and the ash box was clean. Thank God it's a pull-out-and-dump kind and I won't have to shovel ashes into a little bucket. All the doors, dampers, draft slides were in place and closely fitted, but not easy to move. A little WD-40 took care of that.

Trent had a chimney sweep come by to clean out the stovepipe and fireplace chimney. Fortunate, because there was a bird's nest about halfway up that I couldn't see, even with a flashlight. He sold me some stove black and pronounced the thing "a great stove and ready to use."

That afternoon I lit a test fire—a slow, easy one. I opened all the windows in case of a smoke leak, but it was good and tight. Standing there in my twilight kitchen listening to the gentle little ticking and popping of the cast iron warming up, I thought about the old monster stove at Armonía, the Dragon, and I decided to christen this one Dragonfly.

The sound of tires crunching on gravel pulls my eyes to the road. Scott's pickup bounces across the drainage ditch and down the drive—Scott behind the wheel, Trish waving from the passenger seat, Bailey balancing like a surfer in the cargo bed. I stand up, smiling. They pile out of the truck, Trish carrying a huge enameled stockpot, Scott hefting a brown grocery bag and a six-pack of beer.

The dog jumps down and comes immediately to me, sticking his nose in my crotch.

"Bailey, no!" Trish scolds him. "You know, I really love dogs, but damn, can't they find some other way to introduce themselves?"

Scott's eyes crinkle when he smiles. "Maybe we could get him some little business cards."

Chastened, Bailey lopes off to survey the meadow.

"So, he's yours?"

Scott shakes his head. "He's JT's dog, but he's sort of a gypsy. He was hanging around outside Forsthoff's when we stopped for beer, and he decided to come with us."

"Who's JT?"

"A friend of ours." Trish shifts the stockpot in her arms. "Lives on his boat. I hope you like mussels."

"I've never actually had them. But I'll eat almost anything. As long as the beer's cold."

Scott twists the cap off a bottle and hands it to me. I take a mouthful and let it trickle down my grateful throat.

"So Trent came through with the fridge." Trish nods approvingly and sets the pot on the table. "But you still don't have any cupboards or workspace."

"I've got two shelves and a table."

"That's not enough. And you don't have any storage in the bedroom. Where are you going to put your clothes?"

I laugh. "My clothes will all fit in that chest with room left over for a bowling alley."

"I guess that blows the scenario about you being a runaway heiress," Scott says.

Trish gives him a sideways look. "And you really need to think about getting a cell phone. You shouldn't be out here all by yourself with no phone. Just go see Wayne over at Harmony Wireless on Broad Street. Tell him I sent you."

"Okay, I promise. Now, what do we need to do with the mussels?"

"Clean 'em and cook 'em. Does this thing work?" She eyes the stove.

"Beautifully. I'll just get a fire going."

"Let Scott do that."

I smile and say firmly, "No, thanks."

I clear the grate, throw on a handful of tinder, stack the kindling, and scrape a large kitchen match on the side of the stove. The tinder blossoms into delicate yellow petals of flame.

"Trish tells me you grew up on a commune." When I don't reply immediately, he adds, "I guess it gets old, people saying *so what was it like*? When what they really want to know about is sex and drugs."

"Don't forget rock 'n' roll."

"So . . . what *was* it like?"

I replace the T and back lid over the firebox, lay in a few larger pieces of wood. In a minute the fire is burning briskly. "It was just a way of living. Like a lot of other ways. Only weirder."

Trish admires my firecraft. "Pretty slick," she says wistfully.

"You're some kind of frontier woman. I wish you could've met Luke. Our son. He'd have really liked you."

The way she talks about him it sounds like he's dead.

She pulls a huge plastic bag full of mussels out of the stockpot and shows me how to scrub the black shells with a brush and pull off the stringy beards, while Scott chops garlic and halves lemons and slices the crusty, chewy bread from Harmony Bakers.

"If you find any that are open, they're dead, so toss them in here." She waves a small plastic veggie bag.

Scott sniffs. "Is this thing on fire or something?"

I look around at the wisps of black smoke rising off the surface of the stove. "No, it's okay. I just blacked it. It usually takes one good firing to burn off the residue."

Trish makes a face. "Smells like road tar."

"I always kind of liked it," I say. "But we can eat outside."

Scott opens a bottle of white wine and pours half of it into the stockpot along with the garlic, a chunk of butter, a mixed bunch of herbs and a few grinds of pepper. I set the stockpot on the stove over the firebox. In a few minutes the contents are boiling energetically, and Trish dumps the mussels in and clamps the lid on.

"Where does your son live?" I ask conversationally.

Scott says, "Seattle. Well, Bellevue, actually. He's a lawyer, and Mary Beth works in human relations for Adobe."

Trish giggles. "Human *resources*, honey. They've got the cutest, sweetest little girl. And smart. Bree's only six and she knows all the state capitals."

"Could that possibly be Sarah's daughter Mary Beth?"

Trish's smile pulls tight for just a second. "The very same."

So Trish's baby boy is the befuddled-looking groom in the photo on Sarah's TV.

Suddenly a heavenly, briny smell fills the kitchen. Scott uses my dishtowel to move the pot off the fire. He lifts the lid and offers me a sniff. "Better than stove black?"

In five minutes we're sitting on the porch with steaming bowlfuls of glistening black shells and cream-colored mussels. I pry one out of its shell and chew it slowly, savoring the plump, garlicky sweetness.

Scott says, "What's the verdict?"

"Love it," I say, with my mouth full.

Trish hands me a piece of bread. "To soak up the broth," she says.

After we've polished off every mussel, they help me assemble the bed, and then the three of us sit on the porch sipping the rest of the now-tepid wine.

Out of the blue Scott says, "I can put in some cabinets and a countertop for you. And build a closet in the corner of that bedroom."

"That's really nice of you, Scott, but to be perfectly honest, I can't afford it right now."

"I bet we could pry some money out of Trent." He rubs his lower lip thoughtfully. "It's not right, him renting you the place in this condition. Let me just talk to him about it."

"No, really, you guys have done enough—more than enough—and I really appreciate it, but this—"

Trish cuts me off. "Sunny, don't be a pain in the ass. You're going to have to get used to people being nice if you're going to live here."

"But I don't know if I'm going to live here."

"Of course you are." Her blue eyes are wide and confident. "Where else would you go? Besides, it's the third law: a body in Harmony tends to remain in Harmony."

Chapter 16

The box has been sitting unopened for over a week—a small collection of my remaining worldly goods, which I left with Artie to forward when I got settled. I guess the fact that I asked him to send it amounts to an admission that I am settled. Or as settled as I'm going to be for a while. Then it arrived, and I procrastinated about opening it. I reasoned that there wasn't much point in unpacking it over at Sarah's. Now my reluctance to open it, I think, has more to do with my wish to leave the past in a sealed container.

But there are a few items I could use, so after Trish and Scott leave, I drag the box out of the corner and slit the tape with a kitchen knife. Everything seems to have arrived in one piece. The first thing I do is pull my computer out of its padded carrying case and plug it in to recharge it. The boom box goes on the shelf near the door, along with my CD case. Next, I take the upside-down lid off the bean pot and lift out my jewelry, a squash blossom necklace I couldn't bear to sell, and some silver beads and chains. One wide silver cuff. My little alarm clock, wrapped in newspaper. A few paperbacks. The metal box Michael used for documents. Now it holds my birth certificate and the two photos from his desk. The frames went fast at the yard sale, but I knew nobody would want the pictures, and somehow I couldn't throw them in the trash. Maybe for the same reason Freddie could deface her wedding photo but couldn't quite bring herself to part with it.

I put the bean pot on the warming shelf above the stove. I set the time on the clock and plug it in on the night table in the bedroom. Back in the living room I chase down the Styrofoam peanuts and crumple the newspapers to toss in the firebox.

Then a headline catches my eye and I stand motionless, waiting for the world to stop.

KIRBY DOLEN, "SOFTWARE ROCK STAR," FOUND DEAD.

Gingerly, as if it might turn to ash in my hands, I carry the page into the kitchen and spread it on the table, pressing out the wrinkles till my fingers are smudged with newsprint. There's a photo—probably from the UNM yearbook—his funny owlish face, ears sticking out from his closely cropped head like open taxicab doors, black, square-framed glasses, and an earnest expression. The cutline reads *Kirby Dolen Dead at 35*.

I ease down into a chair and begin to read the article, dated April 23. The day after Michael's accident.

Taos, NM.—Local software entrepreneur Kirby Childs Dolen, 35, was found dead early yesterday morning in the smoldering remains of his home on Kiva Ridge, 13 miles north of Taos. Dolen, founder of DolenWare and Dolen Consulting Group, was well known locally for his eccentric and reclusive lifestyle as well as for his generosity to area schools. The Kiva Ridge Volunteer Fire Department was alerted to the blaze by a truck driver who noticed black smoke pouring out of Boca Canyon in the early morning hours. The fire, which gutted the home, apparently started in the office, where Dolen's body was found, according to a police spokesperson. The cause of death has not yet been determined.

Dolen is survived by his mother, Anita Dolen, of Deming, NM.

I read the story two more times, unnerved by the timing of his death and his connection to Michael. I stare until the words blur and my eyes burn and a sudden wave of exhaustion breaks over me. I've been up and working since 6:00 a.m. I fold the piece of newspaper and stick it in the middle of a big, fat paperback that I thought sounded interesting but never got around to reading—and I stack it, along with the other paperbacks, on the shelf with the boom box.

I dig out my toothbrush and the new towels I bought at the dry goods store. I make up the bed with new sheets and crawl under the covers, fully prepared to toss and turn, thinking about Michael and Kirby Dolen, but the somewhat embarrassing truth is that after a brief moment of gratitude that I'm not in Sarah Lakes's garage, I close my eyes and don't open them again until the sun shines in my bedroom window.

Piggy and Laura's cabin sits at the crest of a hill that slopes down to a marshy pond. It's far enough off the road to be completely private, but as if that weren't enough, the little valley is ringed by dense stands of spruce and fir.

A covered porch runs across the front of the house and Laura has furnished it like a second living room. The two of them are ensconced in fan-backed wicker chairs that resemble thrones—King Piggy and Queen Laura of the Valley, surveying their domain. I approach their royal dais, offering my tribute: a pan of cornbread.

"I feel like I should prostrate myself at your feet," I say.

"A simple curtsy will do." Laura pushes her curly blond hair back and smiles as she takes the foil-wrapped package. "Um. Smells good." She peels back the top. "Kind of smoky?"

"That would be the wood cookstove."

"Mmm." She slaps Piggy's hand as he nicks a piece of crust off the corner. "We'll have it with lunch, Brendan."

I lower myself to the steps. "Sorry I'm late. It took a while to get a ride. Not a lot of traffic on Lavender Road."

"I could've picked you up," Piggy says.

"That's okay. I hitched a ride with a guy named Bonner. He has a farm on the north end."

"I'm going to make some more tea." Laura rises from her chair. "You two better get down and take a look at that bike in case there's anything I need to do to it." The screen door bangs behind her and I get up to follow Piggy across the yard.

The shop is more barn than garage, dust motes suspended in shafts of sunlight and bales of hay stacked around. Closer inspection reveals various engine parts sitting on the hay bales, Laura's grimy coveralls hanging on a peg next to a workbench cluttered with screwdrivers, pliers, a drill set, boxes of screws and bolts. A set of socket wrenches arrayed in a dusty black case reminds me of my father's workshop at Armonía.

I used to sit on his workbench, surrounded by tools and curly wood shavings. There would be music playing—usually the Grateful Dead or the Allman Brothers, but Rob had a thing

for old R&B, and his favorite song was "Handy Man." He held
my elbows and moved my arms, in a funky version of the twist,
while he sang,

> *If your broken heart needs repair, I'm the man to see.*
> *I whisper sweet things . . .*

. . . at which point he'd lean over and make a buzzing noise
in my ear, sending me into a fit of giggles.

> *You tell all your friends*
> *And they'll come running to me.*

Everyone did come running to Rob, with their cars and
vans and pickup trucks and power tools. He could put in a
new window, shave the edges of the door so it would shut tight
against the snow, make the cabinet hinges stop squeaking, fix
the leaky pipe under the sink, mend a boot heel. He could do
anything. Except fix broken hearts. But when he sang that song
to me in the workshop, I thought he could do that, too.

"There ya go," Piggy's proud voice booms, startling me back
to the present. "Needs a new side stand, but I know Laura's got
a few of those around here, and it won't take a second to put
one on." When my eyes adjust to the dim light, I stare first,
then burst out laughing.

"Piggy, when you said you had an old bike—I want a bicycle, not a motorcycle."

"Really?" He seems completely baffled. "Why?"

"Because I haven't the faintest idea how to ride a motorcycle. And I don't have a death wish."

"Death wish?" he sputters, indignant. "What kind of trash you talkin', woman? This ain't no crotch rocket, it's a Honda CB500, for God's sake—the sweetest little beginner's bike ever made. It's tame, it's housebroke, it practically eats out of your hand."

"Any motorcycle is dangerous if you don't know how to ride it," I point out.

"True. But this little baby is gentle, it's reliable, and way easy to ride. Laura's got an extra full-face helmet you can use. Of course, you don't want to be taking it out on the I-5 or anything, but for island transport—shit! It just doesn't get any better than this."

"I don't think so . . ."

"Now, come on, Sunny. I guarantee I can teach you how to ride this baby in a few afternoons. It'll change your life."

"End it, you mean. Besides, don't you have to have a different license?"

"Just a stamp on your driver's license, but you can get a special island learner's permit from Zack Eden."

"Oh, great. The law west of the Pecos. He hates me."

"Does not. I happen to know for a fact that he thought Sarah was totally out of line that night and a rippin' big pain the ass to boot."

"Okay, fine, but I really need to get something for the short term. Just to go to work."

"Tell you what, for the short term, if you want to walk in to work, I can at least run you home."

"Oh no. You can't be running me all over the—"

"It's practically on my way. Trust me, when you see what a gas it is to ride this baby, you'll be throwing rocks at bicycles."

• • •

Monday morning I'm up with the predawn bird chorus, drinking my coffee outside, pacing off my garden squares in the silver half-light. After a hasty bowl of cereal, I mark the boundaries with stakes and string, and begin working in the lime and composted cow shit. My plot is tiny, but it's still backbreaking work. Even so, it's easier than gardening on the mesa, where we had to hack through a cement-like layer of *caliche*, a hardpan mineral deposit, before we could start to work in the soil amendments.

By the time I finish, the sun has cleared the tops of the trees that ring the meadow and the tall grass waves like a field of new wheat spiked with purple thistle. Curious ravens circle overhead chattering in their strange language. If I stand quiet, I can actually hear their wing beats.

When I kneel in the damp earth to plant the seedlings— tomatoes and peppers, carrots and lettuce and radishes—it calls up an indelible memory, one of my very earliest. I'm not sure how old I was, but the image is clear. Gwen digging rows in the Armonía garden, Hart following her, dropping corn kernels at regular intervals—even as a child he was careful, precise— me following him. Supposedly my job was to cover them with earth, but I was too young to be very efficient. A lot of the dirt ended up in the cuffs of my overalls and in my shoes, which came out of the Free Box and were too big. As I scuffed along, I kicked some of the seeds out of their beds and Hart kept turning around to see how it was going, replacing seeds that I had dislodged, patiently covering and tamping down what I'd missed.

In the summer, Gwen led us through the garden again, the

picture of a farmer's wife from a folktale, barefoot, filling her apron with tomatoes and peppers still warm from the sun. She would show us what was ready and how to pick it. My favorite things were the radishes and carrots and beets. I was thrilled by the notion of grabbing the soft green tops and pulling up a totally unexpected, bright-colored treasure from deep in the earth.

I pat the mound of soil around the last plant and sit back on my heels. My hands are encased in a thick coating of mud, partially dried into dun-colored gloves. A slow breeze cools the sweat on my forehead and my body aches in that pleasant way that I'd almost forgotten. This is the solitude, the stillness that I always wished for, even though I'd never experienced it. Until something makes the hair prickle on the back of my neck and I sense that I'm not alone after all. I turn my head slowly.

A face. At the top of a small rise about twenty yards away, wary eyes study me. A luxurious red tail, tipped with white, waves like a signal flag. The fox and I check each other out for a few minutes. My feet are numb and tingling, but I don't move. I barely breathe. Finally he decides that I'm neither interesting nor threatening enough for further attention, and weaves his way through the tall grass, melting back into the woods, and something rises in my chest that might be happiness.

That night I get my first ride home with Piggy. He gives me the extra helmet, which feels like wearing a pumpkin on my head, and I stand patiently on the back porch of the Ale House listening to myself breathe inside it, while Piggy dons his leather jacket, ties his bandana around his head.

"Don't get on till I've got it started," he says. "And fasten the chinstrap. Not gonna do you any good if it falls off."

"How come you don't wear one?"

He gives me a look that plainly says, *Because I'm a grown-up, that's why*.

"Sit as far forward as you can and hold on to my waist. Hold on tight." He laughs. "Don't want to lose you."

I nod.

"Keep your feet on the foot pegs, even when we stop, and keep your legs away from the mufflers. They get hot." He grabs the handlebars. "Oh yeah. When we go into a turn, lean with me, not against me. I promise we aren't gonna fall. Okay?"

I nod again. Piggy throws one huge leg over the bike, does some kind of little hop-step, and the Indian roars to life. I climb on behind him and put my arms around his waist, which is sort of like trying to hug a Sequoia, prop my feet on the foot pegs and we take off.

He takes it slow through town, but when we pull away from the stop sign at Otter Crest, he digs in and we start flying. The wind, which was pretty benign back at the Ale House, turns icy, cutting through my jacket and sweatshirt, and the vibration of the engine makes a weird tickle starting in my pelvis and rising up my spine. I can't imagine what the function of the mufflers might be, since they don't seem to be muffling much of anything. Why is he not deaf by now?

We wind north on Rand Road, through the woods. There's at least one way to Lavender Road that's shorter than this, but I assume he knows that. Everything is black except for the Indian's headlamp, its long finger of light pointing into the darkness. I worry about possums and raccoons and skunks crossing the road. I worry about falling off when he leans into the curves. If I lean, too, won't it be too heavy, and we'll just tip over, like a canoe? I hide my face in his jacket and feel him shaking. Is he just vibrating like I am, or is he laughing at me?

We zoom out of the woods, and the road begins to rise. I open my eyes just as we crest a hill, and the sight takes my breath away. The light from the big yellow moon bathes the meadows on either side of us, silhouetting a barn and a house with lamplight in the windows, and turning the road ahead into a streak of silver between blue-black hills.

Ten minutes later we're at my place, and I climb off, a little wobbly, pull off the helmet, handing it to Piggy. He hands it back to me and grins. "Sleep with it tonight and bring it with you tomorrow."

I stand in the pool of my porch light and watch him scramble back up the driveway, the bike spitting gravel out both sides of its path. Even after he turns on to the road and disappears, I hear the Indian's voice like thunder in the night.

Tuesday morning Scott shows up on my front porch, apparently having convinced The Trent that regardless of how long I stay there, the cottage should be upgraded.

"I just told him that he could rent it for more money next summer," Scott says and winks at me. He turns and waves at someone in a rust-spotted orange truck parked behind his. A tall kid clambers out of the cab, pulls a toolkit out of the back, and follows us inside.

"Hi, Sunny." He grins engagingly. "I'm JT."

In contrast to Scott, whose neatly pressed jeans and clean plaid shirt could land him a spot on *This Old House*, JT wears faded jeans, inside-out sweatshirt minus sleeves, ratty loafers with no socks, and a blue knitted cap. He has one of those soul patch things growing like a fungus on his chin, which makes him look like the drummer in a grunge band, and an earring with some kind of black stone. Even so, he reminds me of my brother . . . there's an openness in his face that holds my eyes.

"So Bailey's your dog."

He laughs. "No, I'm Bailey's person."

The two of them spend an hour drinking my coffee, talking about somebody's new boat—a forty-five-foot something or other—and taking measurements in the kitchen and bedroom.

"Wouldn't it be easier to get some of those cabinets that are already put together?" I ask.

Scott looks at me like I've just spit in his food. "Those things aren't worth the powder to blow 'em up," he says. "These will be way better built, better-looking, last longer . . ."

I hold up my hands in surrender. "I was just trying to keep things simple."

"Not to mention those prefab things are loaded with VOCs and they'd be out-gassing for months," JT says, frowning.

"You want to run that by me again?"

"Volatile organic compounds," he says. "They give off toxic fumes."

"I still think you should go to law school, JT. You could change the world." Scott smiles and hooks his tape measure on the back pocket of his jeans. "I'm off to Henderson's to get the wood. JT, you coming?"

"I'll stay here and get the saw set up."

I leave him to his work and, grabbing a plastic bucket, head across the patch of meadow, high grass tickling my bare legs. The pond is still and cool, sage green in the cloudy morning. I plunge the bucket in, scattering the water striders on the surface.

By the time I reach the edge of the garden, I'm breathless and my arms ache. I set the bucket down and tip the water slowly into the first square, watch it race through the little channels I've dug out, bubble and sink into the rich black earth. It still amazes me the way things grow here.

"You put in a garden?" JT's voice startles me, and I look up.

"Not much of a garden. I just stuck in a few plants to see what would happen."

"I'll tell you what's going to happen: unless you put a fence all around it, the deer'll be using it for a breakfast buffet."

"I haven't seen any deer around here."

"They just haven't discovered you yet."

I shrug, irrationally annoyed that I haven't thought of this.

"What's the rim for?" he says.

"It's the way the Pueblo Indians grew crops. You build up the sides of the beds to hold water around the plants. That's how they could grow food with the minuscule amount of rainfall in the Southwest."

"You won't have that problem here."

"No, but I have to irrigate from the pond, so I want to make the most of every drop."

"So you're from New Mexico?"

I look sideways at him.

"Scott told me."

I keep waiting for him to say I'm a long way from home, but he doesn't. He just stands there, hands shoved down in his pockets, watching me watching the water. Finally he sits down on the wet grass.

"Don't they have deer in New Mexico?"

"Not in . . . Albuquerque." I stumble over the word, thinking instead of Armonía, the way Hart and I and the other kids
were always shooing the goats out of the garden.

I scoop up a handful of loose dirt and sniff it. "The soil here
is amazing. It's so alive. Not like at home." He leans toward me,
and I scrunch it under his nose.

He smiles. "Smells exactly like dirt."

"Can't you smell the layers?" I take another hit. "Leaves.
Tobacco. Maybe even chocolate."

"You must have a better nose than I do."

"Probably. I remember one time we had a dead rat in the
wall of our apartment. The stench was truly disgusting. I was
going around with Vicks plastered on my upper lip, and Michael couldn't even smell it—"

"Michael is your . . . ?"

I crumble the dirt and open my hand, letting it sift through
my fingers to the ground. "Fiancé."

He looks casually back toward the house, as if Michael
might wander out onto the porch. "And where's your fiancé
these days?"

"Dead."

"Oh." He seems completely unsettled. "Sorry. I shouldn't
have—"

I dust my hands together. "That's okay. It's history."

His cell phone saves us from the awkward silence. The ring
tone is a riff from Nirvana. I don't remember the name of the
song, but Michael loved it.

"Hey, Scott. No problem. Yep, I'll take care of it." He puts
the phone back in his pocket. "Scott has to go over to Orcas to
check on a job over there."

I can't hide my disappointment. "So he won't be back this afternoon, I guess. Shall I help you put the stuff back in the truck?"

"The wood's all ready to go; I just need to get over to Henderson's and pick it up. Want to go with? We could grab a sandwich somewhere."

"Thanks, but I'll just stay here. I've got stuff to do."

He looks directly into my eyes now, the same way Hart used to do. It's a child's look, innocently self-absorbed and making no apologies for it. "Like what?" he says.

"Just some unpacking and stuff."

"I didn't see any boxes." He gets to his feet, reaches down for my hand, and pulls me up. "Come on. You can pick out some wood for a countertop."

"I don't think . . ." I say quickly, but he's already walking toward the truck.

"And you can look at some deer fencing." He grins over his shoulder.

At the Main Street Café we find a table on the deck, looking out over the ferry landing. A chubby girl in a short skirt brings us water with a few forlorn slivers of ice floating in it and takes our order.

"I don't mean to sound like your mother, but why don't you take that thing off your head?"

He puts a hand up to the knitted cap and laughs. "Believe me, you don't sound like my mother." When he pulls the cap off, his hair springs free in all directions, blond, thick, and curly. Suddenly I realize why he looked familiar. He notices my stare and puts his hand on top of this head. "What?"

"Are you Sarah Lakes's son?"

He frowns. "That is still to be determined. I've always suspected there was a mix-up at the hospital."

"I saw your picture on the mantel. When I was living in the apartment."

"Along with the Mary Beth shrine?"

"That was on top of the TV."

He nods grimly. "She's moved it since I was there. Probably ran out of room on the mantel."

A change of subject seems in order. "Are you in law school or did I misunderstand?"

"The short answer is no. I was planning to go, then I changed my mind."

"Why?"

"I don't know." He looks out at the ferry terminal, where cars are already waiting in the lanes for the boat to Victoria. "I went to Chambers Northwest for undergrad. At first I liked it— being off the island. I've never lived anywhere but here, and it was so different being in Seattle . . ."

"But then what?"

"I don't know. I got tired of crowds of strangers. Traffic. Having to lock the truck every time I parked it . . ."

I try not to smile at the thought of anyone stealing his giraffe-spotted truck.

"I missed sailing," he says.

"You can sail in Seattle, can't you?"

"Sure, if you can afford a slip. Anyway, it's not the same as being here. I just didn't feel like another three years. Besides"— he grins—"there's a surplus of lawyers out there."

"So you're working with Scott now?"

"And taking tourons out to see the whales. A little maintenance around the marina." He shrugs. "Trying to figure things out." When he turns to the window again the sun flashes on his earring. The stone, which looked black when I saw it before, seems now to ripple darkly with green and blue.

"I like your earring. What kind of stone is it?"

He touches it absently as if to remind himself. "Black pearl. From Tahiti."

"I love the way it shows different colors when the light hits it. Did you buy it in Tahiti?"

"I wish. Actually it was a present from my sister. She was in Tahiti on her honeymoon and she heard the story that sailors should always wear a black pearl. Then if you're ever in trouble at sea you can trade it to Poseidon for your life."

This last part he says very matter-of-factly, as if it's some generally accepted system of barter. He seems about to say something else, but our server appears suddenly, slapping plastic plates down in front of us.

I eat my chicken sandwich and watch JT dismantle the house special, a cheeseburger with a fried egg and fried onions on top. We split a huge basket of sweet potato fries, dipping them in blue cheese dressing, and the salt-sweet combination is addictive. He eats like his last meal was two days ago, and when the girl brings the check, we both reach for it. He wrests it out of my grasp.

"I want to at least pay my half," I protest.

He gives me a forbidding look. "Don't fight me on this; you'll be making yourself a rep as a ballbuster."

By the time we swing by Henderson's and pick up the wood and get back to my place, it's 2:30 p.m.

He drags the two-by-fours out of the truck and goes back

for a sheet of plywood. "You want me to run you over to the Ale House before I get started?"

"No thanks. I need to walk off that lunch."

"You don't walk home at night, do you?"

I laugh. "No, Piggy's bringing me home. He's trying to make me into a biker chick."

His eyebrows lift. "Cool. I could see you in black leather." He holds out his hand. "Why don't you give me your key. I'll work on this the rest of the afternoon, then I'll lock up and bring it over to you when I'm done."

My hesitation lasts only a second, but he notices.

"It's okay," he says gently. "I promise I won't clean out the family silver."

Chapter 17

Friday afternoon at 3:20, the Ale House is humming and will only get more frantic when the first wave of weekenders arrives on the five-forty ferry.

"Hey, girlchik." Freddie comes up behind me, runs her card through the reader and starts inputting an order. "Check out Sugar Daddy and his little buckarette." She cuts her eyes to a table in the corner, near the end of the bar. I try to look discreetly: an older guy—Tommy Bahama shirt, big gold Rolex, hair combed over his bald spot—and his much younger, blatantly gorgeous girlfriend, boobs spilling out of her orange halter top.

"What's she got that I haven't got?" Freddie says.

I laugh. "Implants. You think it would be worth it?"

"What, a boob job?"

"Having to have sex with him."

"I don't know. I've got friends who swear they all look the same in the dark."

"I don't think I could do it." I sigh. "But then nobody's asked me lately."

"Except JT," she says. "And he's practically on welfare."

I look up quickly. "That's crazy."

"What's crazy about it? He's cute as a bug's ear."

"He's a kid."

"Young ones are good. They've got stamina."

"Will you stop?"

"Just an observation," she says mildly. "Don't forget it's a small island. Not much sneaks by unnoticed."

"Like what?"

"Like having lunch on the Main Street Café deck. Like him bringing you your house key."

"He's building me some kitchen cabinets. He and Scott. Next thing I'll be hearing I'm having an affair with Scott."

She smiles. "Nah. You wouldn't survive that. Trish'd stick an ice pick in your ear."

"Hey, Sunny, can you check the tables?" Piggy hollers at me. "We're gonna be getting slammed pretty soon."

I pick up the bus tray that holds the packets of sugar, sweetener, the containers of salt, pepper, ketchup, and mustard, and the big bag of peanuts to refill the little dishes on each table. By the time I work my way around the room to where the couple sits, Freddie has brought their food and is setting down two more Cosmopolitans. The guy has some bulk to him, so he seems to be holding his liquor, but the woman is looking a little smeary.

"You lied to me." Her voice is full of tears, and I can't help feeling a sympathetic twinge. "You said you were moving out."

The guy mutters something I can't hear. I scoop out a dish of peanuts and set it down, unscrew the salt shaker.

"The surgery could have been scheduled anytime. I can't reschedule my vacation." She hoists her breasts, rearranging them inside the halter top as if they were some foreign objects she was carrying home in a sack. Again his reply is inaudible.

I take the tray back to the refill station and pick up two waters. Freddie's still watching the couple. "Damn. I thought for sure they were going to spring for dessert. Maybe Irish coffee."

From the corner of my eye I watch her cautiously deposit the check on the guy's side of the table. He picks it up without looking at it and slaps it down on the woman's plate. "Maybe you should pay your own way for a change."

The noise level in the room edges downward as everyone around them strains to hear, and there's a collective combination gasp-snicker as the woman scoops up the check along with a handful of quiche and lobs the whole mess at him.

"You're a pig, Ron!" She stands abruptly, her chair scraping across the floor. "And you're an *old* pig." The glass rattles in the door as it slams shut behind her.

A woman sitting alone at the bar laughs unabashedly and holds up her napkin, displaying her scribbled performance rating: 9.6.

Somewhere in the background, the phone is ringing. Piggy answers it, and I watch him put a hand over his other ear to exclude the noise. "Hold on." He presses the phone against his chest and looks at me. "Your friend Betsy."

My heart stumbles. For some weird reason I think about the time I went with her to have a lump in her breast aspirated. I remember her gripping my hand so tightly when they stuck the needle in I thought she'd crush my fingers.

"You can take it in the office," he says.

I hesitate for a minute. "Could you just say I can't come to the phone?"

He looks at me quizzically. "Sorry," he says into the receiver, "she's gone for the night. Yep, I'll tell her."

"You ever drive a stick-shift?"

It's 6:00 a.m. on Sunday and we're standing in the empty parking lot behind Harmony High School. Actually, Piggy's sitting astride his Indian, looking like a warrior on horseback. I, meanwhile, stand beside the little "housebroke" Honda, twisting my red bandana nervously.

My provisional island permit is in the pocket of the black leather jacket I've borrowed from Laura. I have to say, I like the costume, which also features jeans and some old cowboy boots I bought from Freddie. My medicine bundle is tucked inside my shirt, next to my heart, to make me brave and ward off mishaps.

"No. I've driven a bakery truck, though."

"Did it have a clutch?"

"Usually."

"Good, then you get the concept of shifting. You're gonna take right to this." He grins disarmingly. "So what do you think we're gonna do first?"

"Get on the bike?"

"No, that's the second thing. First thing is, you check your bike." He gets off the Indian, and I follow him around the machine from nose to tail, checking wheels, controls, lights and signals, oil and other gauges, chassis and side stand. Of course, thanks to Laura, there's nothing at all wrong on this bike. When he's pointed out all the stuff to look for, and which I promptly forget, he says, "Now . . . the controls. Front brake." He points to a lever in front of the right handgrip. "Squeeze it, throw your leg over the saddle, and straighten the handle bars."

Okay, not so bad. It's like a bicycle.

"This"—he points at the right hand grip—"is the throttle."

"I thought it was the front brake."

"The lever's the brake. The grip is the throttle. You roll it toward you to speed up, away from you to slow down. When you let go—"

"I'm not planning to ever let go."

"When you let go," he repeats, "it goes back to idle position. Now this—" He points at the lever in front of the left handgrip.

"Rear brake," I suggest.

He shakes his head. "Clutch."

"But that doesn't make sense. Where's the rear brake?"

"Down by your right foot, just like in a car."

I point out that in a car, your right foot takes care of all the brakes. "So what's the left hand grip?"

"Nothing. Just the grip. Down here"—he points to a lever in front of my left foot—"there's the gearshift. It's a little different from a car because the gear pattern is vertical. At the bottom is first, a step up is second, then third, fourth, fifth. Neutral's a half step up from first or down from second. Now you tell me where you think reverse is."

I shoot him a look. "The same place it is on a bicycle, I guess."

He roars with laughter. "Good answer."

"Piggy, I can't remember all this stuff. It's so illogical."

"Here's the deal. Everything on the right side has to do with stopping and starting. Everything on the left side has to do with changing gears. Okay? Now I'm gonna show you how to get her started."

"Wait a minute. How come it's suddenly a girl?"

"Shit, make it a boy if you want. Call him Myron."

"Myron?"

"Okay, the way we start the engine is called FINE-C. That's *F* for fuel. Turn the fuel valve on. Right here, under the gas tank. Turn it till it's pointing back. *I*, turn on the ignition switch. *N*, make sure it's in neutral. See here, the little green *N*? *E*, turn the engine cutoff switch to run. C, pull out the choke and squeeze the clutch. Then hit the starter button. This thing here, by your right thumb. Got it?"

"No."

"Good." He presses my back. "Sit up tall. Arms are for steering, not propping yourself up. Scoot up forward so your elbows are bent. That's good. Now hug the gas tank with your knees and keep your feet on the footrests." He backs up and looks at me like an artist surveying his creation. "Slicker 'n owl shit."

I spend the next twenty minutes straddle-walking the bike with the engine off, from one end of the parking lot to the other so I can get used to the weight, how it maneuvers—which I imagine is comparable to a rhinoceros on a wet clay bank. Then, with the engine running and my feet on the ground, I get to rock back and forth, letting the clutch out just enough to make the bike move. At eight o'clock we walk over to Harmony Bakers to get an espresso. I've been sitting on Myron for almost two hours and my butt hurts.

When we come back, Piggy says, "Okay, get on the bike. Zip up your jacket. Put on the helmet."

I gulp down my terror and do as instructed.

"We're gonna ride from here to the driveway in first gear. No shifting, okay? Start her—I mean him—up."

I go through the FINE-C ritual, jolting as the engine growls awake. I stomp on the shifter, and first gear engages with a solid thunk. Piggy grins and jerks both thumbs up. I roll on the throttle, too much at first, and the thing roars at me. I scale back, let the clutch out ever so gently, and start to roll. Piggy's jogging alongside me.

"Feet up!" he yells, and the bike magically balances itself. It feels like flying. I hear myself laughing inside the helmet, like a little kid with the training wheels off for the first time. Suddenly I understand the thrill of this, and then almost as suddenly I see the driveway fast approaching. Shit! How do I brake? My mind's gone blank.

I think Piggy's trying to tell me something; I can see him in my peripheral vision, making hand signals, but I can't turn my head to look at him and I can't hear him anymore. Abruptly I start squeezing the left lever. No power to the rear wheel, but I'm still rolling, so I clench the right one in a vise grip and the next thing I know I'm on the ground with four hundred pounds of motorcycle resting on my leg.

Piggy comes running, drops down next to me. "You okay?"

"Swell. Get this goddamned thing off me."

"Easy, easy. Hold still." He grabs the handlebars and lifts the bike just enough for me to crawl out.

"This is stupid. I'm going to kill myself." I scramble to a seated position and start massaging my right calf.

He shakes his head. "No you're not. You just did what all beginners do. If you only remember one thing from today, it's don't try to stop with just the front brake. Always, always, always use both brakes. At the same time." He takes my hand and pulls me to my feet. "Okay?"

I nod slowly, limping a circle around Myron, who's lying on the ground like an injured horse, his engine silenced.

"Hey, relax those shoulders." Piggy's big hand kneads the knots around the base of my neck. "Come on, level with me. For a few minutes there it felt awesome."

I don't say anything.

"Come on, Sunny. I saw you laughin' in there. That's how it's gonna feel all the time with a little more practice."

I let out a long whoosh of breath and turn my head from side to side, trying to loosen my neck. I rub what I know is going to be a very ugly bruise on my thigh.

"This is actually good, because now I can show you how to pick up the bike. Ready?"

Anger burns my throat. "Are you crazy? I can't lift that thing."

"Yeah, you can and I'm gonna show you how."

"No, I can't and I'm not going to try." I fold my arms and glare at him. "All I need is to throw my back out."

Suddenly the humor disappears from his eyes and I can see his jaw lock. He hooks his thumbs behind his belt buckle. His voice is quiet, but it has the presence of a brick wall. "Here's the rule, Sunny. You drop the bike, you pick up the bike. You think you can't do it, but you can. I'm going to show you how. Take hold of the bars."

Something in the green depths of his eyes makes me bend to the bike and put my hands on the handlebars. "Good. Now turn them as far as they'll go so the wheel's pointing down.

Okay. Now come over here and squat down with your butt against the saddle."

He keeps talking, quietly, steadily, while I'm grasping the handgrip with one hand, the bike's frame with the other, pushing with my legs, taking little backward steps one at a time, straining against the weight and heft of the machine, and then abruptly, it begins to lift.

"That's it, keep going. You're almost there."

Myron and I gain the magic balance point, and it's like he's waking up and standing alone. I'm so astonished I nearly drop him over on the other side.

"Put the side stand down and turn the bars," Piggy commands, and I do. His face is transformed by his grin. "See?"

Sweat runs in private rivulets down my back and under my breasts. I barely nod.

"Okay, breathe deep and turn 'im around. We're goin' back the other way."

By eleven o'clock, I feel like yesterday's French toast. I'm also on intimate terms with every bump and crack and pothole in this parking lot. More important, I've learned how to turn, how to shift up to second and how to brake . . . sort of. I've got a rudimentary understanding of counter-steering and I know that as long as I inhabit Planet Earth, I'll forever hear Piggy's voice in my head shouting, "Look where you want to go! Turn your head! Look where you want to go and you'll go there!"

As my final test of the day, I have to follow Piggy—*on the street*—back to the Ale House, where he's keeping the bike until he feels confident enough in my abilities to let me ride it home. This is a humbling experience. The sun is baking me like a potato in my black leather jacket. I'm sweating so much that the faceplate on my helmet keeps fogging up, and there are enough tourists to populate a small country wandering around in the streets by this time. To the amusement of most of them, I end up stalling out the bike five times in the four blocks between the high school and the Ale House.

At the back door, I put the side stand down and climb off Myron. The breeze feels heavenly when I pull off the helmet and wipe my face. My hair is plastered to my scalp in soggy clumps.

"Sunny, I know you don't think you did good, but you really did," Piggy says. "You're gonna be ridin' that baby in no time. Come on in and I'll buy you a beer."

"I need to go home and take a bath."

"You need a beer first," he says firmly. "You earned it."

I follow him in the back door, struggling out of the leather jacket.

In the kitchen, Freddie and Barbara and Justin burst into spontaneous applause.

Freddie says, "We went out and watched you on break, girl. You are awesome! A goddess in black leather!" She pauses, light infusing her expression. "Damn, what a bitchin' great title for a book!"

Barbara stops singing "Motorcycle Mama" long enough to tell me that I should wear a bandana to prevent Helmet Hair. Or at least hide it.

"Right." My face is red from heat and embarrassment as I follow Piggy through the swinging door to the bar. "No parking lot is safe from me now."

But as I drag my aching bones up on to a barstool, a tiny smile cracks the thin rime of salt on my face.

Chapter 18

I wake up early and lie still, eyes closed, reaching back into sleep to grasp the thread of a dream. Except it's not a dream.

It's June 21, the Summer Solstice, the anniversary of Mari's death. I used to fight the memory, the way it comes every year on this long day, but I've discovered it's impossible, so I just lie there and let it roll over me, like the little kid who goes limp, lets the bully pummel him, figuring he can't stop it; might as well get it over with.

It was June 21, 1979, a warm, cloudless morning on the mesa. I had just turned eight years old.

At Armonía everyone was running around, getting ready to go over to Morning Glory commune where the summer solstice party would be held. Things hadn't been good there for a while—a hepatitis outbreak, a feud with some farmers about water rights, a dwindling population. Morning Glory was sinking. But they were hoping a good solstice party would jump-start their revival. I remember Gwen saying they were expecting more than five hundred people to show up.

That's a lot, but not like the old days, she said, when we had it at Armonía and nearly a thousand people came, mostly wandering hippies and the other commune tribes, but also some friends from town, the curious among our ranching neighbors. It was sort of a blended holiday, borrowed from the pagan and the Indian traditions, the hippies adding their own spin on things. My mother was always up for a party, but she particularly adored all things pagan. We didn't have the solstice celebrations at Armonía anymore because we'd developed into a full-fledged farm and we didn't want a bunch of people parking in our plowed fields, trampling the alfalfa crop, and spooking the animals.

There would be tons of food at Morning Glory, enough to last all day and into the night—roasted pig and barbecued beef and cabrito, the stew made from baby goat. There would be green chile stew, enchiladas, coleslaw, potato salad, baked beans, homemade breads. Women from all the communes would bake their specialties—banana cakes, chocolate chip cookies, lemon pies. You could always spot the healthy stuff made with whole grains, fruit, honey (not sugar), and carob (not chocolate). It would sit in the pans, settling into itself, crust getting soggy, attracting bugs—until the munchies set in and everyone got desperate for something sweet. Then it would taste good.

Of course there would be the loaded brownies. There would be THC tea and pipes of hash. There would be cheap wine and kegs of beer and the stuff they called Purple Jesus—a punch made from grape juice and grain alcohol. If the partiers were really lucky, somebody from California would show up with a bagful of acid tabs.

There would be bands—at least three or four—and they would spell each other, playing all day till no one could stand up any longer, much less dance. There would be volleyball and improvised baskets to shoot hoops. The kids would run around playing, shrieking, getting into everything, till their mothers came to retrieve them for a while. And by late afternoon, most of the adults would be too wasted to retrieve them, but by then, the littlest ones were usually curled up asleep in somebody's van or in the corner of a room, while the party dwindled down into fights and clandestine sex.

The parties scared me. I never liked crowds. Although, the truth is, after a while, you get caught up in the light and the heat, the noise and the music. There's an image in my head to this day: looking out across the field from the roof of a pueblo over a sea of wildly painted and/or rusting cars, trucks, buses, vans, wagons, to the bandstand where hundreds of bodies moved in the sunlight—a field of strange flowers in a chaotic wind.

By the time we got on the road to Morning Glory, the sun was high and so was Rob. He had the Grateful Dead on the truck's eight-track and he and Gwen were singing "U.S. Blues" at the top of their lungs. Hart and Mari and I rode in the back, eating dust.

We were part of a slow-moving caravan, rumbling over the back roads, following the makeshift signs that pointed the way to Morning Glory. Behind us was an old school bus painted all over with psychedelic designs, flowers, comets, planets, sunrise on the mountains, and across the top of the hood the oddly foreboding message NOTHING LASTS.

When we arrived, my mother headed for the pueblo kitchen, loaded down with her baked goods. Rob hooked up with some friends from California. Hart disappeared into the barn to check out the horses, and I took Mari by the hand and went looking for Sage, who was sort of a friend. She and her mother, Robyn, had lived at Armonía for a few months the year before, till Robyn decided life there was too much work and moved over to Morning Glory.

I found Sage down by the river. We discarded our clothes and waded into the icy water, gasping and splashing each other, while Mari played in the mud with her ratty old stuffed dog, Woof. All afternoon we wore a path between the river and the courtyard, eating multiple desserts and having mud fights with a bunch of boys.

Mari was a mess, caked with mud, hair plastered to her face, which was red from too much sun. I used the hem of her dress, dipped in water, to clean her up a little bit. She was sleepy by then, and she nodded heavily against my chest, still clutching the now sopping wet Woof.

At some point the band retired for a break, leaving the air empty of music. This was the time of day I hated most. The adults were all tripping, and a lot of the kids seized the opportunity to help themselves to controlled substances. The ones who weren't getting drunk on PJ or stoned on pot brownies were getting wired on sugar. I was ready to go home, but I knew from experience that it would be hours before Rob and Gwen would leave. Right at the moment, they probably weren't even speaking to each other.

The next band started up then, a little bit quieter than the one before, just as the sun was beginning to slip behind the mountains. The air had cooled.

"Let's go up on the roof and watch the sun," Sage said.

I always liked that vantage point at these gatherings. I could see what was going on, but didn't have to feel included in it.

Between the two of us, we got Mari up the ladder to the

roof of the main pueblo. People lounged against the walls, one or two sprawled unconscious, others sat around the skylights, using the glass tops like tables to read the Tarot or play Chinese checkers, or just to set their food and drinks on.

We sat down, and Mari curled up with her head in my lap. She smelled of wet river mud and little kid sweat. A few chocolate crumbs languished in the corner of her mouth. She was almost asleep when Hart appeared on the ladder, jumped over the parapet. He had something—a scarf or a table cloth or something—tied to both wrists so that it floated out behind him like a cape.

"I'm Pueblo Man," he announced. He whipped part of his cape across his face and peered over the top at us. Mari opened her eyes and shrieked with delighted laughter.

"They locked me in jail, but I escaped." He gave us a loopy smile. "No prison can hold Pueblo Man."

People stood at the edge of the roof, watching the changing colors—bands of gold and pink, a blaze of red-orange, cooling to lavender and dusky blue. Some held on to each other, swaying back and forth in a group hug. The band was playing something slow and spacey.

Hart bent down and grabbed Woof. "You are my prisoner." And he took off.

Mari howled like a siren, and a few sunset watchers turned to glare at us.

"Stop it! Give me that dog!" I jumped up and took off after him.

He was running and laughing, and people watched us through bleary eyes. Someone said, "You kids stop running around before someone gets hurt."

"Help me!" I yelled over my shoulder at Sage. The three

of us ran, skirting the chimneys and skylights. Once, I got my hand on Woof, but Hart jerked him away and darted behind a card table covered with half-empty drinks, toppling some of them. I slipped in a puddle of beer. I don't know when I realized that Mari was now following us, laughing.

Hart was headed for the ladder, with Sage and me getting closer. Suddenly he leaped like a broad jumper, flying over the big skylight in the middle of the roof. Sage dodged to the side and I jumped, following my brother.

Somewhere in midair I must have understood that Mari was right behind me. It was one of those moments you see in dreams forever after. My body twisting, trying to defy the momentum of the leap, to catch Mari, to stop her. My foot snagging on the skylight's rim. My sister and me, crashing through the glass together.

For years my memory of what followed was intermittent, coming in pieces that obligingly knit themselves together, since I didn't have the dexterity. People running and Hart screaming, his face so contorted that I hardly recognized him, still clutching Woof. Me, standing somehow, a sticky warmth collecting on my left hand.

Mari was lying on the packed-earth floor; her eyes were open and moving slowly, like she was looking for me and couldn't find me.

Later there were sirens. I remember the back of my mother's head as she bent over, her long hair hiding my sister. Somebody pulling the piece of glass out of my arm. Riding with my mother to the hospital in Taos.

The doctor said it would hurt when he stitched up the jagged tear in my arm, but I didn't feel anything.

• • •

I must have drifted halfway back to sleep because a sudden noise prods me fully awake. Someone's knocking on my door. I pull on my jeans, hollering,

"Just a second."

JT stands on my porch. "Sorry. Did I wake you up?"

"No problem. I had to get up to answer the door."

He smiles. "You shouldn't be sleeping in on a day like this anyway."

I frown and comb my fingers through my hair. "Some of us worked till midnight."

"I didn't have your phone number or I could've called first—"

"Then I'd have to get up to answer the phone. What is it you want?"

"Are you always this grouchy in the morning?"

"Pretty much. I'm a bitch till I've had coffee." I turn around and head for the kitchen. "After that I'm only mildly irritable."

He follows me in and leans against the counter that he and Scott built, watching me make a fire.

"I just came by because I left my toolbox here."

"I know. I tripped over it and nearly broke my leg when I came in."

I give the pump a few strokes, then open the spigot and fill my blue enameled tin coffee pot, set it over the firebox.

He says, "We used to have a coffee pot like that. For when we went camping."

I pull the jar of coarse-ground coffee off the shelf and look at him over my shoulder. "You want some?"

"Sure. Thanks."

I set the cups on a corner of the stove to warm up, pull the milk out of the little fridge, and set it on the table.

"Are you hungry?"

"I had breakfast," he says.

"That's not what I asked you. I'm going to have some toast. Do you want some?"

"Sure. Thanks." He looks around. "Can I help you?"

"Yes." I point at the chair. "Sit down there and don't talk. And take off that damn hat."

While I wait for the water to boil, I slice some wheat bread from the Harmony Bakers and lay it on the oven floor to toast. Then I ease down into the other chair and look at him bleary-eyed and thoroughly annoyed. I should probably be grateful that he interrupted my foray into the past, but it was too sudden. I feel disoriented, one foot in Armonía, the other in Harmony. And the memories will be back soon enough.

Eventually, with caffeine racing through my veins, I feel somewhat better. I take a bite of toast and chew it slowly, noticing that he's already devoured his two pieces.

He rests his elbows on the table. "I guess you could say I left the toolbox here on purpose."

"I guess I'm supposed to ask why."

He grins. "Not if you already know the answer. So . . . uh . . . would you like to go sailing sometime?"

"Actually, no. But thanks."

"Why not?"

"I can't swim and I don't like being farther than walking distance from the nearest solid ground."

"You like tennis? There are some courts up at Rocky Harbor Resort. They're supposed to be just for guests, but I'm not without contacts."

"I don't play tennis."

"What about hiking?"

"Don't you have any playmates your own age?"

"None as interesting as you."

"I'm not all that interesting. Plus I'm too old for you. There's a cultural gap. Like that Steely Dan song 'Hey, Nineteen.'"

"Who's Steely Dan?"

I point my coffee spoon at him. "See what I mean?"

He laughs. "I know who they are. But age is an artificial obstacle. If you're not interested in me, you can just say so."

"I thought I just did."

"No, you said there's a cultural gap. It's not the same thing as not being interested."

"JT, I like you—"

"Well, that's a start."

"No, it's not a start. We can be friends. That's all."

"Because of Michael?"

I don't bother to answer.

He drums his fingers on the table. "I notice you don't talk much about where you came from."

"That's because I came here to get away from where I came from."

"Okay. But probably if you talked a little more, people wouldn't ask so many questions."

"What do you want to know?"

"Nothing too personal. How long did you live in Albuquerque?"

"Since I graduated from high school."

"Where did you grow up before Albuquerque?"

"Northern New Mexico. Armonía."

"Is that a town?"

"More or less."

"More or less?"

"It's a commune. *Was* a commune. Now it's a bed-and-breakfast."

"Well, shit. That's pretty interesting. What made you come all the way out here?"

"I decided I wanted to try something different."

"So do you still have your place in Albuquerque?"

I sit back in my chair. "No."

"I just wondered. I mean, you don't have a lot of stuff . . . I thought maybe you left it all there or . . ."

"I got rid of it."

"Everything?"

My head is suddenly full. My empty apartment. How dirty the walls looked when all the furniture was gone. The box of Michael's clothes waiting by the door for the Salvation Army truck. My belongings piled around the courtyard, bargain hunters picking through them. Betsy . . . or the space left empty by her absence.

He looks down at his unlaced high-tops. "I guess this hasn't been a very good year for you."

The sound explodes from my chest—great shuddering spasms of uncontrollable laughter. It's been a long time since anything seemed so oddly and excruciatingly hilarious. I laugh and laugh and I can't seem to stop. And about the time I start to hear the hysterical overtones, it turns to crying. Noisy crying. Sobbing. He watches me with a mixture of curiosity and alarm.

"I'm sorry. Sunny? I didn't mean to—Sunny? I'm really sorry."

He hands me the dish towel lying next to the sink. I use it to blot my face. I clamp my teeth together and try to concentrate on breathing. When things are relatively quiet, he says, "Shit, I didn't know whether to hug you or slap you or call 911."

I almost start laughing again, but I hold it in tight. "Please, don't be amusing."

His smile is nice. "Normally that's not a problem for me."

"I'm sorry. I don't know what's wrong with me lately." I look at him through my puffy eyelids.

"Hey, don't apologize. Not to me." His gaze switches from my face to somewhere over my head and he pulls the cap back on. I expect him to head for the door. Instead he says, "Go get your sunglasses."

I look at him, totally blank.

"Come on," he says. "You need to get out. I'll show you the lighthouse. Come on. You'll feel better."

Bailey's lounging in the bed of the orange truck, and we head south on Rainy Road, a twisting ribbon of alternating gravel and blacktop, which JT explains was named not for the weather, but for early settler Charles Rainy, who brought the first sheep to the island. It's a perfect day—clear and breezy, the sun, warm through the windshield, making me drowsy. Twenty minutes later he parks the truck on a windy bluff.

Bailey is out of the pickup almost before we stop, running through the meadow on the other side of the road.

"How can you let him run loose like that? Don't you worry about him?"

He smiles. "Bailey and I have an understanding. I don't try to run his life, and he doesn't try to run mine. He's smarter than I am, anyway. At least he doesn't crap in his own bed."

I'm not sure what he means, and I don't ask. In my experience, people tell you these kinds of things as part of a bargain. They're looking for an exchange of information. But I don't want to know his secrets. I don't even want to know mine.

He steers me to the edge of the bluff. Clumps of golden California poppies blaze from crevices along a steeply winding path down to a small white crescent of beach.

"So here's where they've been hiding the beach. Where's the lighthouse?"

"Down here and around the point. Take it slow," he warns. "There's loose gravel on the trail."

We pick our way down using the plentiful nooks and crannies in the rock for handholds, and stopping every few minutes to enjoy the view. Halfway down, invisible from the top, an old brick building sits on a wide ledge, snug against the face of the cliff, its windows and doors neatly cut out.

"This was a radio transmitting station in the twenties and thirties," he says.

I read the plaque posted next to the door.

A radioman would be stationed here on stormy nights to listen for QTE messages broadcast by lost ships. The radioman would then use an Azimuth compass to pinpoint the radio signal and tell the ship its location.

The wind blows my hair into my eyes, and I push it back. "What's a QTE message?"

"I'm not sure what it stands for, but it means 'What's my true position?'"

"Interesting. You have to have somebody else tell you where you are."

"Come on." He nudges me back toward the path. "We've still got a ways to go."

The lighthouse requires a vigorous scramble around the point, over boulders slick with seaweed. We stop at intervals to catch our breath and inspect the creatures left behind by the retreating tide. Below the beacon, a series of natural terraced ledges leads down to where the water foams in a semicircular cauldron of rock.

"Along about August it's a good place to swim," he says, "fairly warm and protected from the tides."

I gaze down into the blue-green depths, wondering how deep it is, how it would feel, those strands of kelp brushing against my bare skin. It makes me shiver.

The lighthouse looms almost directly above us now, the paint faded and peeled, the brass trim a tarnished green. Some of the windows are broken out.

"Can we go inside?"

He shakes his head. "It's all boarded up. Two kids came out here a couple years ago and were climbing up to the light. One of the stair treads was rotten and they went right through. The boy broke his neck."

A feeling moves through me, weighted, falling slowly. "Oh, God. That's terrible."

"Yeah. Every once in a while some civic group gets a bug to restore the thing, tries to raise money, but then it always sort of loses steam. Too many bad memories, I guess. It'll probably just stand here till it falls down."

When I realize I'm rubbing the scar on my left arm, I drop my hand abruptly.

"You really should learn how to swim," he says.

"I might do that someday. And learn to play the cello. And finish reading Proust."

The corner of his mouth lifts in a slow grin. "You're one strange chick, Sunny Cooper."

"I know. I think it's genetic."

He gets to his feet and offers his hand to help me up. "The tide's starting to come in. We should get going."

Since there's no phone line at the cottage, Piggy lets me use the office computer at the Ale House. Mostly I read the *Albuquerque Journal* online, send an occasional message to Artie, shop for cooking essentials—like masa harina, posole, piloncillo, tomatillo salsa, red and green chile, Mexican chocolate, piñon coffee, the spiced honey from the Santa Fe School of Cooking. This afternoon, when I check my Hotmail account there's one message. From FoodMaven.

Sunny—I'm sorry. I miss you. Betsy

I think about writing back, but what would I say? *I miss you too, but I'd like to cut your favorite dress into ribbons and serve it to you with Hatch green chile.*

I hit the Delete key and sit for a minute, waiting for my mind to engage. It takes so long I nearly nod off. I rub my eyes and suddenly remember what it was I wanted to check. In Dogpile metasearch I type KIRBY DOLEN. Several pages of entries pop up, the majority of which are old links to stories about his hacker days at UNM and later the companies he founded. There's one photo of him donating some desktops and printers to a private school in Santa Fe. About halfway through the second page I find his obituary, which runs on and on about his accomplishments and says he was found dead in his office.

Next is the story I've already seen in the *Taos Sun*, and the following week there's a tiny follow-up. Only a paragraph.

The probable cause of death of software entrepreneur Kirby Dolen was being struck by a vehicle, according to Taos police spokesperson Allison Cuatro. The Medical Investigator's report, released Monday, said his injuries were consistent with having been hit by a vehicle traveling at a high rate of speed. Dolen's body was discovered in his office shortly after 5:00 a.m. on April 22 by firefighters who were called to his Kiva Ridge home to extinguish a fire. Police are asking anyone who has any information about Dolen's activities that evening to call the Crimestoppers Tipline at 1-888-992-9787.

Chapter 19

Breathing is one of those things you take for granted till you can't do it.

Nearly every night for the last week I keep waking up with my mouth so dry I can barely swallow, sinuses blocked solid. Trish says it's allergies; Freddie thinks it's a cold or a virus. I'm not so sure.

Growing up as Nature Girl out on the mesa, I was exposed to every bacteria and virus, every allergen, and plenty of plain old American dirt early in life, and I developed the immune system of an Orc. I can count on the fingers of one hand the number of prescription drugs I've ingested in my life, so first I try inhaling saltwater and putting Vicks under my nose. Then I stop having a glass of wine before bed. In desperation, I try an OTC antihistamine/decongestant. Nothing works, and the decongestant makes me wide awake and jittery. Nosebleeds follow, along with relentless headaches.

The only thing that seems to help at all is sitting upright, which is not conducive to sleeping. So I lie down and sleep, then I sit up and wait for my head to clear. Then I lie back down, then I sit up . . . repeat as necessary throughout the night.

Monday morning I'm up at 4:30, groggy and frustrated and very pissed off. I'm supposed to be going for my first real bike ride with Piggy at six, and I'm not exactly in prime condition. I make the coffee even stronger than usual and drink it sitting on the porch, wrapped in the green afghan.

The shadows recede slowly, but still it takes several minutes for my brain to understand exactly what it's seeing. The large shape at the edge of the garden, the smaller one beside it. The movements are unhurried, graceful.

Deer.

"Hey!" I stand up, and they raise their heads to look at me, seeming more annoyed than afraid. When I step off the porch, they turn and bound into the woods. I trot over, trailing the afghan through the damp grass, to inspect the damage. Breakfast buffet wasn't too far off. They've nibbled everything except the rosemary, pruning my lettuce back to the ground. Damn. If only deer weren't so beautiful and fences so ugly.

There's no fog this morning; that means it's going to be hot later, but right now it's perfect. Cool and bright and still. At the top of my driveway, I can hear the Indian's aftermarket straight pipes, the change in the engine's song as Piggy downshifts. Then he's in view, leaning around the curve. He executes a perfect full stop effortlessly, inches from my booted feet, and gives me a wicked grin.

"Mount up, woman," he says.

I kick up the side stand and press the starter button. Myron sings out with a throaty baritone. We sit for a few minutes, idling, letting him warm up, and then Piggy shouts over the noise, "Follow me."

"Not too fast," I holler back. I can't tell if he hears. I step down on the shifter, roll over on the throttle, ease out on the clutch, spray a little gravel, and then find traction on the pavement, heading north on Lavender Road. The toe of my boot kicks the shifter up to second, and then I begin to weave, the way Piggy taught me, to warm up the tires, dipping left, then right, left, right, drawing a shallow S-curve down the road.

Piggy's gaining distance on me, so I kick it up again into third, feeling the accompanying jolt of power like a horse springing from a trot to a canter. I realize then how tightly I'm clenched, from my hand on the throttle to my toes curling inside my boots, and I make myself relax. It's 6:15 in the morning, a gorgeous day, and the road that dips and lifts and curves beneath our wheels belongs to Piggy and me. For nearly an hour, I follow him. We shoot through tunnels of shade, and ride through sunlit curves, slowing, speeding up, leaning and straightening in a dance of power and gravity.

When we pull into a dirt turnout, I realize I'm trembling, exhausted from sheer exhilaration. I put the side stand down, pull off the helmet and the bandana I wear under it, and shake out my hair. Piggy climbs off the Indian, grinning like a pirate, his beard blown into a fan by the wind.

"Couple more rides, you'll be ready for Sturgis," he says.

"What's that?"

He adjusts his bandana. "Just the biggest, baddest bike rally in the world is all. Every August, in Sturgis, South Dakota."

We leave the bikes and move down the rocky path that disappears into the shade of scrubby shore pines.

"So what goes on at a bike rally?"

His laugh is a muted version of the Indian's exhaust note.

"A lot of drinking, a lot of lying. A lot of music and checking out other guys' bikes. Riding around, buying shit for your bike and yourself. It's really just an excuse for a party."

A breeze rushes up from the beach to meet us.

"Have you gone to it?"

"Me and my buddy Denny went a few times."

"When you lived in San Francisco?"

He nods.

"What's he doing now? Your friend."

"He's dead."

We step out of the shade into a splash of morning sun reflecting on the water and I turn to see his face. He's looking straight ahead, no longer smiling.

"I'm sorry. Was it a bike accident?"

"No."

That feels like the end of the conversation. A few steps later we reach the high-tide mark where the wet, packed sand makes walking easier, and I hurry to keep pace with his long strides.

"Killed himself," he says. "At least that was the official verdict."

When I don't say anything, he begins to talk, almost to himself, eyes focused on a point somewhere past the farthest tip of the rocky half-moon beach.

He talks about Denny, how handsome he was, how they grew up together, discovered bikes together, rode with a biker group called the Devil's Spawn. He talks about sitting on the roof of Denny's mother's house the muggy August night his own mother died, drinking beer and chain-smoking. He says Denny just sat with him and matched him "beer for beer and butt for butt," not saying a word until the hot, red sun rose over the city.

He talks about the way they lived, the drinking, the drugs, the fighting, the riding. Waking up on the floor of somebody's kitchen, panicking until you found your bike safe in the garage. The taste of cigarettes and bad coffee on top of hangover breath. Grease under your fingernails, wind in your hair. Cuts and bruises and scraped knuckles and stitches in your scalp from being hit with a broken beer bottle. Concussions and broken bones. Wearing the same grimy shirt for weeks. He somehow manages to make it sound like fun.

Our progress is stopped by a huge rock outcropping that neither of us feels like scrambling over. Instead, we lean against it. I take off my jacket.

"How long have you been here?"

"Three years," he says. "Almost four. Long enough to know I want to die here." He gives a half-embarrassed laugh. "But not anytime soon." He bends down to pick up a piece of amber sea glass, turning it between his fingers. "At first I thought—well, it just didn't seem like my kind of place. You know? But there was Laura . . ." A slow grin steals across his face.

"Of course." I stick my hands in my pockets.

"This place is—it's almost like when you get on a bus and it's packed full, but everybody kind of scoots over." He's facing the water, but his eyes slant in my direction. "They make room for you here. All you gotta do is sit down."

Freddie and Hallie are sunning themselves like two cats in the bookstore's bay window, feet propped on a stack of book cartons, drinking iced tea. Otherwise the place is deserted.

Hallie looks over her shoulder when the bell jingles. "Oh, it's just Sunny. I was hoping you were a rich patron of literature here to stock up on hardcovers for the summer."

"Sorry to disappoint you. I was looking for some—"

"Want some raspberry tea?" Freddie raises her glass.

"No, thanks. What I want is a book that'll tell me how to keep the deer from clear-cutting my garden." I sit down next to her and nudge my clogs off, wiggle my toes in a warm puddle of sun.

"The only thing that really works is a six-foot fence," Hallie says.

"I don't want a six-foot fence. There has to be some other way."

Freddie says, "Have you tried coyote urine?"

I look at her. "Actually, no."

"You just spray it around the perimeter. It really works. Least, it did in Texas. I don't know if Patterson's carries it, but you can order it online. 'Course you don't want to do it on a windy day . . ."

Hallie laughs, slapping her thigh. "Can't you just see it? You're at a party, chatting up some stockbroker, and he says, So, what do you do for a living? And you say, actually, I harvest coyote urine. Definitely a conversation killer."

Freddie looks thoughtful. "There's a couple things you can try. It has to be something that smells. Like rotten eggs mixed with garlic and hot pepper."

Hallie's still choking back little giggles that keep threatening to break out like brush fire. "Or you could just put the radio outside and play it all night."

"With my luck, the deer would think it's a party and invite all their friends over."

"My granny used to hang pieces of soap . . ." Freddie's voice fades away as she peers into the corner at the base of the window seat.

Hallie leans forward. "What is it?"

"Just one of the girls." She takes a sip of tea. "Got us a black widow there in the corner. Sunny, you might want to—"

Before she can finish the sentence my feet are up on the cushion. They both look at me in surprise.

"They're more scared of you than you are of them," Freddie says.

"Yeah, that's what Gwen always used to say, and it's a big fat lie. If they were more afraid than I am, they'd never get anywhere near me." I wipe my palms on my jeans. "Could you just kill the thing?"

On the mesa, black widows were ubiquitous. I dreamed about them—hanging from vigas over my bed, crawling on my face, building webs in my hair, trailing my arms and legs with their silky threads. The worst time was fall, when cold nights drove them indoors to colonize the dusty corners behind chairs and under windowsills. I vividly recall Wendy pulling on a pair of jeans that had been draped over a rock wall to dry and getting bitten on the butt. She was sick—sweating and crying with fever and wrenching cramps—for days.

I learned to recognize their shiny round bodies, with the telltale red hourglass on the underside, although I couldn't bring myself to even get close enough to smash them with a shoe or a folded newspaper. My unarticulated fear was getting so close that they could jump on me. Hart explained repeatedly, but patiently, that black widows don't jump, and he would scoop up the offender on a stick and carry it outside to a new home. I firmly believed that the same spider kept coming back inside to torment me.

"She's not interested in you," Freddie says. "She's waiting for

Bubba to come home—sex and a nice dinner. In that order." She gets down on the floor and smiles at the spider. "You go, girl."

Hallie rests her head against the window frame. "So what wine does one pour with male of the species?"

Freddie purses her lips thoughtfully. "I guess that depends on whether you barbecue him or sauté him. Or maybe deep-fry. Actually if you fried him up crispy, that would probably call for a beer."

"Oops," Hallie says. "I think we're making Sunny sick." She looks at me over the tops of her glasses. "Are you okay? You're looking a bit peaked."

"I'm fine," I say, although my face feels slightly damp.

Freddie reaches for a pencil sitting on one of the boxes. "I have a no-kill relocation policy."

On her knees, she sticks the pencil into the sticky web and slowly rotates it until she's collected the whole thing, including the spider. I watch her carry it carefully out the door and deposit it on the deck.

"Don't worry, I won't let her back in." Hallie laughs. "She never buys anything anyway."

There's a pink message slip paper-clipped to my time card. When I open it up and register the name, it's like stepping off a cliff, that weightless second before you plummet.

Sergeant Tim Bagley of the New Mexico State Police has called. He's the next-to-last person on this earth I want to talk to . . . the last being Betsy. And I sure as hell don't plan to call him from here.

"Hey, girlchik." Freddie's voice startles me and I turn, crumpling the message slip and jamming it into my pocket. "You okay?"

My mouth feels odd, numb, like when the dentist gives you Novocain. "I think I'm having a sinking spell. Low blood sugar or something." My forehead is damp. "Is it hot in here?"

"No more'n usual." She paws through one of the table baskets and hands me two packages of saltines. "Go on, eat 'em. Right now. Can't have you doing a face plant on the floor. It's *so* bad for business."

"Thanks." I take the crackers, turn to punch my time card, and collide painfully with the corner of the little hand sink that juts out from the wall. "Ow, shit!" I rub my hip.

"Are you okay?" Freddie says again.

"Other than being a total klutz, you mean?"

"Why don't you sit down for a minute and eat those crackers?"

"I'm fine. It's just a good thing—" When I turn back to look at her, my field of vision narrows swiftly as some unseen hand closes the drapes. Over Freddie's head the clock on the wall flies toward me like a bird.

I open my eyes to the ceiling. Freddie's face is down close to mine. Piggy's is farther north. Barbara's is upside down so that her smile looks like a grimace.

"Drunk again, huh?" Barbara says.

Freddie glares at her. "Barb, zip it shut, okay?"

"I was *kidding*!" She slinks away.

Now I see Justin, holding a dish towel. It's wet and it's dripping in my face.

"Ack!" I throw my arm over my eyes and try to sit up, but six hands are holding me down.

"Just hold still, darlin'. Put this on your forehead." Freddie is lowering the wet cloth to my face.

"I'm clean. I took a bath this morning. Come on, you guys,

let me up." I feel incredibly stupid, as if I've showed up for work
with my underwear outside my jeans.

"Help her up," Piggy orders. "Put her over here."

They arrange me in a plastic chair like a blow-up doll at a
bachelor party.

"I must've slipped or something."

"Honey, you fainted," Freddie says. "Passed clean out. Eye-
balls rolled back and the whole nine yards."

Piggy says, "Freddie can take you home—"

"No! Come on, it was nothing. Let me just sit for a minute
and I'll be fine. Really."

He looks dubious.

"I haven't been sleeping well. My sinuses are driving me
crazy. I'm okay to work tonight, really."

"Barbara! Get her a glass of orange juice! See how you feel.
If you start getting dizzy again, you get your butt in a chair and
call me or Freddie. Understood?"

"I will. But I'm fine."

He folds his arms and looks down at me from his full
height. "You don't pass out for no reason, Sunny. You can work
tonight, but I want you to go see a doctor."

"I don't have a doctor."

"Well, get one. I'm not just being nice. We've got some li-
ability issues here."

"Okay, I will. I promise." When he goes back to the bar, I
throw Freddie a pleading look. "I hate doctors. I haven't had a
physical since college, when I needed a prescription for birth
control pills. Do you know one here?"

"No, but Trish does. Been going to the same guy for years."

"I was just kidding, Sunny." Barbara hands me a plastic cup
of orange juice.

"Don't worry about it."

Freddie pulls out her cell phone. "I'm calling Trish right now and we're getting you a date with Dr. Ralph."

It rained in the night—the kind the Navajos call a female rain—slow and steady, soaking into the earth. As opposed to a male rain, which is hard, fast, and runs off immediately.

I hang my helmet on the sissy bar and wander into the crowded parking lot of Harmony High School, where the farmers market is just getting under way. Some of the vendors are still setting up their makeshift booths. The cool smell of wet pavement is rapidly being overlaid with the welcoming scents of brewed coffee and sausages sizzling on a grill.

The official opening gong sounds at 8:15, but it's a lot like a garage sale. If you go early, you're more likely to get what you want, and by nine, the tables of some of the best purveyors have been picked clean by the folks from the big boats.

I buy a double espresso from a woman who has a little cart set up right by the entrance every Saturday and head for Heather the Bread Lady's table, piled with crusty brown loaves that she and her family bake in their wood-burning brick oven. With a loaf of still-warm country French in my pack, I move on to the tables of fresh goat cheese, bins of vegetables with crumbs of dirt still clinging to their roots, pastured chicken and eggs, organic beef, the cookie guy.

"Hey, Albuquerque . . . Got some kick-ass king salmon today. Flown in last night from Dora Bay." Mick sneaks a sip of beer from a can in a brown paper bag. "Breakfast of champions." He grins and winks.

There's no avoiding Mick. Not only does he have great fish,

but he's extra generous, always giving me a few ounces more than I'm paying for. Maybe it's guilt. He's convinced that he got me evicted from Sarah's garage, and I haven't contradicted that notion. It's hard to get a word in edgewise with him anyway.

"Okay, I'll take a pound."

He raises his eyebrows. "You must be havin' company for dinner. Am I right?"

"No, you're wrong. I'm going to freeze half of it."

"Why freeze it when you can buy it anytime all summer long?"

"For a rainy day." I smile.

"Hey, you know what, Albuquerque, you've got about the cutest little smile there is. Why don't I take you out for dinner tonight? I'll even take a bath. We could go to the Tree House and then sit around and listen to some music and get mellow . . ."

"Mick, your idea of mellow is not mine."

"Hey, are you still pissed about that little episode at Sarah's? That was nothing but an aberration, I swear. Ask anybody, I'm really a nice guy."

"I know you are. And you have great fish, so weigh me out some king salmon and then you can take care of all these people standing behind me."

"You're breakin' my heart here."

"I feel really bad about it."

"I'm gonna have to start chargin' you regular prices," he grumbles, laying the package in my hand. "Hey, come on out to the marina and see me," he calls after me. "I got some new jokes . . . What d'you get if you mix Viagra with ginger ale? Mount 'n' Do . . . The rest of 'em are better than that, I promise . . ."

His booming laugh follows me to the end of the aisle.

I hit the booth with all different kinds of fresh sprouts, the hippie girl whose salad greens are always sold out by ten o'clock, and the woman offering little French pastries called *cannelés de Bordeaux*, which are indescribable—crusty, chewy, caramelized, custardy, redolent of rum, and totally addictive.

My last stop is a small stand practically hidden by cardboard pints of strawberries, and the smell from ten feet out is intoxicating. Mr. Martin, the vendor, is a diminutive white-haired farmer who always wears a plaid shirt and clean overalls and stands behind his table straight as a Marine on parade.

I load two pints carefully into a bag, place it gently in the top of my pack, and ride home.

Chapter 20

Actually Mick was right. I am having company.

First JT invited me to watch the Fourth of July fireworks on the deck of his boat, *The Lucky Dawg*—but if having lunch with him made us the object of speculation, I can only imagine that going to his boat for the evening would kick-start a veritable gossip frenzy.

So I invited him to dinner as an alternative. Besides, I wanted to do something nice for him. He's made a masterpiece of my kitchen pretty much single-handedly, planing and sanding, oiling and rubbing the wood till it glows warm and golden. He's adjusted the hinges and the hardware so everything opens and closes soundlessly at the gentlest touch.

He put a mirror on the inside of the closet door and he hammered pegs in the wall near the fireplace to hang wet jackets and scarves. When he ran out of things to work on inside, he built a lean-to for wood storage on the side of the house near the porch. Whenever I've tried to talk about payment, he shrugs me off.

He's given me the island like a gift, taken me to places that aren't in any tourist guide—hidden, mysterious, glorious places. Like the hundred-year-old apple orchard, protected by a thorny hedge of brambles on the north end. We wandered through the labyrinth of gnarled trunks with huge, twisted limbs enmeshed in a tangle of blackberry vines and wild roses. Beautiful tiny knobs, no bigger than cherries, flecked with green and red, clustered along the branches. As we walked, he rested his hands on each tree, as if greeting old friends.

"This was part of a farm owned by a family named Westbrook," he said. JT likes knowing the history of things. "The last of them died in the 1950s, and the farm got subdivided. I couldn't find any record of who owns the orchard now."

I was only half listening, lost in a memory of picking apples at the old Padilla farm. Of my brother, tanned and smiling, the picking bag around his neck, sagging with the weight of fruit, Mrs. Padilla, standing on her portal, her old dog Pancho sprawled at her feet. Suddenly I realized I wasn't holding up my end of the conversation.

I said, "We have lots of apple trees at home, but I've never seen any this big." And I wondered if I'd always be calling New Mexico "home."

He showed me a trail, a shortcut from my house into town that winds through woods and across a meadow with a big pond full of ducks and geese, and pointed out the lightning tree—an ancient maple struck years ago and split in two, both halves still living.

But the place that intrigued me most was the lime kiln where, in the early 1900s, limestone was fired to about two thousand degrees Fahrenheit to transform it into pure lime, which was then loaded onto ships at the wharf down below. What's left of the kiln reminded me of a ruined castle from some fantasy kingdom.

We hiked up into the woods, following the rusted cart tracks from the kiln to the quarry. Moss has softened the edges of the gaping pit; wildflowers and grasses have sprung up to hide the scars. Even the forest has grown back. It's silent now, except for the slapping of waves on the rocks below and the haunting, fluty whistle of a meadowlark.

Sunday evening at five thirty I open my door, hair wet and curling, no makeup. JT's golden brown eyes smile at me over the top of a huge bouquet—daisies, baby's breath, black-eyed Susans, and bachelor's buttons. In his other hand is a bottle of wine.

"You're not supposed to be here till six. I haven't even dried my hair."

He looks different—clean scrubbed and smoothly shaven. Even the soul patch is gone . . . just when I was getting used to it.

"I couldn't wait to tell you," he says.

"Tell me what?"

"I'm going to Hawaii!" He grabs me in a bear hug and twirls me around so fast I'm afraid we're both going to end up in the fireplace.

When he finally sets me down, the room continues to revolve. "Hawaii? That's great . . . Here, give me the flowers. And shut the door."

At the kitchen sink, he watches me stuff the flowers into an empty milk carton because I don't have a vase. "These are really beautiful, JT. But you shouldn't have—"

"Don't worry. I stole them out of my mother's garden. So it's this guy Callender. I took him and his wife out whale watching

the other day. He asked me to help him sail his boat to Hawaii.
It's a Hunter 45-CC. The *Princessa*." He pounds on the coun-
ter. "God, I can't believe it! I'd sell my mother for one of those.
That's assuming anyone would buy her, of course."

"How did it happen? Pour us some wine, okay?"

He grabs two glasses off the shelf over the sink and pulls the
pinot gris out of my little fridge. We clink our glasses together
and he sits on the corner of the table.

"Apparently Scott's been crewing for him for the past few
years in the San Juan Regatta. The guy must have about two
dollars more than God. He just bought this boat in L.A., and
he and his wife sailed it up here, and now he wants to take it to
Hawaii, but she won't do the trans-Pac thing, so he asked Scott
to sail with him, but Scott's too busy to go, so he gave the guy
my name. I can't believe it. That's why he wanted to go whale
watching. Not to see whales, but to see how I handled the boat.
So I guess I did okay."

I smile at his modesty.

"And he's paying my airfare back."

"When do you leave?"

"Wednesday." He runs both hands through his hair. "I still
can't believe it. I'm terrified something's going to happen before
we leave. Like I'll sprain my ankle or get hit by a car crossing
First Street."

"How long will it take?"

"Two and a half to three weeks, I guess. Depends on winds
and weather." He seems to be looking at me for the first time.
"Damn. I didn't know you owned a dress."

"Granny Cooper's still got a few surprises left." I pat my
hands on a towel. "I'm going to go finish drying my hair—"

"No, leave it." He reaches over to flip a curl off my forehead and the lightness of his touch makes the hair rise on my neck. It's a silent, oddly intimate moment, almost suffocating. Then his laugh releases the tension like air going out of a balloon. "You look like a mermaid."

"Right. The mermaid who can't swim."

When the fire's burning hot in the stove, I smear the salmon with spice rub, sear it in my black iron skillet, and pop it into the oven to finish cooking. JT refills our glasses, and sets out dishes and silverware while I toss the salad with raspberry vinaigrette, slice the bread, and heat the cooked orzo in a spoonful of olive oil.

"Why don't you find us some dinner music while I fix the plates. The CD carrier's in the living room on the shelf next to the boom box."

Finally we sit down. "Do you always cook like this?"

"I always cook real food, if that's what you mean. I don't do frozen dinners or anything like that."

"Come on, you're talking to a guy who eats Nestlé's Quik out of the box. You've gotta have at least one food vice."

"Okay. I confess. My name is Sunny Cooper, and I'm a Sarah Lee cheesecake addict."

Suddenly I'm there. In front of the TV, watching *Star Trek* and eating frozen cheesecake the night I waited for Michael to come home from Taos. I still haven't called Sergeant Bagley; the message slip is still in the pocket of my jeans. I reach for my glass, and the wine rushes through me, liquid heat and light.

Then I hear the music. The CD he's picked is a Charlie Haden/Pat Metheny collaboration called *Beyond the Missouri Sky*. Acoustic, just guitar and bass, the arrangements spare and open as the prairie.

JT says, "What are you thinking about?"

"The music."

"Does it remind you of Michael?"

"Yes. But probably not in the way you imagine."

"I wouldn't presume to imagine anything about your memories."

"We both liked this album, but for different reasons . . ." The thought trails off like an interrupted dream.

"How did you two get together?" he says.

I push the lettuce around on my plate, pick up the bread and break off a small piece. "I was dating a friend of his," I say. "When Addison and I broke up, Michael was just sort of there." I dip my piece of bread in the saucer of olive oil.

"Did he give you the necklace?" He's looking at the medicine bundle.

"No. My father did."

He studies me for a minute, then smiles and picks up his fork. "This is nice," he says. "Really nice. Thanks for inviting me."

Dessert is very thin, very gingery ginger snaps, fresh goat cheese from the market, and a big bowl of strawberries.

I hand him a bottle of pinot noir and the corkscrew. "Have you told your mother yet? About Hawaii?"

"It wouldn't interest her." He gives me an oddly cheerful smile. "We're a pretty weird family. I used to seriously believe I was adopted. I even asked her once. She just looked at me, totally straight, and she said, 'No, you're mine.'" He scoots forward and rests his arms on the table. "Almost like she was wondering about it too."

There it is, then—it's like some kind of radar, the way we

recognize each other, all the asymmetrical ones, the odd ones, whose edges don't quite fit, the way one combat veteran can spot another.

"Were you close with your sister?"

He raises his head. "Basically, there's two kinds of islanders. The ones who leave and they can never come back. And the ones who leave and then realize they can't stay away. When Mary Beth went to college I knew she'd never live here again."

"What about your dad?"

"He wasn't around much. The best time I remember was when he gave me my first boat. It was just a dinghy with a little sail. I must've been eight or nine. He taught me to sail it by standing on the dock and shouting things I couldn't hear. Eventually I figured it out for myself."

A sudden impulse makes me say, "Was your mother disappointed that you didn't go to law school?"

His eyes darken. He ignores the coffee and refills his wineglass. "Major," he says. "Major disappointed. And totally pissed." He takes a long swallow of wine and looks at me over the rim of his glass. "I didn't tell you why I ended up not going."

"You said you were tired of living in the city."

"That's true, but it's not the reason."

I wait, watching him twirl the glass around and around between his fingers.

"It wasn't my decision. I cheated on a final exam. I got caught."

"Why did you do that?"

"The usual reason, I guess: I needed to ace the class. My law school acceptance was conditional on my final semester GPA. The professor called me in and said that he suspected me. He gave me the choice of voluntarily withdrawing or being called up before honor council. So I left. Two weeks before graduation."

"Could you go back? To school."

"No," he says quickly. "It was a permanent dismissal. I never told anyone."

"But they must have asked why you left."

He looks at the ceiling. "God, yes. Everyone. A million times. That was the hardest part. Every time someone asked me, I wanted to cry. I just said I'd decided to quit. So now they don't think I'm a scumbag, they just think I'm crazy." His smile tugs at me. "The worst part was Luke."

"Who?"

"Luke Carver. He's married to my sister, but we were friends a long time before that. He's a lawyer in Seattle. He wrote this great recommendation for me . . ."

"That's what you meant about Bailey. Not messing in his own bed."

"Yeah. Really stupid, huh?"

"It was. But it's not the end of the world."

"I thought so at first." He shrugs. "But honestly . . . I don't think I ever really wanted to be a lawyer anyway."

"Then why was it so important to get in?"

"She wanted me to. I think it's the only thing she ever wanted from me. It sounds insane, but I guess I wanted my little place on the television shrine. I thought if I gave her that one thing, it would make her happy. I finally figured out that it wouldn't. I could be on the Supreme Court, and I'd never be on the same exalted plane as Mary Beth."

I rest my elbows on the table and cup my chin in one hand. "I hope you know I'd never tell anyone."

Suddenly it's quiet and we're sitting there looking at each other.

"Why don't you go put on another CD?" I smile and stir my coffee energetically.

From the other room he says, "You must have your CDs mixed up. Actually this one doesn't even look like an audio CD." A pause. "It says . . . 'Dolen Consulting.'"

I nearly spit out my coffee.

Later, after we've emptied the bottle of pinot noir, he offers to help with the dishes. He's shocked that I have to heat the water on the stove.

"At Armonía we had to heat water for everything on the stove. You get used to it."

"Someday you're going to quit teasing me with these little sound bites and tell me what it was really like in the commune."

"Right. Granny Cooper tells tales of the olden days."

His face reddens. "I didn't mean it like that. I was just curious, that's all."

I turn and face him. "Everybody's just curious. It makes me nuts."

"There's curious and then there's curious, you know. I'm not a reporter for the *National Enquirer*. I'm curious about you, not about Ammonia or whatever the place was called."

I try not to laugh, but I do. "Armonía."

"Whatever. I like you, so I'm interested in how you got to be who you are. That's not so unnatural. Is it?" He moves toward me. One more step and we'll be in that zone where things happen.

"Sorry. Sometimes I overreact." I fold the dish towel and hang it over the pump.

We stand awkwardly on the porch. The sound of fireworks drifts up from the harbor, a series of short, sharp pops punctuated by a long, descending whistle. Bursts of light flash behind the trees like summer heat lightning.

I rub my arms. "Let me know what time you're leaving Wednesday so I can come down to the marina and wave a lace hanky as you sail away."

"I will," he says. "That would be a nice thing to see when we're leaving the harbor."

I lean toward him to bestow a friendly goodnight kiss on the cheek, but the little shit turns his head at the last minute. His mouth is cool and smooth and it produces a small shiver of pleasure. By the time my brain kicks in, his arms have slipped around me and we are trampling all over that crooked line between friendship and whatever comes next.

"Oops." His attempt to look contrite fails utterly. "Lost my head there for a minute."

I try not to sound breathless. "JT, I really think—"

"Don't, okay?" He kisses me again, and it's more serious this time, causing me to forget that he's nine years younger than I am, to disregard the proddings of common sense, to ignore the certainty that this can only end badly. The thought of Kirby Dolen's CD sitting on the coffee table just inside the door has already evaporated in the heat we're generating. If we could just stand here like this and kiss for about an hour, I'd go for it. But of course, that's not how it works.

Reluctantly I extricate myself. "JT, I can't do this. Not tonight."

"Okay. I'll bookmark the place." His hands rest lightly on my shoulders.

He's still grinning when he gets into the truck and the engine wheezes in the cool night. I go back inside, shut the door, and turn off the lights, but I stand at the kitchen sink watching the truck's taillights disappear up the driveway and feeling strange. Glad he was here. And very glad he's gone.

I sit at the kitchen table, open my laptop, and turn it on. I pop the CD in and close the player, boot up, and wait. In a few seconds I'm looking at a black-and-red dialog box that reads SECURED ACCESS. ENTER USER NAME AND PASSWORD.

I try Michael Graham and Bluedog, which was the password he used for his bank accounts. I try using his birthday and his cell phone number and his e-mail address. The machine beeps after each attempt and stubbornly displays the same answer.

I shut down the computer and take out the CD, worrying this thing in my mind like a new mosquito bite. Did Michael put it in my CD carrier? And when? And why? I suppose it could just as easily have been me on one of my cleaning binges, sweeping CDs off the coffee table and stuffing them absent-mindedly into the wrong cases. I've done it before.

And what should I do with it? Keep it? Send it off to Sergeant Bagley? Throw it in the fireplace and watch it melt?

I get up, put the CD in the metal file box, and climb in bed. I turn over a few times, yawn, a huge jaw-cracker, and pull up the covers. But I lie there for a very long time, eyes shut but still awake, seeing red letters burned into the black screen of my eyelids: USER UNKNOWN.

The Fourth of July holiday weekend is the unofficial apex of high season, and all those Californians Justin warned me about have arrived. The village seems like a different place, sidewalks thronged with people. The cafés are full from lunch to closing, and at night you can hear music and laughter from the boats anchored in the harbor. For island residents who don't derive their income from the hordes, this is a good time to go on vacation.

The *Princessa* sails on that first sunny Wednesday morning in July. Trish and Scott and I go down to see them off. Laura and Hallie are there, too, and some young things I don't recognize—I assume they're school friends of JT's. A few of the other marina rats stop by to wish them safe voyage. Bev Callender, the boat owner's wife, is there with Casey, their daughter. She looks about eighteen, and is blond, tan, leggy, and clearly peeved that she's not been invited along on this trip.

Pete Callender, who looks exactly as I expected—graying but fit, weathered from years of sailing, wearing a faded pink polo shirt, baggy shorts, and a giant black diver's watch—kisses the top of his daughter's head. "Next time, Kitten," he says, while she sulks and shrugs him off.

I was halfway hoping that Sarah Lakes might show up, although her grim-faced presence would probably have put a curse on the whole undertaking. JT seems not to notice. He seems not to notice much of anything except the boat as he runs around checking lines and winches and sails, and stopping every few minutes to look around and break into a helpless grin.

Finally they get everything lashed down and stowed below. People have brought presents—food and CDs and a stuffed dolphin. The kissing and hugging are over. Bev is snapping photos with her digital camera while her husband takes his place at the wheel and JT casts off the lines. Very slowly they start to motor away from the dock. I know, because he told me, that they won't put the sails up till they get outside of the harbor.

Scott and Trish are hollering, "Have a great trip, you guys! Have fun!"

Bev calls, "Be careful, you two. No wild wahines in the cockpit."

Casey forgives her father long enough to shout, "Bye, JT. Love you, Daddy."

My hand goes automatically to the medicine bundle. The thought of that tiny sailboat in the empty ocean somewhere between here and Hawaii gives me the same feeling I always get in a fast elevator. I was irrationally relieved to see that JT was wearing his black pearl earring.

I mean, this Callender guy looks in his fifties at least. He could have a heart attack. What if he keeled over in the middle of the Pacific? How could JT possibly sail the boat alone? I wish I knew if he has his appendix, because I read about some guy whose appendix ruptured a hundred miles from the nearest hospital in Fiji and he had to be airlifted off the boat. I've heard about pirates hijacking boats, killing everyone on board, and using the boat for drug smuggling. And shipping traffic. One of those huge container ships could squash them like a bug without even knowing it.

For a few seconds JT stops what he's doing and stands motionless on the deck, a line coiled in his hand, looking straight at me. He touches two fingers to his temple in an offhand salute, and gives me a crooked smile that makes me blush. I glance around surreptitiously to see if anyone's taking note.

Part Three

Sometimes the things that seem lost are only hidden, and they may yet be seen again.

WILLIAM deBUYS

Chapter 21

If Dr. Ralph Tomball lived in a city, he would have retired by now. He'd be on a golf course several times a week or sailing his boat or fishing at some mountain getaway. Instead, he's sitting behind a desk in a small white office that carries a faint smell of pipe tobacco and antiseptic in an old house now called The Harmony Clinic. Behind him is a huge window that looks out into the woods. Three different bird feeders hang from various tree branches and birds of all shapes and sizes mill around them. He sees me watching them and a smile crinkles his long face.

"Better than Prozac," he says with a glance over his shoulder. Then he stands up and reaches across the desk to shake my hand. "Ralph Tomball. Come in, sit down."

Mary Jo, his receptionist-nurse, looks about my age, but acts like a mom, plumping a pillow in the chair, offering a glass of water, which I decline.

"Okay then." She smiles, pushes her glasses back up on her nose, and closes the door behind her.

Dr. Ralph and I go through the small talk that I've learned is a prerequisite to every interaction on the island (where am I from?) followed immediately by the observation that I'm a long way from home (what am I doing here and how long do I plan to stay? And of course, how do I like the island?).

That out of the way, he opens a manila folder with a single sheet of paper inside, uncaps an old fountain pen, and gives me his full attention. "Why don't you start by telling me why you decided to see a doctor?"

I run through my litany of complaints while he scratches out notes—constant fatigue, sinus congestion, nosebleeds, headaches, peeing constantly, and low back pain.

"Any digestive problems?"

I shake my head.

"Have you been under any stress in the last few months?"

I choke out a laugh. "You could say that."

He waits, never looking away from me.

"The main thing is, my fiancé was . . . killed in April. And I just sort of . . . ran away from home."

"I'm sorry," he says. "That's a pretty fresh wound."

"So what do you think is wrong with me?"

He gets up and comes around the desk. "Before I go making any wild guesses, why don't we have a look first." He calls, "Mary Jo!"

The door springs open so fast I have to believe she was standing there with her ear pressed against it. "Let's get a urine specimen and some blood from this young lady and then you can get her set up in the examining room."

I pee into a plastic cup and Mary Jo draws my blood. Then I'm shivering in a faded cotton "gown" that gaps open everywhere while Dr. Ralph looks in my ears, eyes, nose, and mouth. He takes my blood pressure, listens to my heart from the front and my lungs from the back. He taps my knee with a little rubber hammer, making my leg kick out straight. He presses lightly on the lymph nodes under my jaw and under my arms.

Then he says, "When was your last period?"

"I don't know . . . about a month ago, I guess. I've never been very regular."

"When was the last time you had a pelvic exam?"

Just the sound of the words makes all my bodily orifices clamp shut. "A few years ago."

He calls for Mary Jo again and she appears in her nurse persona. "You're going to want to start getting a pap smear done annually," he says.

I decide not to tell him that's probably the last thing I'm going to want to start doing annually. He's clanking instruments around on a tray while Mary Jo slips little pink crocheted socks on my bare feet.

"Those metal stirrups are cold," she explains, smiling.

Very thoughtful. Too bad they don't have a little crocheted thing to take the chill off that speculum.

"Try to relax, Ms. Cooper."

Mary Jo shoots him an impatient look. "You just try to relax with a hunk of cold metal up your butt, Ralph. It's not that easy."

He looks at the ceiling while she and I laugh, and finally I do relax a little. After he's poked and prodded around to his satisfaction, he withdraws the torture device.

"Go ahead and get dressed," he says, "and I'll see you in my office."

I stand at the window, waiting for the doctor and watching a little red-breasted bird creep headfirst down a tree trunk, prying his bill into the bark. All around him, other birds are tanking up at the feeders or grazing as they make their way up the tree.

"Nuthatch," says Dr. Ralph behind me. "I love those little guys." He taps the window gently. "I wonder if it feels strange eating upside down."

"So what is it?" I say, impatient. "What have I got? Hepatitis? Mono? CFS? Bladder infection?"

"I see you've done some research. Please, sit down." His expression is serious, almost grave, and it's scaring me. "Actually, what you've got"—he sets my folder on the blotter—"is a baby."

"What?" The room tilts abruptly and I grab for the corner of his desk. In a second his hands are on my shoulders, guiding me back into the chair. Mary Jo materializes with a glass of water.

"Drink it slowly," he cautions as she vanishes back to the waiting room.

The glass is at my mouth, but I can't feel it. "Are you saying . . . ?"

"You're pregnant," he says.

"That's not possible." I hear the sharp whine of desperation in my voice. Beads of sweat are forming on my upper lip. "I mean . . . the last time I . . . it's been so long I can't even remember—and I was on the pill. Sort of."

But then I do remember. The Monday before Michael was killed. The night he came home late from playing poker . . . or whatever he was doing. I look up to find Dr. Ralph studying me. "April," I say weakly. "Mid-April."

He nods. "I was going to say twelve to fourteen weeks."

I look out the window again. All the birds are in motion

now, images swimming before my eyes. I can't pick out my little nuthatch. "But—wouldn't I have felt something before now?"

"Not necessarily. It's usual to experience nausea or breast tenderness or fatigue right away. Sometimes within a few days of fertilization. But it's certainly not unheard of to go as long as you have without symptoms."

"So the fatigue . . . ?"

"Yes."

"And the sinus congestion . . . ?"

"It's caused by higher-than-usual levels of estrogen and progesterone. They increase blood flow to all the body's mucous membranes. Unfortunately, including the sinuses—"

"But—"

"You've got the elevated levels of HCG—that's the pregnancy hormone—in your urine, and the size of your uterus is consistent with . . ."

I put my face in my hands and the tears pour out, hot and wet. For a while all I can hear is myself crying.

Dr. Ralph waits patiently, watching his feathered legions outside, while I run through half a box of his tissues. As my sniffles and hiccups begin to taper off, he comes around to sit on the edge of his desk. I look up at him.

"This is a pretty heavy load of news to dump on you, but I have to tell you one more thing, I'm afraid. I don't know how you feel about this . . . but if you want to terminate the pregnancy, it's your choice. The thing is, you're right on the borderline of the second trimester. There's a very, very small window of time here."

"How small?"

"I'd say next Friday at the latest."

I swallow and dab at my red eyes with a crumpled tissue. "I don't know what to do."

"You don't right now, but you will. And whatever you decide, it will be the right choice." He reaches for a card in his little cardholder made from a pair of glasses. "My exchange can reach me anytime, day or night. I hope you'll call me if you need anything. Even if it's just a friendly voice on the other end of the line."

I sit on Myron in the little four-space parking lot for the longest time, blank as a clean blackboard, and numb. I keep hearing his words: *A very, very small window of time.*

I heard those exact words one day in March. A Tuesday, I think. The Albuquerque Art Museum. I'd just dropped off some cookies and truffles for the Visual Arts Society board meeting and I decided to detour through some of the exhibits on my way out.

I wandered around for an hour, looking at Spanish Colonial paintings of saints and Madonnas, and ended up in a narrow, high-ceilinged room housing an exhibit on time-lapse photography.

Both long walls were lined with video screens, and you could push buttons to watch film and video clips, and read about the filmmakers. I stopped at a nature documentary screen, pushing the button over and over to watch a pink flower open into lush bloom on a barrel cactus, furred with dangerous looking spikes. It was mesmerizing, the way the bud unfurled while the voiceover described the "very small window of time" for desert plants to bloom. The rains had to come at just the right time, he said, or that year's bloom would be lost.

I drove home in a sort of trance. It was like one of those

computer games where you just steer and try to avoid hitting things while the scenery flashes past. A window of time. The idea embedded in my brain. He was talking to me. This was the feeling that had haunted me lately—so vague and ephemeral that I couldn't even be sure something was really there, much less identify it.

I'd find myself at odd moments thinking about people I knew at UNM and what they were doing now. It wasn't that I envied Ali her house in Cedar Crest and her husband who was gone all the time. It wasn't that I wanted to be Frankie, starving in New York, going to cattle calls, and finally landing a role in an Off-Off-Broadway production that probably paid next to nothing and yet demanded huge commitments of energy and time and passion.

It was more that they'd made their choices and I hadn't. I saw it so clearly—how I'd dreaded actually getting the life that I seemed to be forever chasing. How much easier it was to drift along in the present, hoping that if I didn't get too greedy, the gods might not notice how well things were going.

It was time, I decided, to reach out and take what I wanted.

But by then, other events were already in motion.

At 10:40 p.m. I escape to the break room, slump into a chair, and pillow my head on my arms. The table is covered with crumbs and smears of sauce and moisture from sweating glasses. A piece of spinach curls limply about two inches from my nose, but I can't make myself do anything about it. I feel like a million little grains of sand in a box—all of a piece, but not quite connected.

I'm almost in a doze when I hear the door shut and I open one eye to see Freddie slide into the chair beside me. She sets down a steaming cup of tea.

"For you," she says. Her smile is nervous. "For God's sake tell me what the doc said. I been watching you all night and you look like a zombie."

With great effort, I push myself into a sitting position and grasp the hot mug in my hands. "Thanks." I take a breathy sip.

A furrow appears on the bridge of her nose. "Is it bad news?"

I set down the cup and inhale deeply. "I'm pregnant."

"You're *what*? But how . . . I mean, how long . . ." She gives up and just stares at me.

I watch the steam rising from my tea. "Apparently, I was pregnant when I left New Mexico."

"No. *Way*." Her eyes sweep over me, looking for telltale bulges.

I smile. "That's pretty much what I said. Dr. Ralph says it's not unheard of not to have any symptoms till your second trimester . . ."

"What are you going to do?"

"I don't know, Freddie." My eyes are filling up again and I look away quickly, but she's already handing me a paper napkin. "I have till next Friday to make up my mind."

"Oh, swell. Plenty of time to think."

I flick the spinach leaf onto the floor. "I'm not sure having more time to think would be helpful."

"Sunny, if there's anything, I mean, *anything* at all . . ."

The door flies open, banging on the wall behind it, and Piggy glares at us. "Damn! I could've sworn I had four servers working tonight. Must've been my imagination, because there's only two on the floor."

I scramble out of the chair. The last thing I need right now is to get fired. "Sorry. I just needed to sit—"

"Oh, back off, Murphy," Freddie snaps. "She's not feeling good and I brought her a cup of tea."

"There's some people at your tables who'd probably like a cup of something."

She stands up and meets his gaze. "Yeah, well, if they can't take a joke, they're dinin' at the wrong establishment."

I manage to last out my shift. Freddie follows me around discreetly, checking with the customers at my tables, making sure they have everything they need—covering for me, in essence. I think I should be insulted, but I know her only intention is to spare us both the wrath of Piggy, and anyway, I'm beyond caring.

As we're clocking out, she leans closer. "Are you coming in tomorrow?"

"I don't know."

"You want me to run you home?"

"I'm okay, Freddie, but thanks. I'll be extra careful."

I say that, but in fifteen minutes I'm standing on my porch with no idea how I got here. I unlock the door and go in. The silence is total.

Sleep is out of the question even though I'm exhausted. I stoke up the fire in the stove and put the kettle on for tea. Then I walk around turning on all the lights. Then I retrace my steps, turning most of them off. When the kettle boils I make a cup of chamomile tea and stand at the window. After a couple of sips I take off my jacket and toss it on one of the kitchen chairs. A small stream of light spills out the window and onto the porch, but beyond that, the world is dark.

If there is a God, I think now would be an appropriate time to come forward. Sir or Madam, as the case may be, I could use a little help here. You probably don't know me; I don't remember ever calling on you before, because I always figured I should look out for myself and not bother you. I mean, since there were plenty of other people who needed help worse than I did. Until now.

I'm sure there's something I could do that would make sense, but I'm drawing a blank. So I'll try listening. I'll look for signs. Omens. Hints. Indications. Or specific instructions. Whatever works for you is fine with me.

I hang my jacket on one of the pegs JT hammered into the wall by the front door. I undress and brush my teeth and wash my face and climb into bed. I punch the pillows up behind me and reach over to turn out the light. The green numbers on the clock say it's 2:35 a.m. I breathe through my mouth, staring into the dark until my eyes adjust and I can see everything in the room. It will be daylight in three hours and then my eyes will have to adjust back. I scoot down a little, almost prone but not quite, and when I lean my head back, sleep comes quickly.

Birds wake me and I blink in the light. Noisy little buggers. Hallie and Freddie have tried valiantly to instruct me in recognizing their different songs. They can't understand why I don't feel compelled to learn the names of every bird, their songs, their habitat. Just to see them and hear them is enough for me. So maybe I don't know a scaup from a scoter or a wigeon from a pigeon, but to me, it's preferable to feeling like I'm working on some Girl Scout merit badge.

I lie drowsing, massaging the crick in my neck, and then I remember. My neck hurts from sleeping with my head propped up. I have to sleep that way because my sinuses are blocked. My sinuses are blocked because of excess hormones. Because I'm pregnant. I screw my eyes shut, but the tears force their way out. *Damn*.

The most frightening thing about imagining myself as a mother is not only what it would do to my life—and it would definitely change things—but also what I might do to a child's life. It suddenly occurs to me that at some point I must have decided not to want that . . . the way you decide not to want something you know you can't have. But now I'm having it. Whether I want it or not. Oh God.

I can't lie here and cry all day, tempting as it is. I use the hem of the sheet to blot my face, then get up and pull on my sweats and a T-shirt and head for the kitchen. There are still live embers from last night's fire in the stove.

I go through the motions of breakfast. Two soft-boiled eggs, toast, and coffee. In spite of everything, I'm hungry. I pour a second cup, add milk, and carry it outside along with the last scrap of toast. It's barely seven o'clock. The pond is gray and still; mist rises from the garden like breath. Strips of Mylar flash in the barely discernable breeze. Between them, the slivers of soap, the hair and garlic sachets twist slowly on a fishing line. The overall impression is of some otherworldly shooting gallery . . . like in a dream. And the deer don't seem to be deterred by any of it.

I sit down on the steps and put the cup down beside me.

Do I want to have a baby? Am I prepared to take responsibility for another life? Never mind whether I want to, am I capable of it? Strong enough, smart enough? Unselfish enough?

Or do I "terminate the pregnancy"? A good neutral term. Reminds me of Betsy and her "terrible situation." Intellectually, I believe in my right to choose. But there's my dilemma. If I have the right to choose, then the choice—and its consequences—are all mine.

The annoying buzz of my cell phone startles me and I fumble in my pocket.

"Hello, Ms. Cooper? This is Ralph Tomball." My heart jumps. He's calling to tell me it was all it a mistake. I'm not really—"How are you doing, Ms. Cooper?"

"I've been better."

"Yes, I imagine you have. That's why I'm calling. Just wanted to be sure you were okay. And to see if you have any questions for me."

I get up and carry my cup back into the kitchen. "Actually, I was wondering how—I mean, if I decided to . . . terminate the . . ." I sit down in a chair. "How is that handled? What's the procedure?"

"I'd want to send you over to Seattle. To a clinic run by a colleague of mine."

"So, it wouldn't be you doing it."

"Dr. Miller is a first-rate gynecologist. I've known her for twenty years." He pauses while I picture Dr. Miller. She'll have a kind face. Very clear skin with no makeup. Honey-colored hair pulled back in a French twist. "As to the procedure, there are two main ones that are used these days. Vacuum aspiration, which is a suction-type method, or dilation and curettage, which is commonly called D-and-C. The method would depend pretty much on the gestational age, and I'd want to have Dr. Miller making the final determination on that."

The clinic will be spotless, the reception area a soothing pale blue and hushed. The patients will be successful, independent women with good haircuts, looking sad but resolute while Bach plays on the sound system.

"Does it hurt?" I ask. The fingertips of my right hand are rubbing my lightning bolt scar. Just like Harry Potter, Hallie said a few days ago.

"It's more of a discomfort than actual pain," he says. "Dr. Miller doesn't like general anesthetic, and I would tend to agree with that, but she usually uses a local—"

"No," I say. "Not me. The baby—fetus. Does it hurt the fetus?"

He hesitates. "Nobody really knows the answer to that. As you can imagine, each side in the abortion debate has its own theories." When I don't respond, he adds, "I can drop off some information if you'd like."

"No. That's okay."

"What other questions can I answer?"

I draw breath. "I've got lots of questions, but I don't think you can answer them for me."

"Then I'll wait to hear from you."

I punch the End Call button and sit for a minute, turning my coffee cup around and around on the table. I didn't even thank him for calling.

"Sunny?"

"Yes." I'm curled up in a ball on my bed. My mouth is dry and my eyes are glued shut with sleep. I don't remember getting back in bed or even hearing the cell phone ring.

"It's Piggy."

"Yes."

He clears his throat. "Do you know what time it is?"

"No."

"It's four o'clock. Are you planning to come to work today?"

"I don't think so."

"You don't think so? Sunny, what the hell is wrong with you?"

"I'm pregnant."

The silence rebounds over the airwaves.

"You're . . . Tell you what, we'll call this a sick day. We can talk tomorrow, okay?"

"Maybe."

"You need anything? You want to talk to Freddie?"

"No thanks. I'll call you, Piggy. Bye." I shut the phone off and roll over on my back.

Shit. I'm done with this. With Michael. With New Mexico. With everything from before. It's supposed to be over. I just need to get past this. Get wherever the hell I'm supposed to be going.

I can. I still can. I can take the ferry over to Seattle and go see Dr. Miller. It can be a nonproblem in twenty-four hours. I can pick up right where I left off.

It's not cold, but I pull the blanket up to my neck.

I wake up at dusk, hungry.

There's not much in the refrigerator. A few dehydrated strawberries. Three eggs. Oil-cured olives. A head of romaine and a quart of milk. On the shelves I have rice and chicken broth cubes. In a few minutes, I've got a fire going in the stove and I'm putting together my favorite easy supper. This Greek guy who stayed at Armonía for a couple of weeks one summer showed us how to make it. He called it *avgolemono* or something, but I could never pronounce it right, so to me it was always chicken soup with rice, egg, and lemon. It's the perfect antidote for fatigue or too much alcohol or just the blues.

When I was living alone and had to work late or I came home hungry from a party, it was what I made myself to spoon up slowly, ensconced in front of the TV watching a Japanese monster movie. You just bring the broth to a boil, cook the rice in it, then at the last minute stir in a beaten egg or two, a squeeze of lemon, and a grind of black pepper.

In lieu of Japanese monster movies I have Eva Cassidy singing "Songbird" on the boom box. I sit in the living room, no lights on, the front door open. The sun is on the other side of the road now and night seems to hang above the tree tops, waiting to come down. There's something comforting about eating my soup in the dusky purple light with only Cassidy's pure, haunting voice for company.

At about 8:30 Friday morning, I'm shuffling around in my sleep shirt, still groggy, the green afghan wrapped around me like a nomad's robe. The coffee is ready, sitting on the back of the stove, but I'm so out of it I haven't poured any in my cup. And it hasn't registered that a car has driven up and parked out front until someone knocks on the door.

Trish. She's obviously trying out a new shade of blond on her hair. Her blue eye shadow matches her eyes and her blue T-shirt. She smiles at me.

"Did I get our appointment mixed up yesterday? I thought it was at eleven a.m., but . . ."

I pinch the bridge of my nose. "I'm sorry, Trish. I totally spaced."

"That's okay. I left a message on your voice mail . . ." She looks past me. "Can I come in?"

"Sure." I step back, catching a whiff of her musky perfume. "You want some coffee?"

"Thanks."

I pour two cups and we settle at the table.

"How are you feeling?"

I shrug. "About the same."

"Did you see Dr. Ralph?"

She knows. I can tell by the casual way she's not looking at me.

"You and Scott went to the Ale House last night and Freddie told you. Right?"

She puts her hand on my arm. "She was worried about you, that's all. Don't be mad at her."

I sigh. "I'm not mad at anyone. Except maybe myself. And Michael, that son of a bitch." My eyes flood with useless water. "What the hell am I going to do?"

"Well . . . I guess that depends on what you want."

"I'm so confused, I have no idea what I want. And I'm scared shitless."

"I know."

I frown at her. "No, you don't. You have no idea—all the things Michael was doing, things I never knew about and probably don't want to. Everything he told me was a lie. How am I supposed to feel about having his baby?"

"It's not just his baby," she says. "It's yours, too." She takes a sip of coffee, leaving a perfect pink lip print on the cup. "I want to tell you something. Something I never thought I'd tell any-one. Ever. In my whole life."

"So you're telling me because . . . ?"

"Because I think you need to know it. And because you don't talk a lot. And if you do tell anyone, I'll just drug you and color your hair chartreuse. Understand?"

"Got it."

"Now listen. I know you think I'm just a silly twit hairdresser—"

"Trish, I never—"

"It's what everybody thinks. Even people who've known me a long time. They've all forgotten that I had a full scholarship to Blakely College . . . in California. And then I was going to come back to UW for grad school. Oh, I had such big plans." She sits a little straighter.

"So what happened?"

"I didn't want to go to California. To be that far away from Scott . . . But my parents convinced me I should go, and my teachers said what an honor it was, so I went. And I was miser-able and lonely. And I met this guy. Richard Gordon. He was a junior. Sort of an intellectual—or what passed for one then. But the thing is"—she raises her eyes to me—"he looked so much like Scott . . . I sort of got involved; that sounds so stupid." She gives her head an impatient shake. "I thought I was in love with him. I mean, it was the best of both worlds, right? He looked like Scott, but he had . . . this intellectual bent. We talked about philosophy and literature and we drank brandy out of snifters. I know. It was incredibly shallow, but I was eighteen. I'd never been off the island. What the hell did I know?"

I stare at her. "What are you saying?"

"I found out I was pregnant after he dumped me, and I came home with my tail between my legs." She rests her chin on her hands. "Fortunately for me, Scott still loved me and we got married." She pauses. "And it was so lucky."

"That you got married?"

"That I got pregnant. Because Scott has a really low sperm count—"

"Trish . . ."

She smiles. "Too much information. I know. But what I'm trying to say is that we might never have had a baby if I hadn't gotten pregnant by Richard."

"Did Scott know?"

Trish inserts her thumbnail between her front teeth. "Maybe not at first—although Luke was born way too big to be premature, but then when I couldn't get pregnant again and we had all those tests, he knew. I was freaking out when we left the clinic, just waiting for him to start demanding explanations. You know what he said? He put his arms around me and he said, 'Just goes to show doctors don't know everything. And we can still have fun trying.'"

"You got yourself a bona fide saint."

She nods, but her expression is unsettled. "The trouble with ignoring the elephant in your living room is you never know when he might decide to take a shit."

I laugh for the first time in days. Then a thought occurs to me. "You mean Luke doesn't know?"

"It's never been discussed." She takes a sip of coffee and exhales slowly. "Did you ever think you wanted kids, Sunny?"

"Not really. For sure not like this. Not by myself."

"I never did, either. I was going to be an executive, a career

woman. I can tell you, it comes as quite a shock to the system the first time they lay that soft, squalling thing on your chest. So perfect and so tiny." She laces her fingers together. "When you love somebody that much, you can rationalize anything— even lying to them—in the name of protecting them."

"That's what scares me. I don't want to love anything that much." Suddenly tears are sheeting down my face. "I don't think I can."

"Of course you can, honey. That's what's so damn scary." She pulls tissues from the box by the sink and hands them to me.

So, am I thinking that I'm actually going to have this baby? I don't feel as if I've decided anything. I haven't made lists of pros and cons, I haven't read any books about childbirth or parenting. I haven't lain awake at night pondering the enormity of the question . . . I've been too busy just trying to breathe. But here I sit, feeling like I've chased down a train I wasn't even sure I wanted to be on and now, like it or not, I'm on board.

I blot my eyes with a soggy tissue. My coffee's stone cold. I dump it in the sink and pour both of us another cup. "Do you know anyone who sews?"

"Couple of people. You want to have some clothes made?"

"Yeah. And maybe a big scarlet *A* I could Velcro to the front of my T-shirts."

E-mails from JT.

They appear like magical flying fish out of the ocean when I sign in on the computer. He tells me about the Transpacific Diet—eat anything you want and still lose weight because it all ends up over the side. By the third day he's over that, and his commentary turns to fifteen-foot seas, learning to use a sextant, catching a twenty-pound fish, which he had to clean, and pouring a shot of Bacardi 151 over the side as an offering to Neptune. He says he misses me.

I keep my replies brief, crisp, and pen-pal casual. I talk about the weather, update him on the Deer Wars, and complain about the tourons. I try to think of questions to ask about the boat and the trip and what he's going to do in Hawaii, but it's hard—sitting here in the Ale House office, trying to sound interested and intelligent about something so far removed from my reality.

Not that reality has much to do with my life at the moment.

I seem stuck in a kind of Neverland where each day exists on its own, separate and distinct from the one before and the one to come. The lone thread that runs through it all, linking the days with loose stitches, is this entity who's taken up residence in my body.

My brain seems to have undergone some kind of experimental surgery that has rearranged everything. The past and the present have exchanged places. Things I thought were long forgotten are suddenly more accessible to me than where I've left my sunglasses.

At night I lie in the dark, listening to the night birds, the cottage's little creaking noises, the scuttling of raccoons across the porch. I listen till it all stops and there's nothing but silence. Silence and the soft sound of rushing memories.

Chapter 22

Summer, 1986. The world had changed since my parents first came to the mesa to create a new society. Ronald Reagan was president, business was big, greed was in fashion, and there were only two communes left in northern New Mexico. One was Lama, which had evolved into a kind of spiritual community. The other was Armonía, which had dwindled to a small group of diehards, led by Gwen and Boone.

Mari was dead. Rob was gone. Half the land had been sold off, along with all the cows, and Boone kept talking about selling the horses, too. Eventually it would come to pass, but Gwen persuaded the others to wait till Hart was gone. Besides the horses, the only animals we still kept were a dozen goats and the fifty-odd chickens. We made money from selling goat cheese, eggs, and vegetables at the farmers market. The alfalfa we raised was sold mostly to local ranches, and now a few people had day jobs in town and contributed their earnings into the pot.

I had turned fifteen in June. I would be a sophomore at the county high school in Taos in the fall, and Hart would be a senior at the Taos Free School. We were both restless. Every morning we hurried to finish our chores and then we'd saddle the horses and take off. It was a blistering hot summer, not much rain so far. We'd head for the mountains, for the relief of altitude and the shade of the woods. There was always that first moment when we crossed from the blinding sun into the cool silence, when the horses' steps were suddenly muffled by pine straw.

We climbed straight to the top first, moving as fast as we could between the trees, Hart in the lead. He knew the way even when the trail was lost in brush. He guided us around the deadfalls. He knew the places where we could still cross the river when it was swollen with snowmelt or summer rains. He showed me the scarred trees and told me the story he'd learned at the free school.

A long time ago, the Indians would peel off the orange outer bark of the Ponderosa pines to get at the cambium, the inner bark, which was full of sugars. They knew not to girdle the trees, because that would kill them. They just peeled a narrow vertical strip. The tree would keep living, he said, but it would always bear the scar where its skin had been peeled back.

At the top of the mountain we'd pause, looking out over the valley, the fields, marked by the acequias, the flanks of the hills slashed with dark canyons. A few scattered houses and barns, the curving wall of cottonwoods marking the river's path.

Then we'd turn and pick our way down along the stream to the place where a granite slab thrust up from the riverbed, slowing the water's flow so that it formed a perfect natural swimming hole. Well, we called it a swimming hole, even though it was only about three feet deep. That was fine with me, because I couldn't swim. It was the perfect place to pass the hot afternoons splashing and wading, lying on the rocks or picking berries and talking about the future.

"I'll be sad to leave here," he told me more than once.

"Fine," I said. "You stay here, and I'll go."

He gave me that sweet, sad smile of his. "Aren't you going to miss me?"

"Of course I will."

I would miss him. Terribly. My big brother was my best and only friend. He was the one who knew everything I knew, the one who had been through it with me; we two were the survivors.

"The thing is I don't know what I'm going to do."

"I think you should be a veterinarian."

He slapped water at me. "I'm tired of school."

"How would you know? That stuff they teach you about making bricks isn't real school." I splashed him in retaliation, sparking a major water battle, and after a few minutes we hauled ourselves out and collapsed, laughing and sputtering on the narrow ledge above the water.

"If I was a vet, you could come work for me," he said with his eyes closed.

"I thought you didn't want to go to school anymore."

"Just if I was, that's all. Maybe I'll be a dog trainer."

I sat bolt upright. "Hey, you could train animals for the movies. Or you could get a job with the circus, taking care of the animals. And I could come meet you in all the different towns. That would be so far out."

He opened one eye partway. "I don't want to travel all the time. Maybe I'll just have a farm. Raise horses or something."

"You are so fucking boring."

He looked hurt. "Don't say that word."

"Boring?"

"Ha, ha. Very funny."

"Gwen says it," I said.

"She's old. She can say what she wants. It doesn't sound right coming out of you." He turned his head toward me. "Am I boring?"

"No, flea brain. I was kidding."

"Are you sure?"

"Come on, you're my brother. I can't be too nice to you."

He put his arm back over his eyes and smiled.

While Hart and I cooled ourselves in the Rio Embuste, Kris Stanton was hitchhiking from Baltimore to Los Angeles. Through a conjunction of fate and timing he got picked up just outside of Nashville by Wally, who was on his way back to Armonía from visiting his mom in New Jersey. They sort of hit it off and Wally told him about Armonía and invited him to stop there for awhile. I was in the kitchen with Gwen when they walked in, shaking the dust off. I was glazing a loaf cake with honey and lemon juice, and I didn't bother to look up. People were always dropping in for dinner unannounced.

Then I heard Gwen say, "This is my daughter, Soleil."

Kris smiled at me almost shyly. I couldn't have said what color his eyes were at that point, but later I knew they were sort of a hazel. He was wearing jeans and work boots and a faded orange T-shirt, a wide leather band on his left wrist. His dark hair was long on the sides, tucked behind his ears, and he was holding a dirty black guitar case.

I think I said hi, and he said it was nice to meet me. That's all I remember before Wally led him away to find a place to sleep.

"He seems nice," Gwen said after they left.

"He was only here five minutes," I said. "How can you tell?"

She said, "Good vibes, that's how. I'm usually right about people."

Kris had lived a lot of places because of his father's job: Utica, Trenton, Philadelphia, Washington. He'd graduated from high school in Baltimore and gone to George Washington University, but he dropped out after his freshman year because he didn't see the meaning of anything he was supposed to be studying.

He told us all this at dinner that first night, pausing politely to look at each person around the table. When his eyes met mine, I felt my heart stall out and go into a dive. I wanted to look away, but for a few seconds I couldn't, and he went on talking about how he'd decided to go visit his cousin Jesse in L.A.

Dave mopped up some spaghetti sauce with a piece of bread. "Well, you're welcome here, brother. You can stay as long as you want, but if you want to stay more than three days, we'll ask you to help with the farm chores." This was what had been decided at the last commune meeting.

Kris nodded and said he was tired tonight, but he'd think about it and let us know tomorrow what he wanted to do.

I was up before dawn, pulling on my shorts and a clean T-shirt, my psychedelic American flag T-shirt that I got at the Taos Art Fair the previous summer. It had lately become a bit tighter across the chest, but I figured that was okay. I heard noise in the kitchen and I knew Gwen was up stoking the stove. But when I came through the doorway I saw Kris loading wood into the oven. He turned when he heard me. "I guess if I'm going to stay, I should start making myself useful," he said, smiling.

"That's great, but if you build a fire in the oven you'll smoke us out. The firebox is on the left."

He laughed, not at all embarrassed, and started moving the wood.

He built a fire while I filled the coffee pot with water from the pump. I poured milk in a pan and put it on the stove next to the coffee pot. I got out the honey and some clean mugs and spoons.

Then he said, "How long have you guys lived here?"

"Always," I said. "Hart was born in San Francisco, but I was born here."

"You mean here on the commune?"

"Right in there." I nodded toward the room Gwen now shared with Boone.

"Wow," he said. "It must be cool, growing up here."

I might have tried to disabuse him of that notion, but Gwen chose that moment to make her entrance. When she saw us, right before she smiled, I caught a glimmer of something in her eyes.

In a few minutes I was sitting on the cool sand by the river, holding the warm, sweet taste of coffee in my mouth and pondering the oddly pleasant feeling the thought of Kris produced—sort of a hollow sensation down low in my stomach. I wondered if he'd ever milked a goat—if he hadn't before, he probably had by now. That was the first thing Hart liked to show visitors. I wondered how old he was. If he had a girlfriend back in Baltimore. If he thought I was pretty. And I wondered if he was going to stay at Armonía.

Sure, he said he wanted to stay. But he could easily change his mind and slip away without even saying goodbye. He wouldn't have been the first. People were always crashing at

Armonía for a few nights, saying they loved it and wanted to become part of the family, and then you'd wake up one morning and they were gone. People who'd been around for months or even years were capable of going on a vacation somewhere and never coming back.

But Kris fit in well. He was a hard worker, kind of shy, not obnoxious like most guys that age, didn't drink much, would take a toke once in a while; everyone liked him. He worked with Hart some, but he didn't share Hart's devotion to "the critters." Kris was into building things. Tucson and Larry showed him how to make adobe bricks, and the three of them got busy rebuilding the greenhouse that had been damaged in a spring storm.

The plan was also to build a separate entrance to the greenhouse from the kitchen so you didn't have to go outside to get to it. Tucson was just about to put a sledgehammer through the kitchen wall when Kris diplomatically suggested that they wait to punch through until the repairs to the greenhouse were done; that way the kitchen wouldn't be full of dust and debris while they were working. Everyone looked at him like he was Einstein and agreed that, yes, it was a great idea.

So for the next week, Kris was always either just on the other side of the kitchen wall or down in the mud pit near the river, where they made the bricks. This was good and bad. I was thinking about him too much. So much that it stopped being something I did and became part of me, a hollow ache in my center. Sometimes, in the hot afternoons, Gwen would send me out with lemonade or iced tea. The guys would have taken off their shirts and I'd hand them the cups and try not to stare at Kris—his long torso, the way the low-rise jeans hugged his hips, his brown skin, smooth as river rock.

Always close, but he might as well have been on Mars. He seemed to appear in the kitchen only when Gwen was there. Several times I came in from the garden or the washhouse to find them deep in conversation. Working, eating meals, wading in the river, picking berries, going to town—there were always people around. It was almost as if he was trying to avoid being alone with me. I couldn't figure it out, because there were unguarded moments when our eyes would meet or I'd pass him a plate or a cup and his hand would brush mine accidentally, and my heart would tremble and sink. It was inconceivable to me that he might not feel it, too.

The only time I ever saw him alone was occasionally first thing in the morning, which was hard, because I was not by nature an early riser. In fact, the few times I managed to get up when Hart did, he'd give me a strange look and say, "What are you doing up?"

I'd shrug and say, "I just can't sleep."

He would laugh, his magical, wide-open laugh. "Coulda fooled me."

Of course, I wasn't fooling him. Or anybody else.

There was a peyote meeting scheduled for the last night in July, up near Questa. It was about an hour's drive up and then the meeting would go all night in the tipi. I'd been to my first one on Earth Day this past spring, and had no interest in repeating the experience.

For the July meeting, Hart volunteered to stay at Armonía and look after things. Gwen asked me if I wanted to stay with him, which I'd planned to do, but I let her think it was her idea. Then Kris said he would stay, too.

The caravan pulled out about three thirty in the afternoon. They'd get up there in plenty of time to visit with friends and prepare the food for the next morning, before the meeting started at sundown. Kris and I helped Hart with the evening milking, and then I went to the washhouse and took a shower while they sat in the shade and had a beer.

We cooked hamburgers out in the courtyard and I made a salad and we ate outside just as the sun was going down. They drank more beer and Hart gave me some of his. I didn't really like it that much, but I didn't want Kris to think of me as a little girl, so I'd take a sip and chase it with a bite of hamburger to kill the taste.

After dinner, we lingered around the glowing coals in the fire pit. Kris got out his guitar and strummed it softly without actually playing a song. Hart was nodding off, and I pulled my sweater around myself in the evening chill, mesmerized by the movement of Kris's long fingers, spiderlike, over the guitar strings.

"I always wished I had a brother or sister," he said suddenly.

My heart sank. Now he was going tell me that I was like the sister he never had.

"You two seem to get along great," he said.

Hart let out a little puttering snore and I giggled, clamping my hand over my mouth.

"He's my best friend," I said. "My only friend, actually."

"No girlfriends?"

I shook my head. "It's hard here. We're still the hippie kids. A lot of the locals still don't like us."

"Why not?" He frowned.

"Because their families have been here a long time and they

don't have much money. So back in the late sixties a bunch of Anglo freaks move in and start buying up the land . . . then all these crazy people are here, swimming naked in the hot springs and giving dope to their kids and having sex—" I stopped, feeling myself blush. "I mean basically we went against everything they believed in."

He quit playing. "I don't see a lot of that here. People seem to work pretty hard. I haven't seen anybody getting totally wasted."

"It's calmed down a lot since the old days. There were about twenty communes, and it was pretty wild then."

He considered it for a minute. "Still, I think I'd rather grow up in a place like this than the way I did: No sibs. Moving a lot. It takes me a while to get to know people; then every time I made friends with somebody, we'd move again. It got to where I didn't even try."

"You get along with your parents?"

"My dad's never home long enough for a major battle. My mom drinks too much when he's gone. Then when we're together . . . I don't know. We don't seem to have much to say. I remember a lot of long, quiet dinners."

I smiled. "I'd kill for a long, quiet dinner. Here there are always people around, too many strangers."

"I'm a stranger," he said.

Suddenly Hart regained consciousness and sat up. "What's going on?"

"We were just listening to you snore. Kris was accompanying you on the guitar." I got up and started picking up our plates.

Hart rubbed his eyes. "I'll take these cans to the recycle bin."

Kris followed me into the kitchen. "I'll dry," he said.

I poured hot water from the teakettle into the dishpans,

then pumped a little soap and cold water in to one of them, scraped the leftover salad into the compost bucket, all the time feeling him watching me.

"How old are you?" he asked me.

I didn't look at him. "Sixteen. Why?"

If he knew I was lying, he didn't let on. "Just wondered. You don't seem as silly as a lot of girls I know."

I set the plates in the soapy water and swished the dishcloth over the top one, wondering how many girls he was talking about and what he meant by silly.

"If I'd grown up in a normal place, I'd probably be just like everyone else." I finished washing the plates and laid them in the rinse pan. "That's what I always wanted."

"It must be hard right now," he said. "Maybe later you'll be glad you grew up here."

This conversation wasn't going the way I hoped. "You don't have to dry these. I'll just let them drain overnight."

"I don't mind," he said.

"Fine. I'm going to bed." I turned quickly, headed for the dark refuge of my room. I didn't bother lighting the kerosene lamp; I just slipped out of my shorts, unhooked my bra and pulled it out from under my shirt, and slid under the covers. A while later Hart came in and undressed in the dark.

"Sunny?" he whispered.

I didn't answer.

I heard car doors slam. Then voices. I tried groggily to figure out what they were saying. Then I sat up in bed gasping, wide awake. Everyone was gone. No one was supposed to be coming home tonight.

"Hart!" I jumped up and reached for my jeans, hanging on

the back of the chair. "Hart, wake up! Someone's in the court-yard."

"Hunh?"

"Get up. Listen."

The voices were louder now. One of them was singing.

"Bunch of drunk motherfuckers," Hart bolted from bed, and I heard him pulling on his clothes. "You stay here," he said.

"No way." I fumbled with the matches, lit the lamp, and we crept out to the Circle Room. The singer was doing a very off-key rendition of "Whiskey River, Take My Mind." Another voice hollered, "Wake up, longhairs! Let's party! Where the fuck is everybody?"

Hart shushed me. "If they can't find anybody, maybe they'll go away."

"Sure." My voice sounded amazingly calm, but my knees were shaking. This had happened more than once at other communes on the mesa, although not in a while. A bunch of drunks would show up on Saturday night and, finding only a couple of caretakers, they'd trash the place and set a few fires. Just to let the hippies know they weren't welcome. Occasionally people got beat up, and once or twice women had been raped. "Where's Kris?" I said.

"In Tucson's room."

Shit. That was in the other building, at the opposite end of the compound.

Hart leaned over and blew out the light, opened the door just enough to peer out. A pickup truck sat in the courtyard, headlights illuminating a wheelbarrow full of adobe bricks. Two guys were urinating on them. I couldn't see anyone else.

They finished their business and started walking around

the courtyard. One of them tripped over something and swore. "Place is a fucking pig pen. How'd ya like to live here?"

"Maybe they moved out."

Hart said casually, "No, we haven't moved out. Everybody's asleep. So we'd appreciate it if you guys would be quiet." His voice echoed in the dark.

"Hey! Where the fuck are you?"

"Turn on the goddamn lights, why don't ya."

Hart stepped outside and I was right behind him. The night chill made goose bumps on my bare arms.

One guy held up a six-pack. "We came to party with y'all."

"That's real nice of you," I said. "But we worked in the fields all day and everyone's tired."

"Hey, it's a girl. What's your name, hon?"

"Well, for starters, it's not 'hon.'"

Hart poked me.

The other one slapped his thigh. "Ain't she a pisser?"

The first one started toward us, and Hart stepped in front of me. "You're probably as tired as we are, so I think you guys should go home now."

The two looked at each other. One had on a cowboy hat. "You tired, Ed?"

"Nope. You?"

"Nope. In fact, I always wanted to see inside one of these places. See how pigs live. Hey, you guys got any of that funny tobacco?"

My throat was starting to close up.

Hart said, "Look, if everybody else wakes up, there's gonna be a problem, so why don't you—"

"Listen, boy"—now I could smell the beer; shit, it smelled

like they'd taken a bath in it—"I heard there's a big peyote meeting tonight and I bet all your long-haired buddies are up in that tent in Questa pukin' their guts out."

"That leaves you and Miss Honey here mindin' the store," the bareheaded one said. "So Bobby and me thought you might need some company."

"Thanks, but we've got all the company we can use right now." They both spun around trying to see where Kris's voice had come from.

"Now where the hell are you, sonny?"

"The only thing you need to know is that I'm holding a thirty-thirty and it's aimed right at your Stetson." His voice was pitched low.

The two beer-necks hesitated. Then one laughed. "You're so full of shit, sonny."

A sharp crack was the next sound, along with the shattering of the truck's back window.

"What the fuck?"

The boys were suddenly falling over each other to get into the truck, one hollering that we owed them a new window, the other bellowing that we owed them a new truck.

Sand, dirt, and gravel plumed as they backed up, turned around, and peeled off, scraping the edge of the bumper as they shot through the arched gate.

That's when my knees gave out and I sat down hard on the wooden stool by the door.

Hart was looking around. "Kris? Where are you?"

"Over here. On the roof."

In a few seconds he was beside us. Hart studied him, eyes narrowed.

"Where'd the gun come from?" I said.

"It's Tucson's hunting rifle," Hart said. "You better put it back."

Kris nodded, but I looked at my brother, surprised. "Geez, of course he'll put it back. Meantime, he just saved our butts."

"I guess it's good you know how to use it." Hart's tone was grudging.

Kris said, "I've never shot a gun in my life. I was aiming at the side mirror."

There was a bare second of silence before the three of us doubled over, laughing with giddy, hysterical release.

I told Gwen the story the next day when they all came home. I don't know what I expected. That maybe she'd hug me tight and say thank God you weren't hurt. Or that she'd thank Kris. Or that she'd rant about the ignorant assholes and threaten to call the sheriff.

Instead, she gave me a quick little one-armed squeeze, took a giant industrial-size can of tuna fish out of the pantry, and started making tuna salad for lunch. Finally she said, "Well, I wondered what all the tire tracks were from. And the gate— looks like they took a chunk out of it. You missed a good meeting. Lots of people from Morning Glory showed up. Sage said to say hi. Her mom's in law school at UNM now. Would you fill that big plastic container and make some sun tea?"

Everything that happened after that would probably have happened anyway; our tangle with the beernecks just speeded it up. After all, I was a fifteen-year-old girl who read novels, and suddenly there was Kris Stanton, gun blazing, saving us from the bad guys—even if he wasn't the best marksman in New Mexico. That put him about as close to a romantic hero as I was likely to see at Armonía.

I never doubted that if either one of those guys had laid a hand on me, Hart would have jumped on him like a wildcat. But it would never have occurred to my brother to pick up a gun to defend me . . . or himself, or anyone else. Kris Stanton—the stranger, the outsider—had to step up and do it for him. Things were never quite the same after that night. A distance sprang up between Hart and me. We both preferred not to see it, but it was definitely there, a vacuum that Kris came to fill.

The moon was about three-quarters full and the rabbit brush shimmered like silver between the dark clumps of grass and stunted junipers. The air smelled of sage and the river, and it made me high. I wanted to run, but I had to walk slowly, keeping an eye out for snakes and rocks. One hand shined a little flashlight on the path; the other rested in my jeans pocket on the plastic wrapping of the rubber I'd stolen from the box under Hart's bed.

Kris was waiting by the river. I walked up to him and for a minute we just stood together, holding hands, watching the moonlight flash where it touched the water.

"Sunny . . ." His voice cracked and he coughed a little bit and then tried again. "Are you sure you . . ."

"Of course. Why else would I be here?"

When he reached for me, the whole world went up like a brush fire in a hot wind.

We finally stopped for breath, and he bent his head to my shoulder. Wait," he said. "Wait. I have to think. We have to be careful."

"I don't think I can," I said.

He looked at me very seriously. "You have to. Unless you want to be bringing me a cake with a file in it."

"What?"

His smile had that unbearable sweetness—like Hart. "It's an old movie cliché. The guy's in jail and his girlfriend brings him a cake with a metal file in it so he can cut through the bars."

I turned my face up to his. "You want chocolate or vanilla?"

He'd brought blankets, and he spread one on the ground and pulled me down next to him. He reached into the pocket of his flannel shirt the same time that I reached into my jeans, each of us producing a condom in its crackly wrapper, and we shared a nervous laugh. I found myself wondering how many he'd used on his trip. But I forgot about that and everything else when he started unbuttoning my shirt—Hart's shirt, actually, and that thought distracted me for about a second. Did he suspect? He'd been snoring his little motorboat snore when I tiptoed out of our room in the dark.

I sat motionless, looking down at the blanket while Kris carefully undid each button then pulled the shirttails out of my jeans.

"You haven't done this before, have you?"

I looked up quickly. No use lying. He'd know soon enough. "No," I said.

"I'll try not to hurt you, but it probably will. A little bit."

"I'll be okay. Just tell me what to do."

"You're so pretty," he said.

Nobody had ever said that to me. Except Rob, and that didn't count. The guys at school I'd met at the movies in Taos and kissed in the dark—their idea of romance was *Hey, come on, Sunny, let me just put it in for a minute. I promise I won't come.*

I took a careful breath and held it along with those words. *Pretty. You're so pretty.*

He said, "Why don't you take off your jeans. It'll be easier."

I did and then shivered in the dark, watching him undress. I wanted to touch his flat, smooth stomach, but I was too afraid of doing something stupid, so I sat there while he kicked off his boots and peeled off his jeans and lay down. I was shaking.

"Are you cold? Come here." He pulled another blanket over us, but it didn't matter, because as soon as our bodies touched, skin to skin, I wasn't nervous and I wasn't cold. I was overwhelmed by the rightness of it, and thrilled by the way his breath would catch when I touched him.

It did hurt, but only for a minute, and he waited, letting me get used to the feeling of him inside me and then we started to move together. At some point I opened my eyes and saw, over his shoulder, a falling star. It was a sign.

Afterward, he held me, rubbing my back and talking softly. He told me about his parents, how they still lived together but had separate lives. He talked about college, how he'd always thought that maybe when he got to GW he'd figure out the problem with his parents, along with the rest of life. But before long he was lonely and restless again.

"When I got on academic probation, I didn't know what to do. I didn't want to go back to Baltimore and live at home, so I called Jesse and she said I could come and stay with her for a while. Till I figured out what to do."

There was a slight disconnect when I realized that Jesse was a girl. Was she really his cousin? But I didn't say anything. He asked me if I had any plans, and I told him my only plan was to get out of Armonía.

"At least you have that," he said.

For one minute the future opened to me and I saw him wandering around the country, hitchhiking with his guitar, like the weary pilgrims who were always turning up here, thinking this was it, the place they'd been looking for . . . until something happened. They got dumped by their lover or there was a disagreement about work or somebody told them about a place not far away where the living was easier or more fun or just warmer. Then they were back on the road.

Kris would leave Armonía; it was only a question of when, but that was okay. I would still have this, and it was mine alone, shared with no one but him. Tonight. With the river running quietly at our feet and the stars falling down.

Chapter 23

The living room of Piggy and Laura's cabin is strewn with fat pillows and cushions supporting women's bodies in varying states of repose. Laura is pouring boiling water into a teapot full of chamomile tea bags, although most everybody is drinking wine at the moment. Everybody but me, of course, because *I'm pregnant.*

By now, it's common knowledge. I'm certain of this, although no one has actually said anything to me. But their smiles are too cheery, and the simple question *How are you?* feels loaded with subtext. They look me in the face when they speak to me, but their eyes keep furtively darting to my boobs (Are they huge yet? I wouldn't say *huge*) and my stomach (Is it showing yet?) I leave my jeans undone and wear big shirts.

Freddie is shuffling the pages of her manuscript while Barbara nibbles a tortilla chip. The front door opens and Trish appears with a Saran-wrapped plate of cookies. She sets the plate down next to the ginger espresso cake I brought and unzips her nylon windbreaker. "Freddie, what's this I hear about you going to Mexico?"

"It's true, darlin'. Just got to work out a few minor details.

Like getting Piggy to give me a week off before September thirtieth."

"When did all this happen?" Trish lowers herself onto the couch and accepts the glass of white wine Laura passes her way.

"Oh, lordy, must be a month ago now." Freddie's told the story a dozen times since it happened, how the guy in the Tommy Bahama shirt came back to the Ale House and gave her vouchers for a vacation in Puerto Vallarta after his girlfriend walked out on him, but she launches into it again, with gusto, embellishing the details for those who weren't on site at the conflict.

"She actually threw food at him?" Trish says. "How come I always miss all the excitement?"

"Shoot, yeah. I haven't seen such cussin' and carryin' on since Grandpa slammed his dick in the outhouse door."

Heather appears from the bathroom. "Freddie, all she did was call him a pig. Every time you tell the story, it gets more sensational." She tosses her hair back over her shoulder. "Laura, can I smoke?"

"Sure. Just don't exhale."

"Sensational." Freddie lowers her eyelashes. "That's what Amber Kincaid is all about, ladies."

Barbara pops a Diet Coke. "So, Freddie, have you got some more to read us?"

"I do. You're gonna love this chapter, too. It's got more pumping and thrusting than your average internal combustion engine."

Laura sits down next to Hallie. "Before we get to the sex, ladies, we have a few other things on the agenda." She smiles apologetically in my direction. "Sorry, Sunny. This won't take long. But feel free to jump in if you have any ideas."

Barbara and Heather boo and hiss, but Laura silences them with a look. "This is the first meeting of the production committee of the Harmony Players. Unfortunately, Tracey's got a bad cold, so I asked her not to come. She'll give us a financial report at the next meeting, but suffice it to say, there's not a lot to talk about in the financial department. We have only enough money in the treasury to do one play, so I've asked Hallie, as our resident literary authority, to come up with some suggestions." She looks at her sister. "Hallie?"

"After much research and pondering, I have only one suggestion. So if you guys don't like the idea, we'll have to drop back and punt, but I think we should do *Our Town*."

"*Our Town*?" Barbara makes a face. "I think we should do a musical."

"Can I explain my rationale before we throw things open for debate?" Hallie's voice is testy. "*Our Town* is an American classic. At the same time, it's very nearly avant garde, because of the simple, stark staging. Which dovetails rather neatly with our simple, stark financial situation—we don't have a lot of cash for fancy costumes, sets, and props. Also, it's got good name recognition, and because it's been around so long and been produced so many times, it's fairly inexpensive to acquire the rights." She levels her gaze at Barbara. "Any discussion?"

"Nobody's going to pay good money to see *Our Town*," Barbara grouses. "It's been done to death. A musical would have more pizzazz."

"That's assuming you can find people who can actually sing and dance," Trish says.

Barbara sits up taller. "Well, I know some people who can."

"Barb," Heather's voice is surprisingly gentle. "You can't do all the parts by yourself."

"Plus a musical would be more expensive and a lot more time-consuming to stage," Laura says. "Personally, I like *Our Town*. And it's a play that parents could bring their kids to see."

"Could we tinker with it?" Trish asks. "You know, they're always doing different stagings of old plays. Like when they did one of those old operas and everybody was dressed like the forties."

"I don't know if we want to be changing the era," Hallie chews her lower lip. "A lot of the dialogue is time-specific. But we might be able to come up with something to give it a little twist."

Barbara grimaces. "Like we could have it take place on Pluto and everyone could dress like ET."

"Let's see hands," Laura says. "Everyone for *Our Town*?" All the women raise their hands except Barbara.

"Does this mean that you don't care to participate?" I detect a note of hopefulness in Hallie's voice.

"No, it just means I dissent."

"Duly noted," says Laura. "The next order of business is thinking up some new ways to promote the production. Something besides the usual press releases, posters, public service announcements, yada, yada, yada. Something that will reach more people. And motivate them to buy tickets. Something a little more . . . professional."

At this point I realize that six pairs of eyes are focused on me, and I suddenly understand why I was invited to this gathering. I swallow the orange shortbread cookie in my mouth.

"What have you got in mind?"

"We were hoping you could tell us," Laura says.

"I don't know anything about promoting plays."

"You've been living in a big city," Trish says. "You've done commercials."

"True." I take a sip of tea from the delicate china cup. "But I don't plan campaigns and I don't write spots. I just take the scripts they hand me and read them into a microphone."

"I told you she wouldn't know anything," Barbara says.

Hallie shoots her a poisonous look. "But at least you know what other groups are doing," she says to me. "We thought you might be able to give us some idea of what works."

"Maybe you could record some spots," Heather says.

"I could, and I would. But I doubt seriously that the sound of my voice is going to generate a big audience for you."

Laura reaches behind her for the chips and salsa and sets them on the coffee table. "At least it would sound professional—not like the ones we always do. I mean, we have fun doing them, but they sound so dorky."

Trish licks salt off her thumb. "We always have a booth at the fair. With posters and flyers. We raffle off tickets . . ."

The teacup clinks against the saucer as I set it down. "Laura just said that you guys have fun doing your own spots. That sort of confirms something I've always thought—that inside most people there's a voiceover artist trying to get out. So instead of getting me to do a 'professional' voiceover, why don't you let people in town do it?"

Hallie slaps her thigh, nearly spilling her wine. "At the fair!"

"How do we do that?" Trish says. "Don't you have to be in the studio to record?"

"Not anymore," I say. "These days all you need is a mike, headset, and a laptop. I'm sure the radio station could do it if they're willing—"

Laura says, "Brendan can go over there and talk to Joe. What would we need him to do?"

"I was just thinking about this contest that one of the rock stations in Albuquerque did. Anyone could make a tape and send it in. They chose the best ones and let each winner be the morning drive-time DJ for an hour on Friday morning for a couple of months."

I nibble on my cuticle. "How about this: if you can get him to set up a little recording area in your booth, then, instead of raffling tickets—or maybe in addition to raffling tickets—you sell people the chance to audition. Maybe five bucks for adults, two for kids. And the best ones get aired as promos for the play."

"Who decides which ones are the best?" Barbara asks.

"I don't know. You guys. Or the radio station staff. Or . . ."

"Since it's a community effort, why not let the listeners decide," Hallie says. "They can e-mail their votes to the station."

Suddenly everybody's talking at once, converging on the card table by the window to fill their plates with veggies and dip, cheese, crackers, cookies, nuts, pretzels—all pretense of etiquette abandoned. While I'm refilling my teacup, Heather stands next to me, frowning, rummaging in her hot pink leather backpack. "I have *got* to have a cigarette. Right now."

"Outside." Trish lays her arm across my shoulders. "Sunny's breathing for two, and she doesn't need your secondhand smoke."

A pause ensues that can only be described as pregnant. I

feel the twin spots of color in my face, heat prickling my scalp. I can't believe I've got six more months of this ahead of me—being treated like some hothouse flower. Heather raises her eyes briefly and continues to dig for her cigarettes.

"Which brings us to the second half of the program," Laura says. She disappears around the corner into the kitchen and comes back rolling a small white crib full of packages wrapped in pretty pastel paper and ribbons. *Oh. God.*

I stare at it for a second too long and my whole body goes cold. Six faces are turned toward me, uncertain smiles, hopeful eyes.

I find my voice somewhere in the back of my throat. "You shouldn't have done this."

Trish says, "Of course we should. We're your friends and we—"

Freddie inserts herself. "We knew you wouldn't want a fuss, but you're going to be needing things, Sunny. We just want to help."

They wait in silence for me to redeem myself. *Why can't I be happy? Shit, why can't I at least be grateful?* I choose my words carefully. "I think . . . I haven't quite gotten used to the idea yet, I guess. But thank you all so much for . . . this."

Their disappointment is palpable; I've blown it.

"We understand," Hallie says quickly, "and you don't even have to open the presents right now if you don't want to. Let's just eat and listen to Freddie's chapter, and it'll be a regular girls' night out."

I take a deep breath and force a smile. "No naming games or guessing how many jelly beans in the baby bottle?"

"Never even crossed our minds." Laura smiles encouragingly.

Freddie squints into a nearly empty pack of Virginia Slims. "Heather, let's go outside and blacken our lungs. Then I can read the latest installment."

Hallie smiles and empties her glass. "I thought you were supposed to smoke after sex, not before."

Freddie has volunteered to drive me to the clinic in Seattle. Dr. Ralph and Mary Jo are adamant about my having an ultrasound, since I didn't even know I was pregnant. I'm concerned about the cost, but Dr. Ralph assures me that Dr. Miller's fees are based on a sliding scale taking into consideration your ability to pay.

"Guess that means this one's on the house," I grump.

"It will be, if necessary," he says, unperturbed. "Meanwhile, you need to get busy and fill out those assistance applications."

Just what I always wanted to be: a welfare mother.

Turns out Mary Jo is a certified nurse-midwife and she'll be my "birth practitioner"—lots cheaper than an ob-gyn. She was surprised and thrilled to find out that I was delivered by a midwife myself. She says, "The ultrasound is just a little insurance. Not having to worry about all the what-if's will make for a happier and more relaxed pregnancy."

Happy and *relaxed* are not words I associate with pregnancy. In fact, underneath my grouchy exterior lurks a black tide of panic made worse by the memory of Gwen's experience with Mari.

That summer was hot and dry and still.

The thunderstorms that usually brought afternoon relief during that season had been absent from the mesa. Every day we watched the clouds pile up in the West, turning from white to an ugly bruised color, lightning, thunder, and then curtains of rain hanging in the air, evaporating before they touched the ground. Gwen's feet and ankles were fat and rubbery by afternoon, full of fluid that never seemed to go away no matter how many times a day she peed. I recall with a four-year-old's selective memory that she was tired all the time and "mean."

And then, at 8:30 a.m., on August 19, I wandered out to the kitchen in my pajama top to see her standing in a puddle, crying. Her water had just broken. I couldn't have known that her tears were from relief and happiness at finally being in labor. She sent Hart out to the fields to get Rob, and Wendy ran down to the shop to call Señora Aurelia, the midwife.

I have only a few memories of the day. The terrifying noises coming from Gwen's bedroom, my absolute certainty that she would die, Rob asking Boone to take me somewhere.

Boone put me in the Dream Machine and drove to Taos while I cried and called for Gwen. He bought ice cream, which I wouldn't eat. He put me on a pony that some friend of his had tied up at the feed store and walked me around town while I cried some more. Finally he gave up and drove back to Armonía.

The circle room was quiet when we came in, till someone blurted out that Rob had taken Gwen to the hospital. I started to scream, and Boone scooped me up, holding me against his chest.

"Don't cry, Soleil. Everything's all right. Your momma's okay. She has to finish having the baby at the hospital so the doctor can help. She's gonna be fine. Hey, let's see if we can find Hart. Where d'you think we should look? Maybe the barn? I bet he's down there with the horses. Come on, let's go find him."

He turned and ducked through the low doorway, walked toward the barn in measured strides, with me still sobbing and squirming in his arms.

A week later Gwen returned, looking tired but radiant and holding the most beautiful baby ever born in New Mexico. Because of her breech position, which had necessitated the C-section, Mari's face and head never endured the trauma of the birth canal. Rob explained to Hart and me that our little sister Mari had been in Gwen's tummy the wrong way and that the doctor had had to cut her open to get the baby out. I was confused, grossed out, and thoroughly pissed off at that baby.

That evening, when Hart and I were finally allowed in the bedroom, Gwen was propped up against the pillows, nursing Mari. All I could see was a tiny head covered with pale fuzz. I stood aloof at the foot of the bed, arms folded, trying to decide if I wanted Mari in the family or if I should suggest we send her back and get one that was less trouble.

Gwen smiled at me. "Come closer, Soleil. Don't you want to see her?"

I inched around to the side.

"Pull the blanket down a little so you can see her face."

I stepped up next to Hart and reached for the blanket. At that moment, Gwen's nipple slipped from the little sucking mouth. The baby's flailing hand brushed my pinky finger and locked on to it while her huge blue eyes gazed calmly into mine.

"She knows you," Gwen said. "She knows you're her big sister and you're going to take care of her."

• • •

Freddie and I leave the Dodgemonster on the car deck and head upstairs. On this early sailing, it's mostly business commuters, who huddle over their laptops and newspapers in the café, leaving the aft deck to us. The morning is clear with a cool wind, and we stand at the rail sipping our drinks—a latte for her, the last installment of the required thirty-two ounces of water for me—and watching the boiling white foam under the stern of the ferry. There's an air of unreality about this whole expedition, especially when I recall my arrival in Harmony, not all that long ago. The sense of relief, the certainty that the past was lying dead by the side of the road somewhere behind me.

"You haven't told your momma yet, have you?" Freddie says above the engine noise.

"There's a lot of people I haven't told yet."

"You're going to tell her, aren't you?"

"Yes."

"When?"

"When I get ready."

Her pink iridescent fingernails make a light tapping sound on the metal railing. "Just from a purely practical standpoint, you should. She might know stuff that you need to know."

I look back at the marina, still quiet in the early morning, the masts making long shadows across the boats and piers. I think about JT, somewhere in this same ocean. I'm sure there's a lot of work to do when you're sailing, but somehow I just picture him standing at the wheel—the helm, he informed me—smiling, tan, the wind blowing his curly blond hair. And then I picture him back in Harmony. Standing on my front porch. *Home is the sailor, home from the sea.* When it comes time to picture telling him that I'm pregnant, the picture starts to break up and fade to black.

"Genetic stuff," Freddie says. "About your family. Her parents and your daddy's."

"She was hardly speaking to her parents, and she never met Rob's. Both of his died before he was out of high school."

"Yeah, but what did they die from? Like heart attack or stroke or—"

I burst out laughing. "Freddie, for God's sake, I worry enough as it is without you suggesting additional topics."

She leans out over the rail and the breeze ruffles her bangs. "So you're pissed off at your momma."

"It's a gross oversimplification, but I suppose you could say that."

"Why?"

I don't answer, but that doesn't seem to faze her.

"Come on. What did the woman do to you? Beat you? Starve you? Make you take violin lessons?"

"It's too complicated to explain."

"Just try for a minute. Pretend your momma's standing right here where I am and she says, 'Sunny, I want to know exactly why you're so pissed off at me.'" She raises her eyebrows. "What do you say to her?"

"One of us is going overboard."

She shakes her head. "Hey, how about this: pretend you wrote a book about your fucked-up childhood and you gotta have a one-sentence description for the talk show host." She pulls a hairbrush out of her purse and holds it like a microphone. "Tell us, Ms. Cooper, just what your new book, *My Fucked-Up Childhood*, is all about."

"Okay. My parents and their friends were too busy remodeling the world and getting stoned and making love not war to notice what was going on with their kids. All those little things you're supposed to learn from your parents. Basic things like how to dress yourself, and when. Personal hygiene. How to tell time. All that boring stuff." I turn to face her. "And little things everyone takes for granted, like nursery rhymes and fairy tales . . . You learned 'Mary had a little lamb'; I learned 'One, two three, four, We don't want your fucking war.'"

I can tell she's trying not to laugh. "That's more than one sentence, but that's good. Listen, I know lots of women, and every single one's got some kinda issues with their momma. There was a lot of bad feelings between me and my momma, too. For a long time."

"About what?" I jump at the chance to turn the conversation away from Gwen and me.

"About Daddy. About men in general, and what women were allowed or not allowed to do. About religion. I was the evil daughter. Ginger, my sister, she was the good one."

"But you get along with your mother now?"

"Better than we used to, for sure. I called her up one day and invited her to come up here and see me—"

"Gwen would never come up here. She doesn't leave the mesa."

"I didn't think my momma would come, either. The only place she ever went in her whole life was Dallas—once for her honeymoon and then when my cousin Faith-Anne got married. But when I invited her to come here, she was just about on the next plane out of Lubbock."

"When was that?"

"Last July. She stayed for a week. At first it was kinda weird, but then, little by little, we got used to each other again and we started talking. I think it was the first time she and I were ever together for any length of time without Daddy or my sister or my aunts and uncles or somebody else being around. It made a big difference."

"Like how?"

"Like the kind of things we said to each other. She talked about Daddy like he was a real person, not the Head of the Family. She left off all that crap about how we owed him obedience because he was to the family like Jesus was to the Church. That's the kind of stuff I grew up with."

"Gwen and I've had plenty of time for girl talk. It hasn't helped."

"You still need to tell her she's got a grandbaby on the way. It doesn't seem right for her to not even know."

"I'll tell her. I just need to be a little more comfortable with the whole idea myself first."

She grins broadly. "Well, that's starting today. When you find out if you've got a boy or a girl. I'm excited as a flea in a dog house!"

"Good that one of us is." I fold my hands on the rail and rest my forehead on them.

Freddie says, "You're not going to barf, are you?"

"No." I laugh. "That's the amazing thing. Except for the low back pain, I feel really good. I never would have guessed . . ."

"Well, if you feel so good, that must mean something."

I turn my head and squint up at her. "Like what?"

"Like this is a good thing. You know . . ." She turns away, flustered by my glare. "Well, darlin' it's happening, so you might as well try to see the sunny side."

I stand up and give her a look that would bend a fork. "Don't you dare go Pollyanna on me."

"Dammit, Sunny. You gonna spend the rest of your life

being pissed off about having a kid by somebody you don't like anymore?"

"I just might," I snap at her.

She looks right back at me. "Then maybe you should have had the abortion."

The drive to the clinic is accomplished in total silence. She pulls into the parking garage, takes a ticket, and finds a place to park on the second floor right near the pedestrian walkway across to the clinic. "I've got good parking karma," she says with determined cheer.

I open the door and get out.

She's right behind me.

"Why don't you go get some coffee," I say. "I think I can handle this myself."

She looks stricken. "Sunny, please don't be mad at me. I'm sorry. I had no right to say that to you—"

"True."

"I was upset—"

"*You're* upset?" I wheel on her. "*I'm* the one who's having the baby. And I'm so goddamned *sick* of everyone petting me and telling me how wonderful it all is and looking at me like I'm some kind of ogre freak because I'm not sitting around starry-eyed knitting booties. I didn't fucking ask for this and I can't help how I feel!"

By the time I reach the end of my tirade, I'm screaming, and people getting out of their cars are turning to stare. Freddie tries to put her arm around me, but I shove her away. "In fact, why don't you just head on back? I can get myself home."

"Sunny, for Pete's sake—"

I hear her slam her hand against the car and curse the pain, but I'm halfway over the bridge, and the automatic glass doors are about to open and swallow me up.

My fantasy image of the South Seattle Women's Reproductive Health Clinic wasn't too far off the mark. Pale blue walls with tasteful watercolor landscapes, Pachelbel's Canon playing on the sound system, comfortable love seats and wingback chairs in soft floral prints. There's a marked absence of baby stuff, except for the brochure rack, which is full of pamphlets about pregnancy, childbirth, nursing. No matter how you decorate a clinic, though, they all have that smell. I swallow my queasiness.

Everybody else has someone with them. Husband, partner, girlfriend. I could have had someone too, if I hadn't been a complete and total bitch. But maybe they all need someone with them. I don't.

I finished my thirty-two ounces of water on the ferry and I'm now painfully crossing and uncrossing my legs and flipping the pages of *O* magazine without so much as glancing at the pictures. I keep checking the clock. It's three minutes past my appointment time. I stare at the receptionist. She smiles.

"Dr. Miller will be right with you," she says.

"Is there somebody else who could do this? Because if I don't pee pretty soon, I'm going to explode."

"No, I'm sorry." She runs the tip of her tongue over her perfect lipstick. "Dr. Tomball wanted Dr. Miller to see you. I know it's uncomfortable, but it should be only a few more minutes."

Uncomfortable is not the word I would have used. No, I would've described it as something like having a live ferret resident in my bladder.

The clock's second hand makes a few more revolutions,

and finally I hear my name. A nurse is standing in the doorway holding a clipboard. I follow her down a hallway lined with black-and-white landscape photographs.

"Put your purse on that chair and step up on this scale," she says.

"I'll weigh a lot less after I evacuate Puget Sound from my bladder," I say.

She just fiddles with the weights, sliding them back and forth on the balance. "One-forty-five," she says. She picks up the chart. "What's your normal weight?"

"I have no idea."

She gives me a look that she probably reserves for uncooperative patients.

"I don't own a scale."

"Haven't you ever been weighed by a doctor?"

"Last week I weighed one-forty-two, but that's obviously not my normal weight."

She sighs, scribbles something on my chart, and leaves me in a small, dimly lit room with an examining table and lots of *Star Wars* equipment. I take off my T-shirt and bra, slither out of my jeans and underwear, and pull the paper gown around my shoulders.

I pace. I try to avoid thinking about how bad I have to go. I make a game out of walking as if I'm on a tightrope, one foot directly in front of the other.

There's a door on the opposite side of the room. I open it and peer in. Oh God, it's a *toilet*. No Queen Anne chair with cabriole legs and ball feet ever looked as beautiful to me as that piece of white porcelain. I feel like whimpering. Then I wonder . . . maybe I could just let a tiny bit out. Bleed off a little of the pressure like you do with espresso machines.

Just as I'm about to succumb to temptation, the outer door clicks open and I whirl around, flashing Dr. Miller the full monty.

She's very cool. "Hello, Sunny. I'm Vera Miller. I know you're anxious to get this over with, so hop up on the table and we'll do it. We can talk afterward."

She washes her hands in the sink, unwinds a cord, flips some switches, and then squirts something that feels like ice cold Vaseline on my stomach and smears it around while I dig my fingernails into the palms of my hands. I wonder if anyone's ever peed on her table.

She turns a rack of equipment around so I can see. I think of the studio at SoundsGood, of Artie and Ron Wyler. I think of Jack Piper, all dressed up like John Wayne. Suddenly I'm thinking about Betsy and the Twin Oaks Café, Montoya's green chile bread and Sissy's Castro convertible.

"Watch the monitor," Dr. Miller says. She traces a wide arc below my navel with what she calls the transducer. It looks like a computer mouse standing on end.

At first the screen is full of oozing gray liquid with staticky white flecks. Then I see something. It's gray, rounded at both ends, and it seems to be floating in the middle of a black pocket.

"Is that it?" I whisper, momentarily forgetting about my bladder.

"Yes." She points out the face, which looks like a tiny space alien, two black holes for eyes and a sort of triangle for the nose.

I frown. "What's that big black spot on top?"

"The baby's head is still developing," she says.

The machine makes clicking noises while she looks at the fetus from other angles. She asks if I want to know the sex.

"I don't know. Should I?"

She chuckles dryly. "It's your choice. Some people want to know; others want to be surprised."

"I don't need any more surprises."

"Well, I'd say it looks like a girl," she says.

I stare at the blobs on the screen. "How on earth can you tell?"

She points to an area where there are three dark parallel lines. That's the beginning of her labia. A pretty clear indication."

Finally she switches the machine off and starts gathering up papers. "You can use the bathroom—" she begins, but I'm already in there with the door closed. "I'll see you in my office," she calls.

Dr. Miller doesn't look anything like I imagined. She's short, sort of chubby, and dark-haired. She has big, dark eyes and wears bright red lipstick, which is smeared onto her front teeth. However, she does have beautiful skin.

When I come into her office, she motions for me to shut the door behind me. She puts down her Diet Coke.

"Nice to meet you, Sunny," she says. "You can call me Vera. Feeling better?"

"Yes, thanks."

"Ralph told me a little bit about you. Apparently you didn't know you were pregnant until recently."

I nod. "I didn't have symptoms. Or I guess I had them and didn't recognize them."

"It's a lot more common than people think," she says. "But everything appears to be just fine. I understand you're interested in a home birth."

"It's more a necessity than an interest. I don't have insurance."

"At all?" She frowns and doodles on her desk blotter.

"Except for catastrophic. I've always been disgustingly healthy."

"Well, that much is good. So you'll be working with Mary Jo? She's a wonderful midwife. Do you have any questions for me?"

"I know I should, but I haven't quite . . . digested the news yet."

"That's okay. If you think of any as we go along, you can always call me. I've put together a packet of information for you. Renee will give it to you when you check out. I assume Ralph told you about my fees?"

I look away, embarrassed. "He said something about a sliding scale."

"Right. There are a couple of financial forms in the packet, but the main thing I want you to do regarding the money is not worry about it. You've got more important things to think about for a while."

"I've applied for . . . assistance. Or whatever they call it now."

"Just concentrate on taking care of yourself and the baby. Nobody's going to throw you out in the snow because you can't pay. What I'd like you to do is look over the information in the packet. If you have any questions at all—even if you think they're dumb—call Ralph or Mary Jo or me. And I'd like you to get on a regular schedule of visits with Mary Jo. Can you do that?"

"Yes."

"Well, then . . ." She looks at her watch and I stand up.

"Thanks, Dr. Miller. Vera."

"You're welcome, Sunny. I'll see you again."

When I come out into the reception area, Freddie is sitting on a love seat with an unopened magazine on her lap. Our eyes meet briefly before I turn to the receptionist, who hands me my information packet.

Freddie follows me out.

"Sunny."

"What?" I keep walking.

"Nobody thinks you're an ogre freak. Except maybe you. Are you that scared that you might really love this kid?"

A hot rush of dizziness washes over me and I put my hand against the cool tile wall for balance. "Freddie, I'm sorry," I manage just before the knot in my throat becomes weeping. Freddie puts her arms around me and hugs me. She smells clean, like soap and some kind of grassy shampoo.

"I'm sorry, too," she says. "No way I should've said that to you."

"You're entitled to defend yourself." I sniffle. "Shit, I can't believe I'm doing this again. I've cried more in the last two weeks than the whole rest of my life put together."

"Hormones," she says, then brightens. "Hey, remember that old joke: How d'you make a hormone?" She pauses a beat. "Don't pay her."

I laugh helplessly, clutching my stomach. "Oh God, that's terrible. I've got to use the bathroom again before we leave here."

Chapter 24

Justin is off today, so the kitchen is quiet. Manolo's wearing headphones while he cuts potatoes for French fries, rocking back and forth, nodding in time to the jumpy Latin music only he can hear. He smiles and waves at me when I come in, bumping the screen door on Bailey's inquisitive nose.

I hang up the leather jacket and walk back into the storeroom. A dozen cartons are stacked against the wall, and I find the box cutter on the window ledge, slit open the first one.

I don't even bother turning on the light switch. I like working in the cool, damp darkness, lit only by the daylight from the small window high up on the wall. I like the smells of cardboard cartons and more faintly of hot deep fryer fat and simmering tomato sauce.

I stack cans of the black beans and tomato paste and some giant plastic bottles of extra-virgin olive oil. I unpack roasted red peppers and sun-dried tomatoes and anchovy paste and huge jars of peeled garlic cloves, hermetically sealed plastic bags of capers and olives and pine nuts.

The rhythm of it—turning and bending to the box, reaching to the shelf and turning again—puts me in a trance. Inside the flow, I don't think. I can almost forget the image of cells dividing inside me, cells that don't belong to me, faster than I want to imagine, each one reporting to its position for duty assignments like little soldiers. Fingers—here. Eyes—over there. Brain—upstairs.

"Sunny?" The light comes on and I spin around. "What are you doing in here?" Piggy adjusts the Irish tweed cap he likes to wear at the bar.

"I'm just unpacking some stuff. I thought you were off today."

"I'm supposed to be, but Dave's sick. Or so he says. You don't have to unpack deliveries, you know. The guys can do it."

I shrug. "I don't mind. I didn't have anything thrilling to do this afternoon." I heave a sixty-ounce can of garbanzo beans onto the shelf and pull another out of the carton.

"But you probably shouldn't be . . ."

"Piggy, I'm pregnant, not crippled."

The little wooden bench we use as a step stool disappears under his bulk, and he sits there stroking his beard, watching me. I put another can on the metal shelf and push them back to the wall to make room for more.

"Your friend Betsy called again. She left her number."

"I know her number." I go back to unloading cans of tomatoes.

"I guess there's a reason you don't want to talk to her."

"Yes." I flip over the empty carton, slit it down the middle, and stomp it flat. Then I drag the next box over to the shelves and slit it open. More crushed tomatoes. They clink on the shelves.

Piggy waits till I stop making noise. "Sunny, we need to talk about some stuff."

"Now?"

"Yeah, I'd say now's a pretty good time. Here." He gets up off the stool.

"I don't need to sit down."

"Just put your butt on the stool, okay?"

"You can't fire me; it's illegal."

"What the hell are you talking about?"

"I know how it works." I fold my arms. "If I start slacking off, sitting down all the time, you can say I'm not doing the job."

"Jesus Christ. Does being pregnant make you paranoid? You're in here an hour before your shift unpacking boxes and I'm going to say you're slacking off?"

"I've seen it happen."

"Goddamn, Sunny. You know me better than that."

Tears are welling up in my eyes. "Funny how I always think I know someone better than that."

"Hey, cut it out. Don't cry, okay?"

I sit down on the stool and rest my forearms on my thighs. "I'm trying not to, but it seems to go with the territory. Every ten minutes. Spilled coffee, dead rabbit in the road, missing button—it doesn't take much." I brush at my eyes.

"I want you to work just as long as you want to. As long as you can."

"I'm going to work till I'm five centimeters dilated."

The thought seems to make him slightly queasy. "Sunny, you might not be able—"

"I *will*," I say fiercely.

He shakes his head. "Okay. Whatever. You've got a job as long as you want it." He heads for the kitchen.

"Piggy . . ."

He turns in the doorway.

"Thanks. And could you turn the light off?"

I've already written and mailed actual—not virtual—thank-you notes to everyone who gave me gifts. I ended up opening the presents that night, displaying as much gratitude as I could muster. I tried to be enthusiastic about little yellow duck play-suits and pink kitty-cat rattles—actually my greatest pleasure came from imagining how horrified Gwen would be at all this stuff—the little white crib with a set of pink bedding, a soft plush teddy bear, a diaper bag with green cartoon frogs all over it, a set of onesies—something I'd never heard of; but then, why would I have? They're little one-piece all-purpose baby suits for newborns. There are seven, in different pastel colors, each with a day of the week monogrammed on the front. There are little white socks and impossibly tiny crocheted booties and a match-ing hat with pink ribbon trim.

These things have occupied my house, taking up strategic positions like mini alien invaders. It's jarring to look up from a book and see a fuzzy teddy bear leering at me from the shelf, or to grab for underwear and come up with a sunny yellow one-sie that says FRIDAY or to reach for a pen and wrap my fingers around a kitty rattle with an evil pink smile. The crib is the worst, screamingly white against all the natural wood and the age-darkened maple of the spool bed. I think about stripping the paint off and just sealing the wood, but I don't think I'm supposed to mess around with chemicals like paint stripper and varnish. But then, this is not about baby accessories taking over my decor; it's about a baby taking over my life.

How did Gwen do it? Twenty-three years old. She was JT's

age when she had me. Out in the middle of the mesa. The nearest clinic in Arroyo Embuste. The closest hospital in Taos. No
disposable diapers or baby wipes or diaper bags with green cartoon frogs and built-in bottle holders.

And what do you do all day with a baby? I try to imagine
it. Waking up early, and before you can even get out of bed and
pee, the baby is crying because she's hungry or has a wet diaper.
Or just because she feels like crying. How do you know? Is
there a hungry cry? A thirsty cry? A cry that means *my diaper is
full of poop*? What about *my stomach hurts*? Or *hey, I'm tired of
this stupid kitty rattle.*

How do you get anything done? How do you hold down a
job? So many things to buy and so little money. I can't afford
a full-time sitter. I probably can't even afford daycare. And if I
could afford it, do I really want to leave a new baby with strangers all day, every day? How do I find a job on San Miguel Island
where I can keep her with me? And what if I can't? Do I pick
up and move again?

I could go back to the mesa.

As soon as the thought materializes, I blast it with a .357
magnum shot of reality. I couldn't make a living there . . .
being strictly practical. And I couldn't stand being that close
to Gwen. She'd be in my face all the time. Lecturing me about
non-biodegradable disposable diapers and the additives in commercial baby food. Teaching my child to roll a joint and that
microwaves cause cancer and that the Internet is the antichrist.
Filling her head with stories of the good old days at Armonía,
tales of peace, love, and brotherhood.

• • •

It's not until JT appears on my doorstep, brown as a walnut, his hair sun-bleached almost white on top, dazzling me with his crooked grin, that I realize how much I've missed him. How the island seemed half empty in his absence. With that awareness, all my carefully rehearsed words skitter off and disappear like water on a hot griddle. When he moves toward me, I let myself be drawn in; when he kisses me, I kiss him right back. Just because I want to and because I'm sick of pretending I don't.

It's a really good kiss, too. All those little hormones cruising through my bloodstream shift on down into overdrive. Rampant, raging, rampaging hormones. I'm totally oversexed because I'm pregnant. Forget all the stuff that has to be said. It doesn't interest me nearly as much as the idea of lying down in my bed, the full length of me pressed against him.

I hit the brakes.

"Wait a second, wait. JT—come in." I rearrange my shirt, newly conscious of the gentle mound underneath. "When did you get back?" I hadn't even noticed Bailey standing behind him, tail waving slowly, nose pressed against JT's thigh. He follows us in.

"Last night." He kicks the door shut behind us and he's already reaching for my hands again. "If it hadn't been so late I would've come over right then."

My laugh is a quick, nervous flutter. "Good grief, look at you. Didn't you ever hear of sunscreen?"

He pulls me closer, touching his forehead to mine. "I can't believe how much I missed you."

"I missed you too, but we need to talk."

He grins. "Okay." He flops down in one of the chairs, stretches his long legs out in front of himself. Even the hair on his legs is sun-bleached. His sockless feet are tan, the ankles smooth and slender, like a young boy's. Bailey wanders around sniffing everything and finally lies down beside the hearth.

I sit in the other chair. I have to say it now. Fast, before I lose my nerve. "JT, I want to hear all about the trip, but there's something I need to tell you. I'm pregnant."

At first, it's like he hasn't heard me. Then there's a wary little smile, as if it might be a joke. When he finally understands that it's not, I watch the sequence of reactions move across his face like cloud shadows.

"Pregnant?" He says the word as if it's some foreign language he's never heard. "Like you're having a . . ."

"Baby. Yes."

"What are you saying? God, Sunny. Tell me . . . something. What happened?"

I sit forward on the chair, my hands bunched in my lap. "I was pregnant when I left Albuquerque, only I didn't know it."

"When did you find out?"

"Just after you left."

A silence settles over the room. He studies his hands. He looks at Bailey. He gets up slowly, eyes on me, but not seeing me. "Can I have some water?"

In the kitchen he stands at the sink holding an empty glass while I sit at the table. Three weeks ago we were having dinner here. I was at the sink, putting flowers in a milk carton; he was telling me about the trip to come.

"There's cold water in the fridge."

He doesn't move. "What are you going to do?"

"Well, right now, it looks like I'm going to have a baby in about six months."

I can tell he's trying to see if I look pregnant without looking like he's trying. "This is so weird."

"I couldn't agree with you more."

He opens the refrigerator and pours water from the pitcher into his glass. He swallows some, then sets the glass on the counter, contemplates it. "I really don't know what to say."

I fold my arms and wait for him to look at me. "So far, most people have said congratulations. Or *Sunny, if you need help with anything, let me know.*"

"I guess I'm not most people." He drinks some more water. "But you know I'd help you if you needed me to." His voice is flat, all traces of feeling carefully removed.

"That's very generous."

"I thought . . ." He takes a breath. "I thought you were starting to feel the way I do. I thought we'd . . ."

I lean forward, looking up at him, trying to make eye contact. "JT, I was. I do. But this is a big time-out for me. I have to figure out what the hell I'm going to do with my life. Because now I've got two lives to worry about."

He nods. "Understood."

"*Understood?* What the hell does that mean?"

"I thought about you," he says.

Great. Now we're having two separate conversations.

"Especially when I was lying on deck watching the stars. I thought about the sound of your voice. I could hear it in my head, you know? Like when you hold a shell to your ear and you can hear the ocean."

I sigh and lean against the back of the chair. "How sorry do you need me to be?"

He frowns. "What do you mean?"

"I'm getting the distinct impression that you think I've done something terrible. Something that offends you. You want me to apologize for getting pregnant?"

"No . . . I don't want you to apologize. It just changes things, that's all."

"It changes some things. It doesn't have to change everything."

He waits a few seconds, turning the glass around and around on the counter that he built. "I don't know what you want from me."

"Nothing. I don't want anything. No, I take that back. I want you to tell me how you feel."

"Okay." He shifts his weight uncomfortably. "Here's how I feel. I feel like somebody just dumped a bucket of cold water on me from two stories up. I feel like you want me to say it's no big deal, like we can just sit down and have coffee, take up where we left off—"

"No, really. That's not what I want. Believe me, I know it's a big deal. A very big deal. But can't we just sort of *be* . . . I'm not asking you to make any kind of a . . . statement. I don't expect you to—"

"Sunny, we can't just *be*. I can't, anyway. It's all different now." He hesitates. "That's my problem, I guess."

Finally we make eye contact. Direct. No obstructions. We look at each other, and all at once I know what I'm seeing. There's a child in there—a sad, lonely child—perfectly preserved like a fossil inside those amber eyes. And if there's one thing I don't need right now, it's another child.

"I mean, what am I supposed to do?" he says.

"Do what you want to do, JT. What you have to do."

I feel diminished somehow. Whatever it was in me that was so open and expansive, whatever made me so happy around him is gone.

"Look, I'm sorry," he says after a minute. "I know I'm not handling this the way I should—"

"'Should' has nothing to do with it. You can't change how you feel. I guess I could have been a little more tactful."

"It's just so out of left field . . . I need to get used to it. Give me a few days, okay?"

"Take your time. I'm not going anywhere."

"I'll call you this weekend. Okay? We can talk or something." Then, without waiting for me to respond, he calls Bailey and the two of them walk out my door.

I watch the orange truck disappear up the driveway while I drink the rest of the water, putting my mouth on the glass where his mouth was. Then I wash the glass, dry it, and put it back on the shelf.

What is it with me? How is it that I think I'm asking for nothing, but end up expecting everything?

In my bedroom, there are shreds of paper scattered on the floor. I bend to gather them up, seeing them, but not seeing them. Thinking about JT and bad timing and great expectations. The shreds are wet. And then I realize they're not paper. They're soft. Spongy. Like leather. *Oh shit*. I stand up and my eyes go immediately to the night table. The empty place where my medicine bundle used to be. I stare at the floor. Shreds. A couple of red beads. The remains of my father's present. And a few feet away the turquoise bear, neatly deposited, like the discarded seed of some petrified fruit.

It's so horrible it's funny. Bailey ate my medicine bundle. Well, why not?

I'm sure he found the deerskin a tasty morsel. I think I read somewhere that they tanned the hides with urine, which probably made it even more piquant.

I can't be mad at him. He's a dog, after all, just doing his dog thing. I can, however, be mad at JT. For letting him run wild. Not teaching him better manners—*And remember, Bailey, you must never under any circumstances eat the hostess's jewelry.* How can he be so blind? *I don't try to run Bailey's life and he doesn't try to run mine.* Dammit. Can we take some responsibility here? If somebody doesn't try to run somebody's life, you get anarchy. You get chaos. You get Armonía. Where every person thought they had a plan, but they couldn't possibly be so uncool as to impose their vision on anyone else. So the place looked like a big box of those little windup toys, everybody running around doing their own thing, spinning off in every direction—it's a wonder it lasted as long as it did.

I inhale deeply. Does being pregnant do these strange things to your brain?

I sit on the edge of my bed, turning the bear over and over in my palm. The woman who has cried at least once a day for the last three weeks over everything from broken fingernails to broken dishes has no more tears.

I've reached the point where my balance is getting uncertain, so as of tomorrow Myron is retired for the duration of gestation.

To take up the slack, Laura has found me an island beater. "Ten years old, reliable, fair gas mileage, not much rust."

"Not much?"

"Well, you know . . ." She grins. "Every vehicle on the island has a little bit of rust. It's like proof that you live here. I've done all the maintenance on this one, so I know it's in good shape."

It's a truck, a white Toyota, compact and sensible, with automatic transmission and a decent-size cargo bed. It has blue cloth seats, AM/FM radio, and a working heater. It's not a vehicle with which I could ever form an intimate attachment, like I have with Myron—it would never occur to me to talk to the truck, or even name it—but it's sort of like a plain older sister, the one who takes care of you when your parents go out.

It's in my price range—cheap—and the owner was willing to let me pay it off in four installments.

For my last ride with Myron, I retrace the route Piggy showed me that very first time, and I hold that morning in my mind like a dream. I remember being wound tight, the ache in my hands from gripping the bars, the exhausting thrill of it. The long hairpin turn just past the beach that made me so nervous that first time, slips beneath Myron's wheels today like a silk ribbon. Vistas of rock and ocean, meadow and woods and farms, open up around almost every curve, and the road appears and disappears in front of me as the sun ducks in and out of the clouds.

I'll never see these things in exactly the same way, ever again, and it makes me sad. It also makes me afraid. Not of riding or of falling. It makes me afraid of being afraid. Later, after the baby comes. Afraid to ride. Afraid that if I do ride I'll always be worrying about what would happen to the baby if anything happened to me. Afraid that I'll be one of those mothers who wants to bundle the kid in bubble wrap so nothing can hurt her. I could easily go that way. I have those tendencies.

How did Gwen do it? How did she let go of us, let us find our own way, let us learn to be strong for ourselves? Maybe she was able to do it because, until the accident, she viewed the world as essentially benign. She truly believed in the Age of Aquarius. She was convinced that materialism was bad but that people were good, or at worst, misguided. That society was perfectible *if only* we could be true to our best selves, try to love and understand everyone, live a simple life in harmony with the earth, if we could raise the next generation to do the same . . . If only.

The problem was all those good intentions didn't stop people from being selfish and lazy. It didn't eliminate lust or jealousy or anger. It didn't keep some people from looking for the free ride, taking advantage of somebody else's hard work. When I lived at Armonía, all I could see was the gap between what was professed and what actually happened.

Now, suddenly, I recognize that they were trying. As hard as they knew how. They were so young. Most of the people who begat Armonía were younger than I am now. When you think about it, it was sort of amazing they accomplished as much as they did. And then, having created their utopia, they left. Things fell apart. Do they all sit around reminiscing about how wonderful that life was and how much they loved it there? All those ones who went back to the cities, to law school and med school, who became teachers or stockbrokers or learned to sell insurance.

All except Gwen. She's the last one left, still living the dream. I guess you could call it deluded. You could also call it pretty steely.

I turn into my drive and stop, surprised by the sight of a strange blue sedan in front of my house and a man standing on my porch.

He watches me coast down between the trees, put the side stand down, and pull off my helmet. Probably doesn't see many pregnant bikers.

He steps off the porch and walks over to me. He's tall with light brown hair and eyes a chilly shade of gray that blends with his slacks and jacket. The curving scar on his chin is narrow, as if made by a scalpel or a razor.

"Been waiting long?" I pull the key out of the ignition and climb off Myron, lifting the bandana from my hair.

"Not too long. I've been enjoying your view." His voice is low and raspy. It's a smoker's voice, but he doesn't have the tobacco smell. I remember how Michael and I argued about it till he finally quit.

"I always like to know who's enjoying my view."

"Jonas Bradley." He thrusts a business card into my hand.

A memory stirs. "The last time we spoke, I believe your name was Milton Kaplan. You said you were Michael's partner."

He smiles like his face is unaccustomed to the exercise. "Good ear, Ms. Cooper."

The card is white and stiff with black lettering. No color except the unimaginative globe logo. Gerond Corporate Security is the company name. Under it is a San Francisco address.

I run my finger over the engraved letters. "Anyone can have cards printed up."

"True. However, if you'd returned Sergeant Bagley's phone call, you would've known I was coming."

I stick the card in my pocket and unlock the door. He follows me in.

"Sergeant Bagley called to tell me you were coming?"

"Among other things. Like the DNA samples didn't match."

For a few seconds the thought floats obscurely over my head. Then the earth shifts under my feet and I spin around, swallowing air.

"What did you say?"

He grips my elbow firmly, almost to the point of hurting me, and settles me into one of the chairs. My hands clamp like claws onto the arms. "What are you saying? That Michael's alive?"

He sits down in the other chair. "All we know right now is, he didn't die in the truck."

"*God*. I don't believe it. I can't . . . Why didn't he . . ." Initial shock is followed by another, stranger sensation: disappointment?

He waits a minute or two, watching me rub my arm where he gripped it. Then he says, "I'm looking into some of his business dealings."

"I can't tell you much about that. He liked to start companies and then sell them."

"He·liked to play poker, too." He crosses his legs and straightens the crease of his slacks.

"I know he played with a bunch of guys on Monday nights."

"That group hasn't been together in almost two years, and Graham was already on to bigger things." Bradley leans back in the chair now, looking loose and comfortable. Except for his eyes. He reminds me of those dogs that don't bark before they bite.

"Apparently your boyfriend had a pretty big gambling jones. At the time of his disappearance, he owed a lot of money to some not very nice people. Ever hear of the Campos Syndicate? They run high-stakes poker games and some off-track betting on horses and greyhound racing."

"I've . . . seen the name. I didn't know what it was."

He leans forward slowly. "Are you telling me you had no idea he was gambling?"

I put my fingers to my temples and rub in a circular motion. I'm not sure if I find this guy obnoxious because he actually is, or because he's making it clear to me how stupid I was.

"I knew he liked to gamble. I mean, in the sense of taking risks. But I thought . . . I mean, he said it was because of the businesses. That sometimes things would be good, and other times . . ."

"When he ran through all the money he had and everything he could pull out of his companies, he had to come up with some more creative ways of making money faster."

"Like the Remington stock thing?"

"That, too. My company was called in by a Miami bank to investigate one of their foreign investment VPs. They suspected him of being involved in money laundering. Apparently he was a buddy of Milton Kaplan's."

"Who exactly is Milton Kaplan?"

He presses his palms together and releases them. The Namaste pose. It looks weird on him. "He's sort of a self-styled wheeler-dealer. Apparently he met Michael through this Monday night poker group."

"I thought he lived in Denver."

"He's got lots of addresses. He's a regular world traveler. Except right now he's in residence at the Everglades Correctional Institution in Miami."

"You seem to know a lot more than I do about what Michael was into. So why did you come all the way up here to talk to me?"

"Well, a couple reasons. Bagley said you didn't know Graham was alive." His look is unsettling. "I figured you *did* know."

"Why would you think that?"

"Come on, Ms. Cooper. A guy like Bagley—he's pretty young. Hasn't been around long enough to get cynical. Or maybe you're just a damned good actress."

I stare at him, till I can manage a weak "What are you talking about?"

"Look at it from our perspective . . . You leave town in a hurry—"

"For personal reasons—"

He shrugs. "They're all personal. You sell all your belongings, don't tell anyone where you're going, including your supposed best friend. You don't return Bagley's phone call—what are we supposed to think? Maybe you and Michael planned this whole thing: faking his death, checking out of a bad situation, meeting up again somewhere else."

Anger boils over inside me. "Mr. Bradley, trust me, I haven't planned my life based on what you and Sergeant Bagley might think. And this could have been cleared up a lot sooner if you'd told me who you really were the first time you called instead of pretending to be Kaplan."

"I had no way of knowing how involved you were. Are."

"I'm not. All I'm doing is trying to put my life back together here, and I don't know what was or is going on with Michael or anything else that has to do with this whole mess."

"It's nothing personal, Ms. Cooper," he says with exaggerated politeness. "You're just one link in the chain. Also, we believe you might have some evidence in your possession . . ."

I can feel his eyes on me when I go to the shelf, take down the metal lockbox, and pull out the CD. He takes it from me.

"How did you happen to come by this?"

"I don't know. It was in with a bunch of my music CDs. I just found it a few days ago." I can tell he doesn't believe me.

"Have you looked at it?"

"I tried. It's password protected. What's supposed to be on it?"

"Financial records, I hope. We think Kirby Dolen realized that Kaplan was skimming money that he was supposed to be laundering. It's not clear whether Michael was involved in that or whether Dolen told him. Dolen might have confronted one of them or threatened to go to the police. Or he could have attempted to blackmail Kaplan. It's complicated. We're still piecing things together."

By now it's pretty clear that Jonas Bradley thinks I'm an idiot. He looks at me down the bridge of his very straight nose. "So you really had no idea what he was into?"

"This probably sounds strange to you, but I was happy for a while there. I didn't want to rock the boat."

He fishes in his pocket for the rental car key and his eyes rest on my abdomen. "Is it his?"

Heat jumps into my face. "That's really none of your business."

"True. But if he's in touch with you, it becomes my business. There are several law enforcement agencies involved, including federal. We all have a lot of questions right now." He pauses. "You know what happened to Kirby Dolen?"

"I know he's—he died."

"He was killed," he corrects me tersely.

"You don't think Michael . . ."

"He's officially a 'person of interest' with regard to Dolen's death. So if he should contact you, try to resist the urge to be helpful. Call us right away—either myself or Sergeant Bagley."

Out on the porch I watch him climb into the blue sedan. He rolls down the window. "By the way, if you decide to move again, please keep us informed."

I sit on the edge of my bed, struggle the cowboy boots off. My toes feel cool in the damp socks. I ease myself down against the pillows, turning on my side to curl around the baby. I close my eyes.

So Michael's alive. Do I laugh or cry?

So many questions. What happened, and where has he been all this time? Why did he let me believe he was dead? And what will I do when he shows up on my doorstep? Because he will. Never mind all the things I don't know; of this I feel absolutely certain. He'll find me. Sooner or later I'll have to deal with him.

And what about Betsy? Did Michael contact her? I assumed she kept calling me because she was sorry for what happened, but what if she wanted to tell me he was alive? Or that Jonas Bradley was around asking questions.

I reach across to the night table for my medicine bundle, momentarily forgetting that it's gone. Instead, my hand finds the brown plush teddy bear. Unthinking, I pick him up and bring him into the crook of my arm.

Chapter 25

When I come in the back door of the Ale House, there's a big cardboard box of apples, a couple of bowls, and a paring knife on the counter.

"Hey, Sunny, how you feeling today?" Justin says.

I smile. "Pretty good for a fat lady."

"No, you ain't fat. Hey, I need some apples for apple tarts. Can you handle it?"

I pull one out of the box. It's an odd little round apple with pretty greenish yellow skin marked with broad red stripes. "What are these?"

"Gravensteins," he says. "Best summer apple I ever did eat. Taste one. You don't even have to wash it. They're organic."

I dust it off with my shirttail and take a bite. The apple responds with a great crunch and a gush of tart-sweet juice that runs down my chin.

"Wow," I say around the apple in my mouth. I lean over the box and inhale. "Are these local?"

"Nah. Too bad. A friend of Trent's brought 'em up from Sonoma. So this is it; there ain't no more."

I find an apron and settle myself on the stool and begin my

task. The pile of curling skin grows bigger, and my hands get sticky from the juice, and the flowery scent of the Gravensteins calls up a memory that's piercing and tart-sweet as a summer apple.

The hills of northern New Mexico are honeycombed with valleys where small family farms grow apples. Depending on the weather, some of the varieties are ready to pick in late July or early August and there never seems to be enough help for the harvest, for the cider making or taking the apples, the cider, the applesauce, apple butter, and dried apples to the farmers markets in Espanola, Santa Fe, and Albuquerque. So Armonía would sometimes send workers out to the farms to help with the harvest in exchange for wages or apples, sometimes both. Hart and I had been going on these expeditions since he was fourteen and I was twelve, and it was something I always looked forward to.

For one thing, Gwen never went. So it was a chance for me to get away from her and from Armonía. I loved working all day in the hot sun, surrounded by the heady sweet smell of ripe apples. I loved lying in the afternoon shade in tall grass, too tired to care about the ants and pill bugs that I knew were invading my underwear, while the cool breeze dried the sweat on my skin into a salty shell, and then sipping an icy Coke with a burrito or tamale from the vendors who came down the road in the afternoons during picking season.

Sometimes we even got to spend a night or two in our sleeping bags on the flatbed truck or on top of the rock 'n' roll school bus or the Dream Machine. We would lie there smelling the campfires, listening to guitars and voices, waiting for sleep under a high, black New Mexico sky full of stars. In the mornings the farm people would bring breakfast—scrambled eggs and ham wrapped in tortillas or beans and bacon, washed down with freshly pressed cider and strong coffee before another day of work began.

During the summer of Kris Stanton, we met Serafina Padilla when we came to her farm to pick apples because Boone had overheard her at the feed store in Arroyo Embuste complaining to Matt Jankel that the men she'd hired to pick her trees had gotten drunk on their first day's pay and never come back to finish the job. Boone had smiled and told her he could have a crew there in the morning to finish the rest of her orchard. And because Boone was always clean-shaven and soft-spoken, she believed him and gave him directions to her place.

Our crew, which consisted of Boone, Hart, Wendy, Topper, and me, had a lot of experience, and even though Wendy and I couldn't climb as high with a heavy picking bag on our chest as the men could, we put in a good day's work. Kris said he would go too, but in the morning he came up to me after breakfast and said his back was hurting and he thought he should stay at the compound and take it easy.

I hung out the back window as the van started up to the road. He smiled and waved, yelled at me to be careful climbing the trees. I noticed everything—how long his hair had gotten, the sun streaks on top, the way his eyes were serious even when he smiled. And I noticed that he'd taken off his leather cuff, leaving a wide band of pale skin that had escaped the sun.

The Padilla farm was like most farms in northern New Mexico—the house close to the blacktop for easy access during bad weather, the pasture and orchard farther back, hidden from view, down a long dirt-and-gravel road badly rutted by last winter's runoff.

Serafina lived alone. She was old—I wasn't sure how old, but she was as bent and gnarled as her apple trees—and she had never married. She and her brother, Segundo, had grown up on the farm, inherited it from their parents, and worked it together until he died; then she soldiered on by herself.

She used to have livestock, she said—geese, goats, and a mule. They had all died off, and she never replaced them because it was too much work. The only animals around now were a barn cat, an ancient dog named Pancho who hobbled around after her, and a few slow and dignified hens she kept for eggs.

Of course Pancho made straight for my brother, laying his face against Hart's leg. You could tell Serafina was surprised, maybe even a bit miffed, but she led us back to the orchard, showed us where to park the van. She pointed out the shed where the ladders and pruning saws and bushel baskets were neatly stored and said she would bring us ice water in the afternoon. And then she disappeared.

All morning I picked quickly and quietly, listening to the others joke and sing, trying not to think about anything, especially not about Kris standing in the road, waving goodbye. When Serafina didn't come in the afternoon, Hart said he would go ask her for water. Our bottles were all empty.

He was gone for so long that Boone was about to go up to the house and see if something was wrong, when we saw them coming down the road. Serafina carrying a basket, Hart pulling a child's wagon with a couple of Igloo coolers, Pancho limping between them, but with his eyes firmly fixed on my brother.

"He wouldn't take his medicine," Hart explained, "so I had to help give it to him."

"I'm sorry about the water." Serafina looked embarrassed. "I forgot the time and I couldn't get Pancho to swallow his pill." She held out the basket, which was full of cookies, and we fell on it like starving wolves.

Serafina took Hart's hand and looked up at him. "You're a good one," she said, her wrinkled old chin quivering. "You have the touch. Will you come for his medicine tonight?"

"Sure," he said. When she left, she had to call Pancho several times. He'd take a couple of steps, stop and whine and look at my brother, then turn back toward Serafina. Finally Hart told him to go, and he trotted off after her.

Hart and I moved to the next row, and he was picking at the top of the tree while I worked at the bottom.

"You feel okay?" he asked me.

"Fine," I said, and kept picking.

"You're just so quiet, that's all. I thought something was wrong."

"Nope."

A minute later he said, "Are you sad that Kris didn't come?"

"It's no biggie."

"I know you like him."

"Everybody likes him."

He let out an exasperated sigh. "I mean everybody knows you two are together. I just don't want you to get—"

"Could we please not talk about this?" I said through gritted teeth.

"You don't tell me anything anymore," he said, and his voice was soft with hurt. "Just like Gwen."

I stepped away from the tree, dumped my apples into the bushel basket, threw my bag on the ground, and walked away.

"Sunny! Wait a second."

"Leave. Me. Alone!"

Hart didn't try to speak to me the rest of the day, although he cast an occasional sympathetic glance my way. Being mean to him made me feel shriveled and unlovely, but I didn't want to talk about Kris with anyone, not even Hart. And being compared to Gwen was really more than I could bear. Especially since I secretly feared it might be true.

For supper we heated vegetable soup over the fire and ate huge chunks of Gwen's seven-grain bread. Hart sat next to me and we talked, very politely, about nothing important. Then he took a flashlight and headed up to the house to help Serafina with Pancho. I volunteered to do cleanup, since I'd sort of slacked off during the afternoon, and there was an audible sigh of relief from Wendy. She had taken up with Topper after Boone dumped her for my mother, and they snuggled up together by the fire while Boone lit a pipe and proceeded to get pleasantly stoned.

I didn't mind cleaning up. It was something I could do without thinking—scraping the bowls clean, scouring the cooking pot with sand, boiling water for a final rinse, and setting everything on the fire ring to dry. By the time I finished, Wendy and Topper had disappeared inside the van and Boone was stretched out on top of his sleeping bag, snoring. I knew I had to talk to Hart or I wouldn't be able to sleep, so I took another flashlight and headed up the road.

The batteries in my light were old and weak. The light kept fading out, and I was hoping they'd last till I could see the lights from the house, because there was no moon. But before I could see the house, I saw a small bright spot swinging toward me and then catching me in its glow.

"Sunny Bunny?" Hart called out.

I ran toward the light and nearly bowled him over with my hug. He smelled so good to me, like grass and apples and sweat. "I'm sorry I was horrible to you."

He grabbed me around the waist and picked me up. "Forget it. Guess what!"

"What?"

"Serafina wants to teach me all about apples," he said breathlessly. "She's going to let me work for her, and instead of money, she's going to give me part of the orchard!"

"Oh Hart! That's so cool I can't believe it!"

"So I'll be working here every weekend this fall helping her pick and make cider. I'll have a job and I won't even have to leave New Mexico." He swung me around, laughing. I dropped my flashlight and it went out, but his burned steadily in the dark, and in its yellow glow I could see my brother's smile.

By three o'clock the next afternoon, we were finished picking. We cleaned up our campsite and collected our wages. Serafina came down and shook hands with all of us, but she kissed Hart on both cheeks and made him blush, and then we took off for Armonía, singing, with ten bushels of apples packed around us in the van.

I was happy for Hart, but on the bumpy ride home, my thoughts were full of nothing but Kris. How we would talk and laugh and touch, the sweetness of those first few minutes alone tonight in the dark. I could hardly sit still. No more sneaking off to the barn. Tonight I would go to his room. I didn't care if the whole world found out.

Armonía was quiet when we pulled through the gate. We piled out and started unloading our gear and the apples. The whole time, I was looking around for Kris. Wendy went inside, calling for help. When she came back, Gwen was with her. One look at my mother and I knew.

She examined a few of the apples and smiled. "These look great. We'll make some applesauce tomorrow and we can slice some for drying."

I planted myself in front of her. "Where's Kris?"

When she looked at me I saw her pity. "He left," she said. "Yesterday morning. He said it was time for him to go to Los—"

The rest was drowned out by my explosion. "You made him go!"

"Soleil . . ." She touched my arm and I jerked away.

"He was afraid of you."

She shook her head. "That's not true."

"It is so!" I hissed at her. "He was afraid you'd have him arrested."

Everybody stood there, watching us, Wendy, Boone, Topper, not in the way of rubberneckers watching an accident, but as participant-observers, waiting their chance to contribute to the discussion. It made me even angrier.

"Sunny, remember the song, 'to everything there is a season'?" Wendy said. "Love is like that, honey." Gwen flashed her a look and she shut up.

"You're upset, Soleil, and I understand." My mother's voice had taken on that rational, placating tone that I knew so well. It was the same one she used at commune meetings to bring together opposing sides on whether to repair the garden shed or dismantle it, who would be in charge of our irrigation, how much to ask for the cows. She said, "It wasn't me Kris was afraid of. I told him it was okay with me."

"You *what*?" Rage coiled in my throat like a snake.

"Soleil, it was obvious—the attraction between you—I wanted your first time to be good, so I told him I had no objection as long as he used a condom and treated you gently."

"Oh my God!" I screamed at her. "How could you do that to me?"

She looked genuinely puzzled. "How could I do what? I was trying to make sure that—"

"It was supposed to be private. It was mine. Nothing is ever mine. Not even my goddamned vagina."

"Really, Soleil, you need to calm down. Nobody's trying to take anything away from you, but you're my daughter—"

"That's what it is," I sobbed. "Right there. That's my whole problem." I turned my back on her and ran for the river. I thought for a minute that Hart might come after me, but he didn't, and that was a relief.

Gwen and I had had plenty of fights, but this was different. Always before, after I'd thrashed around for a while, we'd settle back into some kind of normalcy, but not this time. I'd been manipulated and humiliated and my resentment solidified, a kind of permanent blockage in my heart.

Months later, when the white heat of my anger had cooled to a soft glowing red, I remembered her words. "It wasn't *me* Kris was afraid of." And I finally understood. It was Hart. Everything made sense now. The way he'd tried to warn me off in the orchard, telling me that everyone knew about Kris and me, that he didn't want me to get hurt. The way he didn't come to comfort me when I stormed off to the river that day.

But by the time I figured it out, my brother was experiencing his own heartbreak. After working all fall for Serafina Padilla, he found her one morning, dead in her kitchen. Greedy cousins swarmed up from Velarde to sell off the farm, and apparently she had never told anyone or put in writing her promise to pay Hart for his work with a couple of acres. Her relatives gave him twenty bucks and showed him the door. Pancho came with him back to Armonía but died a few weeks later.

The Island County Fair is the second week in August.

At nine o'clock on a Saturday morning, Freddie picks me up and we drive to the fairgrounds, me holding the pan of brownies in my rapidly dwindling lap. We leave the car in the shade of a big hemlock tree and join the trickle of early birds walking along the road in the cool morning breeze, stopping to pick blackberries and pop them in our mouths. A few are still a little tart, but most of them are plump and ripe. I don't chew them; I crush them between my tongue and the roof of my mouth to prolong the musty sweetness. They are the secret ingredient in my brownies.

We leave the pan at the baked goods table under the tin roof of the main building and then make our way to the Harmony Players' booth in the arena. In addition to building our "sound booth" out of sheets of plywood, Piggy has painted a sign that says YOU'RE ON THE AIR and surrounded it with flashing Christmas tree lights. It looks a lot different from all the other booths, where island artists and craftspeople, farmers and homemakers, display their work for show and sale. Even though there's nobody there, nothing going on yet, people have gravitated to the lights, curious about what's coming.

Freddie takes out a manila envelope full of copies of the spot she's written and lays it on the counter with the cash box and the registration forms, the raffle tickets, a cup crammed with pens and pencils, and the giant glass bowl for the drawing.

Joe McAffee, the program director of KILE-FM, looks like a satyr—black wavy hair, beak of a nose, warm brown eyes, and killer smile. "So you're the VO," he says when he shakes my hand. He's about an inch shorter than I am, but energy seems to crackle in the air around him.

"I'll just get this all set up and we'll do one or two, and then I'll turn it over to you." He's opening up his PowerBook as we speak, turning it on, plugging in the headphones and the mixer. The mike is a well-used Shure 58, the kind bands use because it filters out background noise and picks up the singer. He sets it in a stand on the table.

"Running this thing's a piece of cake. Let's do a test." He plops the headphones on me and I sit at the table. "We'll go on one. Okay? Five, four, three, two . . ." he points at me and I read Freddie's copy.

Change comes slowly to a small New Hampshire town in the first days of the twentieth century. People grow up, get married, live, and die. Newspapers and milk get delivered every morning, and nobody locks their front doors.

It's Our Town, *Thornton Wilder's Pulitzer Prize—winning play, presented by The Harmony Players, a dream of small-town America, full of simplicity and charm. It's also a contemplative work about the nature of human existence. But we sneak that part in so it doesn't even hurt.*

Arrive early, walk slowly, hold hands, greet friends. Don't miss Our Town. *Three shows only at Harmony*

High School Auditorium. Friday and Saturday, October 10 and 11 at 7 pm, Sunday, October 12 at 2 pm. Tickets available at the Ale House, the Library, Different Drummer Books, and the Chamber of Commerce.

"Got it. Want to hear what you did?"

I shake my head. "That's okay. I know what I sound like."

He plays it back on the computer anyway. "You've got a terrific sound," he says. "You ever want to work, come see me."

"Thanks. I might do that."

"We ready back there?" Freddie hollers from out front. "We got some American Idols out here."

The first contestant is a girl who looks about fifteen. She's beautiful in that way only a very young girl can be—skin soft as a flower, wisps of light brown hair curled around her face. She has a sprinkling of freckles, very long eyelashes that dust her cheeks, and a gap between her front teeth big enough to drive a bike through. She hands me her registration: Tiffany George. Tiffany's nervous, but Joe puts her at ease with jokes about her jewelry store. He puts the headphones on her.

"Just relax, speak clearly, and in your normal voice. It's a little bit noisy, so I want you to get right on top of that mike, okay? Don't worry if you fluff it; we can do another take. Okay, we'll go on one. Ready? Five, four, three, two . . ." He points.

Tiffany reads.

"That was great," he says. You're a natural."

She laughs and blushes, and when she leaves I hear Freddie telling her to have all her friends e-mail the station and vote for her.

"Sunny, you do this next one. All you need to do is hit the

Space bar to start and stop. See, it brings up the wave file so you can see the elapsed time. Then you can save each one as a file under the person's name."

He gets up and holds the chair for me. I wonder if he's always such a gentleman or if it's because I'm pregnant.

"I'm going to get some coffee," he says. "I'll come back and spell you in a while."

As soon as he leaves, we're inundated. News travels fast that there's something really cool going on at the Harmony Players booth, and by ten thirty, the line out front is halfway down the aisle to the entrance.

When Joe comes back at 11:00 to check on us, the sun is high, the arena's hot, and our little sound booth should be labeled SAUNA.

"Joe, honey, can you see if you can find us a fan?" Freddie gives him a persuasive smile. "It's hot enough to fry a horned toad in here. I think Sunny's going to be ten pounds lighter by the time we're done, bless her heart."

I mop my face with a paper napkin left over from coffee somebody brought us.

"Tell you what," he says. "Why don't you guys take a break? Have some lunch. When you come back, I'll go back to the station and grab my little desk fan."

Freddie and I walk along the sawdust midway, where the barkers try to get you to knock over pyramids of wooden milk bottles with baseballs and the tilt-a-whirl careens around and up and down and the little rollercoaster roars by with its cargo of screaming kids. I see Laura and Piggy on the carousel, riding side-by-side horses and holding hands. We pass the music stage where a group of high-school girls with guitars are singing old folk songs. Children gnaw on corn dogs or clutch wands of spun cotton candy, their mouths outlined in sticky red sugar. Toddlers lick the ice cream cones that dribble down their arms—all of them caught up in the fair's magic, sweetly oblivious.

We buy lunch at the Rotary Club salmon barbecue and sit on a bench eating it and drinking icy lemonade, watching the people, smelling the damp, grassy smell of animals from over in the livestock barn.

"There's Most Popular Couple." Freddie points across the arena at Trish and Scott.

They walk slowly, arms around each other's waists, followed by JT, hands in his back pockets. He's never called me or come over; in fact this is the first time I've seen him since the scene at my house. Freddie ratchets up the Texas twang. "And look at that. The little maverick's trailin' them—unroped, unbranded, and lookin' for love."

I tilt my head back too far and the ice in my cup shifts, sloshing lemonade down the front of my shirt. "Damn!" I brush pieces of ice off my rounded tummy. "We better get back and relieve Joe."

At three o'clock Hallie and Laura arrive to run the booth till the fair closes at 9:00 p.m. Freddie and I head for the food fair where the crowd around the tables is already six deep even though winners won't be announced for another thirty minutes. There are so many categories, I can't keep track of all of them, but it seems they're doing desserts last. We wander around looking at the gorgeous produce, the jams and jellies, the home-canned goods, the chili.

Freddie makes a face. "These are all nice folks, but they don't know thing damn one about chili. Look at these . . . every last one of them's got beans in it."

The judges are finally moving—slowly but steadily—from one table to the next, laying out the ribbons next to the winners, saying a few words about their choices, chatting with contestants and their partisans. Every few minutes there's a burst of applause.

At last they get to the desserts. Cakes are first, then pies. When it's time for the cookies, Freddie steers me up front.

"So you can pick up your prize," she whispers.

"Why are you so sure—did you bribe somebody?"

"Didn't have to. Hush! Here they come."

And sure enough. The gold ribbon goes to a plate of lemon bars, the red to triple chocolate chippers, and the blue ribbon is laid with great ceremony in front of my brownies.

"Hot diggy damn doggies!" Freddie pounds me on the back so hard I bite my tongue. "I told you!"

"Hey, Sunny! Good job, babe!" Piggy shoulders through the crowd, which parts for him like the Red Sea.

The head judge, a chubby guy with perfectly manicured nails, who works at Forsthoff's market, beams at me, then his eyes stray to Piggy. "You must be the biker—baker. I mean baker."

"She's both," Piggy says.

I nod, still sort of in shock, amused and amazed.

"These are simply fantastic." He clears his throat and addresses the crowd. "The judges felt that not only were the brownies prize-worthy in terms of taste, crumb, and texture, but the addition of blackberries makes them particularly northwestern, and gives them a haunting taste that evokes the end of summer. Congratulations, Mrs. Cooper." He hands me an envelope, while the crowd applauds politely and a frizzy-haired guy wearing an *Island Times* T-shirt leaps around taking photos of me with my blue ribbon.

Trish grins broadly. "And you thought they just tasted good."

Thirty minutes later everyone's dispersed, agreeing to meet at 6:30 for dinner. Freddie and I are waiting for the photographer to finish snapping the entries. Across the way, in front of another stage, the next band is setting up. Suddenly JT steps out of the press of bodies and my heart turns over.

Just in time, I manage to stop my hand from waving at him, diverting it to brush the hair away from my sweaty forehead. He's with someone. Blond and eye-catching even at a distance, moving with an easy, athletic grace. Casey Callender. She grabs his arm, pulling him toward the midway, and they disappear into the crowd, holding hands.

Freddie stands next to me, arms folded. "If you could see the look on your face, honey."

"What are you talking about?" I try to sound puzzled, not annoyed.

"What happened with you guys? Couldn't he handle it?"

My temper, which is unpredictable at best these days, flares up. I open my mouth to tell her to mind her own business, and then it happens. Just below my navel, something moves. Not a jab or a kick, but a sudden swimming motion.

The entity has put me on notice.

Chapter 26

No good deed goes unpunished.

Sunday I offer to work for Barbara, who's gone down to Seattle to visit a friend in the hospital. Otherwise I wouldn't even be on the floor at 1:30 in the afternoon when Dean, who's behind the bar for brunch, comes back in the kitchen to say there's a guy asking for me.

I've been expecting him, and there's no one else it could be, but it still hits me like a wrecking ball when I step through the swinging doors and see him standing there, one arm resting on the bar. Feelings bear down on me, too many, too mixed. I feel cold and hot and sick.

He's wearing jeans and a black T-shirt. His hair is long and pulled into a ponytail. His face seems thinner. Could be the new beard. Or maybe it's just the things I know about him now that make him look different.

"Sunny . . ." His smile is uncertain. "You look . . . great."

"Yeah, you too. Especially considering how long you've been dead."

"I was hoping we could talk."

"Why?"

"So I could explain—"

"It won't make any difference."

"I know." He lets out a breath. "But I was thinking you might at least be curious . . . You don't seem very surprised to see me."

"I heard about your miraculous revival when the DNA lab report came back. They thought I'd want to know." From the corner of my eye, I see Dean regarding us with interest and several people at tables trying to get my attention. "As you can probably tell, I'm working at the moment."

"What time are you off? I could meet you at your place—"

"Absolutely not."

"Well . . . is there someplace we can go?" He leans toward me slightly, lowering his voice. "Someplace quiet?"

"I'll think about it. I'm off at seven."

He smiles again; this time his glance avoids the bulge under my shirt. "I'll see—"

Before he can finish, I grab the iced tea pitcher and the water pitcher and head for my tables. When I look over at the bar again, he's gone.

Eventually my hands quit shaking.

I mark the afternoon's progress by where the sun lies on the Ale House floor, by the shadows inching across the street, and by the dread building a nest in my stomach. I could leave early and take the ferry over to Friday Harbor or Anacortes. Get a room someplace and just wait it out. He can't hang around here forever. I consider that option and discard it several times during the afternoon. He just happened to hit on the one thing that could move me now.

I want to know what happened.

At some point Dean reminds me that I haven't taken my breaks or my lunch. I tell him I don't feel like eating, and he gives me a questioning look but doesn't ask. I find myself wishing Piggy was here.

Not that I want him to do anything specific. I just miss the comfort of his bulky presence. It surprises me to realize that of all the people I know—here in Harmony or back in New Mexico—it's Piggy that I trust, unquestioningly and completely. I would trust him with my life.

I know I'm not in any kind of danger. Not from Michael. I admit I've been wrong about him, but not that wrong.

And yet . . . when I come out the front door at 7:15, behind two couples, and he's waiting more patiently than I ever remember and his eyes find me, I have the sensation of meeting a total stranger who only resembles someone I knew—and the dread ramps up.

For a minute neither of us speaks.

"Are you . . . pregnant?" he asks. His voice is subdued.

"I think that's fairly obvious."

Either he doesn't know what to ask next or he's afraid to ask anything. I start walking, and he falls in beside me as if our going somewhere together were entirely natural.

The Bayshore is a seedy little pub behind the ferry terminal frequented mostly by fishermen, construction workers, and ferry crews—or so I've heard—and I can feel the stares on us before my eyes adjust to the dim light. The combined smell of beer and old hamburger grease is oddly comforting. All at once I'm hungry.

We order at the bar and take our drinks to a booth in the back, where we sit across from each other. I dunk the wedge of lime in my club soda and watch the bubbles rise, and he pulls the wrapper off the straw in his Coke.

"Look, Sunny, before I say anything else, I want you to know that I'm really sorry."

"For what? Letting me think you were dead? Leaving me to deal with the people you ripped off? Sleeping with my best friend?"

"I don't blame you if you hate me."

"That's good, because I do."

He reaches for the pack of Marlboros in his shirt pocket, draws one out, and taps it on the table, one end, then the other. He quit over a year ago.

"You can't smoke in here," I say.

"I just need one in my hand sometimes."

"How did you find me? Did Betsy tell you?"

He doesn't react to her name. "I traced you online. You bought a cell phone here . . . Harmony Wireless." He laughs a little, regaining some of his confidence. "Don't look so shocked. It's easy to do these days. I just looked at your MasterCard bill."

"So much for online security."

"I helped you set up your account, remember?" he says modestly. "I had your password."

"Of course you did." After everything else he's done to me, my outrage at this revelation seems somehow beside the point.

"I figured you'd probably try to get a job at a restaurant, and there aren't that many. I just started calling till I found you. So . . ."

"So you thought you'd just drop by. Since you were in the neighborhood."

He scans the drinkers at the bar. "Actually I'm on my way to Mexico and I . . . just wanted to see you before—" He waves the empty aluminum dish and the annoyed-looking waitress appears to refill it with peanuts. "It's been a bad time for me," he says.

"If I've said or done anything to make you think I care, I sincerely apologize."

In spite of the darkness and the fact that I can hardly stand looking at him, I'm acutely aware of his eyes, that deep, clear blue with points of light like a crown of fire.

He lets go a long, exhausted breath. "All right, I won't bore you with sentiment. There's a Dolen CD. I think you have it."

"Michael, what have you gotten yourself involved in?"

He smiles wanly. "I thought you didn't care."

"I don't. Except as it concerns me."

"It doesn't concern you. I'm trying not to have it concern you, but I want the disk."

"And I want to know what the hell happened. How everything could be so totally and completely different from what I thought."

When the waitress brings the food, I immediately regret ordering it. The hamburger is overdone and too salty. I put it down after one bite and squeeze a blob of ketchup next to the fries, glistening with grease. I wait for him to talk. I want to know what happened, but I also want to know what he's going to tell me, how much he's willing to volunteer without being interrogated.

Michael tucks into his cheeseburger, apparently oblivious to the fact that it's terrible. Half of it's gone before he says, "I had some money problems."

"You always had money problems. You told me up front that it would always be possible. You said—"

"Listen. Just listen to me, okay? This was different. I was playing poker."

I study him. The way his eyes keep darting away from mine, the way he clenches his jaw, the nervous tapping of the cigarette. "I guess we're not talking about the Monday night group."

"No. It was some other people."

"The Campos Syndicate?"

He looks surprised. "What do you know about Campos?"

"Nothing. I saw the name in your check register."

"Campos run these poker games that I sat in on, every now and then. High-stakes games," he says. "And I had a run of bad luck. Not a huge deal; it happens to everybody. But it's not like owing money to a bank or to investors. You can't just file bankruptcy and expect them to go away. It still would've been okay if I could have sold Brookfield."

I stir a French fry around in the puddle of ketchup till it's all but dissolved. "Why couldn't you?"

"Because I took money out of it."

"To finance your gambling habit."

"Sunny . . ." He places his hands on either side of his plate, as if he could push the table away and me with it. "Just so you know, I don't have a gambling habit. I just happen to like playing poker. The money was to finance some other start-ups."

"So who's Milton Kaplan?"

"A friend of Brian's. He lives in Denver, but he was coming down to Albuquerque a lot and he'd show up at the Monday night group once in a while. He said he did some day trading, managed investments for other people. Sometimes we'd go out for a drink after. He knew I needed money, and he had this idea about building up Remington and then promoting the stock to his mailing list of investors."

I roll up my jacket and stuff it behind the small of my back to relieve the ache there. "Yes, I think I've met some of them indirectly. One of them followed me up to my mother's house."

"And then Milton came up with this other thing." He shifts uneasily in the booth and his eyes slide away from mine. "He said he had these associates who needed to distance themselves from the source of their income, and then reintegrate it back into—" He drinks some more Coke. "They could use a couple of companies I already had in place, and they paid us a percentage of what we handled for them. It was a way to make some money fast without having to do much."

"Just out of curiosity, what made you think that getting involved in money laundering would be a good idea?"

He closes his eyes briefly, and it's a gesture of defeat. "I was desperate. I was only going to do it till I could settle up with Campos and repay what I'd borrowed from Brookfield."

"What about Kirby?"

"We needed a tech guy to set up the systems. And I knew he could do just about anything you needed done on a computer."

"So what happened? Did he get greedy?"

Something like real sadness shadows his face. "With him it was never about money. He just loved being able to do what he did. It was sort of his art."

"What happened?"

"I'm not sure. He called that morning and asked me if I'd gotten the CD he sent me. I had, but I hadn't looked at it. I thought it was in my office somewhere. He said there were discrepancies in some of the accounts, and one of Milton's buddies wanted to set up a meeting. He sounded freaked out. We were supposed to meet for dinner, but he never showed up. I waited and I checked different restaurants. I thought maybe I misunderstood the place or the time. I kept trying to call him. I thought about going to his house, but by that time it was dark and he lives . . . lived way up Boca Canyon. I knew I'd never find it on my own.

"I decided to stay up there that night. I thought if he called me we could still get together, but he never did. Then when you told me somebody broke into the apartment and your CDs were gone, I didn't sleep at all. Mostly I walked around the room. Finally I dozed off, and when the clock radio came on I was laying there listening to the local news and I heard it."

He looks longingly at the cigarette. "There was a fire in Boca Canyon. I knew it had to be Kirby. I grabbed my stuff and ran outside. And while I was standing there, trying to decide what the fuck I should do, the airport shuttle pulled up at the Comfort Inn next door. I didn't even think. I just got on and rode back to Albuquerque."

"What happened to the truck?"

"I left it."

"You just walked away from the Blue Dog?"

"I was scared. I needed to be invisible, and driving that truck would have been like wearing a target. With Kirby dead, I'd be—"

"How did you know he was dead?"

"I just knew it, okay?" Impatience hones the edge of his voice. "In my gut. Anyway, I took a cab from the airport back to the apartment. I knew you wouldn't be there and I wanted to look for the CD." He blots his forehead with what's left of the cocktail napkin, leaving a tiny shred of paper over one eyebrow. "But it was gone. I figured whoever broke in had gotten it. So I took a few things and I left." He finishes off the Coke and motions to the waitress, holding up his empty glass.

"Where did you go?"

"To Sandra's. She used to answer the phones a couple of years ago and she's been doing some document prep for me. She let me stay at her place. Don't look at me like that. It's not what you think."

"Nothing ever was. But why couldn't you at least let me know you weren't dead? Why couldn't you trust me that much?"

"I didn't even know I was supposedly dead until Sandra got a call from Milton wanting to know if I'd left any CDs with her— that's when I knew that the CD must still be around somewhere. And it wasn't a question of my not trusting you. I just figured if you didn't know anything, it would be safer. For you."

"But who was driving the truck?"

"I have no idea. Some jerk probably just stole it from the parking lot and took off for Colorado."

"What are you planning to do with the CD?"

"I don't even know what's on it."

"You came all the way up here to get the thing, and you don't know what it is?"

"Not for sure. I don't think anyone else knows, either. But it's leverage."

"Sort of like a grenade without the firing pin. Michael, you need to go to the police. Tell them what you know."

"No way." He shakes his head. "As soon as they found out it wasn't me in the truck, they decided I'd killed Kirby."

"Well, between the police, Milton, and the 'associates,' I think I'd rather be found by the police."

"I don't intend to be found by any of the above."

The waitress sets down a full glass and picks up his empty one. He pulls a money clip out of his pocket and hands her a twenty, then he looks at his watch. "I need to get the CD and get back here for the nine-fifteen ferry."

"Michael, there is no nine-fifteen ferry."

"Yeah, there is. I checked the schedule in Anacortes."

"Well, you didn't check it closely enough. The late ferry doesn't run on Sunday night."

He stares at me for a few seconds. "Shit."

I pull a piece of cheese off the burger and nibble on it.

"Let me guess. You need a place to sleep. Well, you're in luck. The town of Harmony offers several excellent clean and tidy motels."

"Sunny . . ." He gives me a pleading look. "It's not good for me to be staying in motels. If somebody's looking for me, that's the first place they'll check."

"Wrong. They'll expect you to come to me. The first place they'll check is my house. No thanks."

"Okay, look. The truth is, I'm a little short of funds. Getting to Mexico is going to take most of—"

I can't help it. I laugh. "Some things never change."

"Could I just sleep in your car?"

"I don't have a car."

His eyebrows go up. "How do you get around?"

"I have a truck."

"Can I sleep in your truck?"

"The cab's too small. You couldn't—"

"Then just let me sleep on your floor. Please." The last word is almost inaudible.

I don't want to do this. It feels wrong. It makes me sick to my stomach. Or I guess it could be the greasy fries. But I look at him sitting across from me in this painfully upright wooden booth, and it all comes tumbling back, the way it was a few years ago when things were good. Saturday afternoons down by the river, dinners at the Artichoke Café, Sunday mornings in bed, the newspapers that didn't get read.

I sit back and exhale very slowly. "Okay."

Water is running in the bathroom and it seems so completely unlikely that now, after all that's happened, and two thousand miles from where we once had a life together, he's here at my house, taking a bath. I peel an apple into my compost bucket and cut slivers off it to eat while I make a grocery list. In a while he wanders into the kitchen and sits down at the table. His hair is wet and slicked back, and the clean, damp smell of him fills the little room, achingly familiar.

He says, "I wish things hadn't turned out like this."

"Right." I shake a box of rice to see how much is left. "If only we were still in Albuquerque. You could be running your money laundering business and you and Betsy could be—" I turn abruptly. "What is it with you two? You and Betsy. She wished it had never happened. It was a bad situation. You're sorry 'things' turned out like this. Why can't either one of you just take responsibility?"

He's quiet for a minute. Maybe he's thinking about it. Maybe he's only pretending to think about it. "So where's the CD?" he says finally.

I set down my list and pencil carefully and turn to him. "I don't have it."

The color drains from his face. "What do you mean?"

"I gave it to Jonas Bradley."

The chair scrapes on the floor as he gets to his feet, and I lean back reflexively. "Who the fuck is Jonas Bradley?"

"He's a cop. A private security cop. He's the one who told me you were still alive."

He's pacing back and forth in front of me, running a hand through his hair, dislodging the ponytail. "Sunny, how could you do that? Why?"

"Because"—I fold my arms, resting them on top of my stomach—"I wanted him to go away. He accused me of helping you. Of being in on everything. Of planning to meet you here. I thought if I didn't give it to him and they found out later that I had it . . ."

"How would they find out?"

"How do they find out anything? Maybe Milton told them."

"Milton wouldn't tell them anything."

"Somebody did."

"For Chrissakes, even if they knew it existed, they couldn't prove you ever had it."

"Well, you know what? Lying to the cops isn't in my job description. I didn't sign on for the fugitive lifestyle."

He sits down again. "I know. I'm sorry. Shit, Milton's probably in Puerto Vallarta by now anyway. Drinking margaritas on the beach."

"Milton's in Miami," I say. "In jail."

He stares at me for a second, then he starts to laugh, that

kind of teetering-on-the-brink sound, the way you laugh when you're exhausted and nothing is funny but you don't know what else to do.

When the trees outside are fuzzy gray shapes in the fog, I get up and make coffee. I didn't sleep at all. I lay in bed listening to his raspy breathing in the living room. Even when I got up to use the bathroom he didn't stir, and I wondered when he'd last slept through the night in a bed. And whether he was alone. And then I wondered why I was even wondering about that.

I brew my cup of raspberry leaf/nettle tea that Mary Jo prescribed for supplemental iron, calcium, and folic acid and sit at the table sipping and listening. Finally I hear a slight rustling, the change in breathing that means he's awake.

He comes in rumpled and yawning, stretching his arms above his head. His shirt is wrinkled and he slaps the floor dust off his jeans.

"I slept like the dead." He sits down across from me. "Thanks for letting me stay."

I say, "Coffee's ready. Help yourself."

He drinks it fast, sucking in air to cool it as it goes down. He looks at his watch.

"I didn't mean to sleep this late. When's the first ferry?"

"The first one's already gone. There's another one at eight ten."

"Eight ten. Who makes up these schedules? Why not eight fifteen?" He smiles at me. "Crazy."

The word sits there between us like the last cookie on a plate. Yeah, crazy. I'm thinking about how everything might have worked out differently. If I'd been more willing to take chances and he'd been less willing.

"I don't think I did a very good job of explaining things," he says. "I mean, last night. About the gambling . . ."

I smile, but not convincingly. "There's a point where it stops making any difference."

"I guess." He looks at my cup. "What's that you're drinking?"

"Herbal tea."

"You never liked herbal tea," he reminds me, as if I suddenly forgot.

"It's sort of a pregnant lady thing. Then I can have my coffee."

His expression softens and his voice becomes almost tender. "Who's the lucky guy?"

I stare at him. "Michael, are you really such a jackass? You think after you're dead for one month I'm out screwing around, getting myself knocked up?"

Now he's fully awake, and I watch his face go slack with comprehension. "Jesus. No. I didn't. Sunny . . . Why didn't you tell me? I'm . . . I don't know what to say. What can I . . ." He swallows another mouthful of coffee, forgetting that it's scalding hot, and he winces. "This . . . changes things."

I drain the cup and get up to fix my own coffee. "No," I say without looking at him. "It doesn't change anything. As far as I'm concerned, this child's father is dead."

It's about a quarter of a mile down Lavender Road to the trail head. The sun is poking long fingers through the trees. A couple of rental cars are parked by the side of the road. Michael looks around nervously.

"Hikers," I say.

He nods. "Remember that trip to Chaco in the fall? October."

"Yes." *Before everything got weird*, I think, but I don't say it.

The trail is partly choked with summer growth, but it's easy enough to follow. We emerge from the woods by Monarch Pond, and he actually stops to pick a few blackberries before we continue across the meadow. It's strange, walking here, picking berries, watching the birds, as if we were vacationers planning to have breakfast in town.

"How did you find this place?" he asks suddenly.

"I wanted to get as far away from New Mexico as I could without flying over water."

"Are you going to stay?"

"I haven't decided." I let my eyes follow a hawk riding the wind above us. "Why did you lie to me? About being part Indian?"

He looks up, surprised. "I didn't."

"Michael, come on. Frank came to the apartment one morning. He said you'd called him, but he was on a fishing trip—"

"Who's Frank?"

"Your brother, of course."

He comes to a complete stop, turns to me, and grips my arms. "I don't have a brother. I told you that."

"You told me a lot of stuff. None of it was true."

"That part was. Sunny, I swear to God. My mother was Cheyenne. I don't have a brother. At least not that I know about."

I pull my arms out of his grasp. "Then who was he? He said he was your older brother, that he lived in Manitou Springs. That your dad was a contractor and—"

"What did he look like?"

I think for a minute, picturing Frank Graham on the doorstep, in the kitchen, sitting across from me over breakfast at Flying Star. "Not quite as tall as you. Kind of slim. Brown hair. Blue eyes. He drove a blue Jeep Cherokee."

"Son of a bitch." His head falls back and then he looks at me. "That was Milton."

Suddenly things start to settle out. The photo of the Monday night poker group. The guy standing behind Michael, the one who looked familiar, but I couldn't place him: it was Milton.

"But he was . . . *nice*. He was so— I had breakfast with him."

"Yeah. He can turn on the charm if it suits him. When did he show up?"

"It was right after your—the funeral." I look at him. "Why? Why would he do that?"

"He was on a fishing trip, all right. He was trying to find out if you knew anything. And he was probably checking the place out. In case he wanted to come back later when you weren't there."

"But why would he spend so much time concocting this whole story about your family and—"

"Who knows. Maybe he thought if you were pissed off enough at me, you'd tell him something. Or . . ." He smiles, a rueful half-smile. "He's quite an actor. Maybe he just enjoyed playing you."

"And his car , , ," Now every hair on my scalp rises.

"What about it?"

I hit a deer, he said. I felt awful.

I see it like a photograph, the broken headlight, the dented grill. *Oh my God.*

"I think he killed Kirby."

Michael frowns. "Why do you think that?"

"The newspaper said Kirby was hit by a vehicle. The front of the Cherokee was all bashed in. He said he'd hit a deer."

"A deer," Michael says.

We start walking again, both of us silent now. It's damp and cool under the tall firs, and every step we take sends up a burst of evergreen fragrance.

Suddenly we step out of the shadows; the woods give way to tall grass and the path submerges under pavement. At the bottom of the hill, cars are lined up waiting to board the ferry. Some drivers have already started their engines.

I walk with him to the door of the foot passenger waiting room, and we stand, awkward, looking out over the marina. Colorful flags snap in the breeze.

He says, "Will you be okay?"

"I'll be fine."

"Maybe I should get in touch later. After the— in case you need money or—"

"Don't do that. Please." I know he means to be reassuring, but it feels oppressive. I reach down in my jeans pocket and come up with the crumpled scrap of paper, pull it out and offer it to him.

"What's this?"

"Tim Bagley. Sergeant Bagley. He seems like a decent guy."

"I can't—"

"Just take it, okay? In case you change your mind."

He tucks the paper into his T-shirt pocket. The boarding announcement crackles unintelligibly over our heads and drivers start inching forward. He looks at the ferry, then back at me. I'm not even sure his hand is actually moving, but I step back out of range.

"Good-bye, Michael." Something is rising in my throat—maybe all the questions I can't ask because I can't care about the answers. I can hardly breathe.

He hesitates.

"You'd better go on," I say. "They always leave on time."

"Bye, Sunny. I'm sorry."

As soon as he's through the door, I'm walking. Quickly. Back down the trail that will take me home, so nobody I know will see me crying at the terminal.

Chapter 27

September. It's fall.

I know, because I've turned the garden under. Because the tourists are gone. Because quail hoot in the early morning mist and geese honk in the evening. Yellow jackets pester me when I sit outside, and every day I find at least one woolly bear on my porch, endearing in their little orange-and-black fuzzy sweaters. Hallie says you can predict the severity of the coming winter by the width of the black bands.

Bright yellow leaves of alder and big-leaf maple have begun to spike the green woods, and clusters of intense orange-red berries on the madrones around the cottage attract more birds than I ever saw during the summer. Afternoons are filled with their twittering, as well as the raucous squeaks and scolds of Douglas squirrels.

Shopkeepers have relaxed their overworked smile muscles, and when you go in someplace they seem genuinely glad to see you. The smell of woodsmoke lingers in the streets of Harmony.

I do love New Mexico in the fall, all the aspen and cottonwoods flaming gold against the blue sky, clumps of purple asters by the roadsides. Every grocery store parking lot thick with the smell of roasting Hatch chiles and the October sky nearly obscured by bright clouds of hot air balloons. I'd always sort of thought I'd be back there by this time.

Instead I'm sitting in Dr. Ralph's examining room waiting for my six-month checkup. Mary Jo bustles in, wisps of hair escaping from her ponytail, stethoscope draped around her neck.

"Hi, Sunny," she twinkles. "How are you doing?"

"I'm fine."

She looks at me over the tops of her glasses. "And she? How's she doing?"

"She's fine, too."

Mary Jo smiles ingratiatingly. "Have you've talked to your mother?"

"Well, actually . . ."

"Sunny." Her hands are resting on her wide hips, all the twinkle having been replaced with exasperation. "You need to tell her."

I know I need to tell her, but some reluctance—maybe just a stubborn need to deprive her—makes me hold back. I say, "You and Freddie. I wish you guys would give it a rest."

"I don't know what Freddie's interest in the situation is, but mine is the health of you and your baby. So I will not, as you say, give it a rest. What are you planning to do, wait till you're having contractions?"

"What if she was dead? Or backpacking through Katmandu?"

Mary Jo sits down on the little black stool and wheels it over so that she's sitting right in front of me. "I don't know what kind of problems you have with your mother, but I truly believe that you can work around anything." Her voice softens. "This could be such a special time for the two of you. You could probably talk to her about your fears and your hopes for this child and find out that she felt very much the same when she was pregnant with you."

"Mary Jo, talking about fears and hopes is really not my thing."

She sighs and pats my knee. "Okay."

She weighs me, takes my blood pressure, squeezes my ankles and wrists, listens to my stomach with her stethoscope, measures it with a dressmaker's tape.

She laughs. "I think she's going to be a soccer player." Then she meticulously records her findings on my chart. I'm getting ready to hop off the table and grab my clothes, when she stops me.

"What time do you go to work today?"

"I'm off today."

"Good. Can you stop by about four o'clock? I want to check your blood pressure again." Her voice is casual. Too casual.

"What's wrong?"

She smiles and pats my arm. "Nothing's wrong. Your blood pressure's a little elevated, that's all. I want to see if it's just a temporary jump, or if it's something we need to be monitoring a little more closely."

Heat is crawling up the back of my neck. "Don't treat me like a moron, Mary Jo."

"I won't if you promise not to act like one." Her soft blue eyes snap. "This is quite routine. Your systolic is right up around one-twenty-five, which is just a bit on the high side. I want to double-check it. So go do whatever you were planning to do today and swing back by here about four."

I pull on my new baggy pants and the large denim men's work shirt I bought at a yard sale last month. Trish's friend Annette cut off the long shirttails and shortened the sleeves for me so the cuffs button at my wrists, but it's still not a terribly attractive ensemble. I'm in full fretting mode while I pull on my socks and tie my jogging shoes. What if I have high blood pressure and I have to go to bed for three months? Not only will I die from sheer boredom, but I'll die flat broke. I could live for about a month on what I've got in the bank . . . maybe. It would be touch and go. I'm getting checks from the state, but they're not very much. I need to work.

Shit. All this monthly checkup stuff, monitoring weight, blood pressure, sugar and protein in your urine . . . Gwen never had any of that, and she managed to deliver two perfectly healthy babies. Of course, that third one was sort of complicated, but what are the chances?

While my clothes are going around and around at the Laundromat, I drink orange juice and read the pamphlet on PIH (pregnancy-induced hypertension) and preeclampsia that was in my information packet from Dr. Miller. It's not fun reading. While I'm taking my things out of the dryer and folding them into my laundry basket, I resolve to cut salt and fats from my diet, eat more fruits and vegetables, and try to relax more when I'm not working: put my feet up, read, listen to music, take more naps. I promise myself that I will avoid high blood pressure by being a model pregnant person, and through sheer force of will if necessary.

By the time I get back to Dr. Ralph's office at 4:00 p.m.,

I'm feeling like the situation is under control. Until Mary Jo tells me my blood pressure is the same as this morning. I reveal my plan of action to her.

"That's good," she says. "But I also want you to think about the possibility of taking a leave of absence from work."

At that, I burst out laughing. "Mary Jo, I'm a waitress. Make that *server*, if you need to be politically correct. Servers don't take a leave of absence. They either get fired or they quit."

She looks embarrassed, but she doesn't laugh. "Well, then I want you to think about the possibility of quitting early. Being on your feet all day is really hard on you and the baby."

"Excuse me, but I think it would be even harder on me and the baby if we couldn't buy food."

"Sunny, please, listen to me for just a moment." She pushes her wandering glasses back up to the bridge of her nose. "I hear what you're saying, believe me, I do. But we need to explore other possibilities. Maybe there's something you could do where you could sit down and work. I'm bringing it up now because we don't want to be pushing the envelope before you start to look for something."

"I just don't know what I could do. I mean, there's not much, is there?"

"It's true, there's not much going on here, especially this time of year. On the other hand, the last thing you want is a premature labor and delivery."

She could say more, but she doesn't have to. My mind is already swamped with images from television and magazines, tiny preemies looking like little naked birds under plastic domes in neonatal units, hooked up to machines, tubes in their noses. My eyes flood with tears.

"Oh, Sunny, don't cry." But she looks as if she's about to cry herself. "I don't mean to scare you. I'm not saying that's going to happen. We just need to be smart and make contingency plans." She sniffles a bit. "Truth be told, you're in a lot better shape than ninety percent of the women I've worked with. You're healthy and strong. Everything's going to be fine, believe me."

I blot my eyes. "I believe you. What other choice do I have?"

Dear Gwen, I write, and then I stop. Now I'm glad that she has no phone, no computer for e-mail. Writing a letter gives me the perspective of distance. It gives her time to think about my news, and it buffers me from an instantaneous reaction.

> *Following the advice of the I Ching, I crossed the great stream and ended up on San Miguel Island off the coast of Washington in a town called Harmony. I know you'll appreciate the irony. It's very pretty here and I have a job waiting tables at a place called the Ale House. I live in a small cottage outside of the village and I'm writing to tell you that I'm . . .*

I crumple the paper and toss it in the trash, pull out another sheet.

> *Dear Gwen,*
>
> *Believe it or not, I'm living in a place called Harmony.*
> *I'm pregnant and I'm scared. It's a girl. Were there any hereditary diseases in your family? I'm afraid some-*

*thing will go wrong with her because of some gene I'm car-
rying or because of something I did or didn't do. I'm afraid
I won't know how to take care of her when she gets here.
Most of all I'm afraid I'll love her too much and wreck her
life. What if she becomes a terrorist or a Republican? What
if she hates me? What should I do?*

I chew on the pen. Wait. Maybe I'm pushing too hard
again. Where is it written that everything has to be done at
once? I pull the first sheet out of the trash and copy it onto a
fresh page.

*I live in a small cottage outside of the village and I'm writ-
ing to invite you to come for Thanksgiving. You would fly
to Seattle and then take the shuttle to Anacortes and catch
the ferry to San Miguel. I can pick you up at the ferry terminal, so you wouldn't need a rental car. Let me know as
soon as you can. If you need it, my phone number is (360)
706-4161.*

Soleil

I fold the letter and shove it into the waiting envelope. I
can't remember her box number, so I address it to Terry at Arroyo Embuste Café.

JT's gone to Seattle. Weird that I didn't know. The Harmony
telegraph must be malfunctioning. I find out from Bailey.

I've been thinking that I wasn't fair to him, to JT, not
Bailey. The way I just blurted out my delicate condition with

no warning, nothing to help absorb the impact. And then expected him to take it in stride, be selflessly concerned about me. Or possibly so enamored of me that he would say of course it made no difference in the way he felt. That was expecting a bit much.

He's never called me. The only time I've seen him was at the fair. So I start thinking maybe I should go down to the marina and try talking to him. Maybe I could explain things in a way that he'd understand. I'm even prepared actually to tell him some stuff. Back story, as Freddie likes to call it. Not everything, of course, but something. Enough so that the situation makes a little more sense. We might as well be friends. I miss that.

Then this evening I'm just about to sit down to my salt-free, low-fat, high-fiber dinner when I hear something on my porch, sort of a scratching at the door. My first thought is that the raccoons are really getting brazen, but when I open the door, in walks Bailey. He sniffs all around the living room, then the kitchen, and then my bedroom. He scratches at the bathroom door till I open it and let him look inside. That's when it dawns on me. He's looking for JT.

I sit down on the fireplace hearth and he comes over and lays his head in my lap. He just stands there, looking up at me. I'm a sucker for big, sad eyes. I scratch his ears and stroke his head, tell him I forgive him for eating my medicine bundle. He turns around and goes to wait by the front door till I open it. Then he bounds off into the woods.

I leave my dinner on the warming shelf, throw on my jacket, and grab the keys to the truck and zip down to the marina. I wander up and down the rows till I find the *Lucky*

Dawg. Her lights are on, so I holler, "Request permission to come aboard!"

A man emerges from below—older, in desperate need of a shave and shower. He flashes me a grin.

"Hey, Albuquerque. Thought that was you. Where the hell ya been?"

"Oh, hi, Mick. I was looking for JT."

"He's over in the big city. I was just putting Bailey's dinner out, but give me a minute and I can scare up a couple of beers."

I take one step backward. "Thanks, I can't. I'm . . . meeting some friends. Do you know when he'll be back?"

He rubs his whiskered chin. "I think he said November." He cocks his head to one side. "Or was it December? Anyway, not for a while. You want me to tell him anything when he calls?"

"No. That's okay. I'll just . . . It's not urgent."

"Hey, I hear you're gonna be a mom."

I watch his face for any sign of leering sarcasm, but his smile is actually rather sweet. I look down at my stomach. "Yeah, it looks that way, doesn't it."

"Congrats." His eyebrows draw together. "But, hey, you should be eating more fish. Brain food, you know. For you and the kid. Come down and see me. I got a special mom's rate: two for one."

I smile at him without intending to. "Thanks. I'll do that." I turn around and walk back to where the truck sits waiting under a streetlight.

Fall segues into winter almost imperceptibly. It's colder, of course, but not like New Mexico. Things don't die so much as slumber. The air is damp, raw, and muffled with gray clouds, and the prevailing sound is the slow, steady drip of rain, followed by the slow, steady drip of water from the trees after the rain stops.

Among the natives, winter is a time of retreat and relaxation. Drowsing around the woodstove, reading, listening to music. Eating good food and drinking wine with friends. Only Freddie seems more fully alive at this season. She insists on dragging me out on walks through the stripped-down woods. I feel like one of the hot air balloons from the balloon fiesta, only not as graceful, as I lumber along, her hand hovering near my elbow. Just in case.

We traipse through rain-slicked ferns, Oregon grape and salal, mud sucking at our boots, cheered on by the chip-chip of winter wrens. We collect handfuls of lemon-scented needles from the Douglas firs and let them steep in boiling water for an astringent tonic that she swears has more vitamin C than orange juice. One morning in early November, after a light snowfall, we watch, fascinated, as a group of migrating swans feed in a marsh, waggling their wings, chasing each other, and bobbing their heads.

Freddie says, "Aren't you dying to know why they do all that stuff?"

I smile. "Not really."

Thirty minutes later we're back at my place, where Hallie joins us for lunch—ham and lentil soup commandeered from the Ale House kitchen, sourdough bread, and a salad put together with some of the last decent lettuce at Forsthoff's.

After we eat, Hallie stokes up the fireplace while Freddie makes a pot of tea and I sprawl in one of the wingback chairs.

"I can't believe I still have two months left. If I get any bigger, I'll need a forklift to get in the truck."

Freddie dumps a heaping tablespoon of sugar in her tea and stirs it slowly. "Shoot, you're not big. You should've seen my sister when she was pregnant with little Jack. When she'd walk by the corral, the bulls would all get excited 'cause they thought she was a new cow."

"Nice, Freddie. I can't wait to hear what you're saying about me in a couple of weeks."

Hallie stacks a last giant log on the pile and replaces the screen. "That ought to burn for the afternoon," she says, dusting her hands together. She sits on the floor and leans her back against Freddie's chair. "Sunny, who's going to be with you in labor?"

I take a breathy sip of tea. "Mary Jo."

"I mean besides her."

"Nobody, I guess."

"You still haven't told your momma, have you?" Freddie narrows her eyes at me.

"No. But I did invite her to come for Thanksgiving. I figure we'll discuss it when she gets here. If she comes."

"She will."

I don't mention that I mailed the letter several weeks ago and haven't heard anything from Gwen.

"You need someone besides a midwife," Hallie says.

"Why?"

"Because Mary Jo's going to be busy being the labor coach and delivery person. You need somebody else just to be there. To bring you ice water or stuff to nibble on. Read to you or rub your back when it hurts."

"I never thought of it. Are you volunteering?"

She looks at me. "Actually, yes. I'd like to do it. It's probably the closest I'll ever get to having a baby." She looks at Freddie. "Why don't you come, too. It'll be fun."

"Listen to you." I lean my head back and close my eyes. "*Fun.*"

"Um . . ." Freddie hesitates. "I think I'll pass. I'm not real good around blood and body fluids and stuff."

"Sissy." Hallie laughs.

"I don't deny it. If you need someone to run errands or make phone calls, or pace the floor and hand out cigars, I'm your woman. But don't ask me to do birthing. Besides"—she shifts in the chair—"I might not be here. I'm thinking about going home for Christmas."

"I'm going away after the holidays, but I'm flexible," Hallie says.

Freddie gives her a speculative look. "Oh yeah? Where're you going?"

"I don't know. Maybe California." Her voice is elaborately nonchalant.

I open one eye. "Where in California?"

She shrugs. "I'm not sure yet. Maybe Mendocino. I always liked it there."

"Uh-huh," Feddie says. "There's more here than meets the eye, Watson."

Hallie watches the fire. "I'll be gone for a month. Or two."

"*Two months?*" Freddie slaps her hands on her thighs.

I sit up. "What about the bookstore?"

"Well, I was hoping maybe you'd take care of it while I'm gone." She sneaks a look at me. "If you can't do it, that's okay," she says quickly. "I just thought, you know, you don't have to do much; it's pretty quiet after New Year's. And you could keep the baby there. But if you think it would be too much, I—"

"No!" I practically shout at her. "I don't think it's too much. In fact it's perfect. I wouldn't have to be on my feet all day or worry about what to do with the baby. It would buy me some time."

"I'd pay you, of course," she says gruffly.

I poke her with my toe. "I'd hug you, but I can't get up. Really, thank you, Hallie. Thanks so much."

Freddie folds her arms. "So what are you going to do in Mendocino for two months? *All by yourself.*"

"I don't remember saying anything about being all by myself."

Freddie leans over her like a vulture. "Spill it, Winkler. What's going on?"

A tiny smile is beginning to tug Hallie's mouth upward. "Well, I got a postcard from Eric a few months ago."

"Hot damn!" Freddie whoops.

"Don't get carried away. We're going to explore our options, that's all. We've been talking on the phone, and trying to figure out how we could work around the fact that he doesn't want to live here and I don't want to live in Santa Barbara."

"Does it really make that much difference where you live?" Freddie says.

"Yes, it does. It does to me." Hallie regards us gravely. "I don't know, maybe it's just easier and less complicated to love a place than a person. Anyway, we've got a lot of talking to do before we figure things out."

Freddie pours us all some more tea. "Hey, speaking of star-crossed lovers, guess who's back in town?"

I can't tell if the entity's got the hiccups or if it's my heart lurching. I'm so sure she's going to say JT that I can't help feeling deflated—as deflated as you can be at seven months pregnant—when she says, "Luke Carver." She basks for a minute in the reflected glow of inside information. "Rumor has it that Mary Beth dumped him for somebody and he punched the guy out, and now she's got a restraining order against him and he can't even see their little girl."

"Who told you that?" Hallie says.

"A writer never reveals her sources. But Trish introduced me to him day before yesterday at the market. And, ladies, he is a hottie. I do believe Mary Beth Lakes must be a couple sandwiches shy of a picnic to cut him loose. You can look at him and just see what Scott Carver must have looked like about twenty years ago."

I smile. "Can't wait to meet him."

The Tuesday before Thanksgiving is cold. A weak yellow sun radiates feebly in the watery blue sky. I'm working the lunch shift for Gus, who's gone home to Spokane for the holiday. My stomach enters the kitchen first and the rest of me waddles in after it. Sometimes, when I rest my hands on the basketball that is now my abdomen, I swear I can feel the ocean inside. The tides, crashing on the shore and then retreating. Other times there are flurries of bumping and kicking, like tap dancing.

"Hey, Sunny." Justin's ever jolly voice booms out. "How's my favorite *petite maman*?"

I swear, if it was anybody but Justin, I'd brain him with a frozen mackerel.

I smile at him. "Pretty good, thanks. How are you?"

The kitchen is warm and steamy, filled with holiday

smells—cinnamon and sage and citrus. I unwind the long scarf from around my neck and stuff my gloves in my jacket pocket. I pull down a clean apron, tie a bandana over my hair. Justin scoots a stool up to the worktable for me and brings me a paring knife, a bag of potatoes, and one of sweet potatoes.

"Gonna be quiet today," he says. "But tonight, now that's a different kettle of gumbo. Hoo-boy."

Late this afternoon the crowds will start arriving for the long weekend, he tells me. Holiday people and college students and snowbirds who'll stay on the island till after the New Year and then rush back to Phoenix or Hawaii.

"I don't see how you could live like that," I say. "In two places. Wouldn't you wake up in the middle of the night thinking you were in one house, and then when you turned on the light, you'd be in the other? Or maybe you'd be looking for something you thought you had with you and realize you'd left it in the other place."

Justin gives me a long, strange look. Then he clears his throat. "My Vickie, she says you should come take Thanksgiving with us. There's gonna be a crowd and I'm gonna deep-fry a turkey. We got plenty room for one more."

"Oh, Justin, that's sweet of you." Tears rise easily to my eyes. It happens so often I hardly notice them anymore. "Thank Vickie for me, but I'm going to the Grange Hall dinner. Taking my blue corn enchiladas."

"I'm gonna have to try those one day soon," he says. "Maybe you'll bring us the leftovers."

I laugh. "There aren't going to be any leftovers. But I'll make a pan just for you."

The phone rings. He goes to pick it up and I find myself

straining to hear if it's for me. He says, "Oh no, he ain't," and then releases a torrent of Cajun invective. Guess not.

I've never heard from my mother. And why would I think she'd call me here? I only gave her my cell phone number. I went ahead and arranged shift trades so I wouldn't have to work over the weekend, but I know better than to count on her.

Hart and I used to call her Coyote Woman.

In Native American mythology, Coyote is the trickster—contradictory and ambiguous. Coyote is clever, and he gave the magic of fire to the people, but he has been known to pull the rug out from under them on occasion, just for fun.

It doesn't really matter. Things are no better or worse than they've always been with us. I'll just have a nice, quiet Thanksgiving and get some extra sleep.

It's been dark for nearly two hours when I get home, even though it's only seven o'clock. I'm not used to being at loose ends in the evening. I build up the fire in the stove to heat up some corn chowder and I put Trisha Yearwood on the boom box. I want to hear "On a Bus to St. Cloud." I pull a small brown bag out of my daypack. A new lipstick I bought weeks ago and haven't used. Also one of those generic cards—HAPPY THANKSGIVING ACROSS THE MILES. I had some half-assed idea about sending it to Betsy. Not much point in it now.

I slide the card back into the bag and pour myself a glass of nonalcoholic wine. I eat my soup, wash my solitary bowl, spoon, and wineglass. Trisha's moved on to another bittersweet song, "You Can Sleep While I Drive." If I don't snap out of it, pretty soon I'll be listening to Leonard Cohen and staring into the fire.

I flip through the books on my shelf and pull out the one I've been meaning to read. When I open it, a yellowed newspaper clipping flutters to the table like a falling leaf.

SOFTWARE "ROCK STAR" FOUND DEAD.

It takes me a few seconds to recall where it came from, how it ended up in this book. Once the first memory kicks in, it's like cluster bombs. There's no turning it off. All the things that should have happened and didn't, and the ones that shouldn't have happened and did.

In a minute or two I wad up the clipping and throw it in the firebox. I put the book back on the shelf for another day, crawl under the covers on the maple spool bed, and find comfort in the dark.

In the dream, Gwen is standing on my porch. She's wearing a blue skirt and a fisherman's sweater, an old shearling jacket and even older red cowboy boots. Her brown suitcase looks held together with spit and string.

I gape at her for an indecent length of time, trying to make sense of something I must have forgotten.

She says, "You did mean *this* Thanksgiving, right?"

It's not a dream.

"Um . . . yes." I step back to let her in. All this time, she's staring at my belly. Finally she says, "How did this happen?"

"The usual way." I rub my eyes. "Why didn't you let me know you were coming?"

"Long story." She sets down her suitcase and looks around my living room. "Why didn't you let me know you were pregnant?"

"Long story."

We exchange a careful hug.

"Why didn't you at least call?" I pull the door shut. "I only have one twin bed. And no couch. I was going to rent a cot."

"That's okay," she says cheerfully. "I brought my sleeping bag." She slips the bedroll off her shoulders and sets it on one of the chairs. "Were you sleeping?"

"Yes, but it's time to get up." My runover slippers sit on the hearth, where I left them last night. I slide my feet into them and nod toward the bedroom. "You can take your stuff in there.

"Do you want some oatmeal?" I say when she comes into the kitchen, barefoot and having shed her jacket.

"Sure. Whatever it was they served on the plane, it wasn't food, and I didn't have time to eat before I caught the shuttle."

I put water on to boil and take out bowls and spoons, milk and butter, brown sugar and raisins. I measure out the oatmeal more carefully than necessary, still making the transition from sleeping to abruptly waking in the unexpected presence of my mother.

"How did you find me?"

"Real nice girl at the Chamber of Commerce booth . . . Laura? She hijacked some guy into driving me out here. Pretty nice little place."

I set a mug of coffee in front of her. She sits back and looks pointedly at my stomach. "I assume you know who the father is."

I give her an annoyed look. "Of course I do. I was actually pregnant when I came up to see you; I just didn't know it."

"So it's Michael." She gives me a wry little smile. "What do you know—he was good for something after all."

I look away. "I didn't find out till July, and then I was totally pissed off."

"Look at the bright side." She smiles. "You get the fun of having a baby without having to deal with the bullshit of a husband. Is it a girl or a boy?"

Fun? "Girl."

She claps her hands together like a child. "Have you thought of a name?"

"No." I stir the oatmeal into the boiling water and move the pot to the back of the stove.

"Seems like maybe you're still a little . . . ambivalent, hmm?"

"Not really. I'm sort of resigned to the whole thing. It's just . . ."

She's looking at me expectantly.

"It's just that Michael's not exactly dead."

"What?" The mug stops halfway to her lips; her eyes open wide.

"Long story," I say.

"Looks like we'll have plenty to talk about this weekend." She pulls her feet up on the chair, covering her legs with the full skirt. "So that weasely little guy who followed you up to my place was right."

I sigh. "Not exactly. Listen, maybe we could get into this later. Let's just eat breakfast, okay?"

After breakfast she wants to go for a walk, even though the sky looks like a dirty rag and the air smells of rain. I take her on the Otter Ridge path, the one JT showed me, the one where I led Michael to the ferry that morning, through the forest and across Greenaway's meadow, by Monarch Pond. The woods are different now. Flocks of chickadees and nuthatches forage in the treetops as we pass underneath the canopy of trees, wet from morning fog. I point out the madrones, and she examines their peeling bark, as taken with them as I was. We find birds' nests in the bare branches of alders and maples. At the pond we watch a solitary mallard dabbling, its tail in the air like a flag, and Gwen bends down to inspect the salal and ferns.

"It's so green here." She pats her face gently. "If I lived here, I wouldn't even have to use moisturizer."

I look at her sideways. "You'd never leave the mesa."

"No," she says. "Not even feet first."

"Do you ever miss California?"

"Tell me you're joking."

"I don't mean L.A. or San Francisco. But don't you miss the ocean?"

"Not really. I always loved bodysurfing at Malibu when I was young. And Rob and I loved Carmel and Point Reyes. But there's just something about New Mexico. That high desert air, the light on the mountains. There's an energy there. I felt it the first time I saw the mesa. Almost a physical—" She checks to see if I'm rolling my eyes. "I'm serious. I want to be cremated and have my ashes scattered by the river. Where we—"

She stops. She's not ready to say it, and I'm not ready to hear it.

"I don't think Rob liked it as much as you do."

"No. He went because when what's-his-face bought the land—isn't that weird? I can't remember his real name. All I can think of is Moses Strong. Anyway, the way he talked about it, it just seemed like a groovy thing to do. But I think Rob only stayed as long as he did because I loved it there."

It's beginning to rain now, so we pull up the hoods of our parkas and turn back toward the house. She asks about my plans for Thanksgiving, and I explain about the community dinner at the Grange Hall. I probably wouldn't even go if she weren't here, but the way Trish described it, it sounded right up Gwen's alley: lots of warm fuzzies and sharing good food.

"What should I bring?" she says. "I assume everyone brings something."

"You don't have to bring anything. You're coming as my guest; you can help me make the enchiladas."

"I'll help you with the enchiladas, but I want to bring something, too." She looks thoughtful for a minute, then brightens. "How about capirotada?"

I smile. People in Arroyo Embuste have been known to hitchhike to Armonía for a piece of Gwen's capirotada. "Great idea. We can go to the market this afternoon."

At three o'clock, Forsthoff's is deserted except for two clueless guys looking for cranberries and the minimal staff standing around talking and drinking hot apple cider. I didn't realize they were closing at three thirty for the holiday. Gwen pushes the basket through the empty aisles while I toss in loaves of day-old bread, a couple of apples, a package of cream cheese, a hunk of longhorn, and a box of raisins. She insists on wandering through the entire store with me trailing impatiently in her wake, just in case we see something else we might need. I know this is a longtime habit born of living miles from a grocery store, but it irritates me. I want to go home.

I finally get her to the counter, and I'm looking around for a checker, all of whom have mysteriously disappeared, when she announces that the reason she never called to let me know she was coming was that she got mugged and my letter was in her purse. When I turn to stare at her, she laughs. "Sounds like the dog ate my homework, doesn't it?"

"You got mugged? In Arroyo Embuste?"

Another peal of laughter. "Of course not. If you got mugged in Embuste, you'd probably run into the person later at the feed store. I was in Albuquerque. I went down to see Robyn—you know, Sage's mom. She's a lawyer now . . . It's so funny, all these old burned-out hippie women that ended up going to law school; now they're driving Land Rovers and strutting around in their snakeskin boots."

"Wait a minute, wait a minute . . ." I'm practically sputtering. "You got mugged?"

"Yeah, we went out to dinner one night and ended up at some little dive doing shooters, and when we walked out, this guy came up to us and flashed a knife."

I can feel my blood pressure spike. "That has to be the stupidest thing I've ever heard. What the hell were you thinking? Two middle-aged women in a Range Rover doing shooters in some dive; you're lucky you didn't get raped or killed. Jesus, Gwen."

She's looking at me incredulously, and the guy arranging Christmas issues of magazines on a rack a few feet away is trying to act like he's not hanging on every word.

"It was no big deal," she says. "All he wanted was our purses."

"Some guy pulls a knife on you and its *no big deal*? I think all that peyote you ingested totally fried your brain."

"I see your point." Her voice is frosty. "A fifty-five-year-old woman going out with a friend to have a good time? How ridiculous. They should just stay home and knit."

"I didn't mean it that way and you know it."

"Soleil, you can be so arrogant."

"Arrogant?"

"I can't wait till you hit fifty and this child starts telling you not to ride your bike."

"That's hardly the same thing as—"

"Hi, ladies. A few last-minute goodies?" It's one of the checkers, not one I see regularly, thank God. He takes his sweet time, commenting on the superiority of Rome Beauty apples for cooking, making sure we understand the bread is day-old, telling us the generic cream cheese is every bit as good as Philadelphia brand.

Gwen tries to pay for the groceries, and I practically elbow her out of the way, thrusting a twenty into the checker's hand. My next thought—totally irrational—is that she drove down to Albuquerque to see Robyn but she never came down to see me.

We climb into the truck. I grit my teeth and pull out of the parking lot. I promised myself I wouldn't do this with her. She looks out the side window and her breath fogs the glass.

"I'm sorry," I say.

"Me, too," she says. Then, "It's your turn."

"My turn to what?"

"Your turn to tell me a long story. Like why you didn't mention you were pregnant. And what's the deal with Michael?"

I take a deep breath and slide my hands around on the steering wheel. "I didn't tell you because I was pissed off and depressed, and I didn't know what to do. Whether to have the baby or . . . not."

"How did you decide?" She turns sideways in the seat to face me.

"You need to put on your seat belt."

She throws up her hands. "Damnation, Soleil. If that's not just like my mother."

I pull to the side of the road. "I'm not driving till you put on your seat belt. And what's Nana got to do with it?"

"Every time we'd be in the middle of talking about something important, she'd find a way to change the subject. Tell my father he had halitosis or tell me to fasten my seat belt or use hot compresses on a zit. I swear it must skip a generation."

"Excuse me, but I'm not willing to get a ticket so you can exercise your flabby counterculture muscles. Put your seat belt on."

She laughs. "Okay. All right." She pulls the belt across her chest and locks it into place. "Are you happy now? Can we get back to our discussion?"

A few big drops splatter on the windshield and abruptly the clouds open up like eggshells cracked together, releasing a payload of water so intense that my wipers can hardly keep up. I slow to a crawl, peering ahead. I flick on the defroster, but because the truck is cold, the windshield fogs up even worse. I pull over at the next intersection and turn on the hazard blinkers.

"How did you decide?"

Water is rolling off the windshield like a curtain, so I flick the wipers off, leaving a silence filled only with the rain. Nobody has asked me this question before; I've never tried to explain my rationale—or lack of it—even to myself.

"I didn't actually decide," I say, and then pause. "You know how you sometimes really believe something, but you just don't feel it? The idea of right or wrong seems . . ."

"Irrelevant?" she supplies helpfully, and I recall that it was one of her favorite words. Laws were irrelevant. School curriculum. Congressional debates. Organized religion. Any job that required you to wear pantyhose and high heels.

"It was just something I wasn't prepared to do. Ending the pregnancy." Finally I look at her. "Am I making sense?"

"Of course," she says. "The point is it was your choice. Nobody can tell you it was right or wrong."

The rain begins to taper off, and the engine has warmed up enough to clear the windshield. I turn the wipers back on, put the truck in gear, and get back on the pavement.

On the way home I tell her about Michael.

Chapter 28

We've just finished supper. Or I've finished, having wolfed down almost a half pound of turkey meatloaf, a giant baked potato, and a bouquet of broccoli. Gwen is still dousing her potato skin with her home-brewed Worcestershire sauce (no chemicals, no high fructose corn syrup) and munching it contentedly.

"You know, I'm really glad you invited me to come here," she says. "I've been wanting to talk to you."

"About what?" I'm instantly wary.

"I don't know. I guess I just get kind of . . . I was going to say sad, but it probably just happens when you get old." She looks out the window into the early darkness. "It was about this time of year when Nana died."

"I remember."

"I always thought that someday we'd, you know, get back together. I kept putting it off because it always seemed like such a hard thing to do—calling her or even writing a letter. But it could have been so simple. I didn't have to get into all the whys and hows. I didn't even have to apologize. All I needed to say was 'I'm thinking about you.' It just seemed impossible after everything that went down when I left California. So I never did. And she didn't, either. We were both very stubborn."

I smile a little, thinking of the standoff over my wedding outfit.

"Yeah, go on and smile. You think you're immune?"

"I'm really not like you," I begin, but she starts to laugh. "I'm not."

"Yes, you are. In a lot of ways."

"Such as what?"

"Such as: We both tend to feel like being hurt is somehow embarrassing. We'd both rather nurse our wounds in private than accept sympathy or help from anyone. We're both slow to forgive." She pauses for a breath. This is obviously something she's given some thought to. "We both had to leave home to find out where we belong. And . . ."

She takes a sip of wine but before she can say anything else or even set down her glass, somebody's knocking on my door. When I get up from the table I look through the kitchen window at the rusty orange truck parked behind mine, and I catch a glimpse of Bailey running toward the pond.

A nice, quiet Thanksgiving.

JT is standing on my porch looking like he'd rather be somewhere else. His cheeks are ruddy from the cold and one side of his shirt collar sticks up over the neck of his sweater. My fingers want to tuck it back down, but I don't. He looks older suddenly—or maybe it's just because his hair is shorter. The black pearl earring gleams in the yellow porch light.

"Hi," he says, and his breath makes little puffs in the frosty air. "How are you . . . feeling?"

"Fat. Tired. How are you?"

"Is this a good time? I just wanted to talk to you."

"Well, actually . . ."

"Hi. How are you? *Who* are you?" Gwen is standing behind me. "Come on in, it's cold out there."

I'm going to kill her. I'm going to crack her skull with my ten-inch cast-iron skillet.

JT seems confused. "Oh, sorry. I didn't know you had company."

She laughs. "I'm not company. I'm Gwen. Soleil's mom."

His eyes widen ever so slightly. "So-Lay?" he repeats.

"That's her real name, but she hasn't used it since she was twelve. I'm the only one who still calls her that. Come on in; let's shut this door."

JT has the look of someone being sucked into a vortex.

Suddenly he and I are somehow ensconced at the kitchen table making excruciating small talk while Gwen fixes tea and cleans up our dinner dishes. When I get up and reach for the dish towel, she takes it from my hands and pushes me back into my chair.

"It's better if they air-dry," she says with authority. "Fewer germs."

JT says, "I was working. At the Lake Union Sailing School."

I realize that either Gwen or I must have asked what he was doing in Seattle.

He tells us about his job teaching landlubbers to get in touch with their inner sailor while she listens raptly and I say a silent prayer for this to end soon.

"It was okay. I'm pretty good at it," he says modestly.

Gwen says, "You have your own boat?"

This precipitates a whole story about how he came to be the skipper of the *Lucky Dawg*. Gwen is thrilled to discover that he lives aboard. Then he wants to know what she thinks of the island and how long she plans to stay. She ends up telling him the story about getting mugged in Albuquerque, which he finds hilarious, or at least pretends to. In spite of the fact that it's barely 7:15, I'm about to excuse myself to get ready for bed, when Gwen suddenly turns and pours the dregs of her tea in the sink.

Then she turns to me, smiling maternally. "Soleil, can I use your bedroom? I haven't done my meditation today." She kisses my cheek and startles JT by wrapping him in a bear hug and then she disappears into my bedroom, shutting the door behind her.

He and I sit perfectly still for a few minutes, reluctant to look at each other.

"Your mom's nice," he says.

I nod.

More silence.

"Are you mad at me?" he says.

"Yeah. You've been gone two months and I haven't gotten a postcard of the Space Needle."

He shifts his gaze to the window, then down to his hands. "I didn't know what to say."

"Does that mean you now know what to say?"

He nods. "I'm sorry. I acted like a shit. I wasn't even thinking about you and how you must have felt. I was just disappointed that things didn't . . . work out the way I wanted."

I want very much to say *Why didn't they? Why can't they?* But his choice of words makes it clear that I'd only be humiliating myself further.

"I'm sorry, too. I probably shouldn't have just dumped the news on you like that."

"It took me a while to sort of absorb everything. And school was pretty busy. And then when I was off, Casey and I were working out some of the kinks in her dad's new boat."

"That's nice."

"We went out a few times."

"I know."

"How did you know?"

"It's a small island."

He laughs uneasily. "It was pretty casual. She's very young."

"People grow up," I say and look at him sideways.

His expression softens. "You were right, you know."

I push my hair out of my face with both hands. "About what? I'm right about so many things I can't remember them all."

"It's good that we're friends. You and me. I mean, we both have a lot to do. It would've been harder if we'd . . ." His voice trails off like smoke.

I get up and open the refrigerator, stare at its contents. "Are you going back to Seattle on Sunday?"

"No. Pete Callender wants me to come to work for him."

"Doing what?"

A spontaneous smile takes over his face. "Sailing his boat. He keeps a sixty-five-foot ketch in Tortola, to entertain clients and stuff. Somebody just left the crew, so he asked me if I wanted to go. Can you believe it? I'm going to get paid to sail his damn boat around the Caribbean."

"When do you . . . ?"

"As soon as my passport comes through."

"That's . . . great." When I blink, a tear hovers on the tips of my lashes. The baby begins to hiccup. I shut the refrigerator door and grip the counter.

"Hey . . ." He comes over to stand next to me. "What's wrong?"

"I'm out of milk."

"Sunny . . ."

"It's okay. Really. Somebody once told me I have a melancholy streak as wide as the Rio Grande, that's all it is."

His eyes are locked on the surface of my t-shirt. "Did that just move?"

I laugh and swipe at my eyes. "She's got the hiccups."

He can't seem to tear his gaze away, so I pick up his hand and lay it gently on my belly. The look on his face is the funniest thing I've seen in months.

"*Oh my God,*" he whispers. "It's moving."

"She."

He withdraws his hand, and I move toward the table. We sit down again and I drink the last of my tea.

"Oh." He reaches under his sweater and pulls out a small packet, sets it in front of me. "This is for you."

I look at it for a second.

"Go on, open it."

I untie the raffia and unfold the tissue paper slowly, almost certain of the contents before I see it, but still puzzled. The leather is new and not as soft as deerskin, but other than that, the medicine bundle is a nearly exact replica, right down to the black-and-red beaded storm design.

"You didn't have to do that." I turn it over and rub the back with my thumb. "How did you know?"

He looks at the ceiling. "Bailey was shitting beads."

I laugh and rest my hand on his arm. It seems an okay thing to do. "Thanks for thinking of it. And I'm really happy for you."

He puts his hand on top of mine. "Sunny, I want you to know . . ."

I shake my head. "Not now, okay? We'll talk about it some other time."

He nods. "Maybe we could have lunch. I'll call you."

"Sure."

He looks embarrassed. "This time I really will."

Thanksgiving morning, Gwen's up, making coffee and oatmeal, slicing the day-old bread we bought and putting it on the stovetop to dry out when I wander into the kitchen at nine.

"Good afternoon," she chirps.

I glare at her and stretch my hands up to the ceiling.

"Oh, I forgot. You're not fit to live with until you get your coffee. Here, sit." She fixes me coffee with milk and honey. I don't have the heart to tell her I don't drink it that way anymore.

"I'm going to ask my friend Trish if she has a cot or an extra mattress we can borrow," I say.

"Why?" She looks up from scooping brown sugar into a measuring cup. "Hey, don't you have a better saucepan than that flimsy aluminum thing? And you shouldn't use aluminum cookware anyway. It leaches into the food, and you'll get Alzheimer's. And it's not good for the baby."

"Because it's embarrassing to get up in the middle of the night and see my mother lying on the floor."

"I was perfectly comfortable. Didn't even turn over."

"You can make the syrup in my cast-iron frying pan," I say. That seems to satisfy her. "Wouldn't you rather use piloncillo?"

"Do they have a Mexican market here?" she asks.

"Hardly. I order all my supplies online from a place in Albuquerque and they ship UPS."

I point out the southwest cupboard, and she starts pawing through my stash with an enthusiasm most women reserve for a safe full of jewelry. "Oh, you've got canella! And chipotles. And epazote—what's wrong?"

"I should have told you, I don't drink sweet coffee anymore."

"Just pour it out, I made plenty," she says. "By the way, these cabinets are beautiful. They look handmade."

"They are." I picture JT sitting here on the floor, patiently perfecting each door. "JT and another friend made them for me."

"What a cute guy. Is he coming to this happening?"

"I don't think so." I pour fresh coffee in my cup and add some milk.

"Too bad. Doesn't he remind you of Hart?"

"Yes," I say. "He does."

First we make the capirotada—New Mexico's final and definitive answer to bread pudding—because it has to bake long and slow. I soak the raisins in red wine, shred the longhorn cheese, and cut the cream cheese into tiny bits while Gwen makes the syrup with piloncillo, canella, vanilla, cloves, and butter. When that's done we layer the dried bread, cheese, raisins, and piñon nuts in the baking dish and pour the syrup over it, cover it with foil, and stick it in the oven.

Then with the Dixie Chicks wailing in the background, we

tackle the enchiladas. I've already made both red and green chile sauce, so we set up our assembly line on the top of the Dragonfly.

She dips the enchiladas into hot oil, then into the simmering red sauce and places them on a plate in front of me. I throw in a handful of cheese and a few chopped onions, roll them up, and lay them in the giant foil baking pan. Blue corn tortillas can be tricky. Sometimes they shred or crack, depending on the humidity or how long they're dipped in oil and sauce, but Gwen could do it in her sleep, thanks to years of feeding the masses at Armonía. We don't lose a single one.

The grange hall is on Wentworth Street, just around the corner from the courthouse. It's an austere but strangely graceful white building, almost like an old-fashioned church, with tall, narrow gothic windows, but no steeple. We have to park a block away because by four o'clock the parking lot's full and the street is already lined with cars on both sides.

Inside, the air is warm and heady with scents of roasted turkeys and brewing coffee. The rack by the front door is invisible under piles of coats and scarves. Umbrellas are tipi'd into corners. There's a muted roar of happy voices as people wander around sipping mulled wine and hot spiced cider.

Gwen and I make our way through the crowd, and I'm surprised at the number of unfamiliar faces I see. Freddie greets us in the kitchen, looking incongruous in somebody's white lace apron. She gives Gwen a big hug.

"I'm so glad you came," she says. "I been wanting to meet Sunny's older sister."

Gwen laughs. "All you Texas girls know how to lie with a straight face."

I slide the enchiladas into one of the warming ovens, and Gwen pours the heavy cream into a pitcher to put with the capirotada. When she takes it out to the dessert table, Freddie asks me, "So how's it going?"

"Not bad. Surprisingly."

"See? Aren't you glad you told her?"

"Of course, we still have two days to go."

She laughs. "Always the glass-half-full kind of girl."

Someone thrusts an oversize basket of rolls into my hands. "Can you take that out?"

We wander out of the kitchen and over to the makeshift bar.

"Can't believe they don't have margaritas," Freddie grumbles. She has to content herself with a beer, and I squeeze a wedge of lemon into a glass of water.

"Hey, I need to ask you something. Are you interested in my apartment? I know it's a little smaller than your place—"

"Interested in what—living there?"

"Yeah. I gotta go home."

I stare at her. "You mean, move? Back to Texas?"

She jabs her index finger in my bicep. "Don't say it like that. It's not like a life sentence with no parole."

"But, why? Tell me you're not going back to Junior."

She flips the ruffles on the apron bodice. "Oh, please, girl. Actually I think he got married again. Hey, I could be the other woman now instead of the poor little wife." When she sees my expression, she says, "Sunny, I'm kidding."

"Why do you want to leave Harmony?" God, I sound like Trish.

"I don't exactly want to." She takes a slow, careful drink of beer. "My momma's not doing too well. It's not like she's sick or anything, it's just she's getting along. She really needs some help with the ranch, and nobody else in the family cares enough to do it. Besides, I really miss my horse."

"So when are you leaving?"

"I'd kinda like to be home for Christmas, but I just signed a new lease in June, so I'm hoping I can sublet—oh, my soul, will you look who's talking to Sarah Lakes."

I follow her gaze, expecting to see JT. But it's Gwen, having an animated conversation with the woman who hates hippies more than anything in the world. It's hilarious to watch. Sarah standing there, stiff as a Popsicle, clutching her cup of cider and looking frantically for a way to escape, except no one likes her well enough to rescue her, while Gwen laughs and gestures, spilling her wine on the floor.

"Your momma seems pretty cool to me."

"She's like a cat," I say. "Always attaching herself to the one person in a room who's least likely to want her around."

The afternoon passes in a blissful blur of good food and conviviality. By the time the dessert dishes are being cleared, Sarah is asking Gwen for the capirotada recipe. When it's down to mints and coffee, a woman starts playing the slightly out-of-tune upright piano and everybody is singing songs, from Thanksgiving hymns to "Puff the Magic Dragon." Gwen sits between Freddie and me at one of the long tables, singing loudly, swaying to the music, oblivious to the amused glances directed at her.

When I go for a coffee refill, an arm slips around my shoulders. "Happy Thanksgiving, Sunny." I turn around. It's Trish. Behind her is a guy who looks very much like Scott. And a bit like my father.

"Sunny, this is Luke. This is my friend, Sunny Cooper."

She beams at us and stands back, like she's expecting a sudden chemical reaction. Which there is, but probably not the one she had in mind. I stare at him, surprised into silence.

Luke Carver is wearing expensive-looking gray slacks, a beautiful green sweater, and the hollow-eyed look of someone who's recently been emotionally Roto-Rootered.

He knows he knows me; he just can't figure out from where. The first time we met I looked normal; now I look like a momma kangaroo. Do I help him out or just let him twist slowly in the wind?

"Hi. Nice to meet you." We shake hands and he frowns slightly, still trying to figure it out.

Trish says, "Sunny's the one I told you about who grew up on a commune in New Mexico. Hey, is your mom here today? I saw a woman who looked just like you."

"Yes, that's her over there next to Freddie."

"I'll just nip over and introduce myself."

Then she's gone and it's just me and Luke Carver.

"You look so familiar," he says. "Have we met?"

I look up at him. "The Ale House. You: tannic, intense, amusingly pretentious. Me: edgy, unsophisticated, annoyingly underdeveloped."

Suddenly it registers in his eyes. *Oh shit. The waitress.*

He makes a stab at a self-deprecating smile. "If I apologize right out of the gate, maybe you won't tell my mother what an asshole I was."

"Your secret is safe with me."

"By way of mitigation, I'd like to point out that the defendant was under considerable duress at the time of the incident."

"That's okay. I've been there myself recently."

"I appreciate your understanding." His voice is nice—soft,

a little husky. He has Trish's blue eyes and thick, pale hair. "So. My mom says you're living over off Lavender Road. One of Trent's cottages."

"Right. First I was renting from Sarah Lakes—" I stop, remember she's his soon-to-be ex-mother-in-law.

He reaches for a cup and fills it from the decaf urn. "Sarah functions as a screening device, helping to limit island population growth. The weak-willed don't stay long."

I laugh, holding my basketball stomach, striving to maintain bladder control.

He smiles sympathetically. "When are you due?"

"On or about December twenty-seventh."

"Is this your first?"

"Yes."

"Nervous?"

"Terrified."

"As you should be."

"Thanks. I was afraid you were going to be encouraging."

"Sorry. I'm a little weird lately. Sort of in limbo."

"When do you head back to Seattle?" I ask.

For a split second I think he's going to cry. Then he blinks like someone waking up from a nap. "It looks like I'll be around for a while. I'm getting— my wife has filed for divorce . . ."

"I'm sorry."

"I'm going to live with my folks till we can't stand each other, and then I'll probably try to find a place in town." He's looking at me, but he's talking to himself, a man afraid of heights talking himself down off a ladder, convincing himself that he will make it back to the ground and life will resume.

"Oh, I just heard about a place that might be coming available before Christmas. It's small, just a studio."

A spark of interest flickers in his eyes. "Really?"

"Near the marina. It has a great view. Freddie Russell's living there now. That's her over there. The tall blonde with your mother. You should go talk to her about it. If you're interested."

"Thanks," he says. "I will."

There's no heat vent in the ladies' room, but after the warm press of bodies out in the hall, the cold air feels good. Damp linoleum tiles curl up at the corners, and years of drippy faucets have made red iron stains in the old sinks. I blot perspiration from the back of my neck and push my bangs out of my eyes. They need trimming again. My hair has never grown this fast before.

I'm washing my hands under a weak trickle of water when the door opens and Trish peers around the corner at me. "There you are."

"In the john. My new favorite hangout."

"I'm so glad you got to meet Luke."

"He seems very nice," I say carefully. "I'm sorry to hear about the divorce."

She snorts. "Frankly, I'm thrilled." Then she shakes her head. "Oh, I don't mean that. He's so devastated. But Mary Beth Lakes is just a better-looking version of her mother. It's terrible for poor little Bree. Especially since Luke can't even see her till he takes this ridiculous anger management class. *Online*," she adds, as if that proves the insanity of the whole thing. "You know, this is all my fault. It's payback for all the lies I told."

"What lies?"

"You know." She lowers her voice. "About Luke."

"Trish, that's ridiculous. Shit just happens. You can't blame yourself."

She takes out a brush and runs it through her hair a few times, hard, like she's trying to rip it out. Then she stops and looks at me. "No, it's true, Sunny. My mother always used to say the past has a way of coming around again wearing a different hat."

I pull her into a sideways hug and try not to laugh. "Sounds like the fourth law of Harmony to me."

I change into sweats and build a fire in the stone fireplace while Gwen pumps water and rekindles the stove fire and scrapes baked-on sauce out of the enchilada pan. It occurs to me how nice it is that I don't have to show her how to light the stove or pump water. She doesn't complain about having to chop kindling or heat water to do dishes. And having lived through three pregnancies on the mesa, she hasn't once said, *You shouldn't be doing that.* Not even when she discovered Myron out in the lean-to.

When the water boils she pours some into the capirotada pan to loosen the caramelized sugar.

"Have you been seeing anyone?" she asks casually.

The question catches me off-balance. "Seeing, as in having a relationship?"

"Of course." She laughs. "What else?"

"There aren't a lot of guys lining up to get involved with single pregnant women," I say. "Have you?"

"Good Lord, no. I'm beyond that."

"You're only fifty-four."

"Fifty-five." She sighs. "And pickings are slim up on the mesa. You can go with some macho cowboy widower whose gut hangs over the front of his jeans or some glassy-eyed ex-hippie silversmith with three hairs in a ponytail."

I set the serving spoons in the sink and look at her. "Whatever happened with Boone?"

There's a short but definite pause. "He left."

"When? Where did he go?"

"When the new owners turned Armonía into the bed-and-breakfast, I guess he just didn't want to be there anymore."

"You guess? Didn't you guys talk about it?"

She hugs herself, rubbing her arms. "Yeah, we talked. And talked and talked. He was going back to Missouri. His family owns some land there, and he said he wanted to try farming where they have decent soil."

"Did he want you to go?"

"Sure. Of course he did. Wanted to get married and the whole enchilada. He knew I couldn't." She shakes her head. "Can't you just see me in Missouri? Wouldn't I fit in great with the library volunteers? I could've made my secret ingredient brownies for the church bake sale."

"Oh, I bet there's a few unreconstructed hippies in every little corner of the country," I say, smiling. She doesn't smile back.

"Soleil, I'll never leave the mesa. That's where Mari is." Her voice trembles on my sister's name.

It's a relief. Like the murder scene in a scary movie. You anticipate it and dread it and you pretend it might not happen, but you know it will, sooner or later. And when it finally does, you can stop holding your breath.

"That's not where Mari is." I try to keep my own voice from shaking. "Mari is wherever one of us goes. Hart would be the first to tell you that. She was in San Antonio and Ocala and all the other places he ran away to, and I'd be willing to bet that now she's right there in the Kenton County Detention Center."

"I used to wish I'd get Alzheimer's. So I wouldn't remember anything." She reaches for my left arm and turns it underside up, traces the scar gently with a wet, soapy finger. "And now I find myself trying to remember everything. Every detail. Because if you don't remember, it's like it never happened. Like she was never there. And that's worse. Isn't it?" She cocks her head to one side and looks at me. "Do you think I'm losing it?"

"No."

"Good. Because wouldn't that be something? All those years I wanted to forget and couldn't. Now I want to remember and sometimes I forget. Just little things. Like what she was wearing."

"A blue denim sundress."

"And what happened to . . . the dog."

"Woof. He got cremated with her."

"And that stupid song she loved."

" 'Muskrat Love.' "

She studies me. "So you see her, too."

"Sometimes. Not like Hart. He still blames himself."

"Don't we all?"

"No." I lean against the counter. "I miss her every single day and I still love her. Once or twice I even wished it could've been me instead. But at some point I must have figured out that I didn't do it."

Her smile is bleak. "Then I guess that makes you the sole survivor. You're the one who learned something."

"Right. I learned to expect disaster. To be afraid of every day. And to never get too attached to anything or anyone because they'll surely be taken away."

"Soleil, that's about the best reason in the world to get attached." I watch her eyes fill up. "To get attached just as tight as you can." She says it with only a trace of irony.

When I wake up Friday morning, the cottage is quiet.

"Gwen . . . ?"

She must have gone for a walk. Or out to do her Tai Chi or Qi Gong or Kung Fu or whatever she's doing these days. I pull on my sweatpants, throw a flannel shirt over the XXLG Ale House T-shirt that now serves as my nightgown, and pad out to the living room. It's 10:45 in the morning and I probably got about five hours of sleep last night. Most of that was spent dreaming weird, disconnected dreams about losing my keys and gaining so much weight that I couldn't get out of my bedroom, bringing the baby home and not being able to find any diapers.

I fix scrambled eggs with cheddar cheese for my breakfast, wash the dishes, and leave them to drain. I make the bed and light a fire in the fireplace, find my place in the book I've been reading. But I've barely read a page when I hear car doors slamming.

Gwen appears, her hair a wild mass in the cold, wet wind. "Bundle up," she orders. Then to someone outside, "You might need to turn it sideways to get it through the door."

Two men wrestle something wrapped in packing blankets across the threshold, something shaped like a sofa. One of the men is Luke Carver. He looks totally different in jeans, a faded blue shirt, and a down vest.

"Hello again," he says.

I stare at the thing. "What's this?"

"What's it look like?" Gwen laughs and shoves one of the chairs out of the way. "Right there, guys. Thanks a lot."

"Thanks," I echo lamely. "I'm sure you're busy . . ."

"Yeah." A trace of a smile. "I was way overscheduled this morning." He carefully folds up one blanket while his friend wads the other into a ball. "By the way, it looks like I'm taking Freddie Russell's place."

In my muddled state I think he's talking about her job.

Then he says, "Thanks for telling me about it."

"Oh, the apartment. I'm glad it worked out."

They take their leave quickly, as if they're afraid of being held responsible for the pink cabbage rose upholstery.

Gwen beams, delighted. "Ugly, isn't it?"

"Yes, it is. Where did you get it?"

"Rummage sale at a church," she says proudly. "Fifteen bucks. They wanted twenty-five, but . . ."

She scoots the chairs up on either side of it and stands back to admire her acquisition. "Structurally sound. A few quilts will take care of the flowers."

"Well, thanks," I say.

"You needed something to stretch out on in front of the fire."

"And something for you to sleep on besides chair cushions on the floor."

"True. Here." She pats the sofa's curved arm. "Come try it out. I'm going to see what's in the pantry. That's the only trouble with going out for Thanksgiving: no leftovers."

I stretch out on my side, facing the fire, green afghan pulled up under my chin. The couch smells pleasantly musty—eau de rummage sale. The soft patter of rain mingles with sounds from the kitchen, and I doze off, my eyes flickering open when Gwen sets two cups of tea on the little square end table.

I prop myself up. "I'm getting spoiled. Everybody's treating me like some kind of princess."

Gwen laughs. "Better milk it while you can. After the baby gets here you won't have two minutes to sit down. Except when she's asleep. And then you'll be so tired, you'll be asleep, too." She hesitates. "I wish I could be here to help you."

I bite my lip. *I have the right to remain silent. Anything I say can and will be used against me . . .* We seem to have settled into an uneasy truce, but what would it be like with me, my mother, and a new baby all in this very small house?

"I wouldn't have to stay here," she says, as if reading my mind. "I could probably get a room in town."

I force a laugh. "Yeah, Sarah Lakes has a great little place."

The silence turns awkward.

"But you'll be fine," she says, to convince both of us. She holds her cup in front of her mouth. "And I can always come if you need me."

I spend the afternoon trying to read and dozing off.

Whenever I'm conscious I look over at Gwen sitting in the chair, her beading paraphernalia spread out next to her tea mug on the end table. I study her through my eyelashes, not wanting her to know I'm awake, not wanting her to hover over me, bring me tea, or plump the pillows. I just want to look at her, to figure her out.

I remember her trying to explain to me what Armonía was intended to be, how they wanted to live as family, value everyone's humanity, teach peace, eat food that they grew themselves, expand their consciousness, let their children grow up free from society's artificial constraints and emotional hang-ups.

I remember trying to explain to her that I didn't want a

family of twenty-five people. I didn't want to share my food and my clothes and my bathroom with them. I didn't want to see them lolling around stoned or dancing naked. I couldn't make her see that I could live with a few constraints and hang-ups if I could just have my own room. Why couldn't we understand each other? It wasn't like we were speaking different dialects.

And why does it matter now?

When I finally push myself upright, it's dark outside and she's switched from tea mug to wineglass. I feel stale and groggy; my mouth tastes awful and my shoulder hurts from lying on it wrong. I blink a few times and inhale.

"Something smells good." How can I be hungry? I haven't done anything but sleep all afternoon.

"Spaghetti. In fact, I should go give it a stir." She goes to check on our dinner and comes back with a glass of fake wine for me. I take it and stare into the garnet-colored liquid. It looks exactly like wine, but the taste is flat and insipid. Amazing the difference a few microscopic organisms make. I set the glass down without drinking any.

"I've been thinking about her name," I say.

She looks at me with interest. "There's no hurry, you know." She holds up her beading project, a geometric design in green and white with purple and gold accents.

"It's pretty. What is it?"

"I'm not sure." She smiles. "Sometimes I just get an idea for a design. So I go ahead and start working on it, and then, after a while, I start to see what it is. Sometimes I don't know till it's finished. Like the way I had all these names picked out for you—Kachina, Sage, River—and then you were born just at sunrise and you seemed all pinky gold to me. And Soleil just popped into my mind. Maybe when your daughter comes, you'll know what her name is."

My daughter. I repeat it a few times in my head, getting used to the sound of it. The way it unfolds gently, making room for one or two possibilities, then a third. Then clusters of them, soft and pale as morning clouds.

"I've decided to call her Willa," I say, as if the idea hadn't just occurred to me. "After Nana."

"That's a lovely idea." She bends her head quickly and picks up the work.

I clear my throat. "Tomorrow, we'll go for a ride."

"If it doesn't rain," she says.

I laugh. "If it doesn't rain or if it does. Here, if you waited for the sun to come out you'd never do anything. There are some places on the island I want to show you."

"Okay, fun! And I have to figure out the ferry thing for Sunday. My flight leaves Seattle at three."

Something bulky and unfamiliar fills my chest—it takes me a few minutes to recognize it as regret. For fourteen years, my mother and I lived a few hours' drive apart and we saw each other three times. Suddenly I realize that she's going back to New Mexico the day after tomorrow and I'm not. Ever.

"I'll be back soon," she says, reading me again. "I have to come see Miss Willa Cooper while she's still a baby."

Willa Cooper.

I lean my head back and close my eyes and lay my hand on my belly, on the miniature ocean welling just beneath the taut skin, restless, salty, mysterious. For a long minute it's frighteningly quiet and still. And then it comes again—the flutter-kick of my daughter: Willa Cooper, a tiny swimmer, moving fearlessly through the dark waters toward Harmony.

ACKNOWLEDGMENTS

Every time I start a new book, there's that moment of sheer terror when I realize I've forgotten everything I thought I knew about writing. Writing *The Laws of Harmony* was even scarier because there were so many aspects of the story about which I also knew nothing.

What saved me is the same thing that always saves me. I may not know a lot of things, but I know people who know a lot of things. Once again, I got by with a little help from my friends. So I offer sincere thanks to:

Barbara Brumer, a.k.a. the Cookie Lady, and Carol Eason for giving me a glimpse into the world of the voiceover artist.

JT Tunnell, my audio guru, for giving me the technical side of recording spots . . . and also for letting me steal his name.

Myron Nickerson . . . if I did have a motorcycle I could talk to, I would name it after you.

Everyone at Santa Fe Harley-Davidson, especially Murrae Haynes and Mabel Chin, for their humor and patience and stories of the riding life.

Marilyn Clagett for being my best friend and for giving me the book that sparked my interest in this magical mystery tour—so what if we're forty years late!

My friend and teacher Jo-Ann Mapson for equal dollops of encouragement and honesty.

Patricia McFall for dropping everything to read and critique my unwieldy first draft, and Grace Marcus for plowing through early drafts and patiently listening to my endless musings.

Phaedra Greenwood for her beautiful memoir, *Beside the Rio Hondo*, and Phaedra Haywood for enlightening tales of growing up hippie.

No words of thanks can repay the debts I owe to two extraordinary women:

Claire Wachtel, my editor, who somehow knows where I'm going even when I haven't gotten there yet, for her sure instincts and steady guidance.

Marly Rusoff, my writer's dream of an agent, for wisdom, faith in me and in the book, and for friendship.

There's a special place in heaven for publishers who show their authors the support and kindness that I've received from HarperCollins. Thanks to Carrie Kania, Jennifer Hart, Nicole Reardon and Catherine Serpico, Alberto Rojas, and Audrey Harris.

To copyeditor Jennifer Dolan for catching all those annoying discrepancies that I overlooked and designer Robin Bilardello for the striking and evocative cover. And to the unflappable Julia Novitch . . . for remembering everything and doing everything and still being nice.

The Laws of Harmony, like its three predecessors, could never have been written without my husband, Geoff. Thanks, honey, for timely gas pipeline explosions, for knowing what year Mazda RX7s were introduced, for your continuing enthusiasm for dinner at Harry's Roadhouse, and most of all for your love.

The LAWS *of* HARMONY

A NOVEL

JUDITH RYAN HENDRICKS

A READER'S GUIDE

QUESTIONS FOR DISCUSSION

1) What does Sunny Cooper's flexible assortment of occupations—voice-over artist, personal errand runner, obsessive baker—suggest about her personality and her professional focus?

2) How do the suspicious circumstances surrounding Michael Graham's death and his behavior prior to his disappearance make him seem like a stranger to Sunny?

3) How do the detailed descriptions of food and cooking in *The Laws of Harmony* affect your reading experience? Which were most memorable to you and why?

4) Why does Betsy Chambliss conceal her betrayal from Sunny, and could there be any possible justification for her behavior?

5) Sunny can't wait to get away from Armonía, but after almost 14 years on her own, the normality and stability she craves still elude her. Why is this? To what extent is the summer idyll with her grandparents in California responsible for her sense of living an unmoored life?

6) Why do you think the author chose to explore the strange coincidence of Sunny's having been raised in Armonía, and her having turned up in a town called Harmony? What does this convergence suggest, and to what extent do you think the names might be intended ironically?

7) How would you characterize Sunny's feelings about her mother, Gwen, returning to her life? To what extent is their relationship irretrievably fractured?

8) What does JT's reaction to the news of Sunny's pregnancy reveal about his character and their romantic potential as a couple?

9) What do you think the ending of the book suggests for Sunny, her future life in San Miguel, and her relationships with JT, Gwen, and the others on whom she has come to depend?

AN INTERVIEW WITH JUDITH RYAN HENDRICKS

Q: Why is food and cooking so important to your fictional characters?

A: I guess because food is so important to me. It's one of those things that gives life texture and rhythm. Music is another. Those things link us to each other and mark places in our lives. Which is why I can't remember where I put my sunglasses or the name of somebody I met last week, but I can remember the carrot cake I shared with my mom at the little upstairs café in LaConner, Washington, twenty years ago, and all the words to "Rocky Raccoon."

Q: How closely is the setting of San Miguel Island intended to imitate any real-life Pacific Northwest island?

A: Some books could be set anywhere, which gives the elements of character and plot more responsibility for carrying the story. But I always visualize my stories in very particular settings—sometimes real, sometimes wholly invented, sometimes a bit of both. San Miguel Island is an amalgam of places I know and love in the Pacific Northwest.

Q: *The Laws of Harmony* is your fourth novel. What do you know about writing now that you wished you had known when you started out as a novelist?

A: I wish I'd known that each book is utterly different and it's always like starting over. That probably would have saved me from panic on many occasions. I wish I'd known that you have to be gentle with yourself and patient with the story. No matter how many times I've thought I'd never find my way through the maze, or how many times I've been ready to quit in frustration, things have always worked themselves out . . . and I mean that literally. The knots have unraveled with very little help from me. The problem is that what I know now I could only learn through the experience of writing four novels. And still, I forget.

Q: To what extent do you actively resist writing works that can be categorized by genre or theme? For example, *The Laws of Harmony* seems to introduce and combine mystery, romance, self-discovery, and all things culinary.

A: I enjoy reading certain genres, such as mysteries, but when someone who's a school teacher or a cab driver keeps stumbling over dead bodies, there's a part of me that thinks, "oh come on. You just solved a murder last month. What are the chances?" When I write, I like to include different elements in the story because real life is a fascinating pastiche of mystery, romance, self-discovery, and—at least for me—all things culinary.

Q: How did you decide at what point in your story to conclude *The Laws of Harmony*? Is there any possibility readers might encounter these characters again in a sequel?

A: This question makes me smile because the ending came at three different points in earlier drafts. It finally came down to the relationships between Sunny and the other major characters and deciding which one was most important, what the story was really about. Sequels can be tricky. Just because you like the characters and still have questions about what might happen to them doesn't mean there's enough material for a sequel. Having said that, I admit to a certain fondness for the mother-daughter dynamic, and that I'm curious about what might happen between Sunny and Willa . . .

BOOKS BY JUDITH RYAN HENDRICKS

THE LAWS OF HARMONY
A Novel

ISBN 978-0-06-168736-5 (paperback)

An emotionally gripping tale of one woman's struggle to remake herself in the wake of loss and deception, told in the wise, empowering, and heart-renewing prose of an accomplished writer.

BREAD ALONE
A Novel

ISBN 978-0-06-008440-0 (paperback)

"Hendricks creates a compelling character whose wry, bemused, and ultimately wise voice hooks the reader. . . . A well-written, imaginative debut."

—*Publishers Weekly*

ISABEL'S DAUGHTER
A Novel

ISBN 978-0-06-050347-5 (paperback)

After a childhood spent in an institution and a series of foster homes, Avery James has trained herself not to wonder about the mother who gave her up. But her safe, predictable life changes one night when she stumbles upon the portrait of a woman who is the mirror image of herself.

THE BAKER'S APPRENTICE
A Novel

ISBN 978-0-06-072618-8 (paperback)

"Hendricks rolls out a delicious sequel in *Baker's Apprentice*. . . . Prepare to have your appetite teased and stimulated, often."

—*Seattle Post-Intelligencer*